Unclaimed Son
Day K Altair

Unclaimed Son

John DeWitt – Publishing

Copyright © 2021 by Day K Altair

ISBN-13-978-0-578-88344-1

DEDICATION

To John Dewitt, anti-federalist, who warned of the pernicious danger of centralized government.

And, to my loving wife, Jeannette, whose computer skills made this book possible.

Table of Contents

… and when the ship began to flounder,
and the sea grasped for their souls,
they gathered the best among them
and cast them to the sky, I'm told.

Chapter 1
On Raven's Wing

A utumn was a special time in the small community of Riverdale by the Eastern Sea. The foliage was changing from summer greens to the bright colors of fall. The breeze whispered the approach of winter, and the people of Riverdale began their preparation for the coming inclement weather. These were busy days for James Walker, the local coaler. Each morning before the sun touched the day with light, James Walker would travel to the railroad coal yard east of town and shovel several tons of coal into his large ore wagon. Then, as he had done a hundred times before, James Walker would climb onto the front of the wagon and command his draft mule, Halcyon, to pull a load of coal to Riverdale. James Walker was highly successful in delivering coal. He would buy coal by the ton from the railroad and sell it by the wheelbarrow full. Riverdale's citizens respected James Walker; his prices were fair, and his delivery was prompt. Regardless of the elements, James Walker would deliver his coal to any home in Riverdale to ensure no town member suffered from the harshness of winter or went through any season without heated water.

James Walker would start his deliveries from the top of Main Street, a street with a gentle downward slope, which eased the burden on his mule. Much of the coal would be delivered before his mule had to make the more arduous climb on Second Street to the top of the hill. Most of his deliveries were routine. James Walker would load his wheel-barrow with coal from his wagon and place the coal in the coal slide on the side of homes or businesses on his route. Each establishment had a coal bin in the basement that would catch the sliding coal from above and place it next to the furnace. Three wheelbarrows full of coal would last about a week in the grip of winter.

James loved delivering coal. Years of shoveling had made him robust and healthy. Not an ounce of fat seemed to exist on his body. His heart was as strong as the heart of his draft mule, and he could easily work twelve-hour days with little fatigue. He was a well-liked member of his community. His beautiful wife, Ellen, twenty-nine years of age, was carrying his first child. His home above the butcher shop was free of debt. His bank account held a considerable amount of money earned by his own hands. This was a happy time in what seemed an idyllic world. James was thirty-eight years old and full of life. Fate had treated him well, until now.

Mrs. Wolsworth, a wealthy widow, lived in a grand man-sion at the top of Main Street and was one of James Walker's first deliveries. Her home was three stories tall and painted bright yellow with white trim around the window and porch. Stained-glass windows adorned her home, and the gardens resembled a well-kept park. Her three fireplaces demanded a great deal of coal to keep burning, and her servants were constantly shoveling the black fuel in the winter.

Mrs. Wolsworth was one of James Walker's best patrons. A great iron fence with an intimidating gate, which always remained locked, surrounded her home. James Walker would rise from his wagon bench and ring a large, brass bell he kept next to him, calling out, "Coaling . . . coaling," until one of the servants opened the front door of the grand home, walked a short length of the brick path to the gate and unlocked it, permitting entrance to the premises.

But this day was different. No one looked from the win-dow or opened the front door. He rang his bell again and yelled louder, "Coaling . . . coaling." No one came.

James took a moment to look down Main Street. The street divided the town. Freshly-painted Victorian homes lined each side of the wide cobblestone road. Nestled between the ornate homes were several two-story brick businesses. Many families rented or owned the second story of those storefront buildings and called Main Street their home. Each side of the street had a row of trees slowly changing to fall colors. The four blocks of Main Street formed a perpendicular junction with Ocean Front Boulevard, and beyond was the great Eastern Sea. The early morning light was bringing the town to life. The whisper of voices and the movement of people and horses on the street heralded the waking of the town and the renewal of life.

A Raven's strange, loud cry forced James Walker's attention. The beautifully large bird seemed to stare directly at him and, with a piercing cry, announced his presence. How wonderful this black bird. A sense of serene happiness overcame James Walker. He whispered to himself, "What a beautiful and unique animal." The Raven seemed radiant as the rising sun bathed the bird with nascent light, and the bird's eyes seemed to glow. James Walker was filled with awe, peace, and tranquility. This was his last gift from life, the presence of the Raven.

Donnie was a dull, normal child of twelve. His only faults were his youth, boredom, and slow wit. Hiding in the tall grass across the street in a vacant lot and with little thought, he picked up a small rock, placed the stone in his slingshot and aimed at the draft mule. He was motivated by the image of "coal man" falling into his wagon full of coal when his mule jumped. His actions, he reasoned, would make a funny story to share with his friends. Donnie pulled back on the sling and released the stone. The projectile hit the mule between its ribs and, as predicted, the animal jumped forward with the sting and surprise, throwing James off balance. "Halcyon, halt!" James yelled as he attempted to keep control of the ore wagon.

The mule abruptly stopped. James dropped the bell and grabbed the tall brake lever to prevent himself from falling, releasing the brake. The coaler then tripped on the wagon's bench strut and fell forward between the mule and the wagon, hitting the ground with a thud. He landed on his back, the wind knocked from his lungs. The impact of James's body hitting the ground caused Halcyon to jump once again, and, in an instant, the iron rim of the wagon wheel rolled across Walker's neck, crushing his windpipe and spine. The pulverized mush of his neck no longer connected James Walker's head to his body. He was killed instantly.

Halcyon, sensing the wagon pushing on him, attempted to stop the wagon but could not. The wagon continued rolling, the rear wheel striking James's head by his ear, crushing his skull with a dull pop and spraying grey brain tissue and blood several feet in all directions. James Walker's heart, at first, continued to pump blood through his severed neck, spattering the air for several seconds until his heart grew still.

The draft mule instinctively realized his peril. Unable to stop the heavy ore wagon, the panicked Halcyon attempted to run away from the danger. Within a moment, the helpless mule was running as fast as possible, but he could not escape his fate. Halfway down Main Street, the mule stumbled on the cobblestone, breaking the wagon's wooden tongue and falling on his side. The mule slid for several feet before the front wheels of the wagon crushed the mule's back legs and continued over the mule's ribs, slicing the poor animal in two.

Halcyon screamed an ungodly scream as the wagon flipped, breaking and snapping the leather bridles that once controlled the animal and spilling coal in all directions. The draft mule was a massive and vigorous animal. He did not die for several minutes until he bled out. Severed and mutilated, the mule attempted to right himself, and with another horrifying shriek, managed to stand on his front legs. The mule made one more desperate attempt to escape. He pulled himself forward, dragging his crushed hind quarters behind, blood and intestines sprawling from his body. He heaved and stumbled in shock for nearly a hundred feet before collapsing for the last time, crying in pain. Only then did this magnificent animal die and join his master.

Donnie looked in stunned silence as he watched the fruition of his reckless act. James Walker's body twitched and moaned for several seconds after his head was crushed as air escaped from his torso. Donnie's mind and soul were overwhelmed by the specter he had created. He slowly crawled away and then ran from the carnage. He would cry for weeks—a persistent melancholy becoming his lifelong companion. Donnie would never speak of his deed, but as months turned into years, a dark presence of guilt would consume and change him. He died young from hard drink and opium. He was also a victim of his actions on that terrible day.

The Raven watched the gruesome theater of twisted death play out before him. He spread his large wings and leaped into the air as the rising sun warmed the world. As this silent witness rose above Main Street, the Raven could see the gathering and hear the distressed voices of the town as they became aware of the tragedy. Some stood in mute shock. Others screamed and cried. Someone yelled, "Look! On top of the hill. . . . Someone is lying in the street." Another responded, "It's the coaler, James Walker."

The Raven flew higher now and Main Street grew smaller. The Raven had the advantage: he could see the world in a more complete way than those below him. The Raven watched as many of the people ran uncontrolled in all directions, seeking relief from the horror. Two groups formed circles—one around the dead mule, and the second up the hill, around James Walker's corpse. The bright blood from both victims, the life fluid, slowly flowed down the street before coagulating into dark, unmoving streams. The Raven flew higher still, above the buildings and trees, and took one last look at the confusion below. Then, the Raven caught a warm updraft, a gift from the morning sun, and ascended into the heavens.

The Raven, on this day, was not alone.

∿

Dr. Conrad Forrestal was a young medical doctor and had practiced medicine in Riverdale for more than ten years. He loved Riverdale, and the townspeople trusted and deeply respected him. For many years, Dr. Forrestal's vocation consumed and defined him, and he never considered another kind of life. He never took a wife; his mistress was his never-ending role as the Riverdale physician. Dr. Forrestal was a striking man, lean and handsome, with thick, black hair and a distinctive, chiseled countenance. He was immaculately dressed in a long, black coat, a heavily starched white dress shirt and black vest, and matching black trousers. His tall, leather boots were polished black every morning by one of his servants to ensure they were free of the filthy detritus of dirt, mud, and horse manure accumulated from the day before. Dr. Forrestal was a man of considerable means. Riverdale was a successful and affluent community, and Dr. Forrestal had done quite well treating the town's inhabitants. To the families without means, Dr. Forrestal gladly offered his knowledge and treatment, gratis. He stood sentinel, devoted to the community well-being, and he passionately believed his vocation was his fate.

Dr. Forrestal stood quietly in front of his mansion on Ocean Front Boulevard with his ubiquitous black bag, waiting for the stable boy to bring him his horse and carriage at the beginning of his day. He reached into his vest pocket and retrieved his pocket watch: 7:30 a.m. He glanced to his left and, right on time, Jack, the boy from the livery stable, turned the corner with a bridle in hand, trotting beside Demon, the doctor's three-year-old gelding. The beautiful horse was pulling the doctor's new, shiny black carriage. Upon its arrival, Dr. Forrestal stepped down from the stone curb and placed his hand on Demon's mane, whispering a morning greeting. He turned to Jack, handed the boy a nickel, and thanked him for his promptness. He then checked the tack and ran his hand down his horse before stepping into his carriage. Dr. Forrestal loved the feel of the oncoming fall and paused to sense the season before starting his daily rounds. A small voice interrupted, crying out behind him. He turned and observed young Robert Potter, barefoot, wearing ill-fitting, hand-me-down overalls, face and feet filthy, racing toward him and yelling at the top of his voice, "Mule wreck . . . Mule wreck on Main Street. Come quick."

Upon arrival, Robert's small hands reached out and grabbed the doctor's carriage, clinging to the side for an instant and attempting to catch his breath. Dr. Forrestal pulled back on his reins as Demon lunged forward as the boy clamored next to the carriage and with a firm, authoritative voice: "Robert, catch your breath and then tell me what has happened."

Robert took a long breath, and, with a modicum of sadness in his voice, stated, "The coaler man. The coal wagon rolled over his head and smashed it like a punkin."

"Is he dead?" the doctor asked without hesitation.

"Yeah, the coaler, he is dead, and so is his mule," Robert responded.

"Now, I want you to listen very carefully," Dr. Forrestal spoke with a resolute voice. "I want you to run down to the fire station number seven on Elm and tell the firemen I told you to bring the emergency wagon, a canvas stretcher, and some wool blankets to the coaler man. Can you remember that?"

Robert bobbed his head. "Yeah."

"Where is the coaler man on Main, Robert?" Dr. Forrestal asked.

"By the widow's mansion on the top of the hill," Robert stated as he turned to start running toward the fire station several blocks away.

Dr. Forrestal watched the young boy disappear around the corner and, with slight trepidation in his voice, said, "It begins, Demon. Let's go." With a pull on the reins, Demon turned down Ocean Front toward Main and began to trot.

Several blocks down the cobblestone road, Dr. Forrestal reached Main Street and steered Demon and his carriage into the chaos. People were running in and out buildings, screaming and yelling. A large group stood next to a pile of coal and the overturned ore wagon. Closing the distance between him and the crowd, the doctor was stunned by the horrific sight of the mule's mutilated carcass. Passing a somber group of town members surrounding the dead mule, the doctor saw the agony of their faces and heard the voices of some of the men speculating how the animal could have run so far in such a terrible state. Dr. Forrestal's thoughts quickly shifted from the poor mule to the man lying at the top of Main Street. He prepared himself as he approached the next group of people at the top of the hill.

His tall carriage enabled the doctor to look over the heads of the women and men encircling James Walker. The sight was truly ghastly. James's body appeared unmolested by the tragic events, but his head was crushed beyond recognition. The town members formed a collective unity of stunned witnesses. There was some whimpering, a few people sobbed, some could not gaze upon the specter without becoming ill and vomiting as they turned to escape the sight. Mothers grabbed their children and covered their eyes, dragging them away. A few of the spectators fainted, falling to the hard cobblestones, their countenances ashen as shock consumed their sensibilities. Without hesitation, the doctor jumped from his carriage and handed the horses reins to Arnold, Mrs. Wolsworth's butler. Arnold had ventured out of the mansion to witness the events unfolding in the street just outside his place of employment.

Walking smartly toward James Walker's body, the doctor stated in a loud, authoritative voice, "Stand back. Let me through." The group obediently complied. The doctor then kneeled by Walker's remains, took off his coat, and covered the coaler's head and shoulders from the world. No one would ever look upon the face of James Walker again.

The doctor took a moment to aid the overcome and unconscious spectators. Retrieving a bottle of smelling salts and bandages from his bag, the doctor brought the unconscious back to relative alertness and bandaged the wounds inflicted by an unforgiving stone street. The doctor selected several strong men among the group to help their woozy companions return to their homes so they might recover in private. Once again, no one questioned the doctor's commands.

With the rumble of horse hooves, the emergency fire wagon, Firewagon Seven, arrived with a flurry of dust. Two large draft horses pulled the fire wagon, one pale and one dark. The wagon contained five men. Jake Corvidae, the teamster, oversaw the wagon and the horses. He was required to remain with the wagon. The other four men were field firemen, highly trained for fighting fires and removing deceased victims from fires, drownings, and, in this case, a mule wreck. Oboe Jackson oversaw the team. The doctor had worked with Oboe before and directed his comments to him.

The doctor walked up to the wagon and stated, "James Walker is dead."

Oboe responded without emotion, "Mule wreck."

The three other men grabbed the stretcher and blankets, jumped from the wagon, and quickly covered the body. The doctor faced the firemen and began instructing, "Men, the head is severed. One of you grab his ankles, and I will need one man on each side of the body. Grab Mr. Walker's upper arm, and when I give the word, lift him and place him on the stretcher."

The firemen did not hesitate—they knew the doctor's judgment was sound. The doctor walked to the head of James Walker. He put both of his hands on top of the coat he had placed over the corpse's head. Holding the head down with his hands, he instructed the men to lift the body onto the stretcher. As the men lifted James Walker, Dr. Forrestal felt some pulling of the head. A few neck muscles and other tissues held at first, but snapped with little resistance. While the men place the body in the wagon, the doctor carefully gathered his coat around the remains of James Walker's head.

The doctor then tucked the edges of his coat under the pulverized remains and, holding the sides, formed a cloth bag. Blood soaked the coat, staining the doctor's white shirt and dark trousers. The doctor lifted the head with his coat and, with relief, realized little of the head remained on the street.

With calculated effort, the doctor carried James Walker's head to the wagon and placed it on an open blanket next to his body. The doctor, with care and deep respect, wrapped his coat and James Walker's head in the blanket. The firemen watched in silence. A moment passed. The doctor looked at Oboe and gave instructions again: "Oboe, take Mr. Walker to Maxwell's Funeral Services. Tell the undertaker to place the body in a wooden coffin and nail the lid shut. Tell Mr. Maxwell not to attempt to embalm Mr. Walker's body and to prepare a gravesite for immediate burial. Tell him I will cover the expense if Mr. Walker's survivors need assistance."

Oboe softly responded, "Yes."

The doctor continued, "After the body is delivered, take the wagon back to the fire station and wash all the blood out. Put a clean stretcher and blankets into the wagon, and then bring your men to Mrs. Walker's house on Third. Do you know where she lives?"

"Above the butcher shop," Oboe murmured.

The doctor continued his authoritative instructions, "That's right. Now please hurry. I am going to tell Mrs. Walker that her husband is dead, and I'm concerned because she is with child."

"I understand. How awful. I will clean up the wagon and hurry over as fast as I can," Oboe said, staring at the grotesque sight within the confines of the wagon.

The doctor watched the wagon leave Main Street in a flurry of dust. Dr. Forrestal turned to Arnold, thanked him for holding the reins, grabbed the carriage handle, and, with a quick jump, climbed inside and began his agonizing sojourn to Third Street.

Sadness, anxiety, and apprehension consumed the doctor. The doctor had been Ellen Walker's physician for ten years, and he was deeply fond of her. She had grown into a most handsome woman during that time: petite, and well-proportioned, with long, raven-black hair, brilliant green eyes, and in excellent health except for recurring bouts of profound melancholia prior to and later in her pregnancy. The doctor was concerned that Mrs. Walker's persistent mental condition, seemingly endogenous, might be potentiated by her husband's tragic fate. The morose task of informing Mrs. Walker of her husband's death, of course, belonged to her treating physician. He hoped a naïve, concerned neighbor had not informed Mrs. Walker of her husband's fate before his arrival. Dr. Forrestal feared the tragic news would cause such an emotional reaction that Mrs. Walker would go into labor and the child would be born premature or, worse, stillborn. This day was, after all, terrible and tragic for Mrs. Walker and the community that knew and loved the "coaler," and the day was just beginning.

A few blocks and a few minutes travel brought Dr. Forrestal to the front of Passerine's Meats, the town's butcher shop. Jumping down from his carriage and securing the reins to the hitching post, the doctor began his dreaded ascension up the outside stairs to the Walker's residence. He knocked on the door, took a deep breath, and prepared himself. He could hear movement inside the house. The door opened and there stood Mrs. Walker, pregnant, smiling, and radiant. This moment would be the last time Dr. Forrestal saw Mrs. Walker smile for a long while. The events of this horrendous day would change and define her life until the day she died.

Mrs. Walker realized almost instantly that something was very wrong. The doctor's face was drawn and pale. His white shirt and vest covered with blood. Without a word, apprehension consumed Mrs. Walker, then terror. Her legs buckled as her mind began to process the meaning of the doctor standing in her doorway. She began falling backward, knocking over a small table and breaking a glass vase. Dr. Forrestal stepped through the door and reached with his left arm. Grabbing Ellen's left arm just above her wrist and placing his right arm around her shoulders, he slowly lowered her to the ground as she was overwhelmed and no longer able to stand. The doctor, sitting next to her, pulled her close as she began to scream, "James—not James!"

The doctor held her more tightly and said, "Mrs. Walker, your husband is dead. I am so profoundly sorry." Mrs. Walker seemed to slip away, overwhelmed with grief. She began sobbing uncontrollably, her tears mingling with her husband's blood on the doctor's shirt. Just hours ago, the love of her life kissed her goodbye and walked into the outside world, never to return. Her strong, handsome man, the foundation of her existence, was here and now he was gone. Mrs. Walker's mind could not grasp the incomprehensible. The enormous vacuum of her husband's loss caused her to weep and gasp for air. She was adrift in her grief, and all the doctor could do was hold her and console her.

For what seemed the longest time, Oboe and the others could be heard coming up the stairs. Oboe was the first to enter and found Mrs. Walker being held by the doctor on the floor of the entryway. "I am sorry I took so long." The other men came carrying the stretcher. "Place the stretcher next to her on the floor," Dr. Forrestal directed the firemen.

Oboe obeyed the doctor, and the firemen gently lifted the traumatized woman onto the stretcher and then put several reinforced muslin straps around her to ensure she could not fall.

With great care, the doctor and Oboe carried the grieving woman down the stairs and crossed the short distance to the Station Seven firewagon.

While the doctor still held the stretcher, Oboe placed his end of the stretcher on the back edge of the wagon and jumped into the trailer, being careful not to strike his head on the empty hose rack above the wagon bed.

He then lifted and pulled the stretcher into the wagon. The doctor held his end up and guided the stretcher into the fire wagon. The doctor and the rest of the firemen except for one followed Oboe into the wagon. The doctor asked the last man to follow in his carriage. Oboe began ringing the fire wagon bell as the teamster directed the draft horses to Riverdale Hospital.

Station 7 - Firewagon 1878

The Riverdale Hospital was only a mile away, and the fire wagon took only a few minutes to complete the journey, the ringing bell parting the usual traffic of horses, wagons, and pedestrians. The hospital staff heard the sound as the wagon approached and were standing at attention, prepared for the emergency as the wagon pulled up to the emergency room doors. The hospital orderlies helped the doctor from the wagon and, with the firemen's assistance, carried Mrs. Walker into the hospital. She continued to weep and moan, and appeared disoriented.

Supervising Nurse Russell stood in the entrance hall, waiting for instructions from the doctor. Dr. Forrestal spoke unambiguously, "Mrs. Walker is in shock from the loss of her husband, and she is eight and half months pregnant. Please prepare and place her in the birthing ward for observation. The shock may induce birth. She will need all the emotional support we can give her."

Nurse Russell simply replied, "Yes, doctor." Nurse Russell and the rest of the staff were well trained, understood the medical emergency, and began preparing for the events.

Nine hours had passed since Mrs. Walker's hospitalization, and Dr. Forrestal was exhausted. By any measure of
understanding, this day had been difficult and trying. The
doctor walked into his hospital office and slowly untied and
removed the birthing apron soiled with blood and placental
fluids, placing it into the large tin container labeled "Soiled"
next to his office door. He gasped as he saw his reflection in
the full-length mirror, a sense of guilt rising within him. For
the first time, the extent of Mr. Walker's blood adulterating
his clothing became evident to the doctor. What a terrible
visual presentation Mrs. Walker had to endure while I informed her of her husband's death, the doctor thought,
looking at his ghastly appearance. Self-loathing and then rage
consumed him. He removed his pocket watch, then tore the
blood-soaked vest, shirt, and trousers from his body, disposing the soiled clothing into the container. The doctor stated
loudly, "I told that poor woman her husband had been killed
looking like a butcher from a slaughterhouse. How could I be
so insensitive?"

Pushing the door shut, the doctor walked to the washing
stand in the corner of the room and picked up a pitcher of
water. Pouring water from the pitcher into the bowl, the
doctor scrubbed his hands, arms, and face with a bar of lye
soap. He slowly walked to the small closet in his office and
took from the shelf a freshly laundered shirt, and from the
rack a pair of new trousers stored for such an occasion. The
doctor continued to harangue himself as he walked over to his
desk to complete the needed paperwork depicting the events
of the day. Sitting at his desk, Dr. Forrestal looked around his
office. In front of him and to his right, a tall bookshelf
crowded with medical books and journals covered the walls.
To his back, a large bay window permitted the light of the
afternoon to soak the room. Vast piles of medical documentation waiting for filing and medical journals, read and unread,
covered his desk. Opening a drawer, the doctor selected three
blank birth certificates, three death certificates, and several

blank sheets of paper labeled "physician's notes."

Nurse Russell earlier informed the doctor the mother named her child Benjamin Jeffery Walker.

~

The doctor began with the certificate of live birth. He laid three blank forms in front of him and began to fill them out with a fountain pen in triplicate:

CERTIFICATE OF LIVE BIRTH

Child's name: Benjamin Jeffery Walker
Date of birth: October 21, 1878
Gender: male
Weight: 6 lbs 11 ounces

Child's Health: Excellent with exception of a severely deformed right leg and right club foot.

Mother: Ellen Joy Walker
Age: 29
Father: James Kent Walker (Deceased)
Age: 38
Location of Birth: Riverdale
County: Kent   State: Kenton
Residential Address: 29 Third St. Second Floor (above butcher shop)

Dr. Forrestal then filled out the certificate of death, also in triplicate.

CERTIFICATE OF DEATH
Number: 723

Name of Deceased: James Kent Walker
Date of Death: Oct. 21, 1878
Age of Deceased: Thirty-Eight years
Cause of Death: Employment Accident Head Trauma
Location of Death: Riverdale, County of Kent, Kenton
Survivor: Spouse, Ellen Joy Walker
Age: Twenty-nine
Survivor: Son, Benjamin Jeffery Walker

Dr. Forrestal paused to reflect. This was the first time he had completed both certificates containing the father's date of death coinciding with the birthday of the son. The doctor had witnessed far too many mothers die on the same day the child was born. James Walker and his wife had a different fate.

The doctor then placed one of each of the certifications in the following processing bins on his desk: Survivor's copy, County Records copy, and Hospital copy.

Dr. Forrestal then began documenting the day's events.

The doctor reached for a blank copy of the Physician Notes form and began his documents and began his notes on the patient chart.

PHYSICIAN NOTES:
Date: Oct. 21, 1878
Mrs. Ellen Joy Walker was hospitalized for observation and prophylactic treatment after receiving news of her husband's death in a coaling accident. Mrs. Walker appeared ashen, pulse weak and rapid. Mrs. Walker has a history of debilitating melancholia. The patient was emotionally distraught and incoherent. Mrs. Walker was eight and a half months with child. The patient was under treatment for episodic melancholia prior to and during pregnancy. Prophylactic treatment consisted of avoidance of all causes of

excitement, both mental and physical. Small bleedings and a calming milieu were required when the patient became plethoric shortly after labor pains were observed. Cold sponging was also carefully applied to the face, neck, and abdomen. Mrs. Walker commenced labor within an hour and a half of hospitalization; standard procedures were utilized to meliorate pain: 3% opiate solution-soaked muslin sheets were placed on the patient's abdomen until birth. The live birth of a male child occurred approximately eight hours after the start of labor. Birth was normal without complications. Shortly after birth of child, the patient began to exhibit bouts of violent vomiting, which required treatment with effervescing draught containing a few drops of laudanum in a wineglass portion. The child's weight - 6 pounds, 11 ounces. Child appeared normal without complications except for badly deformed right leg and right foot. The leg was undeveloped and 10% shorter than the normal left leg. Follow-up examination of the child's leg will be required to ascertain remedial actions. Mrs. Walker appears emotionally distraught, morose, and will require close observation and emotional support to ensure the mother and child's health and safety. After birth, melancholia may be exacerbated by the loss of Mrs. Walker's husband on the day of birth. Special attention will be given to bonding of mother to child. Mrs. Walker will remain hospitalized and bedridden for the foreseeable future until both physical and emotional improvement will permit patient to return to her residence.

Signature of Physician: Conrad Forrestal, MD

The doctor had just completed his notes when he was startled by a gentle rapping on his office door. "Come in."

Walter Pickering, a digger at Maxwell's Undertakers, opened the door and entered the office. He appeared disheveled and covered with fresh dirt, a derivative of his occupation.

"Walter," the doctor proclaimed upon recognizing his guest. "What's going on."

Walter, a man of many words, began, "Mr. Maxwell sent me to get you because Mr. Walker is going to be put under because the coffin leaks, and Mr. Maxwell wants him down and needs the death certificate before Mr. Walker is laid down, and Mr. Maxwell wants you at the burial to say a few words because he knows you and Mr. Walker are friends, and no one else is around."

"Of course. I will bring the certificate of death and will be right over," the doctor stated, standing to retrieve a clean coat from the closet. "Do you need a ride?"

"No, I rode Martha. Meet you there," Walter responded as he disappeared from the office.

The doctor grabbed a ribbon tie from his desk drawer and made a quick effort at fashion decorum, straightening his coat and then, peering into the full-length mirror, stated out loud, "That's better." He leaned over the top of his desk and secured the certificate of death, passed through the office door, turned left, and headed down the hall.

The late afternoon sun was reaching the horizon, painting the world in yellow and orange hues. The air was still, without even the slightest breeze. The sea was quiet, and Dr. Forrestal was lost in thought of the man he knew as James Walker. Three blocks from the hospital and at the base of Crescent Hill, the doctor reached Maxwell's Funeral Services, the town's only undertaker. The funeral building was a two-story brick structure with a large front window displaying several rows of coffins. Mr. Maxwell and his family lived upstairs, and behind the funeral home was Riverdale Cemetery.

The doctor halted Demon and descended from his carriage. Securing his horse, he stepped up from the street and entered the building. The sizable main showroom, paneled in dark, polished walnut, contained a dozen coffins mostly made of plain oak with one notable exception—Mr. Maxwell had secured a luxury Mahogany, silk-lined coffin in anticipation of widow Wolsworth's send-off. Of course, Mr. Maxwell would never admit his business model required scrutiny of the town elders for potential business opportunities. He was, however, a highly successful businessman.

Mr. Maxwell entered the showroom and greeted Dr. Forrestal. "Good to see you, doctor. Sorry to put the rush on, but because of Mr. Walker's condition. Well, you know. We have to plant him because of corruption. No embalming, and, well, the coffin is a leaker. Kind of a mess. You understand."

"Of course. Is Mr. Walker by his resting place?" the doctor asked.

"He's outside with the boys. Did you bring the certificate of death?"

The doctor reached into his coat pocket and unfolded the document. "I have it."

Mr. Maxwell took the certificate, turned, and walked into his office. He opened a large, black ledger, and next to information pertaining to James Walker, Mr. Maxwell wrote the certificate of death number. Standing back, Dr. Forrestal retrieved his fountain pen from his coat pocket and signed his name next to the number in the thick tome of death. Between the men, not another word was spoken. This ritual was repeated many times during the years. Mr. Maxwell handed the certificate of death back to the doctor, where the document was secured once again in his coat pocket.

The two men walked through the embalming room toward the back door. The Peters' girl, Nancy, eleven years old, was lying on the embalming table under a muslin sheet with only her head exposed, a victim of Mr. Peters' careless handling of firearms. The doctor looked away from the young girl, not wanting to see her again in death. He hated the smell of embalming formaldehyde and the building reeked of it. The doctor was grateful to complete his short journey through the house of death and filled his lungs with fresh air as he stepped outside.

The two men walked a few hundred feet up the hill. Walter and several other diggers stood next to the grave. Two heavy boards at each end of the coffin supported James Walker over the open grave. All the diggers had removed their hats and stood in respectful silence. Several quiet moments passed before Mr. Maxwell spoke, "We will have a proper memorial when Mrs. Walker is feeling better, of course."

The doctor acknowledged, "Yes, when the time is right."

Mr. Maxwell then asked, "Would you please say a few words, as he was your friend?"

The doctor took a moment to gather his thoughts, then softly spoke: "We all knew the coaler as a strong and fine man. He kept us warm in the cold of winter. He warmed our homes and our businesses. When we needed his help, regardless of time or weather, he would appear with a wagon full of coal and, with a smile and a kind word, filled our coal bins. He was known to help the poor when they needed coal. Many of his deliveries went unpaid. He would only say about such things, 'I have been so fortunate. How could I not help those in need?' James Walker was a good man who warmed more than our homes; he warmed our lives. He warmed our hearts. He will be missed."

The four other men said in unison, as was the custom at such times, "He will be missed."

Mr. Maxwell produced a small copy of The Word and handed the book to the doctor. A small, black ribbon marked the appropriate page. In the fading daylight, Dr. Forrestal read the words that must be said:

"O' sacred dead, we place you now in hallowed soil so your worldly substance may find peaceful sleep while your blessed spirit soars on Raven's wing. We will wait here a while longer among the stars and stones of this, the living realm, and mourn as we speak of you with reverence and hushed tones. Be not troubled on this your burial day when we shall weep; true, we weep that we may no longer embrace you or share our mutual burdens and joys, please know we also weep with elation, aware you now roam the dominion of the afterlife where pain and corruption is no more, and unlimited wisdom and knowledge are the norm. We accept the sanctity of fate, so we shall wait for that day when we too shall soar on Raven's wing and meet again at heaven's gate."

The other men said, again in unison, "On Raven's wing."

The three diggers and Mr. Maxwell placed two heavy canvas straps under the coffin. With each man pulling tight on the straps, Dr. Forrestal removed the boards supporting the coffin over the grave, and the four men lowered James Walker into the ground. With James in his final resting place, the doctor picked up a handful of soft dirt and tossed it into the grave, saying quietly, "We will all be with you soon, our friend. Greet us in the afterlife with your smile and your good nature. We will protect your family and think of you often until fate brings us together again, our dear friend . . . our dear friend."

With those final words, the doctor and Mr. Maxwell turned and walked somberly down the path toward the Eastern Sea. Before reaching the undertaker's brick building, the doctor addressed Mr. Maxwell, "Please let me know the cost of the burial. I will write you a cheque."

Mr. Maxwell smiled and said, "Let me tell you a story. Five years ago, in the middle of winter, I went over to the railroad freight yard at Jakeup's station to pick up a shipment of coffins. I was halfway home when a freak blizzard swirled so dense I could not see a thing. I knew I had to get home or freeze to death, but I could not see my horse in front of me. I panicked and drove my poor horse off the road into a ditch, and that sweet horse broke her leg. There was nothing I could do, so I pulled my pistol from beneath my coat and put a bullet in her head so she would not suffer. I then lay down beside my warm friend and prepared to die. Just then I heard James Walker coming through the storm yelling, 'Maxwell, you better not freeze to death. You are the town's only undertaker, so you cannot die.' He had heard the shot. He and that big, old draft mule saved my life. He picked me up and put his coat around me and helped me onto his ore wagon. He was delivering coal to my home when my wife told him I was late, and she feared I was lost in the storm. James told her not to worry and headed out to find me and brought me home. It is my honor to help this man and his family. Please let me do this."

The doctor nodded. "He was the best of us."

The two men shook hands and went their own ways.

The doctor did not ride back to the livery stable that early evening, he walked beside Demon. He felt like walking. He thought of all the day's events and did not say a word when the livery stable boy came out to take his horse and carriage. He ran his hand down Demon's strong, black neck and whispered, "good night." Then the doctor walked the four blocks to the hospital, entered the building, and ambled down the hall to the birthing ward. He unobtrusively entered Mrs. Walker's room. The young mother was sound asleep, holding her bundled baby in her arms. Karen, the night nurse, was sitting next to her, ensuring her and the baby's safety and observing and documenting both Mrs. Walker and the baby's condition. She smiled at the doctor and whispered, "She is doing just fine. She was smiling at the baby just before she went to sleep. She called the baby Benjamin. I think she will be all right."

The doctor smiled back and said, "Yes, I was told the baby's name earlier by Nurse Russell. I am so glad she is doing well."

The doctor took a long moment and focused his attention on Benjamin Walker. The day consumed his thoughts. The doctor whispered to himself, "How tragic his birthday was the same day as his father's death. He will never know his father. His father will never hold him or claim him in life."

Chapter 2
A Gift from the Grave

D r. Forrestal had anticipated, regardless of Mrs. Walker's initial stability, the probability of his patient's mental decompensation. It was not unusual for a new mother to experience some form of hysterical melancholia. However, with Mrs. Walker's history of melancholia prior to the birth of her son, the terrible shock of losing her husband may exacerbate her mental state. Melancholy, in extreme cases, was challenging to treat, and many of the traditional intervention methods were ineffective. Dr. Forrestal spent many hours reviewing the medical journals and found several promising articles on the experimental use of hydrate of lithia to relieve profound depression. Mrs. Walker's condition prohibited any rational discussion of potential treatment options or possible adverse side effects. The doctor knew he would have to proceed with the experimental remedy without his patient's permission. He was aware that without effective intervention, the child was at risk of neglect or worse, and a real possibility existed that Mrs. Walker might take her own life. The doctor knew of several cases in the medical literature of distraught mothers killing their babies before taking their own lives. Infanticide was Dr. Forrestal's worst fear and he instructed the hospital staff on the importance of keeping Mrs. Walker under close observation. Dr. Forrestal was determined to relieve Mrs. Walker of her terrible burden and ensure Benjamin's safety.

PHYSICIAN'S NOTES
Oct. 27, 1878

Mrs. Walker's physical condition shows considerable improvement with no adverse effects of birth on her physical state. Her mental state remains guarded. Mrs. Walker showed some reduction in grief-related behavior the first few days after her child's birth, then demonstrated rapid decompensation beginning day three after birth. Mrs. Walker would express frequent spells of subdued crying and whimpering with escalating paroxysms of agonizing wails and forceful screams. She would frequently vocalize her husband's name, and related issues of loss. Of considerable concern are her statements of suicidal ideation as a viable mechanism of relief. The nursing notes describe several incidents a day of Mrs. Walker leaving her baby alone in the bed while she was found in a fetal position under the bed or on the floor of other locations within the ward, whimpering and crying. Due to the severity of Mrs. Walker's mental state, a pharmacognosy strategy will be employed, in consultation with the hospital apothecary.

Therapeutics: Emetics; 1) Three drachms (f3j) root of the Cephaelis ipecacuanha will be suspended in alcohol and administered in early morning by mouth. Emetics will be repeated until the vomit is clear, or the patient demonstrates repeated dry heaves. Objective: The removal of improper matter that may have accumulated in the stomach during emotional stress, and to give a shock to the system and thus break up the morbid association. 2) Three drachms (f3j) of castor oil shall be given next to relieve constipation and its attendant evil; thus, the noxious matter of the bowels will be evacuated, preparing the patient's system for maximum absorption of the primary therapeutic: hydrate of lithia. Emetics will not be repeated unless the patient demonstrates need.

Hydrate of lithia: This substance contains lithium salts and has been shown in the medical literature in some cases to improve severe states of melancholia. This therapeutic will aggressively be applied. Three drachms (f3j) of hydrate of lithia will be given three times a day at 6:00 a.m., 12:00 p.m., 6:00 p.m.

A regular balanced diet will be given, and copious notes taken daily of bowel and urine amounts and characteristics.

Mental state will be continuously documented for improvement; specifically, reduction of symptoms of morbid expression. Charting will be done every 15 minutes. Documentation of degrees of cessation of melancholia will be critical in determining the efficacy of application of the prescribed therapeutics.

Physician Signature: Conrad Forrestal, MD.

Oct. 27, 1878

Benjamin Walker appears to be in excellent physical health. The child exhibits no signs of fever and has a healthy weight gain of 4 ounces. The baby's current weight is 7 pounds and 3 ounces. The child's skin is clear, and the body seems well developed and proportional, except for the right leg and foot. The child's urine and feces appear normal with evacuation on a regular and appropriate basis. The baby seems alert and reacts appropriately to external stimuli. The right leg is clearly deformed, and the right foot expresses a severe state of talipes varus, club-foot, from congenital etiology, most likely the result of disturbance of the cerebrospinal system producing irregular contractions of the muscles, by which antagonism is destroyed. The right leg is approximately 1.5 inches shorter than the left leg. The leg upper muscular form appears normal. The knee is clearly congenitally deformed. Observation of the leg's movement and tactile examination strongly indicate deformation of the patella ligament, which is non-functional, severed. The quadriceps muscle flexes appropriately, but the leg is limp. The patella ligament moves under the skin and does not seem attached; thus, the right leg will be useless. Appropriate leg brace to stiffen the leg at the knee and orthopedic shoes will need to be developed and customized to the patient's ambulatory requirements. The child's leg will require daily exercise to prevent atrophy of the upper leg muscles. In conjunction with the leg brace, the exercises should produce a satisfactory means of locomotion for the patient. The child's lower skeletal structure in the right leg is congenitally deformed. It is not readily apparent at what stage of embryonic development the bone was deformed. Most likely, the deformity occurred prior to punctum ossification from lack of adequate blood flow to that portion of the lower leg; hence, calcareous particles failed to be deposited appropriately. The leg may have been twisted or pinned up during this period of critical embryonic development. The leg may have been moved to a more advantageous embryonic position later in development but failed to compensate adequately.

Physician Signature: Conrad Forestall, MD

Three weeks had passed since Mrs. Walker began receiving a trial of hydrate of lithia. Dr. Forrestal supervised the administration, and there were minor improvements in Mrs. Walker's mental state. At the beginning of the fourth week, Dr. Forrestal received a telegraph requesting urgent assistance outside Londonderry, treating victims of a coal mine collapse. He returned to Riverdale Hospital late in the afternoon three days later and headed straight for the birthing ward.

Supervising Nurse Russell welcomed the doctor at the door of the ward. She was beaming with contentment. Dr. Forrestal asked in concern, "How is Mrs. Walker? Any improvement?"

Nurse Russell only smiled and opened the birthing ward, motioning the doctor inside. The birthing ward was mostly empty; at the end of the ward, looking out an open window, Mrs. Walker sat, clothed in street attire, holding Benjamin. The doctor anxiously closed the distance between them. As he drew near, he could see Mrs. Walker's countenance was content and at peace, her long, raven-black hair danced in the sea breeze that passed through the open window invading the ward. The late afternoon sun veiled the new mother and child in a radiant glow, as if an angelic halo covered them. How uniquely beautiful and serene Mrs. Walker appeared at that moment overwhelmed the doctor. He was momentarily without words. When Dr. Forrestal was quite close, Mrs. Walker turned her head from the sea and looked directly at the doctor with her piercing green eyes, and with a smile and a soft, tranquil voice said, "Hello, Dr. Forrestal. I feel like I have been reborn. Is this the way the rest of the world feels? I cannot recall a time. . . . This is a miracle, simply a miracle."

The doctor sat down on the hospital bed next to Mrs. Walker. Her appearance was nothing less than amazing. Dr. Forrestal fought back his tears so as not to tarnish his professional demeanor before replying, "Mrs. Walker, you appear to have improved."

Mrs. Walker turned and looked into the doctor's eyes, "Yes, I have improved. I am a different person." Her eyes filled with tears and she began to cry. "These are tears of joy. You have set me free. I cannot understand how for so long I could have been so sad."

Mrs. Walker leaned toward the doctor, reached with her right hand, and took the doctor's hand. She continued, "I mourn the loss of my beautiful husband, and I will miss him the rest of my life . . . the love of my life . . . but now, I can keep this terrible loss in perspective. I am in control of my feelings. Better control. I have a beautiful new baby that consumes me with joy. I must live for my child now." She paused for a long moment, and with some objectivity stated, "It was like I was falling into the darkest, deepest well, like I was dying . . . a feeling of absolute hopelessness . . . awful. I just wanted to die. I was obsessed with darkness. Life was a terrible existence. Then, when I began to take your potion, and after a while, I could feel the dark curtain rise. My world became warm and light. Please tell me, am I cured? Will I ever go to that dark place again?"

The doctor tried to reassure her.

"We have so little understanding about illness of the mind. This medication has had a most advantageous effect in some cases. It is possible you will have to take this medication for the rest of your life. Of course, I will monitor your progress, Mrs. Walker, after you are discharged from the hospital."

"Doctor, I am ready to take my baby home," Mrs. Walker stated unambiguously. "It's time."

"Yes, I think you are right," the doctor returned. "I would like to take a few minutes and take one last look at your baby, and then I will take you home."

Mrs. Walker carefully handed Benjamin to the doctor. After a few minutes examining the child and reviewing the nurses' notes, Dr. Forrestal pronounced the child and mother fit to leave the hospital.

Mrs. Walker and Dr. Forrestal walked down the long row of empty beds, and as they approached the birthing ward door, Mrs. Walker reached down and grasped the doctor's hand. The hospital staff, the orderlies, and the nurses beamed with happiness watching the doctor and patient walk down the hall together. She continued holding his hand tightly while they walked through the hospital, out the emergency room doors, and to the doctor's waiting carriage. With help, Mrs. Walker climbed into the carriage and a nurse lifted the baby into her arms. Dr. Forrestal directed Demon to Mrs. Walker's home. As they traveled up Main Street, the people of the town saw Mrs. Walker for the first time since her husband's death. Observing custom, they placed their right hand over their heart and patted their chest as a sign of sadness and loss. Mrs. Walker smiled and nodded in recognition of their thoughtful gesture.

Arriving at her home, the doctor helped Mrs. Walker and the baby out of the carriage and escorted her up the stairs to the second floor of the two-story, brick building. The home was clean and orderly, and the furniture placed in proper position throughout the home. The broken glass had been removed from the entryway hall. Mr. Walker's lunch, prepared the day of his death, had been removed from her kitchen and the eating utensils cleaned. Three donated steamer trunks sat in the living room containing James Walker's personal effects. James's clothes no longer hung in the closet, or on the wall coat hangers, and nothing remained in his dresser. Even her husband's personals from the private room were in one of the trunks. In the middle of the living room sat the neighborhood baby crib, complete with soft cotton blankets, so baby Benjamin would have a place to sleep. All these things were the efforts of the helpful and concerned neighbors. Mrs. Walker said simply, tears swelling in her eyes, "How thoughtful the people of this town are."

Dr. Forrestal and the young mother, carrying her child, walked over to the kitchen table and sat. Mrs. Walker looked at the baby, and, realizing the child was in tranquil sleep, softly whispered, "I am going to lay him down in the crib." She stood holding Benjamin, walked over to the gleaming-white crib, and gently placed him under the cotton blankets.

She gazed at her son, her mind swirling with the realization of a new life, a child of her own. The doctor took this opportunity to remove a large envelope from his black bag and placed it on the table. In a few moments, Mrs. Walker returned and sat next to Dr. Forrestal.

The doctor started to explain what would be required of his patient to keep her in good health. "Mrs. Walker, I had the apothecary prepare a two-week supply of hydrate of lithia that you must take three times a day. As you can see, there are twenty-two small envelopes contained in the large envelope. Each small envelope contains one dose of medication. Mix one small envelope in a wine glass full of wine, drink the potion when you rise in the morning, when you prepare lunch, and when you retire at night. I will stop by every few days or so to ensure you are doing well and not running out of medication. Would five or six in the evening be a good time for a visit?"

"Yes, that would be fine. What should I do about Benjamin's poor leg? How do I take care of him?" Mrs. Walker asked.

"It is important to exercise your child's leg before he becomes a toddler and attempts to stand on the leg. I will develop an exercise schedule for you to follow while Benjamin is still an infant. When he is older and begins to experiment with walking, we will need to secure a brace to keep his knee stiff and acquire special shoes to compensate for the clubfoot. Benjamin is a number of months away from being a toddler, and we have time. I also want you to arrange a time to bring Benjamin to the birthing ward at the hospital. Nurse Peterson is an expert in caring for infants. She will be helping you with your baby's care, and I will advise her as to what special attention Benjamin will require. We have enough time to work with your son to help him adapt so he may have as normal a life as possible," Dr. Forrestal explained.

"Thank you. I will make arrangements with the hospital. I think being here alone is going to be difficult at first," Mrs. Walker expressed sadly. "Dr. Forrestal, we have known each other for so many years. I wish you could stay a little while more, as a friend."

"This will be a difficult time of adjustment. Reach out to friends and relatives for support. I wish I could stay longer, but I have patients at the hospital and in town to see . . . you can understand. I will see you soon. If something happens with you or the child before I see you again, please come to the hospital. Will you do that?" Dr. Forrestal asked in a professional tone as he rose to leave.

Mrs. Walker walked with the doctor to the door, then stated, "Of course, I understand." As the doctor reached the door, she placed her hand on his shoulder, reached up, kissed him on the cheek, and whispered, "Thank you for caring for my baby and saving my life."

The doctor nodded with approval and disappeared through the door, being ever so mindful of his patient's vulnerabilities at such times.

Mrs. Walker had a difficult time adjusting to life without her husband. The demands of a newborn child required learning. More experienced mothers in the neighborhood offered Ellen considerable help. Mary Simon, who lived near the middle of the block and had three children, ages three, six, and seven, would stop by and share her knowledge and wisdom about child-rearing. Every visit, without exception, she would bring a large box of vegetables and a supply of baby products. The Solses sisters, elderly twins and childless, also brought copious amounts of food: breads, vegetables, and generous portions of bacon, mutton, and beef. Mrs. Walker realized many in the community thought she was destitute, and the frequent food delivery assured Ellen would be well fed, especially while nursing Benjamin. Although the exceptional generosity of the community embarrassed Mrs. Walker, she tearfully accepted the support and vowed that, in time, she would return the kindness.

It was Martha Passerine, the wife of the butcher downstairs, whom Mrs. Walker found to be the most supporting and comforting. Martha had also recently given birth to a son, Petie. Almost every day, Martha Passerine would escape the commotion of the butcher shop and spend many hours with Mrs. Walker planning the future for their sons. Martha never failed to bring ample supplies of various meats from her husband's butcher shop, and would, from time to time, offer to mind Benjamin if Mrs. Walker needed to run errands. Mrs. Walker reciprocated the offer. When Mrs. Walker and Martha Passerine formed a more intimate friendship, Martha offered to care for Benjamin for extended periods of time during the day if Mrs. Walker needed to secure a source of income. Mrs. Walker thanked her for the generous offer and assured her that her husband had made financial arrangements for her needs. Mrs. Walker, delicately, would explain that her loving husband had saved a fair amount of earnings, and, if careful, she would be all right for a number of years—certainly until the time Benjamin was school age.

Mrs. Walker was very conscientious about providing for her child's needs. She met with Nurse Peterson several times a week to ensure her baby's health was progressing properly. She also faithfully took her potions of hydrate of lithia as Dr.

Forrestal instructed. She always had some fear the feeling of melancholy would return, which motivated her to follow her doctor's directions.

Then fate changed her life again.

A month after Mrs. Walker returned home from the hospital, she received an unexpected visit from Robert Bass, the town lawyer. Mr. Bass was a rotund individual and climbing the stairs to Mrs. Walker's residence was a life-threatening task for this poor, fat man. After ten minutes of huffing, sweating, and resting, Mr. Bass reached the summit of his quest. Mrs. Walker had just finished nursing Benjamin and had placed him in the crib when she heard the knock. Opening the door, she found Mr. Bass grasping a black leather, and a somewhat wet briefcase, his face a brilliant red and profusely sweating.

"My name . . . Robert Bass . . . your husband's attorney. Mr. Walker retained my services to handle several important issues concerning his estate and investments. May I come in, Mrs. Walker, and sit down?" he gasped like a drowning man.

"Of course," Mrs. Walker replied, helping the exhausted lawyer to her kitchen table and, she hoped, to a sturdy chair. Without asking, Mrs. Walker retrieved a cold pitcher of water from the icebox and a glass from the kitchen cupboards. Mr. Bass inhaled the water and took a long moment to recover from his triumph over gravity. "Mr. Walker was my client for several years. He instructed me to give you a letter upon his death."

A stunned Mrs. Walker asked, "What are you saying?"

Reaching into his somewhat sweat-saturated leather case, the fatigued lawyer retrieved and handed Mrs. Walker a heavy parchment envelope. "This note from your husband will explain Mr. Walker's wishes," the recovering attorney gasped between breaths.

Hands trembling, Mrs. Walker opened the waxy envelope and began reading her husband's last written words:

My dearest love. I am so sorry that fate took me from you.

How I loved you in life. When I wrote these last words, you told me last night you were with child. Now I am gone, and I will never hold our child. The very thought fills me with dreadful sorrow. My love, I prepared for my death by securing Mr. Bass's services. I trust him, and I hope you will trust him as well. He is devoted to the teaching of The Word. He is a good man. I have known him for many years. He will explain to you what measures I have taken for your financial well-being. I have also entered into a legal agreement to assist you in the event you should become incapacitated when you periodically suffer from melancholia. I am so sorry for not telling you. I thought this best, not wishing you any further sadness. It was my fervent hope you would never be required to read this letter. I wish you and our child a long, meaningful life. Follow the teaching of The Word, and I will see you again when you are lifted on Raven's wing to me. I so love you.   James Walker

Mrs. Walker's tears rained upon the letter. She stared at her husband's words, then looked up at Robert Bass, "How did he know he was going to die?"

"Mr. Walker wrote many letters to you while you were married. He would rewrite the letter from time to time, as events in your life changed. The letters Mr. Walker wrote to you were always current, but the essence never changed. Your husband's most primal fear was that he would die and you would be incapacitated with your illness. So, Mr. Walker arranged for me to ensure your well-being. He placed me in charge of your legal and financial affairs and, if necessary, to ensure you will receive the appropriate medical service if your mental state would not permit rational decisions," Robert Bass stated without emotion.

"What are you saying?" Mrs. Walker blurted out.

"Your husband, through the Kent superior county court, made me your guardian ad litem, which means I am representing you in financial and other legal issues that may arise. I will not, of course, be involved in your daily life; however, issues concerning significant financial and medical decisions, I am legally required to supervise," Robert Bass returned, looking straight into Mrs. Walker's eyes. "This arrangement is strictly confidential. I will be reviewing all legal documents pertaining to this arrangement at your convenience at my office. You may, of course, secure legal representation and challenge your husband's wishes in this matter, if you so choose. You should know the court, in camera, annually reviews this legal arrangement. This means you will have a private meeting with the judge on a yearly basis and your attorney, if you should so choose, may be present. You may, of course, address the court during this meeting. Also, my fees were agreed upon by your husband and are strictly reviewed by the court."

"So, you are saying if I become ill you will arrange for my child to be cared for and ensure that I receive proper treatment," Mrs. Walker was trying to understand.

Robert Bass took a deep breath, "Yes, and manage the fortune in your husband's estate."

"As I am sure you know, my husband managed to save a fairly significant life savings. I would hardly call it a fortune," Mrs. Walker returned, confused by Robert Bass's strange and unexpected statement.

"Yes, well, let me explain," Robert Bass took another deep breath. "Mr. Walker secured a life insurance policy. This was not an easy thing for him to purchase, and the New Brunswick Life Insurance Company thoroughly investigated your husband and his occupation before granting him the accidental life insurance policy. Even then, he had to pay into it for three years before the beneficiary of the policy would qualify to secure payment in the event of death—"

"What are you talking about? My husband never spoke to me about life insurance," Mrs. Walker interrupted.

"Again, your husband was trying to protect you because you were suffering from melancholia, and he did not want you to become more depressed because the subject was . . . morbid." Mr. Bass took another glass of water and attempted to bring his breathing to a normal pace.

"Oh, my. Even from the grave, he protects me," Mrs. Walker stated, sitting back on her chair.

"Precisely, Mrs. Walker, precisely. Well, brace yourself, Mrs. Walker," Robert Bass stated as he wheezed from what seemed like his dying breath. "I thought your husband was a little demented at the time, spending this much money for a life insurance policy, but he loved you very much, and I think he would do anything to protect you. Your husband shoveled a lot of coal each month to cover the policy premium."

Robert Bass took a bank deposit book from his briefcase and stated, "An account in your name has been opened at the First National Bank of Londonderry with the balance of one million dollars. I have secured a book of personalized cheques, so you may begin accessing the money with my countersignature."

Mr. Bass handed the stunned Mrs. Walker the deposit book and the cheques.

"How is this possible?" Mrs. Walker questioned.

"Yes, this kind of thing is always somewhat of a shock," Robert Bass responded, searching for another document in his briefcase. "Mrs. Walker, I have just one document I need for you to sign, which will indicate I have performed my responsibilities as your guardian and placed in your possession appropriate methods for you to access, as the beneficiary of your husband's insurance policy, the amount of one million dollars. Please keep in mind my fiduciary responsibilities in this matter, and the money you have received will not be revealed to anyone. Do you have any questions?" Mr. Bass stated while his ruddy complexion and pressured breathing began to return to normal.

"A million dollars . . . that is impossible—I am sure I will have many questions when the shock of all this passes."

Robert Bass stoically replied, "This is very real. I believe this makes you the richest woman in Riverdale, maybe the entire county. We will meet in a few days so I may review how best to protect your fortune. We will consider how you may wish to invest your money."

Robert Bass, now fully recovered from his "near-death" experience, continued, "I have here a document entitled Note of Completion of Estate Disbursement. Please sign here, and, as your guardian, I will cosign."

With her signature, Mrs. Walker became a very wealthy widow.

"Thank you, Mrs. Walker. I am leaving you a copy of the Note of Completion of Estate Disbursement and a copy of the insurance policy your husband purchased. Please take my advice. Keep all this confidential. Do not tell anyone. I have done this for a few years, and I have seen what happens when people become instantly wealthy. Just keep it to yourself. When you are feeling better, please come by the office so we may speak of any assets you may wish to secure at this time. Any questions? We should start by spreading your money around a few large banks, you know, just in case. By the way, the widow Wolsworth's mansion has just been placed on the market for a mere two thousand dollars. You may wish to consider acquiring the property. I think the mansion is a good investment. We can speak about it when you drop by the office." Robert Bass continued, "I am looking forward to working with you."

Mrs. Walker shook her head while looking at her bank book and said, "All of this is a bit much. I have a lot to think about."

"I am leaving now. I will show myself out. Goodbye for now," Robert Bass stated, opening the door and bracing himself for his next physical challenge: descending the stairs.

Mrs. Walker issued a soft "thank you" as Robert Bass shut the door behind him. She spent the next few hours in quiet conversation with her husband.

Chapter 3
Love and Fate

As promised, Dr. Forrestal continued visiting several times a week to follow his patient's progress. After all, the doctor had begun an experimental course of treatment that required his closest scrutiny to ensure his patient's continued health and well-being. Mrs. Walker's child also required close monitoring. Baby Benjamin suffered from a unique disability, and arduous rehabilitation would be a significant part of his young life. The doctor was utterly professional in his medical endeavors with Mrs. Walker, arriving promptly at the specified time, greeting Mrs. Walker with proper pleasantries, and immediately beginning his patient's examination with a series of probative questions concerning her allegiance to her medication schedule, any potential side effects, or any recurrent episodes of depression. When satisfied with Mrs. Walker's progress, Dr. Forrestal would turn his attention to baby Benjamin. The doctor would ask Mrs. Walker a series of pertinent questions concerning Benjamin's handicap and determine the precise measurements of the child's affected limb and foot; all information concerning mother and son would be carefully documented. When he completed the examination and documentation of his patients, the doctor concluded with a few more pleasantries and excused himself, returning to his many other patients in the community.

After several such weekly visits, the interaction between doctor and patient, quite imperceptibly, began to change.

After his patients' examinations, the doctor would linger and engage in quiet conversation with Mrs. Walker concerning recent events in her life, many times while Mrs. Walker held and fussed over baby Benjamin. Mrs. Walker would express concern over the doctor's workload and if he were eating properly. The obligatory issues of weather were also an essential element of every conversation. As weeks passed, Mrs. Walker would augment the doctor's visits with milk and cookies. Sometimes Mrs. Walker prepared a light meal, and she and the doctor would spend a pleasant evening in polite conversation about their lives, experiences, and beliefs.

By mid-December, both Dr. Forrestal and Mrs. Walker looked forward to their time together as a welcome relief from their daily routines. However, the doctor always maintained complete propriety during his visits; after all, Mrs. Walker was his patient and had only recently lost her husband. Mrs. Walker was also very appropriate. She was still in mourning, and the thought of another man in her life seemed impossible. They were friends, thrown together under trying circumstances, they would privately tell themselves, and both were happy to have each other for company.

In mid-January, the first significant storm of the season transformed Riverdale into a beautiful image of winter. Mrs. Walker gazed down Third Street from her kitchen window, wondering if the cold weather would prevent Dr. Forrestal from visiting. He was now assessing his patient almost daily. The gas lights lining the street cast a warm glow into the neighborhood in stark contrast to the snow and ice-covered street. To Mrs. Walker's surprise, she observed the doctor walking up the street, black bag in hand, in the storm. The lights cast strange shadows of Dr. Forrestal on the road and buildings as he leaned into the icy wind. Mrs. Walker walked to her front door, anticipating the doctor's knock. She could hear him walking up the stairs and, unable to wait, opened the door just as the doctor was about to knock. The somewhat surprised doctor politely said, "Good evening, Mrs. Walker. How are you?"

Mrs. Walker respectfully responded, "Just fine, Dr. Forrestal, and yourself?"

"Perhaps a little cold," the doctor returned, squeezing his collar closed.

"Then please come in," Mrs. Walker returned while helping the doctor into her home. She assisted him with his coat and hat and placed them on a nearby rack. Lacing her arm with his, she walked him over to the kitchen table. Cookies and a pitcher of milk were strategically placed to enhance their daily routine.

"You did not bring your carriage tonight. Why did you walk?" Mrs. Walker asked.

"To spare Demon from standing in the freezing air," the doctor responded, finding his usual seat at the kitchen table.

"That is very kind of you," Mrs. Walker stated. She walked between various lamps in her home and increased the flow of gas in an effort to create more light in her kitchen, anticipating the medical inquisition the doctor was about to initiate.

Taking her usual place at the table, Mrs. Walker announced a proposition, "Before we start the inquisition, I would like to propose that from this point forward, you call me Ellen and I, in return, will call you Conrad. We have known each other for ten years, and I consider you a good friend. It feels strange to continue such formalities."

Dr. Forrestal hesitated a moment and responded, "I think that would be fine, but only when we are alone. It would not be appropriate at the hospital or in public. It is not professional, you understand."

Ellen placed her elbow on the table and leaned her head against her hand. Her dark hair fell around her arm and flowed down onto the table. The light caused her green eyes to sparkle, and her pupils slowly enlarged, almost covering her irises. "Good. That will work," she replied softly.

Ellen looked beautiful in the kitchen's warm light, and Conrad was becoming increasingly overcome by the tension developing between doctor and patient. "We should begin," he stated, taking his notebook from his bag and trying to focus on his mission.

"Conrad, do you remember the first time you met me?" Ellen asked with a smile.

"How could I forget? You were my first patient when I started at the hospital. I was not expecting a beautiful, nineteen-year-old girl complaining about her menstrual period on my first day of work," the doctor said while playing with the edge of one of the cookies piled on a plate beside him.

"I remember when you asked me to pull my blouse up so you could place some warm opium-soaked towels on my stomach. You turned red and began telling me everything you learned about how the female body worked as fast as you could. I was quite touched. Did you really think I was beautiful?" Ellen breathed.

Conrad hesitated, then continued, "Of course you are beautiful. I think you are well aware you are a beautiful woman."

"Well, thank you, Conrad. I am glad you think I am," Ellen said, looking directly at the doctor.

Conrad, realizing he was drifting, stated in his more formal, physician voice, "Well, I think we should focus on the reason for my visit, don't you?"

"Yes, Conrad. What were we thinking?" Ellen laughed, sitting up in her chair and feigning seriousness.

She placed her hands in front of herself, stretched, and in a playful manner announced, "Okay, I have the questions memorized. Be sure and take detailed notes. Ready? My mood is good without significant depression. I have taken my medications faithfully without missing a dose. Besides, I like the wine. I have not had any headaches, no ringing in my ears, no problems with my balance, no blurred vision, no swollen tongue, no constipation or diarrhea—that is very important—no painful urination, nothing is swollen except for my breasts for obvious reasons, my pulse is steady and regular, my appetite is too good, my digestion is perfect. I have no fatigue. I sleep well—and alone, I might add. I have enough medication for two weeks, and I will pick up another two-week supply next week at the hospital, and everything else is fine as well. Nurse Peterson is helpful. She keeps me well supplied with diapers, the new wonder salve petroleum jelly, as well as copious amounts of talcum powder. She also gave me a bottle of oil of cloves to help the baby with his milk teeth. Did I miss anything?"

Conrad permitted himself a slight smile and indicated, "I think you have touched on all the essential areas of concern . . . Ellen." Conrad returned to his black bag and pulled out a yellow cloth measuring tape: "Now, for Benjamin."

"Conrad, I just got the baby to sleep. He has been crying for hours. I do not think he has changed in the last few days. Perhaps this evening we can let the baby examination slide, please," Ellen pleaded.

"Of course," Conrad responded. A long moment of silence passed as the doctor and patient held each other's eyes. The unspoken bond that had formed over their months of close contact slowly consumed the couple with a very real sexual tension.

Conrad broke the silence to mitigate the unacceptable feeling of losing control with an announcement: "I have some wonderful news. An anonymous donor has just given the hospital three thousand dollars."

"Wonderful. How did that happen?" Ellen asked.

"You know that heavy lawyer, Mr. Bass? Well, last week he walked into the hospital administrator's office and gave him a cashier's cheque for three thousand. He said it was from an individual who wanted to remain anonymous. I find it interesting that Ralph Gorman at First National also told me that another client of Mr. Bass, who also wanted to remain anonymous, just purchased a thousand acres of green valley just west of town for the incredible price of five hundred dollars an acre. Why would anyone do that?"

"Perhaps to diversify their cash assets into real estate to protect against bank failure or inflation," Ellen stated, glancing at the ceiling.

Conrad was a bit confused by her quick response. After a pause he stated, "Yes, that makes sense, I suppose. I am sure the person is one of those importers down on Ocean Front, like Jeffrey Porter—he imports all those exquisite, handmade rugs from Kuttor and ships them throughout the Eastern Coast. It is someone like that."

"That makes sense," Ellen agreed and pressed, "What is the hospital going to do with the money?"

"Well, the board of directors wishes to employ a dentist proficient with pain control using sweet air, also known as nitrous oxide, to control pain while pulling teeth and drilling out tooth decay. We were negotiating with a dentist from the Newhopeland Medical Association for a position at the hospital, and now that we can meet his expectation we have offered him the position. His name is Gardner Colton. Half the children in the town have dental problems and almost all the adults. A dentist was very much needed in Riverdale."

"Well, I am delighted. That sounds like a wonderful use of the money," Ellen stated with a smile.

"There is more good news concerning Benjamin," Conrad began. "I was not going to mention this until the hospital could secure the money. At Newhopeland Medical Hospital there is an expert on infantile prosthetic limbs . . . artificial arms and legs for babies and children. He is a professor of orthopedics, Dr. John Evens, and he has been successful in helping babies with missing or deformed limbs adapt. In Benjamin's case, helping him crawl and walk. He is quite familiar with Benjamin's situation. I have been corresponding with him for these last few months, and he has outlined a procedure I believe will benefit Benjamin greatly."

"That is wonderful," Ellen beamed. "What do we need to do?"

"When Benjamin begins to demonstrate he is ready to start crawling, we will need to make a plaster of Somme of his leg. This procedure will most likely involve sedating Benjamin with a few drops of laudanum in sugar water to make him soporific—sleepy. When the cast hardens, we carefully cut the cast from Benjamin's leg and ship the cast to Dr. Evens. Using vulcanized rubber, Dr. Evens will pour hot rubber into the reassembled cast. When it cools, a rubber replica of Benjamin's leg will be created so a precise brace can be made to fit Benjamin's leg. In addition, special orthopedic shoes will be made to help Benjamin walk and compensate for the shortness of the leg and deformity of his foot. As your child progresses in his ability to walk, we will repeat this procedure to ensure that the brace and special shoe fit him precisely. He will have the most advantageous opportunity to walk and have, as much as possible, a normal life."

Ellen blurted, "That is so wonderful. So, Dr. Evens will have to make many braces over Benjamin's lifetime. The braces must cost a fortune!"

"Yes, because a child grows so fast, many braces will need to be made. Braces and special shoes are required for the rest of his life," Conrad explained, continuing, "It may cost many hundreds of dollars a year. The gift we received will provide a few years of funding, and hopefully we will be able to acquire more funds in the future."

"I have a feeling more funds will be donated to the hospital," Ellen stated confidently.

"I am sure as well. More funds will be secured," Conrad agreed.

There was another long silence as Conrad and Ellen looked at each other. Only the soft hiss of the lamps broke the silence of the room. There was a time the doctor would have stood up and expressed some pleasantries, then excused himself as he slipped back into the storm. This was not that time. The attraction Conrad felt for Ellen had increasingly changed the proper doctor to a simple man who could not, and did not, want to leave. Conrad did not move. The obvious was about to erupt. Ellen stood first and moved closer to Conrad. Conrad also stood. They embraced each other and kissed a long, special first kiss. A kiss that would change both of their lives. A long embrace followed as the couple expressed their mutual feeling for each other without words.

Ellen broke the silence with a whisper, "I think the storm is too fierce for you to leave tonight. I think you should stay here with me until the morning."

"I think . . . you are right. I would love to stay with you," Conrad responded with little hesitation.

"The horse and carriage thing worked out well," Ellen teased, smiling as the couple walked toward the sleep room.

Chapter 4
The Sealing

C onrad and Ellen kept all signs of their affection concealed from Riverdale's small community, so as to respect James Walker. Over a year passed in the clandestine courtship. The people of Riverdale knew the couple was deeply in love, yet no one spoke an unkind word concerning the timing and nature of their relationship. The collective consciousness of the community recognized the hand of fate forming a love bond between the couple, and the consensus was complete acceptance and happiness. When Ellen and Conrad announced the day they would read from The Word, sealing their relationship in marriage, the townspeople received the proclamation with feigned surprise and warm approval.

~

Announcement of the Betrothal and Date of Sealing of Ellen Walker and Conrad Forrestal

On February 10, 1880, Oboe Jackson will ascend Crescent Hill and proclaim the commencement of the act of sealing the union of Ellen and Conrad in sacred marriage. Blessed be their love. Welcome family and friends that shall gather to witness the forming of this, the most perfect union of man and woman.

At precisely noon, Ellen and Conrad will ascend Crescent Hill with arms entwined. Upon reaching the summit, they shall read from the The Word and exchange gifts between them and, by so doing, seal their living souls in harmonious matrimony.

> "So, all shall know—all shall gather," so saith The Word.
> Much merrymaking and carousing shall follow the ceremony.

So it came to pass, on a beautiful day in February, the good people of Riverdale gathered on the west side of Crescent Hill and on the meadow below to witness the sealing of the marriage of Ellen and Conrad. The people of Riverdale were pleased with the union fate had formed. Many had been concerned about Ellen's well-being after her husband's death. Many believed Ellen was financially destitute. Conrad would make the perfect husband, being both a physician and affluent.

As was the custom, the people of Riverdale gifted the couple with food and drink to be enjoyed by all. The wedding preparation took weeks of planning and the coordinated efforts of many enthusiastic organizations and individuals from the town. The fruition of their efforts was expressed in many forms. The Carrion Stockyard Syndicate dug seven giant fire pits piled with many cords of wood. The Syndicate supplied seven large steer carcasses, as well as several burly men to slowly turn the meat for hours before the wedding to ensure a perfect steak for every witness of the sealing. The owners from Johnnie's Pig Yard contributed a dozen young sows. The men from the pig farm dug and manned the oak fire pits to guarantee that the slowly-turned and smoked sows would produce the most delicious pickle and sowbelly sandwiches—a Riverdale piquant specialty.

The Kent Dairy Guild donated fifty pounds of butter and thirty gallons of fresh milk for the children, as well as twenty, ten-gallon steel cylinders full of cream, eggs, vanilla extract, and sugar to be spun inside oak barrels with ice and salt to ensure a sufficient supply of ice cream.

Taylor Farms brought three hundred pounds of potatoes and four hundred ears of corn and a pair of giant iron pots for boiling the potatoes and steaming the corn. The wedding cake was nothing less than a culinary miracle rivaling the construction of "The great towers of the Lost Desert." The Kent County Tinsmith Association made hundreds of triangular-shaped baking pans, so when the many cake pieces were fitted together, the wedding cake would form seven, eight-inch-tall, round vanilla cake layers. The bottom layer was seven feet in diameter, and each layer was six inches smaller until the top layer measured three and a half feet in diameter.

The ladies from the Riverdale Relief and Humanitarian Society, using the tin baking pans and utilizing every baking oven in Riverdale, baked the dozens of cake pieces that would be necessary to construct the giant cake. The husbands of the Society ladies created a humongous pine table, sufficiently stable and robust to hold the enormous cake and a few teenage girls. They built the table in the meadow at the bottom of Crescent Hill, and in the early hours of the wedding day, the ladies brought the vanilla cake pieces, still hot from the oven, to the giant table, and the cake was precisely constructed with love and patience. They covered the cake with gallons of chocolate frosting, concealing the cracks between the pieces of cake. The finished cake was nothing less than a gastronomic triumph, a baking extravaganza that would be discussed for years. Two teenage girls were chosen to sit on the table next to the cake—a responsibility that was considered a great honor—and, with large fans, ensured the wedding cake was consumed by the guests and not by the bees preparing for winter .

The most popular gift to the young couple was a collaboration between Jacob's Icehouse and the Loose Lady Saloon. Six massive ore wagons were hauled to the meadow containing fifteen, fifty-gallon oak barrels of beer packed in ice. Almost every man in attendance brought their beer mug clipped to their belts. Many men felt the need to best other males in the crowd by bringing increasingly large mugs. One man had a tin cup that could hold over a gallon of beer, and his pride was evident as he sauntered through the wedding guests looking for envious glances.

The Riverdale Advanced School, for academically-oriented children from fifteen and eighteen years of age, brought a solid wood, portable dance floor for those so inclined, and the entire thirty-member school orchestra came as well. The student and faculty gift to the wedding couple was music and dance.

Ten minutes before noon, the Riverdale Advanced School Orchestra began playing the slow march, "The Ascension." The music announced the arrival of the betrothed couple before they ascended Crescent Hill for their sealing. The couple arrived in Conrad's black shining carriage at the base of Crescent Hill shortly after the music started. Teamster Jake Corvidae was strategically standing where the carriage stopped to control the deposition of Demon. Conrad exited the carriage first, wearing his best black suit, coat, vest, and highly polished boots. A broad-brim black hat covered his head. His crisp, white shirt contrasted his other apparel, and his demeanor communicated a man of means and confidence. Ellen followed Conrad from the carriage. Conrad held her arm to ensure a safe descent. As was the custom, the bride covered her dress with a grey cloak to conceal the wedding gown, which would be revealed just before the ascension. Ellen's black hair descended to her shoulders and down her back, gently swirling in the wind. Near her right temple, a small tight braid, laced with green ribbon, was a subtle prelude to the bride's apparel soon to be revealed.

The couple approached the crowd. As if practiced, the crowd parted, forming a wide corridor toward Crescent Hill. While the music continued, Oboe Jackson emerged from the gathering and headed to the top of Crescent Hill to proclaim the wedding. Now, Oboe was not accustomed to public speaking, so he spent some time that morning at the beer wagons imbibing liquid courage before his big moment. Oboe's incoherence was apparent as he began ascending the hill in somewhat less than a perfect line. Several witnesses assisted Oboe when he stumbled. The sound of laughter emerging from the collective witnesses diminished the seriousness of the moment. Even Ellen began laughing, hiding her expression with the red copy of The Word she held in her hand. Conrad, seeing his betrothed amused by Oboe's antics, also found himself fighting the impulse to laugh.

Teamster Jake Corvidae, realizing the potential for a wedding catastrophe, summoned one of the witnesses from the crowd to hold Demon's reins, and rapidly proceeded up the hill, arriving at the summit at the same time Oboe had completed his intoxicated sojourn. Upon reaching the top of Crescent Hill, the school band grew quiet. Oboe reached down and picked up a giant tin, cone-shaped megaphone to address the witnesses. Oboe took a breath and began, "I proclaim the commencement of the wedding . . . sealing of the two . . . Helen and Conrad."

The witnesses burst into near-hysterical laughter. Hundreds of guests lost control at what was customarily a solemn moment. Ellen began laughing so hard she required Conrad to hold her from falling, and even Conrad lost his usual composure, joining his betrothed in laughter.

Jake Corvidae, who had a gift of handling unruly animals, placed his hand on Oboe's shoulder, whispered in his ear and gently removed the megaphone from Oboe's possession. Jake then directed Oboe to descend the hill on the opposite side of the witnesses, toward the direction of the Riverdale Cemetery. Jake waited a few seconds for the crowd to regain some formality appropriate for such an occasion. When the witnesses had obtained the proper decorum, Jake lifted the megaphone and began, "I proclaim on this day the most solemn occasion: the commencement of the sealing of Ellen and Conrad in sacred marriage. The bride and groom shall read from The Word, and by so doing they shall become husband and wife. All shall witness, so all shall know, and with the exchange of gifts between the betrothed, this sealing is accomplished."

Jake's memory of the proclamation was not exactly right, but all present sincerely appreciated his efforts. At noon, the school band began playing the "The Ascension." Ellen untied

the knot holding her cloak and allowed the concealing garment to fall. There was a gasp from the witnesses as Ellen's
elegant and very revealing gown was presented to the proceedings. The wedding dress was a beautiful green silk,
which covered her so tightly that the gown, in places, seemed
almost painted on. It flowed down her exquisite form and
spread out near the ground, forming a modest train behind
her. The bodice was low-cut, revealing much of Ellen's
striking breasts—small gold chains kept the bodice from
violating all manner of propriety. The gown was widely split
from the ground to Ellen's waist on the side where Conrad
was standing. Complementing the stunning décolletage, small
gold chains held the dress separation from revealing even
more of Ellen's creamy white, beautiful thigh. A 25-carat
green emerald adorned Ellen's neckline, hanging between her
breasts and held in place by a gold chain that matched the
gold chains in her dress. The gown's shade of green matched
the green of Ellen's eyes. The reflected light from her striking
form made her eyes glow in an eerie and stunning manner.
She was exquisite. Conrad joined the witnesses in a mesmer-
izing silence as he gazed on his bride.

In public, the women of Riverdale dressed in the most
modest manner, with one significant exception: on the day of
marriage. As was the custom at such times, a bride was
permitted, even expected, to display a strong sexual presence
to her future husband with her dress. This tradition, at least in
wedding legend, suggested this was a necessary custom as a
kind of last-minute marriage insurance, to keep the future
husband interested and to prevent any last-minute escape of
the impending commitment. The wedding gown was successful in achieving the desired effect on Conrad and, for that
matter, the rest of the male witnesses. For a brief period, all
thoughts of cold beer and hot steaks were the furthest thing
from collective prurient minds. In the far future, long after the
giant chocolate cake was forgotten, clear memory of Ellen's
wedding dress would persist and be discussed and, at times,
emulated in future weddings.

As the wedding music continued, the crowd settled, and the meadow once again swirled with the beautiful melody of "The Ascension." Conrad held a white copy of The Word, and Ellen held a red copy, the traditional colors of fertility. The couple raised both copies straight in front of them, entwined arms, and began, in rhythm to the music, the long walk through the crowd of witnesses. Upon reaching the top of the hill, Ellen and Conrad turned to the crowd and, as custom required, held each of their copies high above their heads. All the witnesses could see the proper source of their readings, and then the couple turned to face each other to read from the appropriate section, marked by a white ribbon. The music stopped, and the witnesses became absolutely quiet. Even the wind and the birds seemed to fall silent. Conrad began, "I, Conrad, have fallen into irreparable love with Ellen, the woman I proclaim to the blessed witnesses gathered here today, to be for now and for all times my wife and life partner until fate separates us from this, the living world. I promise no other woman will bear children from my seed, and I shall slay any man who should violate my wife for as long as I shall live. I beg all to listen to my words. I pledge to provide sustenance to my wife, so my wife will not know hunger. I pledge to protect my wife, so my wife will not know fear. I pledge to provide my wife shelter, so my wife will be protected from the world. I pledge to comfort my wife when she is sad, heal my wife when she is ill, and provide wealth for my wife's well-being. And when fate calls me to the afterlife, I give my solemn promise to die in my wife's arms. I pledge these things and more to my bride. I give my eternal gratitude to the all-embracing force of fate for this woman and these witnesses."

With tears in her eyes, Ellen read from The Word. "I, Ellen, have fallen into irreparable love with Conrad, the man I proclaim to the blessed witnesses gathered here today, to be for now and for all times my husband and life partner until fate separates us from this, the living world. I promise I will bear only the children of my husband's seed and slay any woman who should violate him as long as I shall live. I beg all to listen to my words. I pledge to support my husband in all his endeavors. I pledge to provide comfort to my husband when he is sad, and heal my husband when he is ill, and defend to my death when my husband stands falsely accused. And when fate calls me to the afterlife, I give my solemn promise to die in my husband's arms. I pledge these things and more to my groom. I give my eternal gratitude to the all-embracing force of fate for this man and these witnesses."

Most of the witnesses could not hear the couple, but they knew the words, having listened to the verbal exchange from The Word in marriage ceremonies many times before. The theater of the visual display between the bride and groom was sufficient to notarize the marriage and sealing by the witnesses.

The final requirement in the sealing ceremony was the exchange of gifts between Ellen and Conrad. With this last act, the gathered witnesses could confirm the authenticity of Ellen and Conrad's marriage. Ellen reached behind her neck, unclasped her emerald necklace, and placed the chain around Conrad's neck. As she drew close to her husband's cheek, she whispered: "Don't lose this, it's real." Hearing his wife's remark, a confused Conrad reached into his vest pocket, took out his gold watch, released the fob, and placed the chain around Ellen's neck. He secured the chain with a small hook, then stated whimsically, "Don't lose it. It's old, like me." The smiling couple turned and faced the witnesses.

As was the custom, the witnesses spoke in unison, "Ellen and Conrad are husband and wife." The crowd cheered, and the band played "Eternal Love" as the closest witnesses embraced the couple. Immediately after the couple finished their proclamation, a cadre of elderly women struggled through the crowd, rushed up to Ellen, and began securing her cloak over the very titillating wedding dress. Such a revealing dress was not, after all, appropriate for a married woman in public. Ellen began thanking the concerned women but a strange, low rumble and a mild shaking of the ground interrupted her. Coinciding with Ellen's return to modesty, shouts and the sound of running feet filled the air as the men crowded and rushed to the beer wagons. Several small children were nearly trampled, and one elderly lady was knocked into the air by the self-absorbed mob. Not one man from the rambunctious group stopped to aid the geriatric casualty; that was left to a group of sympathetic women who had witnessed the disgusting display of male insensitivity. The elderly woman was fortunately unharmed from her short flight. The first responders who provided aid were then required to restrain the elderly victim from pursuing her assailants with her hickory cane. Ellen and Conrad, observing the mayhem from the top of the hill, turned to each other in disbelief and once again began laughing at yet another unplanned wedding event.

The couple walked among the wedding guests thanking them for their witness and their gifts. They walked over to the giant chocolate and vanilla cake and thanked everyone nearby for the culinary gift. As was custom, the bride cut a small piece of cake and fed the cake to her husband. Ellen waited for a brief period until Conrad swallowed, and then kissed her husband, much to the delight of the nearby group of wedding guests. So, for the next hour, Ellen and Conrad sampled all the beautiful gifts provided by the community and repeatedly thanked the wedding participants. When the time was right, Ellen and Conrad climbed into Conrad's carriage and waved goodbye to the wedding guests.

～

The wedding party would continue until dawn the next day. Much joy was shared by all: new loves were found and formed among the young people dancing and flirting near the music; children filled themselves with cake and ice cream; frantic mothers struggled to keep track of their energized children in the vast cacophony of the wedding party; and most of the men consumed an enormous amount of beef and beer, rendering them far too compromised to participate in the world for the next several days after the celebration.

On this day, Riverdale, on the edge of the Eastern Sea, was the most joyful town in the world. The sky was crystal clear, the ocean was calm, the wind whispered a quiet melody of tranquility, and all the people of Riverdale were consumed with happiness. The Raven's flight was not apparent, for on this day, the Raven was heaven-bound and alone..

Chapter 5
Mortilus

Ellen and Conrad leaned against the railing of the iron steamship Mortilus, watching the first setting sun of their first day of marriage. Mortilus slowly moved across the calm sea, departing from Riverdale harbor bound for Newhopeland. Ellen was still wearing her now-concealed wedding dress. Conrad broke the silence as he played with the green emerald hanging around his neck with a question: "Ellen, why did you imply this giant emerald was real? Is the necklace a family heirloom?"

Ellen coyly replied, "Conrad, the emerald is real. I bought the necklace along with my tailored wedding dress in Londonderry. The cost of this trinket was about five hundred dollars, and the dress was almost four hundred dollars. Well worth it, don't you think?"

Agonizing thoughts of economic ruin momentarily terrified Conrad. His financial life flashed through his mind, "How is that possible? How . . . did you borrow the money?"

"Conrad," Ellen began, "do you see all those warehouses and mooring docks across the bay . . . over there?"

"Yes," Conrad said with some trepidation.

With a big smile, Ellen stated, "I own them. I own all the land in Green Valley west of town, several buildings and homes in Riverdale, including the Wolsworth's mansion, a ton of railroad stock, and much more. Conrad, I am the richest woman in Kent County."

"But you live over the butcher shop," Ellen's stunned husband replied.

"Very happily, I might add." Ellen returned, "Oh, your anonymous donor to the hospital—I am she."

"How is this possible?" Conrad was confused.

Ellen took Conrad by the arm and slowly turned him in the direction of their cabin. "Listen, my attorney made me keep my mouth shut and represented me in all kinds of things. Mr. Bass is as smart as he is fat, so I follow his advice. For many matters, he's my lawyer, and Conrad, that's the way it must be—my financial situation is to be confidential. I am sorry about all of this. I am so much in love with you, and my wealth, well, think of it as a wedding night surprise. Wedding nights always have some surprises, right?"

Conrad smiled, "You are always full of surprises. I mean, it could have been some awful surprise. I am still confused. Where are we going to live? In the Wolsworth mansion?"

"No, silly. Well, not unless you want to, I suppose. I want to live in your mansion by the sea. Look, we have a lot to talk about, and when we get back, we can meet with Mr. Bass. He will be able to explain the whole thing to you better than I can. My money is in a kind of living trust. Besides, I am late for my Dr. Forrestal magic happy potion, so let's go back to the cabin, and we can have a long talk about this before we go to bed."

"I hope not too long," Conrad returned with a smile.

"Not too long," Ellen repeated, pulling her husband closer. "Hey, would you like a new carriage, or something else, for a wedding gift?"

Conrad laughed, "How about this ship?"

"Well . . . I don't think I am that rich," Ellen replied.

"What a relief," Conrad returned.

The newlyweds started laughing as they disappeared into the honeymoon cabin.

Ellen and Conrad continued to fall deeper in love. The first few days of their honeymoon, they spoke of how much they wished they could continue their romantic adventure forever. Their three-week honeymoon in Newhopeland was filled with food, theater, purchasing gifts at specialty shops, long walks, and making love all hours of the night, and occasionally on the deserted beach during the day. Both hated the thought of such a wonderfully romantic time together ending.

As days turned to weeks, thoughts of Riverdale increasingly entered the couple's minds and their conversation. The couple began reassuring each other that baby Benjamin was well cared for by Nurse Peterson, and that Dr. Young from Londonderry was taking excellent care of Conrad's patients. They continuously reassured each other that their romance would continue when they returned to Riverdale. By the third week of nuptial bliss, both Ellen and Conrad became increasingly anxious about their awaiting responsibilities. The couple returned as scheduled to Riverdale on the steamship with a mixture of apprehension and joy, still very much in love and ready to begin their long, beautiful life together as they pursued their regular routines. Ellen and Conrad caressed and clung to each other as the vessel entered Riverdale harbor.

As Mortilus slowly maneuvered to the mooring, Conrad studied the waterfront, wondering how much more of the harbor belonged to his new wife. He was increasingly looking forward to his conversation with Mr. Bass and understanding his wife's wealth and holdings. As the ship approached the dock, the couple could see a small group of people waiting to greet them. Ellen focused on Nurse Peterson, holding baby Benjamin, and Conrad focused on Dr. Young. When the ramp was lowered, Ellen raced to baby Benjamin with tears, taking him from Nurse Peterson, holding him in the air, and beginning a frantic monologue of loving reassurance. Conrad, delighted with his wife's happiness, slowly walked over to Dr. Young, and was greeted with a firm handshake and a strong, "Welcome home." Dr. Young immediately reassured Conrad that all was well, and relayed how much he looked forward to reviewing his notes concerning Conrad's patients.

The honeymoon was over, and after lunch with the welcoming committee, Conrad established the location and time the next day for the meeting with Dr. Young. The newlyweds said their goodbyes and, still clinging to each other with Benjamin in their arms, the little family walked to Conrad's home by the sea to begin their new lives together.

~

The next day, Ellen and Conrad, as scheduled, met with Mr. Bass at his law office. Sitting across from Mr. Bass at his large oak desk, Conrad became increasingly concerned that the rotund and increasingly plethoric attorney would suffer from cardiac arrest at any moment. Mr. Bass began the conversation with his usual laconic, linguistic style, "Well, Dr. and Mrs. Forrestal, congratulations on your marriage! I trust your honeymoon was a very pleasurable experience."

Ellen began to laugh and responded, much to Conrad's chagrin, "Yes . . . very pleasurable."

Realizing his verbal gaffe, Mr. Bass continued unabated, "Yes . . . of course. Now, for Mrs. Forrestal's estate holdings and various enterprises. I have prepared a summary of Mrs. Forrestal's assets." Mr. Bass handed Conrad a thick portfolio outlining Ellen's many acquisitions and income sources. "As you can see, your wife is in possession of numerous pieces of real estate and various mortgages, and she has retained several hundred thousand dollars of liquid assets. As I have outlined in the document, Mrs. Forrestal's monthly income is, currently, approximately ten thousand dollars. I thought that item M-6 on page two would be of some interest to you."

Mr. Bass continued, "As you can see, Mrs. Forrestal has leased the former Wolsworth mansion to a Dr. Gardner Colton for nine hundred dollars a month. I believe you may be acquainted with him. He's employed at the same hospital where you have admitting privileges, I believe."

Conrad stared at the document and turned to his wife, "This is all hard to believe."

Ellen proudly responded, "The Word tells us if you give, you will receive. Is that not so, Mr. Bass?"

"Precisely, Mrs. Forrestal. Precisely," Mr. Bass returned with a big smile on his very red face.

Conrad continued, "This asset sheet states that Ellen's net worth is well over one million dollars. How was all this possible?" Conrad turned to Ellen, "Please explain the origin of your fortune. This is most confusing."

Mr. Bass answered, "Mrs. Walker's former husband had a large estate. I cannot discuss the details because Mr. Walker was my client, so all information concerning Mr. Walker is privileged, you do understand. However, Mrs. Forrestal is entirely free to discuss the details of her former husband's estate."

"Conrad, I will tell you anything you want to know. James had a life insurance policy that provided me with a great deal of money. Mr. Bass became my lawyer when James died on that terrible day, and he has been helping me diversify my holdings and grow my principle. James was concerned about my mental stability, so he arranged for Mr. Bass to supervise and approve all my financial dealings. I have been able to increase my fortune with Mr. Bass's help," Ellen said, looking at Conrad while placing her hand on his arm.

"Now, let me explain to you how Mrs. Forrestal's estate is structured, now that you have a better understanding of her assets," Mr. Bass began in a detached sort of way. "I placed Mrs. Forrestal's holdings in a living trust, which can only be accessed by Mrs. Forrestal under my auspices. As such, Mrs. Forrestal's estate is not community property. Mrs. Forrestal may distribute her assets, with approval, as she pleases, of course. Upon her death, her estate will be divided between her surviving children and her spouse. The children will not have access to their inheritance until they reach the age of eighteen. In the event Mrs. Forrestal should pass and have no surviving children, the estate will pass to you, Sir. Mrs. Forrestal's trust and estate are reviewed by the court, in camera, meaning in private, in the judge's chambers annually. Dr. Forrestal, you are welcome to attend these annual reviews if Mrs. Forrestal does not object—"

"Oh, I don't object. I want my husband to be familiar with all my financial activities," Ellen interrupted.

"Very well," Mr. Bass stated and continued, "Mrs. Forrestal is currently employing three individuals to facilitate her various business activities."

"Ellen, you have a staff as well?" Conrad exclaimed.

Ellen moved closer to her husband and entwined her arm with his, "Conrad, my business activities are extensive. I have an accountant, a property manager, and a real estate investigator-negotiator to help me out. These employees also do not know who they are working for, and that's the way I want it, for now. They work out of Mr. Bass's law office, and Mr. Bass supervises them and relays my instructions."

"Please don't take this the wrong way," Conrad began, "but, Mr. Bass . . . how are you paid? I mean, what are your fees?

"That is a perfectly appropriate question, Dr. Forrestal," Mr. Bass responded. "My fees are negotiated with Mrs. Forrestal and reviewed and approved by the court. The documents in your possession outline my pay schedule."

Ellen interrupted, "I trust Mr. Bass, and he has helped me through all of this. This whole thing is set up through the courts, and I want you to be in court to ask any questions you want. I was not in any position to handle all this money, and Mr. Bass has helped me through and made me a very prosperous woman. I want you to be free to ask Mr. Bass any question at any time. Will you do that?"

"How is all this property recorded? County records are public. Whose name appears on the deeds?" Conrad continued.

"The deeds reflect the owner of Mrs. Forrestal's property as the trust, which does not identify the trustee. All inquiries concerning Mrs. Forrestal's holdings are directed to me as the administrator of the estate. I must agree and countersign all acquisition and disbursement of assets," Mr. Bass repeated.

"How did you do it, Mr. Bass? I mean, this is a small town. Everyone was well aware that some anonymous person was buying up the town and making financial gifts, and you were representing that person. I mean, how did you accomplish this? Do you meet in the middle of the night?" Conrad asked, still very confused.

Ellen laughed, "You know better than that, Conrad."

Conrad smiled, "I suppose that's true."

"Dr. Forrestal, Mrs. Forrestal and I communicate by telegraph." Mr. Bass began to explain.

"Telegraph? What?" Conrad was becoming overwhelmed. This was a great deal for him to absorb, "How is that possible?"

Mr. Bass explained, "You are aware that a number of the gas street lights in town have telegraph wires connecting various businesses and the railroad. Well, we simply had a telegraph wire installed behind Ellen's home to my office. Mrs. Forrestal is particularly good at using the telegraph key, and I learned telegraph code as a young man as a hobby. We have been communicating for months using this method . . . highly successfully."

Ellen continued, "Now I will be living with you, I was hoping you would not mind allowing me to use one of the guest sleep rooms as my office. We will have a telegraph line connecting my office to Mr. Bass's law office."

All Conrad could say was, "Of course."

"Mr. Bass, it would seem your efforts assisting my wife through all of this have been very salutary. Clearly, she was in a vulnerable position after her husband died. I cannot thank you enough for all your efforts to protect my wife."

"It was an honor to assist Mrs. Forrestal. Let me tell you a story about James Walker and how I first met him. I was a young and considerably thinner man who had just completed law school and had traveled to Riverdale to begin a law practice after completing my internship in Londonderry. I arrived in Riverdale in the middle of the night in the midst of winter and did not get fifty feet from the train before I was hit in the head and knocked unconscious. I came to consciousness with a young man sponging my face with a wet towel. I had been robbed of all my money and my suitcase, as well as a legal briefcase containing my legal books, credentials, and letters of introduction. Even my coat and boots were gone. I was utterly destitute. The man attending to me was James

Walker. It was about five years before Mr. Walker met Mrs. Forrestal. He was living above the butcher shop on Third Street, and he took me to his home. Well, Mr. Walker fed me, cleaned me up, and gave me a place to sleep. He bought me a new coat and boots. Mr. Walker also loaned me five hundred dollars to rent this office with a place to live on the second story. He, of course, also provided me with free coal that first year of my law practice. When Mr. Walker came through that door about three years before his death and sat down where you are sitting now, Dr. Forrestal, and asked if I could help him, all I could say was, 'I will do anything you ask of me.'"

Ellen was deeply moved, "I had no idea. James never told me about any of this."

Mr. Bass smiled and continued, "He was like that—a very private and magnanimous man. Well, he asked me if I would protect his wife if he should die. Mr. Walker was very sullen and morose. He said he had a premonition of death, and his death was going to be terrible, and he wanted to make arrangements to ensure Mrs. Forrestal would be taken care of when he passed to the afterlife."

"I was very devoted to Mr. Walker," Mr. Bass continued, "and I never saw him so low. He seemed almost lost in fear and deep concern. I helped him secure the best life insurance policy I could find, and I promised I would do everything I could to protect and ensure his wife's health and welfare. James and I reviewed the options, and James felt, upon his death, I should be appointed by the court as guardian ad litem to safeguard her assets. He was concerned Mrs. Forrestal might be exploited, so he made me promise I would do everything in my power to keep her safe. Mr. Walker was also clear he wanted me to provide the best medical services available. He knew his wife suffered from melancholia, and he was afraid his death would cause her to fall into a still deeper depression. Mr. Walker instructed me to prepare guardianship papers for the court and assume that responsibility in the event of his death. Obviously, your medical intervention has been successful, even remarkable, and I believe we can dispense with these legal arrangements very soon. I believe Mr. Walker would be happy that a man like you, a man of means, a professional, deeply respected by the community was brought to Mrs. Forrestal by fate to be her husband."

"I believe that, too, and I am delighted with our legal arrangement," Ellen added, leaning toward Mr. Bass and smiling.

"I am her husband, and I love her and will care for her until my dying day," Conrad stated, taking his wife's hand, squeezing it, and looking into her green eyes.

"I am her lawyer, and James Walker was my friend, and I promise I will also be at her service as long as Mrs. Forrestal requires my expertise," Mr. Bass added, pulling his shoulders back proudly, sitting at attention looking back and forth between husband and wife.

Ellen became increasingly uncomfortable listening to the two most significant men in her life pledging an allegiance to her in such a fawning manner. "Well, I am glad that fate has brought the two of you into my life. So, unless there is anything else . . . Mr. Bass, will you join us for lunch? Hotel Riverdale at, say, one in the afternoon?"

"Oh, yes," Conrad added, "we should have lunch together. I do appreciate everything you have done for my wife. I would like very much if we could be friends."

"I think I would like that very much as well," Mr. Bass replied, though his thoughts had already begun reviewing the hotel's lunch menu, which he had committed to memory

Chapter 6
Coming of Age in the Days of Anger

I n the following years after the marriage of Ellen and Conrad, Riverdale's importance in the world's economy continued to grow. The Riverdale harbor became an increasingly important port for commerce as the consumption of coal, timber, and farming exports grew in demand. Five years after Ellen acquired much of the surplus harbor warehouses and docks, the Eastern Sea Shipping Company purchased Ellen's harbor holdings for six-hundred thousand dollars. The railroad created new tracks to the harbor as trade increased, and Ellen's railroad stock doubled in value. Petroleum was found in the Green Valley, and many petroleum wells developed for the production of kerosene. The continuing stability of Ellen's mental state and marriage allowed Robert Bass to cease all responsibilities pertaining to guardianship. He had fulfilled his promise to James Walker. Ellen was safe. All was well. His role in Ellen's life evolved from legal guardian to business partner. His only client was Ellen Forrestal.

Conrad continued his ever-expanding medical practice, and Ellen's days were divided between the development of baby Benjamin and her expanding business interests. Ellen's philanthropy also continued. The Riverdale Hospital continued to receive large grants from an anonymous patron permitting the facility to secure additional physicians, nurses, and bed space.

Benjamin Walker was also thriving. Learning to walk with his brace and special shoes appeared no more difficult for Benjamin than any other child learning to walk. Conrad carefully measured and made plaster molds of Benjamin's leg and foot to ensure a proper-fitting prosthesis for the growing child. During these early years, they had to replace Benjamin's brace and specialty shoes every month. Benjamin was fortunate that fate had provided him with such caring, knowledgeable, and affluent parents. Ellen hired a governess, Mrs. Lewis—a former middle school teacher—to help care for and educate Benjamin. The house servants were encouraged to bring their children to play with Benjamin, and by the time he was ready for primary school, at the age of six, Benjamin was as happy and active as any child.

As with many young children, Benjamin's initiation to the educational experience was a difficult transition, but his exposure to the outside world would be especially challenging. For the first time in his life Benjamin felt different from the other children. The steel brace on one of his legs and a large, oversized shoe with a sole three inches in height brought many questions from his fellow schoolmates, and, in some cases, ridicule. Some began referring to him as the "cripple" or "bread foot" because his shoe looked like a large loaf of bread. This unexpected teasing from the school children would form his lifetime sense of feeling inadequate and freakish. This early disparagement was the beginning of Benjamin's profound self-image of inferiority, but he would bury it deep within his subconscious, only manifesting his abject self-worth in forms of sporadic rage and condescension.

Primary school was the first time in Benjamin's life he felt anguish and anger. To survive the ensuing years, Benjamin had to adapt to what he perceived as an increasingly hostile environment. With guidance from his governess, Mrs. Lewis, Benjamin would learn to use his anger, and Benjamin resolved to be the best student to compensate for his physical limitations with superior intellectual abilities. Benjamin would channel his anger to make himself academically strong, suppressing feelings of inferiority. Mrs. Lewis encouraged this drive to demonstrate his superiority over his peers in the ways that were most important in life. As a result of Mrs. Lewis's strong influence, and without his parents' knowledge, Benjamin also developed deep animosity toward the other children in his school. His anger, he was taught, would become his friend, and serve him well as he prepared for life.

~

Many years had passed since Benjamin entered school, and Benjamin was now thirteen years old. Fate was about to intervene in his life once again. Late in the afternoon, early in autumn, Mrs. Moore, the principal of Benjamin's school, and Mrs. Stuart, Benjamin's fourth-grade teacher, walked across town to Dr. Forrestal's home by the sea to discuss a matter of some importance concerning Ellen's son. The two educators passed through the iron ornamental gate in front of Dr. Forrestal's house and walked up to the large oak door lit by a nearby gas lamp, and the women introduced their presence with a sharp rap. Ellen opened the door and was surprised to find Benjamin's teacher and another lady staring at her without the slightest suggestion of cordiality. The two ladies were sober in expression with the demeanor of serious business. They were dressed almost identically, each one with a proper, conservative white blouse, arms completely covered, and stiff collars secured with dark ribbon ties. Both ladies had black, fluffy dresses—with hemlines several inches above their ankles—and black, button-up shoes with short heels. Even their hairstyles were similar: tight little buns with ivory hair pins. The only difference in the appearance between these sterling examples of institutional public servants was their age: one looked approximately twenty years older than the other.

Ellen spoke first: "Mrs. Stuart, how nice of you to visit. Please come in, ladies."

Mrs. Stuart responded, "Ellen, may I introduce Mrs. Moore, our school principal."

Ellen raised her hand and shook Mrs. Moore's, "I am pleased to meet you. Please come in."

The two ladies walked through the entrance hall, removed their coats and hats, and continued to the large, formal sitting room. The sitting room was seldom used, reserved for just such an occasion. The room contained fine pieces of furniture and large bookcases displaying hundreds of leather-bound books. The finest cut glass, crystal vases could be found throughout the room. Each vase held a bouquet of fresh flowers. The two profoundly serious ladies sat on the large, silk-covered sofa, and Ellen pulled up a large matching chair, sitting to receive the purpose of their visit.

Jane, the downstairs maid, entered the room and rushed into an apology, "Excuse me madam for failing to receive your visitors. May I bring the ladies some refreshments?"

Both ladies, in unison, gave a stern response, "No, thank you."

Ellen then gave the maid her instructions, "Please keep Benjamin upstairs, and I may wish to have Mrs. Lewis join us, so please have her stay." Ellen then motioned with her hand, an informative gesture for the maid to leave.

"Mrs. Lewis is your son's governess?" Mrs. Moore queried.

"Yes," Ellen responded.

"Well, your governess is doing an excellent job," Mrs. Moore continued.

"Yes, I believe she has helped Benjamin a great deal," Ellen said with a little confusion in her voice.

"I think it is best that Mrs. Stuart and I get to the point of our visit, which concerns Benjamin's situation in our school," Mrs. Moore stated sternly.

Ellen, getting a little annoyed with the pretentiousness of her guest, replied, "Of course."

Mrs. Moore took in a large breath of air and sitting straight up began, "We believe Benjamin would be better served if he were transferred to the Riverdale Advanced School—"

"What!" Ellen exclaimed, "Why?"

"Please hear us out, Ellen." Mrs. Moore demanded. "We

have given this a great deal of thought."

"Fine, excuse me. I was not expecting this," Ellen tried to be civil.

"Thank you, Ellen," Mrs. Moore continued, "Benjamin is a special young man. He is highly intelligent, and his scholastic abilities are significantly more advanced than any child in his classroom or, for that manner, the entire school. Last week, we received Benjamin's scores on the standardized achievement exams. His scores in all major academic areas are far beyond the others. In fact, Benjamin's scores are sufficiently high for him to graduate from secondary school."

"What are you saying? Benjamin is thirteen years old," Ellen stated with increasing prejudice.

"Yes, I understand." Mrs. Moore continued, undeterred, "As you are aware, adjustment to public school has been difficult for Benjamin. As much as we have tried to curtail the other children from disparaging Benjamin concerning his disabilities, the teasing and name-calling has continued. Please believe us, Ellen; we consider this kind of harassment completely unacceptable. We have punished several of the children for their comments and actions. We have, on a few occasions, expelled children for their rude and frankly disgusting behavior."

"Thank you. Dr. Forrestal and I anticipated there would be some prejudice directed at our son. We feel a public education would be his best preparation for life. Fools come in all ages. I think you would agree." Ellen was becoming increasingly concerned that the agenda of these two ladies did not have Benjamin's best interest in mind.

"We don't consider our delinquent pupils fools . . . I would prefer 'under socialized,'" Mrs. Moore responded with perceptible condescension.

"What else?" Ellen asked bluntly.

"It has become obvious to Mrs. Stuart and me that, at this point, we are simply holding Benjamin back academically. Your governess has provided him with the necessary primary and secondary education. In addition, we are simply not equipped to merely socialize your son. His life preparatory experience must not be at the expense of the teaching milieu."

Mrs. Moore was being obtuse.

"I thought you were going straight to the point," Ellen was finding the conversation increasingly tedious.

Mrs. Moore continued, "Yes, of course. Benjamin goes to great lengths to make his peers feel intellectually inferior. He frequently dominates classroom discussions, correcting the students when they are talking. His test scores in class have been perfect for some time, and he makes sure the other children are aware of his scores. His class projects are far superior to the other children. Benjamin has no inhibitions whatsoever with demonstrating his contempt for his peers. Now, this is completely understandable, Ellen. Some of the students have been cruel to your son, and Benjamin has been compensating by demonstrating his intellectual prowess. However, this is not a healthy learning environment for Benjamin or the other children. Mrs. Stuart and I believe Benjamin is angry. Angry with his peers and his physical limitations. In a strange way, he has become a bully. Not physically, but intellectually. This is somewhat of a unique situation, Ellen, and this is difficult. Benjamin is, at times, as cruel to the other children as some of the children have been to him."

Ellen did not like their tone. The thought of her crippled son becoming a bully was ridiculous. Without saying a word, Ellen walked over to a long, blue ribbon hanging out of the ceiling that was connected to the maid's bell in the kitchen. Ellen, looking at the two ladies, gave the ribbon two strong pulls and then returned to her chair and waited. Within a few seconds, the downstairs maid entered the room: "Yes, madam."

Ellen, looked directly at the two educators and stated, "Have Mrs. Lewis join us."

"Yes, madam," the maid responded. She turned and disappeared through the doorway.

For several unconformable moments, the ladies stared at

each other, waiting for the governess to join them. Mrs. Lewis entered the sitting room, looked directly at Ellen, and stated, "Yes, Ellen. How can I be of service?"

Ellen stood and introduced the two ladies, "Mrs. Lewis, I am sure you know Mrs. Stuart, Benjamin's teacher."

Mrs. Lewis stated, "Yes, of course. How are you, Mrs. Stuart?"

Mrs. Stuart managed an awkward smile.

Ellen continued, "And this is Mrs. Moore, the principal at Benjamin's school."

"How do you do, Mrs. Moore?" Mrs. Lewis asked politely, offering her hand and shaking Mrs. Moore's clammy palm.

"Please pull up a chair and join us. Mrs. Stuart and Mrs. Moore have formed an opinion that Benjamin's academic skill levels warrant a more challenging academic environment. They are recommending the Riverdale Advanced School. I was interested in your opinion on the matter?"

"Mrs. Forrestal, I think that is a wonderful idea. Benjamin is far superior academically to other children his age. The public schools are, well, oriented for children somewhat more plebeian than our Benjamin," Mrs. Lewis stated without hesitation.

"Well, Mrs. Forrestal, that explains a great deal," Mrs. Moore returned.

"I see," Ellen continued. "Do you think Benjamin is angry with his situation at school?"

"Yes. I believe he is angry at being constantly degraded by the children in his school. I believe he compensates by excelling academically. I think he is ready for a more challenging learning environment. I also believe he will find a more tolerant culture at the Advanced School. The school is quite costly and limited to parents of means. The children's demeanor at the Advanced School will be more reflective of proper breeding," Mrs. Lewis stated while looking at Ellen.

"Very well," Ellen responded. "I want you to make the necessary contacts at the Advanced Riverdale School and make the transition at your convenience, after Dr. Forrestal and I determine the appropriate time and after Benjamin is prepared. Mrs. Moore, will you be contacting the Advanced School with your recommendations and Benjamin's records?"

"Yes, the necessary documentation will be sent tomorrow. I believe you are making the correct decision," Mrs. Moore stated with some relief.

Ellen replied, "I am concerned with the age and maturity differences of the students at the Advanced Riverdale School. Mrs. Lewis, I want you to meet with Benjamin's future teachers, evaluate the current curriculum, and ensure the transition will not be traumatic for Benjamin. I want his academic success to continue. I may delay Benjamin's entry. I will discuss Benjamin's academic future with his father. Am I making myself clear?"

"Yes, madam, very clear," Mrs. Lewis replied confidently.

Ellen turned to her guests: "Ladies, thank you for bringing this to my attention. I trust you will do all you can to facilitate Benjamin's transfer."

Mrs. Moore replied, "Of course. We will do all within our powers to expedite the transfer."

Ellen abruptly stated, "Mrs. Lewis and I will now have a conversation with my son, so please excuse us. I am sure you know your way out."

After a brief discussion with her son and his governess, Ellen returned to the sitting room. She sat alone on the silk sofa. It was late, and the room was dark except for a single gas table lamp placed next to the sofa and the almost imperceptible pilot flame of the central ceiling chandelier. Ellen's thoughts were with Benjamin and the conversation with Mrs. Moore earlier that night. A strange foreboding consumed her. Did she know her son? What kind of person was Benjamin becoming? Was he healthy otherwise, physically and mentally? Was she leaving too much of her son's upbringing to Mrs. Lewis? Did her business interest consume too much of her time at the expense of her son's development? She felt she needed to speak to Conrad, so she patiently waited alone for him to arrive home from the hospital.

With relief, she heard her husband's footsteps approaching. Ellen stood, walked across the room, and met him in the entrance hall as he opened the door.

"Conrad, I am so happy you are home," Ellen stated as she put her arms around her tired and somewhat startled husband, "I need to talk to you about Benjamin and how he is behaving in school."

"You're trembling. What is it?" Conrad returned, putting his arms around her and pulling her close. "Let's go into the sitting room so we may talk."

Ellen turned toward the room where she had spent most of her day but paused at the archway separating the entrance hall and sitting room. She turned the gas valve on the wall to brighten the large chandelier. Taking her husband's hand, the couple walked over to the sofa and sat down to discuss Ellen's concerns.

"Mrs. Moore, the principal at Benjamin's school, and his middle school teacher, Mrs. Stuart, visited today. They said our Benjamin's academic skills exceeded the requirements to graduate from middle school, and they recommended he be transferred to the Advanced School," Ellen explained in a single breath.

"That's wonderful. Benjamin is very bright and Mrs. Lewis—"

"There's more," Ellen interrupted. "I believe they were either frightened of Benjamin or disgusted with him. When I agreed to the transfer – you could see it in their faces."

Ellen began crying.

"What did they say that was so bothersome? What is it?" Conrad asked, holding Ellen's hand.

"Mrs. Moore said some of the children were cruel to our Benjamin because of his leg and foot. They said they did their best to control the other children, but some were just cruel."

Ellen's face was wet with tears at the thought of her son suffering because of others.

"We knew he would be subjected to prejudice; it is human nature. He must learn more than his school lessons. He must learn the lesson of tolerance—"

"I am afraid he has learned to hate. Mrs. Moore said he uses his superior knowledge to ridicule and denigrate the other children in his class. I think he taunts them, makes them feel stupid."

Ellen was frightened she may have neglected her child.

"She even said Benjamin bullied the other children with the same meanness some of the children directed toward him. This cannot be his fate, Conrad. Please tell me this is not his fate."

"This is not his fate," Conrad answered with a stern voice. "Benjamin is a thirteen-year-old boy. You are listening to a couple of dull, normal grade school teachers. It is a public school. We put him in public school so he would be exposed to the world. We knew we would have to provide him with a proper education separate from what he would learn in school. Public schools are terrible—we knew that. Did you talk to him about all of this?"

"Mrs. Lewis and I had a long conversation with Benjamin about the things his teachers described taking place in school. Benjamin was quiet and then looked at me with a strange glare on his face, and said without hesitation the following . . . I was simply astonished. I wrote it down for you."

Ellen took a paper from her dress pocket and began to read:

I hate them all; some of the children come to school dirty and without shoes, others never bathe, and they smell like pigs and horses. Many children have dirty clothes, even some of the girls dress in dirty clothes, and all of them are stupid. They do not study because they are lazy. These pathetic little people have the audacity to taunt me because of my leg and foot. Some of these disturbed children spit on me and some even trip me in the hallway or in the schoolroom to watch me fall so they can laugh. I hate them all. Crude, mean little people. I would hurt them if I could. I hate them.

"Then he said he was excited to attend the Advanced School, where Benjamin said the children would be smarter. Can you believe he called the other students 'pathetic' and said 'audacity to taunt me'? What thirteen-year-old talks like that?"

Conrad began to explain, "Benjamin is bright, precocious, and well-educated compared to the other more prosaic children at his school, and he is having an adjustment reaction to his school experience. Some of the children teased him and made him feel inadequate, so he repressed his feeling of inferiority and compensated by being academically superior. I think that part is a good thing. Our Benjamin will grow up to be a doctor or a lawyer. He will have to make a living with his brains because of his handicap. Keep this in mind, Ellen, all these concerns will diminish when he hits puberty."

"Conrad, he is not just coping by becoming a good student. Listen to me. Benjamin told me in a cold, matter-of-fact way that he hated the other students. You should have seen his face when he spoke. My little boy seemed so angry for being just thirteen years old. What are we going to do?" Ellen felt lost and frightened.

Conrad took a long moment to consider Ellen's words, and with confidence, he explained what he thought would facilitate Benjamin's maturity into a more happy, balanced human being.

"Ellen, you and I must start giving more of our time to Benjamin. I will make every effort to be home for dinners, barring medical emergencies. We will discuss over supper Benjamin's issues and activities. In this manner, we will be able to guide and teach him. I will also make arrangements for one of the other doctors to cover my patients several times a month so the three of us can do things together, like horse riding or visiting some museums or the zoo in Londonderry. I also think it would be best to wait on the Advanced School for a year or so. I want Mrs. Lewis to help him select some books to read and encourage Benjamin to speak about the things he has read, but no more academics for a while. I strongly believe we should let Benjamin be a little boy. We should allow him a few days each week where he can do anything he would like to do. And when he is older, we should let him take his horse and explore the town and the ocean and the nearby forest. A few days a month, Mrs. Lewis may take him to see different things, like how the lumber mill works, or the shipyard to observe ships being repaired, so those experiences might help to stimulate his mind about the world not found in school books. I want our boy to have some fun without the pressure of school academics or unkind things directed at him. What do you think?"

Ellen came alive, "I think that's wonderful. Would you really start coming home for dinner so we can be a family eating together and taking trips together? Conrad, I love you so much. You make me so happy."

"Ellen, the most important thing to me is my family. I will do my best to help Benjamin grow into a fine man," Conrad promised, putting his arms around Ellen.

In the following days, Benjamin left primary school. He appeared less stressed and more affable. He was free. For the first time in his life, or so it seemed, Benjamin was not studying for an examination, or writing an essay, or preparing for an oral presentation in front of a classroom. Benjamin could awake knowing his entire day had no specific plan. Benjamin could be himself, and he loved the feeling.

Now Benjamin could spend a day at the beach collecting shells or walking through the town of Riverdale looking through the many shops, talking and asking questions of the many adults he encountered. The townspeople were kind to young Benjamin, and he could feel the warmth of their acceptance. Benjamin once spent a whole day sitting on the sea wall watching the many ships come and go, dreaming of the worlds those ships would visit and how he wished he could sail on every one of them.

~

As the year passed, Benjamin enjoyed and loved his horse, Fortune. The horse was a three-year-old gelding. He bonded with his horse, riding in the custom saddle his father had made for him to accommodate his oversize shoe and leg brace. The saddle permitted him to ride like the wind and be as adept as any rider. Benjamin loved having dinner with his father, who shared about his day and would ask Benjamin to describe all that he experienced that day. Benjamin loved how his family laughed together and shared their love for each other. In many ways, these would be the happiest days of Benjamin's life.

The cold winter nights gave way to warm summer days. Benjamin was riding Fortune north of Riverdale, deep in the forest that covered the nearby hills. He carefully walked the young horse through the dense growth beneath the towering pines. Late in the afternoon, he came to a clearing with a small stream pouring into a large pool of clear water. Benjamin carefully dismounted and sat next to the pond to gaze upon this forest wonder. The water was full of life. Small frogs and tadpoles darted. Strange winged spiders walked on the surface. Occasionally, Benjamin saw small fish flashing among the rocks, searching for food, and brilliant red and orange salamanders made their home in the soft soil around the pond. The trees and foliage rustled in the wind and birds and squirrels played among the branches, speaking to one another with the language of the forest. As Benjamin sat among all the living and splendid things he had discovered, Fortune did something quite unexpected. He tucked his legs under his body (front legs first, followed by hind legs) and laid down beside Benjamin, rolling onto his side and placing his head in Benjamin's lap. Benjamin's soul filled with joy and love for his horse and this newly discovered place in the woods. He cherished this, the most perfect of moments in the most magical of places.

When the time was right, Benjamin mounted his horse and slowly walked Fortune through the woods to the gravel road that led home. Benjamin did not see Jonnie York hiding behind a tree, nor did he see the older boy rush up behind him. His first awareness of someone near occurred when he was yanked from his horse and thrown to the ground, the air knocked from his lungs. While Benjamin lay coughing and choking, Fortune turned to face his young master. Jonnie then picked up a fist-sized rock and threw it directly at Fortune as hard as he could, striking the poor horse directly between his eyes, splitting his skin and skull and stunning the horse as blood gushed from the wound. Benjamin screamed for his horse to run. Fortune turned and ran for the safety of the stable in town. Jonnie then knelt over Benjamin, placing his knee squarely in the middle of his chest and pinning him to the ground. Jonnie was seventeen, nearly twice Benjamin's size and fat. Benjamin was helpless beneath Jonnie's weight. Jonnie pulled a hunting knife, nearly seven inches long, from a leather sheath on his waistband and placed the knife against Benjamin's left cheek.

"Why are you doing this?" Benjamin pleaded.

"Because you rich folk think you are so much better than us."

Jonnie's explanation was meaningless to Benjamin.

"I don't even know you," Benjamin screamed, adrenaline coursing through him and his heart pounding.

"Jonnie York is the name, and now I am going to leave my mark so every time you look in the mirror, you will remember me." Then Jonnie plunged his knife through Benjamin's cheek, twisting the wound open and splitting Benjamin's tongue down the middle. Benjamin screamed in pain while choking up blood, holding his hand over the gaping wound on his face and in his mouth. While Benjamin writhed in pain, Jonnie did the unthinkable. He reached down with his knife and cut the leather straps holding Benjamin's brace in place and cut the laces holding the corrective shoe on his foot. He tore the brace and corrective shoe from Benjamin's leg and foot, and, without saying another word, disappeared into the forest, carrying Benjamin's only means of walking home. Benjamin sat in shock by the side of the road, spitting up blood. He feared if he did not stop the bleeding, he would die, so he removed his shirt to form a tourniquet covering. As he put pressure on his wounds, he attempted to crawl the fourteen miles back to town while dragging his withered limb.

Fortune ran into the livery stable drenched in sweat, breathing uncontrollably and bleeding profusely from the gaping wound between his eyes. Samuel Summers, the chief librarian for the town public library, was bringing his horse, Redeemer, and his carriage to the stable when he saw Fortune's deplorable condition. The horse franticly raced about the corral in a panic, attempting to enter his closed stable, running several times into the stable gate. Samuel ordered Ralph Stark, the stable master, to get the horse under control and begin cooling him down before he expired from heat exhaustion.

"That's Benjamin Forrestal's horse, right?" Samuel yelled at Ralph.

"Yep, it is," Ralph returned, preoccupied with the severely injured and fatigued horse.

"Where did he go riding today?" Samuel asked, panicked. Ralph looked blank.

"Think, man, think," Samuel screamed again at Ralph.

Then Ralph uttered the lifesaving phrase, "The Forest Road!"

Samuel jumped into his carriage and raced to Dr. Forrestal's home. Tying the reins of his horse to the fence, Samuel ran to the door and began pounding. Ellen opened and fear consumed her, recognizing the frantic rhythm of the beckoning as some form of emergency. Staring at her was the anxious countenance of Samuel Summers. She felt strength leave her legs and her mind began swirling as Samuel's presence was far too reminiscent of a former tragic day in her life. "Is Benjamin with you?" Samuel blurted out.

All she managed was a feeble, "No . . . riding."

"Benjamin's horse just returned to the stable without Benjamin. I'm afraid he might have been thrown from his horse and is trying to walk home." Samuel explained without mentioning the inexplicable condition and behavior of Benjamin's horse that would certainly cause Ellen additional anguish. "I believe he is out by the old Forest Road."

Ellen unconsciously removed her apron and dropped it as she and Samuel raced to the carriage. Samuel frantically turned his horse in the direction of the forest. Samuel struck his beloved horse repeatedly with a whip, prompting the horse to run as fast as possible while pushing the limits of his abilities to maintain control. Thirteen miles from town, Ellen found her young son covered in blood and non-responsive, lying in a ditch. Benjamin's face and mouth were caked with dry and fresh blood. His back was badly sunburned with patches of blistering, tissue forming translucent islands in a sea of reddish skin. His trousers were frayed from his desperate crawl. His good knee and hands resembled uncooked meat, with dirt and stones smashed into the bleeding wounds and his withered limb was scraped raw. Samuel carefully lifted Benjamin into the back seat of his carriage. His mother, sobbing in disbelief, climbed in after him and held Benjamin's burned and mangled face in her arms. His breathing was labored with the sound of gurgling and shallow coughs as he struggled to inhale. Benjamin was unable to speak, and could only manage an occasional groan as he slipped in and out of consciousness. Benjamin's skin was dull blue and ashen except for his sunburned back.

Ellen desperately probed her finger into Benjamin's mouth and throat, attempting to clear dried blood and debris from Benjamin's airway. She turned his head to the side, expediting the flow of blood from his mouth, keeping him from drowning. Samuel, glancing over his shoulder while racing toward town, realized Benjamin's peril and began to succumb to an emotional frenzy, doing his best to guide his horse and carriage while screaming unintelligibly, fearing young Benjamin was about to die. As they neared town, Ellen first noticed Benjamin's brace and corrective shoe was missing. She knew then that Benjamin had been intentionally harmed. She suppressed her anger as she tried to keep her child alive. Redeemer was soaked in sweat and wheezing very badly as Samuel continued to yell at and whip his horse, draining every ounce of energy from the obedient animal and trying to gain lifesaving seconds returning to Riverdale. Arriving in a panicked flurry at the Riverdale Hospital emergency room, Ellen leaped from the carriage and disappeared into the hospital. Seconds later, several orderlies with a stretcher, accompanied by Ellen, raced out of the hospital and carefully removed Benjamin from the carriage, placing him on the stretcher and rushing him into the hospital.

Samuel, badly shaken and alone, began to sob and sat for a long time without moving before regaining his composure. He then dismounted and methodically uncoupled Redeemer from the carriage. He slowly walked his fatigued and dying horse to the stable. Ralph and Samuel labored for hours, trying to cool and calm the exhausted animal. They bathed the horse with cool water, and repeatedly encouraged Redeemer to drink. Redeemer became increasingly uncoordinated until he could not stand. Samuel stroked the poor animal's face and mane, whispering his goodbyes when Redeemer died just before dawn.

Chapter 7
A Mother's Scorn

T he orderlies carried Benjamin down the hall and placed him on a gurney covered with white sheets. Ellen ran close behind, sobbing and crying out Benjamin's name. Benjamin disappeared behind a pair of large, white doors. Above the doors, a red sign read: "Emergency Room Sterile Protocols." An orderly stopped Ellen at the entrance. "Please, Mrs. Forrestal, you can't go in there."

Supervising Nurse Russell rushed up to Ellen and placed one of her arms around Ellen's shoulders, stating firmly, "Mrs. Forrestal, please, you can't go into the operating room. Come with me."

"Where's Conrad, Nurse Russell?" Ellen demanded.

"Dr. Forrestal is in surgery. Please come with me, and you will be able to see what's going on with your son. Please come with me," Nurse Russell repeated, turning Ellen from the hall to a door next to the operating room marked, "Physician's Observation Theater."

Ellen walked into a dark room with several theater seats facing a large glass window. As Ellen approached the glass, she saw her son lying on the gurney bathed with brilliant light and surrounded by hospital personnel frantically working to save his life. The source of light came from a glass ceiling, permitting the sunlight to illuminate the surgical room, facilitating the physician's efforts. Hundreds of white, square tiles covered the walls and floors. The countertops, carts, trays, and surgical table were covered with polished nickel. A central pillar under the surgical table held it in place. Extending from the central pillar to the end of the table were two heavy rods with pedals for raising and lowering the surgical table. Four nurses and one very tall doctor positioned themselves around an extremely ill Benjamin, all of them covered with white aprons from their neck to their feet. Hoods, secured with white ribbon, completely covered their heads. The white hoods had the face area cut out, permitting the doctor and nurses to see, breathe, and communicate. Everyone had a mask tied around the hood covering their mouth and nose. Tight, white rubber gloves and rubber boots sealed their hands and feet. Ellen was shocked at the sight. She had no idea a place like this existed.

Ellen could see Benjamin lying on the cart. She was only a few feet from him as she pressed her face and hands against the glass. Two of the nurses were cutting Benjamin's trousers off with surgical scissors. The doctor was carefully removing the blood-soaked shirt from the boy's face, exposing the massive wound on Benjamin's left cheek. After removing Benjamin's clothing, one of the nurses grabbed the boy's shoulders, and the other nurse placed her hands under his legs. Another nurse seemed to be counting, and the nurses simultaneously lifted the naked boy onto the surgical table. A third nurse rolled the cart with the stretcher and Benjamin's discarded clothing back through the double doors. A fourth nurse pulled a small nickel table with a tray of medical instruments next to the surgical table. She grabbed a round mirror with a nickel edge and nickel back, about the size of a pie tin, and began to maneuver the mirror to reflect light into Benjamin's mouth so the doctor could examine the injuries. The doctor pointed at a small, glass, curved tube. The nurse handed the tube to the doctor and opened a small pan on the table, dipped a small piece of gauze into a bright, red-orange liquid and, with tweezers, took the soaked gauze and rubbed it at the base of the boy's neck between his collar bones, staining Benjamin's neck reddish-orange. The doctor picked up a small knife, made an incision in the boy's neck, placed the glass tube in the incision, and taped the glass tube.

"What are they doing?" Ellen screamed.

"The doctor is helping Benjamin breathe. The opening allows your son to breathe through the glass tube in his neck.

The doctor has determined that the injury to your boy's throat is too extensive to allow your son to breathe properly," Nurse Russell calmly explained while taking Ellen's hand for reassurance. "Your son's neck was cleaned with tincture of iodine. This bright liquid cleans the skin area where the doctor needed to cut to place the glass tube. This procedure is called a tracheotomy, and the glass tube is called a trach tube. Dr. Lister is keeping your son from suffocating. There must be some blockage in Benjamin's mouth or throat," Nurse Russell repeated to a very frightened and confused mother. "Benjamin's skin color will improve as he gets more air into his lungs. He's going to be all right. Do you want to continue to watch?"

"Yes," Ellen said, barely audible.

Dr. Lister motioned a nurse to bring a nickel rack closer to the surgical table. The frame had a bottle with clear liquid hanging from it. The bottle had a small neck pointed down at the ground. A long, rubber hose ran from the bottle to Benjamin's arm. "Dr. Lister will give your son a saline solution directly into the vein in his arm. The procedure is called intravenous therapy—it is a way for your son to receive fluids into his body without swallowing." Nurse Russell continued to explain. "Your son is dehydrated. Intravenous therapy will put fluids into his body."

Ellen continued to watch, feeling anxious and utterly helpless.

A nurse sitting beside Benjamin wrapped a flat rubber tube around Benjamin's arm and, with a small rubber air bladder, began pumping the flat tube with air.

"What are those nurses doing with that thing around Benjamin's arm?" Ellen asked frantically.

Nurse Russell explained, "The nurse is listening to the blood flow to determine Benjamin's blood pressure, and the pocket watch in the jar helps the nurse determine the strength and rate at which the heart is beating. They will convey this information to the doctor so he can assess Benjamin's medical status. The watch is in the jar because it can't be sterilized."

Benjamin's skin changed from an ashen-blue hue to a more normal pink. "Mrs. Forrestal, can you see how your son's skin color is improving? Benjamin is receiving plenty of air now," Nurse Russell said in uplifting tones.

Ellen could only say, "That's good."

Dr. Lister began examining and swabbing out Benjamin's mouth and throat with a pair of forceps holding moistened gauze. The nurse holding the mirror maneuvered it to enhance the doctor's vision. Two other nurses were beginning to clean Benjamin's wounds on his hands and legs. Within a few minutes, Dr. Lister completed his examination and began cleaning Benjamin's throat, tongue, inner cheek, and face. Ellen could see the doctor speaking to the nurse listening to Benjamin's heart. The nurse secured a small piece of cotton cloth with forceps and handed the material to Dr. Lister. The doctor placed the cloth on top of the glass tube in Benjamin's neck and carefully poured a clear liquid onto the fabric.

"Dr. Lister is giving your son chloroform so Benjamin can sleep as the doctor repairs the injuries to his face and mouth. Your son will not feel pain while the doctor works. See? The other nurse with the stethoscope is talking to the doctor. She is informing Dr. Lister of Benjamin's blood pressure. The doctor is concerned that Benjamin may become conscious during the procedure, so Dr. Lister is going to regulate his artificial sleep by periodically adding small amounts of chloroform. Benjamin is getting plenty of air," Nurse Russell explained, sounding increasingly reassuring.

Dr. Lister picked up a hook-shaped needle with a long thread made from catgut soaked in chromic acid, and began methodically suturing Benjamin's tongue and cheek. The nurses cleaning and debriding Benjamin's abrasions on his hands and legs were now finished and began to wrap the wounds. With Benjamin's face and mouth wounds sutured, the doctor motioned the nurse to roll Benjamin on his side. When Ellen saw her child's raw, sunburned back, she began sobbing louder. The doctor carefully removed some of the grey tissue hanging from Benjamin's back, and one of the nurses began swabbing the burned area with a clear, reddish liquid.

Nurse Russell explained that the nurse was applying sterile water and diluted tomato juice to help the sunburn heal.

Ellen watched as Dr. Lister began examining Benjamin's neck and body for any other signs of trauma when the observation theater's door burst open and Conrad ran to his wife, still wearing a surgery apron covered with blood and filth from several surgeries that day. Conrad wrapped his arms around his wife, "What happened?"

"Someone tried to kill Benjamin," Ellen sobbed.

Nurse Russell informed Dr. Forrestal of his son's condition as he frantically looked through the observation window. "Your son received significant facial trauma on his left cheek and sustained some laceration in his mouth. Dr. Lister has sutured his tongue. Your son also ambulated some distance on his hands and his good knee before he was discovered. As a result, he suffered significant abrasions to his functional knee and both palms of his hands. The malformed leg also suffered significant abrasions from being dragged. Those abrasions were cleaned, debrided, and bandaged. Your son was also suffering from exposure and sunburn. Dr. Lister is currently examining your son for additional injuries. Your son seems to be doing very well, doctor."

Dr. Forrestal then returned, "Thank you, Nurse Russell. Why was he crawling?"

"The monster who cut him also stole his brace and corrective shoe," Ellen said, seething with anger.

This malevolence directed at his son shocked and unnerved the doctor. "We will deal with the assault at the appropriate time," Conrad tried to reassure Ellen. "Benjamin is in good hands, Ellen. Dr. Lister is one of the finest doctors in the country, and his medical knowledge is extensive and significantly more advanced than most of the medical community. We are incredibly lucky to have him in Riverdale."

Nurse Russell agreed, "Dr. Lister is excellent. He has the

best survival rate over any of the other doctors in the hospital."

"That's right, Ellen. He is excellent," Conrad reiterated. "Look, I think Dr. Lister is about to finish."

Dr. Lister looked at the nurse with the pocket watch, and she nodded her head and appeared to be smiling behind her mask. The doctor then ordered an injection of penicillin, an antibiotic. Dr. Lister turned and walked briskly through the double doors and, in a few seconds, entered the observation room while removing his mask, hood, and gloves. Looking directly at Conrad, Dr. Lister said, "Oh, Dr. Forrestal, your surgical apron. It's very understandable why you forgot to remove it in the surgical room. Nurse Russell, please aid Dr. Forrestal in removing his apron."

Nurse Russell responded, "Yes, doctor." Conrad lifted his arms. Nurse Russell untied the apron, lifted the cloth neck hoop over his head, and began folding the contaminated apron. Dr. Lister handed Nurse Russell his hood, surgical gown, and gloves, and stated, "Please have these incinerated."

"Yes, doctor," Nurse Russell replied, taking the soiled garments away.

Dr. Lister approached Conrad and Ellen: "You are Mrs. Forrestal?"

"Yes, I am," Ellen returned with anxiety in her voice.

"My name is Joseph Lister, and your son is going to be fine. He received a nasty laceration of the left cheek, apparently from a knife. The knife penetrated the mouth, slicing the center portion of his tongue. These lacerations required extensive suturing and should heal nicely. There is some concern the nerves in his tongue were damaged. We will have to wait and see. Hopefully, nerve damage will be slight, if any. The abrasions should heal nicely as well. The sunburn was not significant and should not present any problems. Your son was lucky you found him when you did. He was close to suffocation from the swelling and bleeding in his throat and tongue. He was also very dehydrated. I don't believe your son would have survived much longer without medical intervention."

The doctor continued, "When the swelling declines, we will remove the glass tracheotomy tube from the neck in a day or so. Now, there will be some discomfort from the wounds in his mouth, so when Benjamin begins to regain consciousness, we will initiate an IV drip of morphine to control the pain and keep your son sedated for the next few days."

"What is an IV morphine drip?" Ellen asked, looking at Conrad.

Conrad explained, "It's a refined opium that can be placed directly into Benjamin's vein to relieve pain."

"Will he be all right?" Ellen asked, unable to grasp everything the doctor was saying.

"Yes, your son will be well enough to go home in a few weeks. We will be feeding through a nasogastric tube through his nose into his stomach," Dr. Lister said unemotionally.

Ellen felt faint and slumped onto the nearest theater seat. Conrad sat next to his wife and placed his arm around her for comfort. "Benjamin will be all right. You brought him to the hospital in time, and Dr. Lister was able to save him. He will be okay, Ellen."

Dr. Lister said, "Dr. and Mrs. Forrestal, I will be available any time for questions. I will look in on your son every few hours. Your son will be in post-op for a few hours to ensure no further problems before moving to a private room. You will be able to see and speak to him then. You are, of course, welcome to stay here and observe your son until he is moved to his room."

"What is going to happen to him when he recovers? Will he recover completely?" Ellen asked.

"His face will have a substantial scar on his left cheek. If his tongue has significant nerve damage, he may have some problems speaking and eating. I believe that is unlikely, but it is possible. Dr. Forrestal, are there any more questions?" Dr. Lister asked.

Ellen then stated, "When will his father be able to care for him?"

Dr. Forrestal responded, "Ellen, Benjamin is Dr. Lister's patient, and that is how it will remain. Dr. Lister is our most excellent doctor and has pioneered many of the medical techniques you saw here today. We are fortunate we have Dr. Lister at our hospital."

"Thank you, Dr. Forrestal. Please, any time, I will be available to answer your questions," Dr. Lister said as he turned and disappeared through the door.

"Conrad, is he really a good doctor? I don't understand any of this. Is Benjamin safe?"

"Dr. Lister gets results. The survival rate of Dr. Lister's patients is far better than that of any doctor in this hospital or anyplace else. Ellen, what you saw today is the future of medicine. In twenty years, every hospital will have an operating room like this one and subscribe to Dr. Lister's techniques. Some of Dr. Lister's theories are sometimes difficult to accept. Dr. Lister's reasons for his treatments may seem strange, but Ellen, they work. Dr. Lister's childbirth survival rate is significantly more successful using sterile procedures versus traditional techniques. Dr. Lister's methods have revolutionized emergency surgery as well," Conrad explained.

"Why all the clothes and white tile? What is a sterile protocol, and what is it all about?" Ellen asked.

Conrad paused for a second before responding, "Well, Dr. Lister believes small invisible animals are everywhere and must be eliminated before invasive medical procedures like Benjamin's surgery."

Ellen coldly responded, "That's not funny, Conrad. We are talking about my child. That sounds implausible."

"I don't know about the invisible animals. I do know Dr. Lister is the most sophisticated practicing doctor, and he gets results. Our son would have died of suffocation if any other doctor had treated him, including me. Dr. Lister does not utilize bleedings, leeches, or emetics, and Ellen, you paid for it all. The money you gave to the hospital paid for this operating room and Dr. Lister's expensive salary. Your generosity has, and continues, to save lives, and this time that life was your child's. You should be proud of what you have accomplished," Conrad said in the sincerest tone.

Ellen pulled Conrad closer to her, "Conrad, will you wait here with me for a while? Just until Benjamin moves to a room, and we can see him?"

"I will be here for you and Benjamin," Conrad said, putting his arm around the shoulders of the woman he deeply loved.

Conrad and Ellen observed Benjamin for an hour through the observation window. Every fifteen minutes a nurse would check Benjamin's pulse. Every hour, a nurse would relieve the monitoring nurse. Several other nurses carefully watched his breathing and the flow of the saline solution from the glass bottle overhead. Benjamin was responding well to the emergency procedures Dr. Lister had performed to save his life. When Benjamin was stable, the nurses moved him to a private hospital room reserved for hospital personnel and their families. Several hours later, the nurses introduced a morphine IV drip into Benjamin's system. He received nutrients through a feeding tube that passed through his nose to his stomach, and four days later he was able to communicate with his mother by nodding his head and writing short notes.

Ellen remained with Benjamin for days, sitting by his bedside, requesting various things from the nurses, and asking Dr. Lister numerous questions concerning her child's progress. Ellen slept in his room, was provided meals, and given anything she requested. After all, she was the wife of one of the most prominent physicians on the hospital staff, and all of the hospital personnel were well aware of Mrs. Forrestal's status. During the four days of hospitalization, Ellen sat next to her sleeping son, watching his body rise and fall as he breathed. Ellen was saddened by the appearance of the numerous sutures on her son's neck, cheek, and tongue. How horrible Benjamin appeared with bandaged hands and legs, and the awful, ugly brown tube passing through his nose into his stomach. However, she was relieved by her son's recovery, and grateful for Dr. Lister's successful efforts.

Conrad tried to remain stoic while supporting his wife and monitoring his son's progress. On the evening of the fourth day of Benjamin's hospitalization, Conrad stood in the doorway of his son's hospital room and watched his wife sleeping in a chair next to his sedated son. Conrad's arms and legs trembled at the thought of how narrow the razor's edge between survival and death had been for his son on some dirt road a few miles from town. Would his son ever be safe? Conrad grabbed the doorsill to maintain his balance and prevent displaying his ever-increasing loss of control as he contemplated the implications. The stress was overwhelming. He was no longer an objective healer. He would not dare show any emotions—he was a physician. Conrad would act the part. He turned and unsteadily walked down the hallway to the door of his office. He locked the door behind him before walking to his chair behind his desk. He removed his boot and sock from his right leg and foot, he opened the bottom drawer of his desk and took out a small, worn, leather box. He opened the box and retrieved a vial of morphine. He tried to convince himself this would be the last time. Conrad took a syringe and carefully placed the tip of the needle in the clear liquid—he was up to fifty milligrams now. He placed the needle between his two largest toes and filled his body with the most wonderful sensation. Conrad leaned back in his chair and the world faded away. He had escaped.

～～

Early in the evening of the fifth day of hospitalization, Benjamin became much more responsive as the morphine drip was discontinued. Benjamin's body was compensating and growing stronger. With tears in her eyes, his mother sat next to his bed, holding her son's bandaged hand. Benjamin stared at his mother, trying to speak to her, but he was unsuccessful. Benjamin motioned with his hand. He wanted to write something. Ellen stood up and disappeared through the door, returning shortly with a paper and pencil. Benjamin struggled to hold the pencil with the tip of his fingers protruding through the bandages.

His mother held the paper backed by the book retrieved from the night table. Her son wrote one word: "Why?"

Ellen could only cry, and placing her hand on his forehead, she answered, "I just don't know. I cannot explain why this terrible thing happened. No one can. I am so sorry. You are getting well and will be able to go home soon. Everything is going to be better."

Benjamin then scrawled the name of his horse, "Fortune."

Ellen was reassuring. "Fortune is just fine. His head injury is healing, and you will be riding him in a few weeks. He ran back to the stable and Ralph cooled him down, so he is all right and waiting for you to visit him as soon as you can."

Benjamin scrawled again, "My brace and shoe?"

Ellen assured him, "Don't worry, we will have a brace for you when you are ready to get out and play."

A moment passed, and Ellen asked, "Do you know who did this to you?"

Benjamin answered by nodding his head and, with some difficulty, wrote the name of his attacker: "Jonnie York."

Ellen asked, "Are you sure?"

Benjamin nodded. Ellen did not mention the subject again, instead focusing on positive things. Soon, he would be riding his horse, sitting under the stars, or playing in the sea. Later that night, when Benjamin was asleep, Ellen left the hospital and returned to her home office at the top of the stairs and began telegraphing a message to her lawyer and friend.

> I want a thorough profile on Jonnie York and all ancillary issues -Stop- Time is of the essence -Stop-

That was all that was telegraphed—that was all that was necessary. The next day, around noon, Ellen began reading a comprehensive file concerning all aspects of Jonnie York's twisted, insignificant life. When she completed the file, Ellen walked to the livery stable, had her carriage readied, and directed her horse to Jonnie York's home a few miles off the Old Forest Road.

A few miles down the Old Forest Road, Ellen turned her horse to follow a narrow road through a series of low hills and parched, barren land. Ellen located a single-story, run-down cabin with a rusting, corrugated metal roof at the end of the road. Surrounding the cabin was a strange menagerie of farm animals squeezed into several small, fenced areas. Filthy chickens, ducks, and goats pathetically packed together appeared to be living in their waste. Another enclosure contained several dirty dogs and a few hogs also living in deplorable conditions. The dogs suffered from mange and looked starved. A single, aged mare was tied in front of the house. Ellen stepped down from her carriage, carefully walked a few feet across a dirt yard replete with holes, trash, and horse manure, and started up a series of rickety, wooden steps. Before she reached the rusty screen peeling from the doorframe, the door flew open and a giant of a man stepped onto the creaking porch. He was well over six feet high and muscular despite a large, hairy belly that protruded beneath his dirty shirt. He was chewing a gob of tobacco, and his chin and mouth appeared streaked with dark brown spittle. His face was craggy, with unshaven and sunburned skin. His nose resembled bleeding cauliflower, and his eyes were distant storms.

Ellen asked softly, "Are you Jack York, Jonnie York's father?"

"What of it?" he sternly answered, wafting a wave of stinking breath toward Ellen and producing several new streaks of saliva and tobacco to his chin.

"Several days ago, your son attacked my son with a knife on the Old Forest Road, hospitalizing him from the injuries he sustained. Your son also stole his leg brace and corrective shoe without which he will be unable to walk. Will you please ask your son to return them?" Ellen asked, increasingly realizing she was dealing with some mistake of nature.

There are times when some men make a mistake so onerous, so hideous, their lives will be lost by the repercussions. So dreadful the blunder that angels would deny their souls. Such was the misstep Jack York was about to make. He walked up to Ellen, grabbed her right breast as hard as he could, pulled her face into his, and spit a gob of tobacco, splotching her beauty and filling her eyes with the burning incendiary of hate. Her mouth, gaping in horror, became adulterated with the warm, bitter liquid, causing her to uncontrollably gag before she was flung off the porch. Ellen landed on her right side in the dirt and manure, her dress torn at the shoulder and neck, her buttons ripped. Ellen struggled to remove herself from the monster she just engaged.

As she turned and stumbled toward her carriage, she could hear the voice of the man she would utterly destroy singing out the anthem of his demise, "If your rich, scrawny husband wants to do anything about it, if he is man enough to honor his oath to you, I will be right here."

Ellen, overcome with fear and anger, climbed aboard her carriage and directed her horse to return to town. She would not remember her journey home that day, her mind preoccupied with rage. Ellen held her torn dress together as she rode through Riverdale, hoping no one would notice her disheveled appearance. Arriving home, Ellen quickly dismounted, tied up her horse, and ran to the house and up the stairs before the servants saw her. She entered her sleep room and locked the door, ripping her dress from her body. Ellen then removed her undergarments, stockings, and shoes, and stood naked before the full-length mirror. She was overwhelmed with anger and hate, trembling in shock. Her right breast was swollen and discolored, disfigured with a discernible imprint of a man's large hand. As she turned to look at her back, she was stunned by the blackened bruise extending from her right buttock down the back of her right leg, where she had struck the ground. She walked closer to the mirror and peered at her face, stained by the monster's tobacco-laden spit. The monster that begat the demon that nearly killed her son. Ellen entered the master's private room and turned on the shower, waiting for the cold water to become warm. When the time was right, she stepped into the iron tub and tried to clean the violations from her body, tears mingling with the water flowing over her body. Ellen knew, no matter the effort, she would never be able to cleanse off the filth.

Ellen, her naked body covered by her white robe, slowly walked to her office down the hall and unlocked the door with the only key. She entered, then shut and locked the door. The cold sea breeze from the open window caused Ellen to tighten her robe around her still wet and sore body. She sat down by her telegraph and sent a message to Robert Bass.

Urgent -Stop- Please attend a dinner my home Thursday next at seven -Stop- Complete all files prejudicial and otherwise on Jack York -Stop- Father of Jonnie York -Stop- Stratagem -Stop-

---

Robert Bass would completely understand the cryptic telegraph message. He would have a great deal to accomplish in the next seventy-two hours. He would sleep little before he met with Mrs. Forrestal.

At precisely seven o'clock, the doorbell rang at the Forrestal mansion. Jane, the downstairs maid, opened the door with a smile, "Good evening, Mr. Bass. Madam is expecting you. Please come in."

Robert had his usual briefcase and, on this occasion, also an extensive portfolio tucked under his arm. Jane removed Robert Bass's coat and hat and placed them in proper order on the entrance hall rack. The lawyer was directed to the sitting room to wait for Ellen. Robert Bass sat on the silk sofa, placing his legal leather briefcase and extensive portfolio containing his efforts next to him. Jane politely asked,

"May I get something for you. Perhaps some wine?"

"No, I will just wait for Mrs. Forrestal, thank you," Mr. Bass responded, wishing his downstairs maid was as polished as Jane. Robert Bass no longer lived above his law office as his close association and friendship with Ellen had made him extremely wealthy. His home was now a large estate, newly built in a vacant lot across from the old Wolsworth's mansion.

After an appropriate passage of time, Ellen descended the stairs and greeted her business partner with a formal, "Mr. Bass, thank you for coming to dinner. It has been far too long since I have had the pleasure of your company. Unfortunately, Dr. Forrestal is occupied with several medical emergencies at the hospital and will not be able to join us, so we may begin," she feigned, knowing Robert's appetite required immediate satiation.

"Thank you, Madam," Mr. Bass returned, standing and placing his large portfolio under his left arm and his briefcase in his left hand. Ellen entwined her arm with her friend's free arm and walked with him into the formal dining room. The dining table was about eight feet long and five feet wide and covered by a silk, white tablecloth. A crystal vase displayed with freshly cut red roses adorned the center of the table. At each end of the table were numerous pieces of silverware and crystal plates, bowls, and goblets, all strategically placed according to proper etiquette. Robert sat at one end of the table, and Ellen sat the other. Robert carefully tucked his briefcase and portfolio next to his chair, never out of sight or reach.

An enormous crystal, gas chandelier hung from the eighteen-foot ceiling, providing the room with a warm glow. Most of the table's leaves were removed to create a more intimate dining experience. The vast room dwarfed the modified table. Two large windows, covered with exquisite red wool drapes, dominated the dining room, which turned beautiful shades of red when mixed with the glow of gas lights or the morning sun. The walls and ceiling were hand-painted with delicate festoons of flowers, ribbons, leaves, and frolicking birds and butterflies, all superimposing subtle clouds. A large oval on the wall opposite the windows contained a large painting of the proud, black Raven. A glass cabinet, nearly ten feet tall and fourteen feet across, displayed a fantastic collection of clear-cut crystal plates, goblets, and bowls, enough for a hundred dinner guests. The silverware collection was also extensive, representing well over a hundred pounds of the most exceptional, artist-engraved silver. Each utensil displayed an elegant rendition of the Raven proudly perched and, juxtaposed on the other side, the Raven flying to the heavens.

Shortly after Ellen and Robert settled, Jane and the upstairs maid, Margret, entered with the start of a cavalcade of culinary miracles. Robert promptly tucked his silk napkin into his collar and smiled with a distinct twinkle in his eyes as he waited for his caloric adventure to begin. The entrée, first course, was the traditional wild rice and fresh clam soup. Each maid had a large bowl of the soup. Jane served Robert and Margret served Ellen. Serving soup from the same bowl was simply considered too intimate for non-familial guests. The dinner continued with the maids serving a trifecta of roasted fowl, pheasant, duck, and goose for the main course, followed by bread made with bleached flour. Rich stuffing in each bird, made with bread, cherries, nuts, and oranges, complemented the main meal. Three goblets sat before both Robert and Ellen filled with red wine, white wine, and water. Ellen took a small envelope from her dress pocket, poured a white powder, the hydrate of lithia, into her glass containing red wine, stirred the potion with her finger, and drank the wine while the maids served dinner. Formal meals were always served in a series of three sets representing, according to fine dining legend, birth, life, and death, or sunrise, day, and sunset. Whatever the origin of such dining etiquette Robert could care less. He simply consumed each course presented to him and washed his ruminations down with red and white wines. Ellen ate several slices of pheasant breast and pheasant stuffing, some wild rice, and sipped on a glass

98

of white wine.

Ellen reached for a second helping of dressing and accidentally knocked over her recently filled goblet of red wine. No one said a word. Ellen merely glanced at Jane, who promptly produced several thick linens to blot the excess wine from the tablecloth, removed a few items on the table, lifted the affected area, and wiped the dark mahogany table to prevent staining. Jane placed another linen piece between the soiled silk and the table to protect the polished wood. Of course, the silk tablecloth was ruined but that made little difference, as the tablecloths were always discarded after one use. Jane's efforts were completely ignored as if she were invisible. Little discussion ever took place during formal meals—such banter would imply a boring meal and would be considered very impolite. Excellent culinary efforts were praised with silence. Three desserts were served: cherry pie, chocolate cake, and freshly made ice cream. Robert ingested a large portion of all three and Ellen a sliver of cherry pie. The meal was finished.

Robert complimented Ellen on the excellent dinner as the maids hurriedly removed all the items from the table.

"Ellen, without a doubt, your meals are the most exquisite in Riverdale. Please feel free to invite me anytime for these excellent dining experiences."

"Mr. Bass," Mrs. Forrestal responded, "I promise you will be a welcomed guest for many years to come."

Several minutes passed with simple pleasantries. When the table was cleared and the soiled tablecloth removed, the maids and cook were summoned to the dining room to receive a compliment from Ellen for their excellent efforts. She then stated, much to their surprise and some concern, that all three servants may have the rest of the night off.

When the maids made a slight protest concerning the amount of food sitting out in the kitchen and the number of dirty dishes that needed cleaning, Ellen merely stated, "You may finish in the morning. Please have a pleasant evening." With that, the servants gathered their personals and quickly disappeared out the rear door.

Robert and Ellen sat discussing the superficial, then Robert broke the chorus of shallowness, "Do you think they're gone?"

Ellen walked over to the maid's bell ribbon hanging through the ceiling and pulled several times. No one responded. Ellen knew the servants would not provoke upon themselves the anathema of not returning if they were still present in the mansion. "Yes, they're gone," Ellen stated confidently.

"What do you think they're thinking, leaving us alone like this?" Robert, realizing proper etiquette did not permit a man other than a husband or male member of the immediate family to be alone in a house with a married woman.

"I don't care what they think. The servants are not getting paid to think. Don't give it a second thought," Ellen reassured her friend.

Robert was finally able to express his concern, "How is your child? Please tell me Benjamin is recovering from the attack?"

"Benjamin's physical wounds should heal. If there is negligible nerve loss to his tongue, my son should speak and eat normally. His leg brace and the corrective shoe will be replaced in a month or so. My real fear is what this tragedy will do to my son's soul, his innermost being. He has suffered so much ridicule, and now this act of hate and violence from someone he does not know. He asked me why this happened to him. He seemed so lost. What am I to say to him?" Ellen asked with sadness.

"It is truly tragic and I am so deeply sorry for you and your child. I will do anything in my power to help. Please tell me what I can do." Robert was at a loss for an answer to Ellen's question.

Ellen continued as if she did not hear her friend's remarks, "The wounds . . . Benjamin's wounds we can't suture or bandage, these are the wounds that haunt my days. It is the wounds that may never heal and leave a scar so dark and deep. Benjamin will never be the same. My son was so angry before this happened. Childhood is a time for childhood innocence, not hate. Hate comes far too soon to us all. I fear I will struggle for a long time, trying to make my son whole again, complete."

There was a pause between friends with the hiss of the lamps and the distant ticking of a grandfather clock the only sounds.

Ellen broke the silence, "I am interested in reviewing your investigation so I will be able, at least, to protect my family from now on from the Yorks, father and son."

"Of course, Ellen. We should begin, I believe, with the proper compensation for Samuel Summers. The poor man lost his horse and will not have the means to replace the animal for some time with the salary he receives from his library position," Robert advised his client.

"Oh—how could I have been so thoughtless? Mr. Summers saved my son's life just as surely as Dr. Lister, my son's surgeon. By all means, let us secure a dozen carriage horses for him or anything else he wants. I did not know he lost his horse. I will always be indebted to that wonderful man." Ellen placed her head in her hand as she spoke, looking down at the table.

"No, Ellen, you can't do that," Robert said, now speaking as Ellen's lawyer. "I have taken the liberty of securing in Dr. Forrestal's name a Grade A carriage horse from the Londonderry Carriage Horse Farm."

Robert began removing several papers from his briefcase. "I have also secured two open, round-trip, first-class train tickets for Mr. Summers and his wife so they may select their carriage horse from the horses that have completed their training at the farm. I have also secured an open livestock freight ticket so the animal can be shipped back to Riverdale. I believe you should write Mr. Summers a letter expressing how you and Dr. Forrestal are grateful for his life-saving intervention and how Dr. Forrestal insisted on replacing the horse that was sacrificed saving your son's life. Also, from you and Dr. Forrestal, a contribution should be made to the mobile traveling book library Mr. Summers is putting together to serve rural children. I thought something like three hundred dollars should suffice."

Robert hesitated and continued, "Did you know Mr. Summers lost his only child?"

"No. I did not know. How did he die?"

"Mr. Summers's only child was trampled to death six years ago from a runaway horse. When his son was brought to the hospital, he was pronounced dead. I am sure he must have remembered . . . well, I am sure it was painful for him. He must have been very relieved your son survived."

Tears ran down Ellen's face as she sat in silence for a long while.

"Yes, of course. You are quite right. Thank you for your thoughtfulness. The letter will be penned first thing tomorrow, and I will deliver the letter, bill of sale, and the tickets personally. What manner of fate is this that far too often fills our world with such grief and sadness. Why so much sadness, Robert . . . so much sadness."

"So we may know the beauty of the dawn, we endure the night. . . . So saith The Word, Ellen," Robert recalled.

"So saith The Word," Ellen softly repeated.

Wiping the tears from her face, Ellen began the next phase of their discussion.

But Robert probed first, "I was somewhat confused by your earlier statement about protecting your family from the Yorks. You must tell me everything. Has there been a verbal assault from the Yorks directed at Benjamin or someone else in your family? I must have a complete understanding of all the issues."

Ellen sat, looking directly into Robert's eyes. Her face grew cold and stern, "You want to know everything, Robert?"

Ellen stood, walked to a small table next to the glass cabinet with a lamp. She lifted the lamp and carefully brought it to the dining table next to Robert, being ever mindful of the long rubber hose on the base of the lamp. Ellen twisted the gas knob on the lamp, bringing the small, faint pilot flame to a vivid source of diffused light emanating through the milk glass shade. She stood a few feet from Robert, her form bathed with light. To Robert's astonishment, his dear friend unbuttoned and pulled her blouse from her shoulder midway down her right arm. Then, this very proper woman pulled down the strap to her undergarment without hesitation, exposing her entire right breast. Robert was stunned and confused by the ugly bruise in the shape of a man's hand imprinted on Ellen's breast. The contusion was so dark next to Ellen's pale skin. The breast's areola had vanished into the twisted storm of injury and inflicted hate.

Ellen stood in silence, tears running down her face, then spoke with anger, "I went to Jack York's home and asked him to have his son return my son's brace, and that evil, grotesque deviant grabbed my breast and pulled me near to him and spit in my face. Then he taunted me to tell my husband I was violated so he would be forced to honor his marriage oath by returning and confronting him.

"Robert, I have been hiding this man's handprint for days, living in fear that Conrad would see the bruise and try to kill York. I go to bed late and rise early, bathe in private, and make love in the dark, and when my husband touches my breast, I do not feel pleasure—I feel pain and the presence of that animal. Robert, York's fate belongs to me. Will you help? I must not permit Conrad to be put in the position he must kill or be killed. Please believe me. If Conrad finds out, it will come to that. Will you help me protect my family?"

Robert looked into Mrs. Forrestal's face, slowly rose from his chair, and approached his dear friend until he stood directly in front of her. He placed his hand on the table and lowered his large frame to his knees. He took and kissed Ellen's hand and pressed it to his tear-stained cheek, whispering, "I love you like no other person in my adult life. Ellen, you are my closest friend. You have respected me and made me rich. Your son's father protected and provided for me when I was lost. I would do anything for you. Command me and I will kill him myself."

Ellen reached down, helped Mr. Bass to his feet, and faced him. She kissed his cheek and whispered, "Robert, I love you too. You are my dear friend, and I don't want you to kill him. I want you to help me to destroy him."

Robert, with a most determined demeanor, responded, "I am at your service."

With Ellen's assistance, Robert reached for his portfolio and briefcase as Ellen carefully secured her clothing, covering her injured breast. Robert spread a drawing of Mr. York's property and the adjacent parcel acreage with the property owners' names. Lawyer and client stood over the map like two generals preparing for battle.

Robert began: "York is fifty-two years old, has one dependent, Jonnie, age seventeen. He has no other holdings and no known cash reserves. He is illiterate and spends most of his income on hard drink, opium, and prostitutes. York owns one acre of property with a house in poor condition. The surrounding parcels are of little value. No structures exist for miles, except York's excuse for a dwelling. Water is present at approximately a depth of one hundred and fifty feet, and that is the only redeeming feature of the entire area. York has had three years of Kent County tax liens against his property. York manages to come up with one year of back taxes, approximately two dollars, when notified he would be evicted for failure to pay. His pattern has been to wait until the last ten days or so of the thirty-day notice to satisfy the basic legal minimum to remain the owner. The tax laws prohibit the county from seizing his property if he pays one year back taxes before the end of the thirty days. York will be given his next thirty-day notice in approximately one month. County tax laws, inexplicably, also permit another party to gain legal possession of any property in which the owner is three years in arrears with a history of being delinquent for five consecutive years, if the acquiring party pays all the back taxes during the thirty days, and before the current owner makes recompense. York's tax lien has been in effect for ten years. I would not recommend that course of action, however. It may appear too obvious who would be seizing his property. I recommend we set up a dummy corporation out of Londonderry to secure all the property adjacent to York's property and then secure ownership of York's property during the vulnerable period. The adjacent property can be secured for five to ten dollars an acre."

Ellen surveyed the property map, then told her lawyer how to proceed.

"I don't want you to acquire York's property using the tax law. I wish you to acquire all the property surrounding York's property in the manner you have described and develop a contract with the Riverdale Construction Company to construct a pig farm surrounding York's home. The first day of construction, have a sign placed somewhere prominent next to York's property, announcing the coming of the pig farm. Be sure to have a few hogs drawn on the sign so he will be able to comprehend his fate."

Robert simply stated, "Yes, madam, the dummy corporation, property accusation, and construction implementation will be completed in thirty days. We will allow York to remain and live surrounded by hogs."

"Very good. What does my lawyer have next up his legal sleeve?" Ellen asked.

"York is employed at the Ajax Lumber Mill about ten miles from his home at the base of the mountains. He has been employed there for about thirteen years and holds the position of first shift supervisor. It seems he's good at busting heads. He earns thirty-four dollars a month. He is considered a reliable employee. The company is moderately successful, making a small profit for the owner, who is also the onsite superintendent. The company owns no timberland and bids for forest lumber tracts at the annual county timber auctions. The company could be put out of business by bidding up the forest timber and making the lumber mill unprofitable. The mill could be purchased for approximately four hundred dollars. What is my instruction?" Robert asked.

"Set up a dummy lumber corporation out of Newhopeland

and purchase the lumber mill. Offer the owner a good price and guarantee him a good salary to continue to run the mill. If he refuses to sell, the dummy lumber corporation will bid against him at all future timber auctions, making his mill insolvent and York without employment. If a sale is agreed to, ownership is transferred, and York will be fired immediately. How long will this take?"

Robert stated with confidence, "Three weeks, maybe four, before the property can be recorded in the name of the dummy corporation at the county hall of records.

"Excellent, Robert—excellent!" Ellen smiled.

Robert continued, "Now for young master York. Jonnie York is seventeen and eight months of age. He is currently living with his father. Jonnie occasionally works as a day laborer at the harbor, mostly scraping the bottom of boats, and manages to earn about four dollars a month. Jonnie York was expelled from primary school for multiple assaults on children and teachers at the age of ten. He was considered incorrigible, a pathological social deviant. Jonnie has been accused of rape on several occasions. One child was eleven, and one child was thirteen years old. Both assaults occurred when Jonnie was sixteen years of age. In both cases, the victims' fathers were severely beaten when they confronted Jack York after the sexual assault. One of the fathers lost an eye during the melee. Jonnie York has a history of antagonizing children much smaller and younger. On numerous occasions, Jonnie has extorted money from smaller children or physically assaulted them for no apparent reason. I was able to determine that his last three victims before your son's assault involved cutting the victim. Two of the children were cut on the face. It is just a matter of time before he kills someone."

"How is this possible? Why can't he be stopped?" Ellen asked.

"Well, as you know, this type of aberrant behavior is very unusual in a minor. The statutes concerning minors are unambiguous: no child under eighteen years can be charged with committing a crime. Childhood behavior, no matter how horrendous, cannot be considered criminal. The law, of course, is based on the teaching of The Word. Childhood deviancy is usually dealt with by the families involved and sometimes with behavioral professionals from the school. However, Jack York and his son are symbiotic in their pathological behavior. Such deviants are rare in our community. They are both extremely dangerous people and must be stopped."

Ellen paused and said, "Robert, I need to give some thought to Jonnie York. It complicates things since we are dealing with a minor. I need a little time."

"Of course, Ellen, I understand. I will keep you informed of the issues we have spoken of tonight," Robert stated as he began folding his parcel map and gathering his things.

"The objective is to entice York and his deviant son to move from this area. We will manipulate him to move, and we will follow him and his son in a most clandestine manner, ensuring a miserable existence for the monster and his spawn," Ellen stated coldly, staring into the lamplight. "I am his fate now."

After a few seconds of silence, Ellen appeared to return to Robert's presence. "I promised Benjamin I would read to him tonight before he falls asleep. I am grateful you are in my life, Robert, and for all the things you have accomplished for me." She took Mr. Bass's hand and walked him to the door.

"I am very grateful you are in my life as well. Very grateful," Robert returned.

Mrs. Forrestal kissed Mr. Bass on the cheek and whispered in his ear, "Thank you for everything, Robert."

"Thank you, Ellen, for a beautiful dinner and a wonderful relationship." Robert opened the door and disappeared into the night.

Ellen withdrew to her office with tears streaming down her face and paused for a moment of reflection before pulling out stationary to write to Mr. Summers. She would deliver the note personally. They would hold each other for a long while when they met. Ellen would never be so grateful to another person.

November 18, 1894

Dear Mr. Summers,

I do not possess the words which will permit me to express properly the gratitude I feel for your selfless act of valor in saving my child's life. When my Benjamin's horse returned in fear and had been severely injured, you took the initiative to ensure my son was safe. When you learned my son's fate was unknown, you did everything in your power to locate him, and when Benjamin was found in perilous condition and near death, you sacrificed your dear horse, bringing my son to the hospital, thereby saving my son's life.

"No greater joy the mother's child,
No greater grief a child's death can be.
From Raven's wing, a child is spared,
No greater glory conveyed to thee."
Verses 11:22, The Word

As a small token of our gratitude, Dr. Forrestal and I have purchased a Grade A carriage horse from the Londonderry Carriage Horse Farm in Londonderry to replace the carriage horse you lost. We are also enclosing the bill of sale in your name and two open, round-trip rail tickets for Mrs. Summers and yourself so you may travel, at your convenience, to the carriage horse farm and select your horse from the large selection offered. Also enclosed is an open equine freight ticket so you will be able to ship your horse to Riverdale.

Mr. Summers, Dr. Forrestal, and I will always be indebted to you for saving our son's life. If we can be of any service to you in the future, please do not hesitate to convey to us how we may assist you.

Most Sincerely,
Mrs. Ellen Forrestal

Chapter 8
Truth Be Told

Conrad sat on the edge of the bed watching his beautiful wife sleep, her thick, black hair flowing over the pillow in tangled waves of femininity. Her presence was as radiant as the first moment he touched her face, kissed her lips, and felt her warm embrace. Still, with all the love he felt for his wife, he could not deny the palpable loss of intimacy in their marriage. There were secrets between them. He could feel these lies of omission growing between them, subtle and persistent, like a shadow cast across a room from the setting sun.

He realized his wife had been through a terrible week and accepted that such a painful experience may alter her usual demeanor. Yet Conrad still felt an elusive verity, a persistent doubt concerning her fidelity regarding the events surrounding their son's attack, and this doubt created a terrible dissonance between the woman he loved and the woman he increasingly feared he might not know. Such is the insidious nature of secrets between lovers.

He rose quietly and left her side. She had returned late from the hospital, after comforting her son long into the night. He would not deny her the much-needed sleep necessary to renew her strength and spirit. This was not a time for reassurance and complete truths—that time would come soon enough. He walked from their sleep room, normally consummated only with delightful and shared secrets, journeyed down the hall, descended the stairs, and walked to the sitting room to read a newspaper and relax on this rare day of reprieve from his demanding profession. He would resist being held hostage to his insecurities and instead reside contently in this grand room with all the superb, leather-bound books, fine furniture, and fresh-cut flowers. Fate would not permit such a moment again for a long time to come.

The tranquil spell was broken by indiscernible angry voices emanating from the kitchen, causing him to rise and seek the source of the discontent. Conrad walked into the kitchen, a room rarely visited by the master of the house or his wife, and—startled—saw Jane and Margret depositing last night's dinner into a large iron pail to be dumped into the compost pile far behind the mansion. Large portions of freshly prepared fowl, giant bowls of bird stuffing, and huge portions of vegetables were being discarded by servants who may, with considerable effort and planning, afford a single goose once a season on the Winter Solstice Eve. "I heard angry voices. Why are you two so angry?" Conrad asked, not appreciating or comprehending the distance between his world of opulence and his servant's realm of scarcity and sacrifice.

Jane spoke for the two of them, being the most senior, "We are deeply sorry, sir. We did not realize you were near. We will keep to our positions from now on. Many apologies."

Conrad repeated, "Why were you so upset?"

Jane took a circumspect moment and responded, "Well, sir, I am deeply sorry. It doesn't mean anything but voicing an opinion when it is not my place. Still, it is such a waste of all this delightful food because we were not permitted to place the leftovers of last night's dinner in the icebox before we were dismissed for the evening, sir. I mean, my children have never had such food, now it is to the compost pile, and it is such a shame."

"I didn't realize Mrs. Forrestal had a formal dinner last night. Whom did you serve last evening?" Conrad asked suspiciously.

Jane, with considerable angst, responded, "Oh, please, sir, I must not cross madam. Please, I must keep my position. My husband has passed and my children, sir. I must not anger madam."

"I will exculpate your cooperation with my query, Jane, of

course," Conrad tersely reassured the maid.

"Sir?" a confused Jane asked.

"I'm sorry. I will watch your back, Jane," Conrad clarified, "Now tell me what I am asking."

"Mrs. Forrestal invited Mr. Bass, madam's fat friend, to dinner last night, and when they began to speak to each other after dinner, me and Margret and cook Peter were given the rest of the night off. I told madam I needed to place the leftovers in the icebox but I was told to leave with Peter and Margret. I am so sorry, sir," Jane explained.

"What was the time when you were told to leave?" Conrad asked the frightened servant.

"Around eight, sir," Jane estimated, looking at Margret for confirmation.

"Thank you, Jane. You and Margret, please take the remains of the cake and pie home to your children, and anything else you might salvage. I concur with your sentiment, ladies, and please do not worry about any of this," Conrad said most reassuringly.

"Thank you, sir," Jane replied and returned to disposing the spoiled food into the iron pail.

Conrad returned to the master sleep room, processing this new information. His mind was compelled to weave a disquieting tapestry of intrigue between his wife and Mr. Bass. Accompanying his realization was a sad epiphany: his wife's deception was inescapable and unacceptable. He now believed he understood what happened, and he fought the rage and fear emerging within him. Conrad found his wife sitting on the edge of the bed with her turbulent hair, uncombed and covering a fair portion of her drowsy expression, hiding heavy eyelids struggling to begin the day. With Conrad's sudden entrance, Ellen quickly pulled her sleeping gown up to minimize any exposure of her injured breast and her secret. The startled response from his spouse and lover seemed peculiar to Conrad, unless Ellen was hiding something about her body from him—a proposition which he was almost convinced of, and consistent with his suspicion of his wife's deception.

"Conrad, I thought you were at the hospital," Ellen blurted.

Conrad responded suspiciously, "I am reprieved from my duties for a few days. I thought we should look in on Benjamin together for a change. What do you think?"

"Of course. Why don't you wait for me downstairs while I use the private room?" Ellen said, a hint of anxiety in her voice.

"I don't think so," Conrad replied.

"What is the matter? Let me go to the private room, and I will be right down," Ellen restated.

"Ellen, I want you to remove your sleeping gown before you go into the private room," Conrad demanded.

"Oh, Conrad, I think it is a little early for love play, and I would like very much to be there when Benjamin wakes up."

"Remove your gown," Conrad ordered, more harshly this time.

"What is the matter with you? I don't understand your tone. You're scaring me, Conrad."

Ellen was trapped.

"Ellen, last night I visited Benjamin at every opportunity during my rounds. I did not see you until after nine o'clock. I did not think anything of it. I knew you were exhausted by all that happened in the last few days. I thought you were resting. But you were not resting, were you?"

"I was with . . ." Ellen began.

"You were with Robert Bass scheming to bring harm to Jack York and his son. That's what you were doing while I was comforting our child!"

"I was compelled to protect my only son, yes. He was nearly killed by that monster and his twisted son! Any mother would do the same."

"Last night, Benjamin wrote a note asking what you were going to do about Jonnie York. He told me Jonnie York was the boy who stabbed him in the face, and he asked if you were getting his brace back. I asked how long since he told you, and he said he told you some time at the first of the week. Why didn't you say anything to me, Ellen?"

Ellen's voice dropped, "I felt this burden was mine to carry. I know you have a heavy responsibility being a physician with so many depending on you."

"What conceit is this? Am I a father who forsakes his son to care for others and who leaves justice solely to my wife to obtain? Am I such a man?"

"I am sorry, Conrad. I was selfish and arrogant. No, of course not. You would do anything for your family. You would die for our family. I know that," Ellen responded.

Conrad continued, "Let me tell you what I know of Jonnie York and his insane father, Jack York. On numerous occasions, I was required to provide medical intervention to fathers of this town badly assaulted by Jack York when they confronted York after his son attacked their child. One man was beaten so severely he lost an eye. But you knew that, didn't you, Ellen? I think you know everything about Jack York and his son, or you think you do, because Mr. Bass has been investigating him for you and was reporting his findings last night when you dismissed the staff so you could speak in private. I think I know you, Ellen, and I think you would use all your powers to protect your family and destroy anyone who would violate you or Benjamin. That's true, Ellen, is it not?" Conrad probed, knowing the answer.

"Yes," Ellen admitted.

"I didn't hear you!" Conrad yelled.

Ellen jumped and trembled, unaccustomed to Conrad's harsh tone, then yelled back, "I know everything about those twisted monsters, and I will destroy them!"

"Now, you have been very careful the last few days to ensure I didn't see your body. We make love in the dark. You dress out my sight. Your timing has been so precise to evade my presence that it is so obvious . . . so obvious."

Ellen stared at her husband, then said, "Yes."

"This is what happened. When Benjamin told you that Jonnie York attacked him, you had Robert Bass find out who his father was and where he lived. You went out to York's property by Old Forest Road without telling me and confronted that crazy monster, and he knocked down, tore off your clothes from your body and raped you, and your body bears the bruise where that man beat you and held you into submission," Conrad expressed his supposition.

"No! He did not rape me. Please, believe me, Conrad, he didn't do that . . ." Ellen pleaded. Ellen stood up and pulled the straps from her shoulders, allowing her gown to drop to the floor. Hate consumed Conrad as he looked upon the terrible contusion of a man's hand on his wife's breast. She turned, showing her husband the dark bruise from her buttock down the length of her thigh. Conrad's rage turned to pain as he witnessed the terrible wounds inflicted upon his wife.

"When Benjamin told me the identity of his attacker, I asked Robert to determine who he was, and he told me he was a child, and his father was Jack York, and where they lived. I did not give Mr. Bass much time, and the information he gave me pertained mostly to Jonnie York. I did not know Jack York was a monster until I was in his presence. I took a carriage to York's property, and I asked Jack York if he would have his son return our son's brace so he could walk again. He grabbed me by my breast and spat in my face and threw me off his porch. I thought I could get Benjamin's brace back. I thought I could do it myself. I was wrong. Then he taunted me to tell you to honor your wedding oath and avenge me. But Conrad, listen to me," Ellen pleaded, "I do not want you near that animal. He is a monster, and your fate is that of a healer, not someone who would take a life. You cannot lower yourself to the level of that animal. Listen to me. I could not tell you. I was so afraid you might try to hurt that twisted man, or worse, get killed trying. Think! Just think about how many people will not benefit from your gifts. Please, Conrad, I cannot live without you. I love you so much—I cannot lose another husband—I could not go through that again. Please, Conrad, I will destroy that man. I have the power to drive that monster and his spawn from our lives. . .I know all about—"

"Stop, Ellen, just stop. You and Robert Bass don't understand what you are getting into. Robert is a knowledgeable lawyer, and you have all the money in the world, but you can't harass this man from our lives. He will retaliate. He will strike like a rattlesnake. Even if you could manage to keep your influence in his life secret as the two of you seize his property or whatever else you and Bass are conspiring to do, he would still suspect us! How naïve are the two of you? He may not know of your wealth, but he certainly knows of mine. Even if he did not realize his tormentors, which is, of course, ridiculous, this scheme Bass and you have conjured would compel him to strike out at someone else. That psychotic monster would not simply slink into the night; his mental disease does not work like that. Ellen, you don't know what you're doing—this is not some kind of business scheme—you are so naïve, so naïve!" Conrad's voice was loud, his face contorted.

Ellen slumped back onto the edge of their bed and began to sob. Her worst fear was about to become a reality, and she was helpless to stop it. Conrad walked to the chair where Ellen tossed her robe the previous evening, grasped the garment, and covered his wife's nakedness and the terrible violations on her body. Then he knelt beside her.

"Ellen, you are the most important thing in my life. I love you more than anything in this world. Please try and understand what I am going to say. Our lives are bound by the teachings of The Word. We must live by those teachings. There are no ambiguities in these matters."

Ellen cried out a terrible moan, "No, please, no. Conrad. . . no, please, we can move away. Anything, but not that."

"Ellen, I want you to go to the hospital and have Dr. Lister give you a complete examination. I must know the extent this man hurt you. There will be no discussion. Do as I say. I want you to prepare yourself for what I have to do now," Conrad spoke firmly to his frightened and sobbing wife.

Ellen became increasingly frantic, realizing what her husband was preparing to do.

"Ellen, I cannot remain your husband if I don't slay this man that violated you. I stood in front of witnesses and gave my oath. If I do not do this thing, I could not live with myself another day, and I could not be your husband. I promise I will return. Now I must go," Conrad stated, holding his trembling wife.

Ellen, sobbing and clinging to her husband, could only say, "Please, no—do not go."

Conrad forcefully removed her grasping hands from his arms, stood, and disappeared from the room. Ellen, nearly hysterical, moaned and sobbed for a few moments. She did her best to gain control of her emotions. When composed, she closed her robe and ran from the mansion onto the street. She ran as fast as her bare feet would permit to the firehouse and to Oboe Jackson and Jake Corvidae. Running into the firehouse in near hysteria, she found Oboe carefully brushing one of the fire horses tied in front of the stables.

"Oboe!" Ellen screamed, running up to him and grabbing his shoulders, "Conrad is going to Jack York's place to kill him! Please, if you hurry, you can stop him."

By this time, the other men began streaming out of the dining room, drawn by the commotion. Within a few seconds, all seven firemen formed a circle around Ellen as she relayed her assertion her husband was on his way to kill Jack York.

Ellen pleaded with the gathered men, "Please, if you hurry, you can stop him before he reaches York's place."

Ellen would not have to ask again. Oboe directed one of his men to walk Ellen to the hospital so she would be cared for if her husband were severely injured or killed. Oboe knew that Jack York would not hesitate to beat a man to death. He had recovered several severely injured men from in front of York's home, and he knew Conrad was not physically able to win a fight with a brute like Jack York. Oboe ordered to bring the horses to the fire wagon and to intercept Conrad before he was hurt or killed.

Conrad had closed the distance between his mansion and

the stable in a matter of minutes. He took Demon from his stall, had him saddled and bridled, and was headed for Jack York's place before Ellen reached the firehouse. He directed Demon to the Old Forest Road at a quick trot. Hate and resolve to kill Jack York for violating his wife consumed Conrad's mind. Within the hour, Conrad turned his horse down the long dirt road to York's home and the inevitable. Sweat foamed on Demon's neck and body from the hard ride, but the horse never wavered. Conrad rode tall, his long, black coat flying behind him, his boots planted firmly in the stirrups, and his white shirt now stained with the perspiration of a man about to enter a death struggle. His broad-brimmed hat shielded his eyes from the glaring sun, blocking out the sight of clear, blue sky scattered with soft clouds, and the silent dark witness soaring overhead.

Within minutes, York's tattered house came into view. Conrad rode right up to the dilapidated porch and yelled, "Jack York, come out and meet your fate!"

Demon reared, unaccustomed to his master's harsh voice, his front legs kicking into the sky, and released a frightened cry.

Jack York sauntered from his shabby house with a grin. He wore black, smokestack boots and a matching leather belt. His pants were stained and filthy. He was shirtless with a huge barrel chest, and as soon as he spotted Conrad, he lifted his fists. With every confidence, he slowly descended the steps of his porch, stood tall, and waited.

The size of this giant man surprised Conrad, but it made no difference. Jack York would die. Conrad climbed from his nervous horse and released the animal. He walked briskly toward Jack York. Within a few feet from his adversary, he reached under his coat, pulled a large caliber revolver from the back of his belt, and shot Jack York directly in his throat. With bulging, fright-filled eyes, Jack York grabbed his bleeding neck with both hands. His arms and elbows were flung high and perpendicular to his body, as the man seemed frozen in this ghastly stance. Unable to make a sound, Jack

York stepped back to die. Conrad took careful aim with both hands for his second shot; he aimed at Jack York's beating heart and squeezed the trigger. The bullet pierced York's chest and heart before continuing through his back, striking the wooden facade behind him. Jack York was dead before his body hit his porch steps. Conrad walked up to the man he just killed and looked into York's open eyes. York's pupils were spreading into large, black pools. His trousers quickly stained with urine, and the air reeked with feces as Jack York's body relinquished all control.

Jonnie York came screaming from the house and gazed upon the corpse of his father. Jonnie did not see the remains of a cruel and twisted man, he only saw his father who loved him, cared for him, and protected him from an unfair world. His anguish was the same as any son who loved his father. Now, his father lay dead at his feet in an ever-expanding pool of blood. Jonnie, sobbing and moaning, slumped down in incomprehensible loss and struggled to lift and cradle his father's head. A last moment between father and son before the warmth of life vanished from his father's body.

Conrad knew what he had to do. The grieving child must die before he grew into a man seeking his revenge. Conrad lifted his revolver and pointed the barrel at the child's head. This delinquent that nearly killed his child should surely die, yet Conrad could not pull the trigger and kill the boy that set all these terrible events into motion. His hand shook with contradiction. Conrad fought the impulse to allow the child to live. At the last second, Conrad turned his gun back to Jack York, took careful aim, and blew the top of York's head off while his son held him in his arms, spraying brains, skull, and blood all over the child and the house behind. Jonnie scurried back against the house in terror, unscathed by the bullet yet petrified, in shock, and dripping from the remains of his father. His mouth gaped, forming a nightmarish image of a child. The boy did not move. No sound emanated from him; he simply stared motionless like a wax figure. Conrad walked over to his horse, returning the heavy caliber in his belt at the small of his back. He mounted Demon, took one last look at the horrific scene, and turned his horse toward town. The horse walked slowly. There was no hurry. Conrad felt nothing.

Conrad had just reached Old Forest Road when he was confronted by teamster Jake Corvidae and Oboe Jackson, who were seated next to each other on the bench board of the number seven fire wagon racing toward him. The two men were yelling and screaming for Conrad to stop.

Several firemen in the back of the wagon held on for dear life as the wagon flew down the road. Conrad fought to control Demon as the fire wagon roared to a stop, and Oboe jumped to the ground and grabbed Conrad's reins and saddle horn. When the horse was completely stopped, Oboe reached up and opened Conrad's coat, trying to determine if Conrad had suffered any injuries.

"Are you hurt, man?" Oboe asked, frantically examining the body of his friend for any sign of blood.

"No, Oboe. I killed him. He never knew what hit him. I killed him," Conrad's voice was blunt and distant.

"Where do you think you are going now?" Oboe demanded to know.

"I am going to give my statement to the county coroner," Conrad stated matter-of-factly.

"No, you're not," Oboe commanded. "You are going to see Mr. Bass and tell him what has happened and let him decide the best course of action. Timothy, jump down and take Demon's reins and walk Dr. Forrestal back to town. Take him directly to Mr. Bass. You will not let him from your sight, and you will make sure he goes and speaks to Mr. Bass before he speaks to anyone. If you mess this up, I will personally run the fire wagon over your head. Do you understand? He may not talk to anyone until he speaks to Mr. Bass. Do you understand, Tim?" Oboe was never more direct than that moment. Oboe knew what Conrad said and did at this terrible time could affect him for the rest of his life.

Tim looked at Conrad and said, "D0 you understand what

Oboe just said? We are going to Mr. Bass's office. Are you going to cooperate?"

Somewhere in his mind, Conrad knew his friends were right. "I will cooperate, Tim."

Tim then asked, "Dr. Forrestal, are you armed?"

Without a word, Conrad reached behind his coat, grabbed his revolver, and handed Tim the weapon. Tim opened the cylinder then looked at Oboe, "Three shots."

Oboe turned and climbed aboard the fire wagon, looked at Jake, and said, "Let's get the body to the icehouse before it becomes ripe."

Tim started walking to town, holding Demon's reins and whistling some obscure tune. Then stopped, looked up to Dr. Forrestal, and said, "Dr. Forrestal, the more I get to know you, the more I like you." Then Tim started whistling again as he turned to complete his mission.

Chapter 9
Coroner's Inquest

Coroner's Inquest Transcript

November 30, 1894-Riverdale-Kent County

Killing of Jack York by Conrad Forrestal
Recorder: Helen Brook-Lic. 329-78

Bailiff Amsterdam: Attention all who gather here. Attention all who gather here. The coroner's inquest shall begin on this day, November 30, 1894. The location of this inquest is the lecture hall of the Riverdale Advanced School in Riverdale, County of Kent. The Honorable Sinclair Rhinehope presiding. All rise.

Judge Rhinehope: These proceedings are the inquest into the death of Jack York, who was killed on November 19, 1894, by Conrad Forrestal on Jack York's property, located in Kent County in the State of Kenton. This coroner's inquest is convened for the sole purpose of determining whether the homicide of Jack York constituted a criminal act or whether the said homicide was justified under the laws of the State of Kenton. If a determination is made, by my judicial review, using the evidentiary standard of probable cause, that the homicide of Jack York was an act of criminal behavior as defined by the Criminal Code 860 of the State of Kenton, Dr. Forrestal will be bound over to the Londonderry Circuit Court for a determination of criminality for the murder of Jack York.

These proceedings will be somewhat less formal than the standards set forth for criminal adjudication. However, I will demand the same standards of conduct and, for the most part, the Rules of Evidence, which exemplify the high standards

and decorum of the Circuit Court. There will be no participa-
tion of any form by the courtroom observers. Those who fail
to heed my admonitions and are found in contempt of this
court will be dealt with in the harshest of terms. This is a
solemn occasion. The taking of human life by another individual is the most grievous act before any tribunal in civil
society for the establishment of guilt or innocence. May our
efforts in this matter be worthy of the grave responsibility
placed upon us today. Will the defendant and his counsel
please stand, and state and spell your name for the record.

Defendant: C. Forrestal: Your honor, I am Conrad Forrestal. C-o-n-r-a-d F-o-r-r-e-s-t-a-l.

Counsel Bass: Your Honor, I am counsel for Dr. Forrestal, Robert Bass. R-o-b-e-r-t B-a-s-s.

Judge Rhinehope: The representative for the people.

People's Rep. Neill: Yes, your Honor, I am Charles Neill.
C-h-a-r-l-e-s N-e-i-l-l, Deputy Attorney General of the State
of Kenton.

Judge Rhinehope: We will begin this inquest with the
reading of Conrad Forrestal's statement submitted to the
coroner's office. The state and the defendant's counsel should
have copies, and if there are any inconsistencies or objections,
please make the court aware of your concerns. The statement
reads as follows:

I, Conrad Forrestal, freely submit the following description and reasons why, on November 19, 1894, I took the life
of Jack York by discharge of a heavy pistol in front of his
home in Kent County.

I was informed on the morning of November 19, of the
same year, by my legal wife, Ellen Forrestal, that she entered
the property of Jack York to request the return of our son's
leg brace and corrective shoe, which was taken on November
9 of the same year by Jack York's son, Jonnie York, a minor,
age seventeen.

Our son, Benjamin Walker, a minor, age fourteen, a severely handicapped child suffering from a congenital defect
of his leg and foot and requiring a specially made brace to

walk and specially made corrective shoe to compensate for the difference in the length of his legs, was brutally attacked while riding his horse on Old Forest Road by Jonnie York, who identified himself before severely cutting our son's face and tongue, causing life-threatening injuries. In addition, Jonnie York cut from my son's leg and foot his leg brace and corrective shoe, forcing my son to attempt returning to town by crawling on his hands and knees while dragging his deformed leg.

My wife, with the aid of Mr. Samuel Summers, found our son thirteen miles from town unconscious and near death. My son was hospitalized and received lifesaving emergency surgery. On the morning of November 13 of the same year, our son Benjamin Walker was able to identify for his mother his assailant by pen as Jonnie York.

The interlocutory initiated by my wife without malice or prejudice for the sole purpose of retrieval of said brace and corrective shoe occurred on November 14 of the same year between Ellen Forrestal and Jack York at the location described. When a request for the return of the said items was made, Jack York seized my wife's right breast with malice and extreme prejudice, causing a severe contusion in the pattern of a handprint, a striking mark, then proceeded to pull my wife's face into proximity to that of the deceased's face, at which time Jack York discharged tobacco-laced spittle directly in the eyes and nose of my wife causing temporary blindness and severe gagging from noxious spittle into her mouth.

At that point, Jack York threw my wife from the step of his house to the ground. My wife suffered a severe contusion on her right buttock and right thigh. My wife, while returning to her carriage, was repeatedly taunted to advise said husband as to the nature of the violation to her body for the sole purpose of provoking a physical confrontation between myself and the assailant as required by my wedding oath, that is, to slay the perpetrator of violation(s) upon my wife or forfeit my marriage to her.

The Kenton Penal Code, Section 12-A, Justifiable Homicide, states that, "The taking of a life of an individual or individuals who have violated a spouse by sexual conduct voluntarily, including intercourse, sexual touching, or libidinous expression, and/or physical contact including but not limited to genitals, breasts, buttocks, and face for the purpose of prurient gratification, punishment, humiliation, or to provoke the spouse of the victim into confrontation, physically or ideologically, shall be considered Justifiable Homicide."

I submit my statement as true and accurate and pray the court to consider my statement in the adjudication of my conduct in the death of Jack York.

Dr. Conrad Forrestal – November 24, 1894."

Judge Rhinehope: This completes the reading of Conrad Forrestal's statement. Are there any comments or objections?

People's Rep. Neill: Yes, your Honor. The people find the section of Dr. Forrestal's statement beginning with the phrase, "Our son, Benjamin Walker," and ending with "lifesaving surgery" objectionable on the grounds of relevance and the obvious fact the material is highly prejudicial.

Judge Rhinehope: Mr. Bass.

Counsel Bass: Yes, your Honor. We feel the entire statement is germane to the defense, clarifying the extreme nature of the circumstances leading to my client's actions. The entire document should be admissible.

Judge Rhinehope: All right, objection overruled. The court will accept Dr. Forrestal's written statement for consideration. As with a criminal trial, this inquest will require the people to justify why Dr. Forrestal should be bound over for a criminal trial. Do you have an opening statement before you present your argument?

People's Rep. Neill: Yes, your Honor. It is the state's position that Dr. Forrestal has committed the act of involuntary manslaughter, punishable by banishment, in the killing of Jack York. We will show that Dr. Forrestal was manipulated by his wife, Ellen Forrestal, to kill Jack York because of her belief that Jack York's son, Jonnie York, had assaulted her son, Benjamin Walker. We will demonstrate to the court that Ellen Forrestal was motivated by revenge and, with the help of Mr. Robert Bass, her attorney, she faked her injuries, then played an elaborate game of feigning avoidance with her husband with the intent that his inevitable discovery of her injuries would serve as pretext to motivate her husband to honor his wedding vows and kill Jack York. The state will demonstrate there is sufficient evidence to reach the level of "reasonable suspicion" necessary to charge Dr. Forrestal with criminal conduct.

Judge Rhinehope: Do you wish to make a statement before we begin?

Counsel Bass: Yes, your Honor. Dr. Forrestal's actions in the termination of Jack York's life were lawful and consistent with the Penal Code, Section 12-A, hence no criminal act was committed by my client. Dr. Forrestal was compelled to kill Jack York for transgressions perpetrated on his wife or accept the dissolution of his marriage of thirteen years. The facts in this matter will allow no other finding in the killing of Jack York than justifiable homicide.

Judge Rhinehope: Very well, I will at this time note for the record that the court has granted Mr. Bass's petition to serve as Mr. Forrestal's attorney, without objection by the people's representative, in these proceedings recognizing the conflict of Mr. Bass's status. The petition was granted in the interest of time and scarcity of legal representation for the purpose of this inquest. Mr. Neill, please proceed.

People's Rep. Neill: Thank you, your Honor. The people call on Ellen Forrestal to come forth and testify.

Bailiff Amsterdam: Will the witness please place her hand upon The Word. Do you solemnly affirm you will only speak the truth, completely and accurately, knowing the act of perjury will be punished by banishment from the State of Kenton for not less than ten years?

Ellen Forrestal: I will speak the truth and accept my punishment if I transgress.

Judge Rhinehope: Mrs. Forrestal, please spell your entire name for the record.

Ellen Forrestal: E-l-l-e-n F-o-r-r-e-s-t-a-l

People's Rep. Neill: Thank you, Mrs. Forrestal. Are you the legal wife of Dr. Forrestal?

Ellen Forrestal: Yes.

People's Rep. Neill: Mrs. Forrestal, will you tell the court how you encountered Jack York.

Ellen Forrestal: While hospitalized, my son Benjamin Walker informed me by pen that his attacker was Jonnie York. My attorney determined that Jonnie York was a minor, and he was living with his father, and informed me of the location of their home. On November 14 of this year, I went to that location to secure my son's brace and corrective shoe, which were stolen by Jonnie York.

People's Rep. Neill: Did you know Jack York before you entered his property?

Ellen Forrestal: No.

People's Rep. Neill: Please tell the court what you said to Jack York.

Ellen Forrestal: I asked him if he was Jack York, then I explained that his son attacked my son and caused him to be hospitalized, and that his son stole my son's leg brace and corrective shoe. I then asked him if he would return my son's shoe and brace.

People's Rep. Neill: What happened next?

Ellen Forrestal: Jack York grabbed my breast, pulled me to his face, then spit in my face and threw me to the ground. When I got up to return to my carriage, he taunted me to tell my husband to return and fight him if he wanted to honor our wedding oath.

People's Rep. Neill: Did you tell anyone you were going to Jack York's property?

Ellen Forrestal: No.

People's Rep. Neill: Maybe the stable master?

Ellen Forrestal: No.

People's Rep. Neill: Did you tell anyone when you returned to town and your home?

Ellen Forrestal: No.

People's Rep. Neill: Did your servants see you return?

Ellen Forrestal: No.

People's Rep. Neill: Why not? You have several servants. How was that possible?

Ellen Forrestal: I was very careful not to have anyone see me.

People's Rep. Neill: Why was that?

Ellen Forrestal: My blouse was badly torn at the neck, and the buttons were all torn from when he grabbed me.

People's Rep. Neill: So you can show the court the damaged clothing?

Ellen Forrestal: No, I had the clothing burned.

People's Rep. Neill: So, the servants you asked to burn the clothing can verify your clothing was ripped?

Ellen Forrestal: No, I hid the clothing in the trash, so when the trash was burned, the clothes would be destroyed.

People's Rep. Neill: Perhaps someone saw you on Old Forest Road on that day coming or going, yes?

Ellen Forrestal: No one saw me on the road.

People's Rep. Neill: So, the only evidence that you were at Jack York's property are the bruises on your body. Am I correct?

Ellen Forrestal: My word under oath, Mr. Neill.

People's Rep. Neill: Your Honor.

Judge Rhinehope: Please answer the question. Do you have anything else other than your statement under oath to this court?

Ellen Forrestal: No, just the bruises on my body put there by Mr. York.

People's Rep. Neill: On November 18, you had Mr. Bass, your counsel, for dinner. Is that correct?

Ellen Forrestal: Yes.

People's Rep. Neill: Was the dinner for just the two of you?

Ellen Forrestal: Yes.

People's Rep. Neill: Did your husband know you were having dinner with Mr. Bass on the eighteenth of November?

Ellen Forrestal: No.

People's Rep. Neill: Why did you not tell your husband?

Ellen Forrestal: This was dinner with an old friend, and I wanted to discuss some legal matters with my attorney.

People's Rep. Neill: What legal matters required secrecy from your husband?

Counsel Bass: Objection! Privileged, your Honor.

People's Rep. Neill: Your Honor, I recognize attorney-client privilege, the people request the court to determine if, at this meeting, Mr. Bass placed the bruises on Mrs. Forrestal the night before her husband discovered the bruises. In the interest of justice, Mrs. Forrestal should be compelled to waive privilege so the court might realize the truth concerning Mrs. Forrestal and Mr. Bass's interaction.

Judge Rhinehope: Sustained.

People's Rep. Neill: Mrs. Forrestal, do you, on occasion, have men over for dinner without your husband knowing?

Counsel Bass: Objection, your Honor. The question is prejudicial and has complex meaning.

Judge Rhinehope: Sustained. Rephrase your question.

People's Rep. Neill: Yes, your Honor. Was this the first time you had dinner at your home with a guest without informing your husband?

Ellen Forrestal: Yes, I think so.

People's Rep. Neill: Were your servants dismissed while Mr. Bass was still your guest at some point?

Ellen Forrestal: Yes.

People's Rep. Neill: How long were you and Mr. Bass alone in your home?

Counsel Bass: Objection. Privilege, your Honor.

People's Rep. Neill: Your Honor, I am not asking anything of substance concerning the material discussed between Mrs. Forrestal and Mr. Bass. This is no more probative of privilege than establishing that Mrs. Forrestal and Mr. Bass met to have a sort of clandestine meeting, which the court has already allowed.

Judge Rhinehope: Overruled. You may continue along those lines, but be careful, Mr. Neill. Repeat the question.

People's Rep. Neill: Thank you, your Honor. How long were you and Mr. Bass alone together at your home, Mrs. Forrestal?

Ellen Forrestal: I think we were alone for about an hour.

People's Rep. Neill: Did Mr. Bass place the bruises on your body at that meeting?

Counsel Bass: Objection. Privilege, your honor.

People's Rep. Neill: I would think Mrs. Forrestal would like to clear this issue up under oath, your Honor.

Judge Rhinehope: Mr. Neill, Mrs. Forrestal would have to waive her privilege to answer that question because any behavior during the meeting between counsel and client falls under privilege. You have made your point, Mr. Neill, now move on.

People's Rep. Neill: When was the first time your husband noticed the bruises on your body, Mrs. Forrestal?

Ellen Forrestal: On the morning of November 19.

People's Rep. Neill: The day your husband killed Mr. York?

Ellen Forrestal: Yes, on that morning.

People's Rep. Neill: Mrs. Forrestal, did you and your husband have intimate behavior between November 14 and the morning of November 19, 1894?

Counsel Bass: Objection, that is privilege between husband and wife.

Judge Rhinehope: Overruled.

Ellen Forrestal: Yes.

People's Rep. Neill: Do you share the same sleep room and private room?

Ellen Forrestal: Yes.

People's Rep. Neill: The bruise on your breast—was it painful when touched?

Ellen Forrestal: Yes.

People's Rep. Neill: When your husband touched you, it

was painful?

Counsel Bass: Objection. Asked and answered.

Judge Rhinehope: Sustained.

People's Rep. Neill: That is all the questions for now. Your Honor, I would request, at this time the Coroner's Inquest into the matter of Jack York's homicide be terminated, and further adjudications in the matter are heard by the Circuit Court on the grounds—

Judge Rhinehope: Denied, Mr. Neill.

Counsel Bass: Thank you, your Honor. Mrs. Forrestal, please explain how you were able to conceal the injuries you sustained from Mr. York.

People's Rep. Neill: Objection! Prejudicial. Mr. Bass has not established that Mr. York injured Mrs. Forrestal.

Judge Rhinehope: Sustained. Rephrase.

Counsel Bass: How did you hide your injuries from your husband?

Ellen Forrestal: It was a difficult thing to do. I made sure we made love only in the dark. When my husband touched my breast, I said nothing, no matter the pain. I went to bed after he was asleep. I either rose and dressed before my husband was awake or after my husband went to the hospital. I was careful not to allow my husband to see my bruises. It was not easy.

Counsel Bass: Why did you keep the injuries you sustained by Jack York a secret?

People's Rep. Neill: Objection!

Judge Rhinehope: Sustained. Mr. Bass, I am vexed you would continue with such antics. Rephrase.

Counsel Bass: Why did you keep the injuries hidden from your husband?

Ellen Forrestal: I did not want my husband to know because I knew he would honor his wedding vows and kill Jack York or be killed trying.

Counsel Bass: Why did you care if your husband killed Jack York?

Ellen Forrestal: My husband is a healer of men, not a killer of men. If I caused him to take a life because I went out on my own to retrieve my son's brace and shoe . . . I did not want to live with the fact I caused my husband to kill someone. That is not who he is. I did not want to put him in that position.

Counsel Bass: That is all, your Honor.

Judge Rhinehope: Mr. Neill.

People's Rep. Neill: Yes, your Honor. From what you have just testified, Mrs. Forrestal, would you characterize your behavior as manipulating your husband.

Counsel Bass: Objection. He is twisting her words.

Judge Rhinehope: Twisting her words. That is your objection? Overruled.

People's Rep. Neill: Thank you, your Honor. Please answer my question. Would you like me to repeat the question, Mrs. Forrestal?

Ellen Forrestal: No. I understand your question. Yes. I was keeping my husband from killing another human being or being killed. Someone might call my effort manipulative.

People's Rep. Neill: Thank you, Mrs. Forrestal.

Judge Rhinehope: Mrs. Forrestal, you may be seated. Do you have any other witnesses, Mr. Neill?

People's Rep. Neill: Yes, your Honor, I would like to call Jonnie York to testify.

Counsel Bass: Objection, your Honor. Jonnie York is a minor. A minor is not allowed to testify at a coroner's inquest.

People's Rep. Neill: Your Honor, may I please approach the bench?

Judge Rhinehope: Yes. Mr. Bass and Mr. Neill, please approach.

COURT RECESS

Both attorneys approached the bench.

Mr. Neill leaned against the table and whispered, "Your Honor, there is precedent. Jackson vs. Peters, the court ruled in exigent circumstances a minor's testimony may be taken under oath in the interest of justice."

Mr. Bass tried not to scoff. "Your Honor, in that situation, the minor was dying, and the court agreed to allow the child testimony under oath because he was not going to make it to the criminal trial. What are the exigent circumstances in this case?"

But Mr. Neill pressed his point, "Jonnie York was trauma-tized when Mr. Forrestal blew the top of his dead father's head off while he held his father for the last time. He is upset and speaking of taking his life. He is suicidal. His testimony is critical now and for future judicial review. Your Honor, we must get Master York's statement on the record."

Judge Rhinehope looked at Mr. Neill, "Do you have an expert witness willing to testify under oath concerning Master York's mental state?"

There was a brief pause, then Mr. Neill answered, "I just found out a few minutes before the inquest began."

"Then the answer is no. Now, both of you sit down so we can get this inquest finished."

COURT RESUMES

Judge Rhinehope: We are back on the record, and the objection is sustained. Mr. Neill, do you have any more witnesses you wish to call?

People's Rep. Neill: No, your Honor.

Judge Rhinehope: Mr. Bass, do you wish to call any witnesses?

Counsel Bass: Yes, your Honor. I would like to call Ellen Forrestal to testify at this time.

Judge Rhinehope: Mrs. Forrestal, you are still under oath, please answer the questions truthfully.

Ellen Forrestal: Yes, your Honor.

Counsel Bass: Why did you wait to reveal the bruises Mr. York gave you?

People's Rep. Neill: Objection. Once again, we have not

established Mr. York caused any bruises to anyone.

Judge Rhinehope: Sustained. Mr. Bass, this is your last warning. Rephrase.

Counsel Bass: Yes, your Honor. Mrs. Forrestal, when did you reveal your bruises to your husband?

Ellen Forrestal: On November 19, in the morning. My husband entered our sleep room and demanded I show my body to him because he suspected Jonnie York's father may have injured me.

Counsel Bass: What did your husband say concerning his insistence on examining your body?

Ellen Forrestal: He said our son identified to him by pen that Jonnie York was his assailant. My husband said he treated other parents injured by Jonnie York's father. My husband was also made aware that Benjamin had revealed his attacker to me. My husband said the house staff told him I dismissed them so I could be alone with my attorney the previous night. He told me he put it all together and believed that Jack York had raped me. I told him he did not. I then showed him my bruises and told him the truth about my actions and what happened to me at Jack York's property.

Counsel Bass: What did you say? Why did you say you were keeping what happened to you a secret?

Ellen Forrestal: I told him I was afraid he would kill Jack York or be killed trying. I was much more afraid my husband would be killed. I lost one husband to fate . . . I was so afraid I might lose another.

Counsel Bass: What did he say? Why must he kill Jack York?

People's Rep. Neill: Objection, your Honor. Mr. Bass is getting all kinds of hearsay into the court record. Mr. Bass should have his client take the stand to explain his actions for himself.

Judge Rhinehope: I am going to accept what was told to Mrs. Forrestal as valid testimony. If Mr. Bass strays into asking Mrs. Forrestal what Dr. Forrestal saw or heard from another witness, I will reconsider your objection. Mrs.

Forrestal is allowed to speak of things stated to her by her husband to explain her behavior. If Mr. Bass strays too far into hearsay, I will accept your objection, but not at this time. Overruled.

Counsel Bass: Thank you, your Honor. Why did your husband feel he had to kill Jack York?

People's Rep. Neill: Objection, your Honor. This is a state-of-mind question. Please, I thought we were following the rules of evidence as in circuit court?

Judge Rhinehope: I am allowing some latitude because this is a coroner's inquest. Please continue, Mr. Bass.

Ellen Forrestal: He said we could not remain married if he did not kill Jack York. He said he took an oath to slay anyone who violated me.

Counsel Bass: Did you attempt to stop your husband?

Ellen Forrestal: I begged him not to go. I told him we could move away. I told him how afraid I was, but he went anyway.

Counsel Bass: What else did you do to stop him?

Ellen Forrestal: I ran to the fire station in my robe and bare feet and begged Oboe Jackson to stop Conrad before he reached Jack York's place.

Counsel Bass: What happened next?

Ellen Forrestal: Oboe had me taken to Riverdale Hospital, and Dr. Lister examined me, and he gave me some laudanum to help me sleep.

Counsel Bass: I have finished, at this time, with my questions for Mrs. Forrestal, your Honor.

Judge Rhinehope: Very well. Mr. Neill.

People's Rep. Neill: Thank you, your Honor. Mrs. Forrestal, did you immediately run to the fire station, or did you wait before running from the house?

Ellen Forrestal: I was traumatized for a few minutes, then I realized I could still stop him if I could get Oboe in time.

People's Rep. Neill: It would seem you just waited long enough.

Counsel Bass: Objection.

Judge Rhinehope: Sustained. Mr. Neill, sit down. You are finished with this witness.

Mr. Bass: Thank you, your Honor. I would like to call Oboe Jackson to the stand.

Bailiff Amsterdam: Will the witness please place his hand upon The Word. Do you solemnly affirm you will only speak the truth, completely and accurately, knowing the act of perjury will be punished by banishment from the State of Kenton for not less than ten years?

Oboe Jackson: I will speak to the truth, knowing the punishment for false statements is banishment.

Judge Rhinehope: Mr. Jackson, please spell your entire name.

Oboe Jackson: Yes, your Honor. O-b-o-e J-a-c-k-s-o-n.

Counsel Bass: Were you on duty when Mrs. Forrestal entered the fire station on the morning of November 19 of this year?

Oboe Jackson: Yes.

Counsel Bass: How was she acting?

Oboe Jackson: Mrs. Forrestal was hysterical. She was screaming, asking us to stop her husband before he reached Jack York's place because she was afraid Jack York would kill her husband. Frankly, I was afraid he would be killed too.

Counsel Bass: Why would you think that?

Oboe Jackson: We have been called to Jack York's property several times to retrieve men who have been badly beaten by Jack York. Some were near death.

Counsel Bass: Was there some reason you may have been delayed in leaving the fire station?

Oboe Jackson: Yes, the horses were being changed out. We have horses hitched and ready and we keep them standing for about eight hours before we unhitch them and rotate them out to keep the horses fresh. Mrs. Forrestal came into the station when the team was not hitched. We had to bring fresh horses and harness them up, and that takes a few minutes. So, we were delayed from our normal emergency out time.

Counsel Bass: I have no other questions, your Honor.

Judge Rhinehope: Thank you, Mr. Jackson. Your next witness, Mr. Bass.

Counsel Bass: Thank you, your Honor. I would like to call Dr. Joseph Lister to testify.

Bailiff Amsterdam: Will the witness please place his hand upon The Word? Do you solemnly affirm you will only speak the truth, completely and accurately, knowing the act of perjury will be punished by banishment from the State of Kenton for not less than ten years?

Joseph Lister: I will speak the truth and accept banishment for the uttering of any falsehood in this tribunal.

Judge Rhinehope: Dr. Lister, will you please spell your name for the record.

Joseph Lister: Joseph, J-o-s-e-p-h, Lister, L-i-s-t-e-r.

Counsel Bass: Dr. Lister, I would like to ask you a few questions so you may be qualified as an expert witness. Dr. Lister, is it correct that you are a licensed medical doctor and certified in emergency medicine, internal medicine, and anesthesiology?

Joseph Lister: Yes, that is correct.

Counsel Bass: You have also written extensively in the emerging field of utilizing medical science as a tool to solve crimes?

Joseph Lister: Yes, I have written extensively and lectured on the topic. I call the new field forensic medicine. I have testified in at least seventy trials in this and other independent states using medical science to solve crimes.

Counsel Bass: I would ask the People's Representative Neill to acknowledge Dr. Lister as an expert witness.

People's Rep. Neill: The people so stipulate, your Honor.

Counsel Bass: Did you examine Mrs. Forrestal on November 19, at the Riverdale Hospital?

Joseph Lister: Yes. A member of the fire department brought Mrs. Forrestal into the hospital at approximately 7:00 a.m.

Counsel Bass: What was Mrs. Forrestal's condition when you examined her?

Joseph Lister: Mrs. Forrestal was hysterical. She was afraid her husband would be killed by Jack York. She also said her husband wished she would be examined for any injuries that she may have recently suffered. I provided Mrs. Forrestal a complete medical examination after I was able to calm Mrs. Forrestal by the use of laudanum.

Counsel Bass: What were your medical findings when you examined Mrs. Forrestal?

Joseph Lister: Mrs. Forrestal appeared physically normal except for significant contusions on her right breast and her right buttock and thigh from her waist to the popliteal area of the leg—excuse me—the area behind the knee on the back of the leg.

Counsel Bass: Could you estimate how old the contusions were on Mrs. Forrestal?

Joseph Lister: In my opinion, the contusions were a few days old.

Counsel Bass: Were you able to determine the cause of the contusions?

Joseph Lister: The right breast was caused by a very large, powerful hand, most likely male, that grabbed and crushed the breast, causing a most painful injury and a striking contusion in the shape of a hand. The other contusion was representative of an impact bruise, such as falling on that portion of the body from a horse, for example.

Counsel Bass: Was there any evidence of rape?

Joseph Lister: Certainly not.

Counsel Bass: Dr. Lister, did you make detailed remarks to the medical record about the size and shape of the contusion on Mrs. Forrestal's breast?

Joseph Lister: Yes, using the center of the breast nipple as a reference point, I measured each digit's length and the pollicis—or thumb—represented by the contusion. In addition, I covered Mrs. Forrestal with a sheet and cut a section of the sheet out so the breast was exposed, and a photograph was then taken of Mrs. Forrestal's breast. I have the photograph for the court to review.

Judge Rhinehope: Will counsel and Mr. Neill approach the bench?

Judge Rhinehope: All right. The court and Mr. Neill have reviewed the photograph, and there does appear a most striking bruise of a very large hand. Does the people's representative and counsel wish to add anything?

People's Rep. Neill: No, your Honor.

Counsel Bass: No, your Honor, not concerning the photograph.

Judge Rhinehope: Very well. Mr. Bass.

Counsel Bass: Thank you, your Honor. Dr. Lister, did you document any additional descriptions of the contusion on the right breast?

Joseph Lister: Yes, we made a three-dimensional model of Mrs. Forrestal's right breast by covering the breast with plaster of Somme. When the plaster had hardened, I poured liquid rubber into the mold, and, when cooled, the rubber formed an almost perfect replica or prosthesis of Mrs. Forrestal's right breast. I then carefully measured the contusion and, using a number of pins initially, then indelible ink, reproduced the handprint's contusion on the three-dimensional model or prosthesis.

Counsel Bass: Were you able to come to some conclusion as to the origin of the hand-shaped contusion?

Joseph Lister: Mrs. Forrestal claimed the contusion was the result of an assault by Jack York, now deceased. To verify the claim, we removed the right hand from the body of Jack York, where he was being stored at the local icehouse . . . I cannot remember the name . . . the one on Fourth Street. We removed the hand about four inches above the wrist. When the hand was thawed and pliable, I placed the hand on the prostheses and the hand was a perfect match. I also photographed the deceased hand placed on the breast prosthesis. The hand is now preserved in ice. I have the prosthesis and the photograph of the hand on the artificial breast in this box for the court's examinations.

Counsel Bass: For this next portion of the inquest, I would

ask the Judge to clear the room of spectators.

Judge Rhinehope: Bailiff, please clear the court except for the principles.

Judge Rhinehope: We are back on the record. The court is cleared. Please proceed, Mr. Bass.

Counsel Bass: Please hold up the prosthesis with the outline of the contusion. Did you come to any conclusion when you placed Mr. York's hand on the replica?

Joseph Lister: Yes. Mr. York's hand was a perfect match.

Counsel Bass: Did you outline the deceased's hand on a piece of paper?

Joseph Lister: Yes, I have the tracing of the hand with me.

Counsel Bass: What are your conclusions concerning the handprint tracing?

Joseph Lister: The handprint is about thirty percent larger than a standard handprint.

Counsel Bass: Would you, for example, consider my handprint a standard-size hand?

Joseph Lister: Your handprint is a little smaller than average.

Counsel Bass: So, when I put my hand in the outline of Jack York's hand tracing, it is apparent the tracing is much larger.

People's Rep. Neill: Objection, your Honor. Mr. Bass is entering his own hand into evidence.

Counsel Bass: I am demonstrating for the court that Jack York's hand was larger than average.

Judge Rhinehope: Overruled. You made your point, Mr. Bass. Very clever.

Counsel Bass: I have completed my questions with this witness, your Honor.

Judge Rhinehope: Mr. Neill?

People's Rep Neill: Dr. Lister, the fact the hand matched the contusion of the prosthesis, of course, does not prove Jack York's hand was the hand that made the contusion. Is that correct?

Joseph Lister: You are correct.

People's Rep. Neill: That is all, your Honor.
Judge Rhinehope: Mr. Bass?
Counsel Bass: Yes, your Honor, one more question. Dr. Lister, what percentage of the adult male population would a handprint of this size represent?
Joseph Lister: I would say the size of the hand represents no more than one or two percent of the male population.
Counsel Bass: No more questions, your Honor.
Judge Rhinehope: Do you have any more witnesses?
Counsel Bass: No, your Honor. The defendant has completed his defense.
People's Rep. Neill: Your Honor, the people rest.
Judge Rhinehope: Very well. We will recess for one hour and hear the closing arguments for the People and the Defense.

RECESS

Judge Rhinehope: The inquest into the death of Jack York is now in session. The court participants that were requested to leave earlier have been permitted back into the courtroom. Mr. Bass, will you present your argument why the killing of Jack York was justified by your client under the statute of the State of Kenton?
Counsel Bass: Yes, your Honor. Dr. Forrestal did not commit a crime in the killing of Jack York. The Kenton Penal Code, Section 12-A, is clear in defining justifiable homicide, and the application of this statue to this case is equally clear.
On November 14, of this year, Mrs. Forrestal approached Jack York to retrieve her son's brace, which was taken by Jonnie York—a minor and the son of Jack York—in an unprovoked attack on her son several days before, on November 9 of this year. Without cause or warning, Jack York grabbed Mrs. Forrestal's right breast with his large and powerful right hand, spit in her face, and threw her to the ground. Then, Jack York taunted Mrs. Forrestal to tell her husband to provoke a confrontation. How do we know this

happened? Mrs. Forrestal, under oath, said to us that is what happened. The people have not provided any inconsistencies in her testimony. In addition, Dr. Lister testified that he had treated several parents that were injured by Jack York when those parents attempted to discuss his son's behavior. Dr. Lister was also able to prove the handprint contusion on Mrs. Forrestal's right breast was the result of a large and powerful male hand grabbing the breast, and the handprint was a perfect match with the right hand of Jack York; this is also consistent with Mrs. Forrestal's testimony. Joseph Lister is an accepted expert witness in this field of criminal medicine by this court.

On November 19, of this year, Dr. Forrestal discovered the contusions on his wife's body and was told by his wife that Jack York injured her and taunted her to tell her husband of the violation to her body for the sole purpose of provoking a confrontation between Dr. Forrestal and Jack York or accept the voiding of his wedding oath and his marriage. Penal Code, Section 12-A, states, among other things, if an individual violates a spouse by humiliating her by having physical contact with any part of the body and uses the incident to provoke a confrontation with the spouse, then the code section is very clear. The spouse, in this case, Dr. Forrestal, is wholly justified in taking the life of his wife's violator—in this case, Jack York.

Your Honor, there is no ambiguity in this area; the fact pattern matches statutory intent perfectly. Dr. Forrestal is a pillar of integrity in this community and faced with this terrible situation, he chose to honor his marriage and the love of his wife by slaying the man who trespassed on his spouse most egregiously. We pray the court finds his actions justified.

Judge Rhinehope: Mr. Neill, do the people have an argument to present?

People's Rep. Neill: Yes, your Honor. The threshold standard in this inquest is reasonable suspicion, an extremely low evidentiary standard. In the case of the killing of Jack

York by Conrad Forrestal, the entire situation reeks with suspicion.

There are mysteries concerning Mrs. Forrestal and her lawyer meeting in secret without her husband's knowledge a few days after the alleged attack on Mrs. Forrestal. Why would Mrs. Forrestal confront Jack York alone without her husband's knowledge? How could a wife conceal such injuries from her husband only to tell him every detail a few days later? Why was Mrs. Forrestal's delay in notifying the fire department to intercede in her husband's intention to kill Jack York just long enough to ensure her husband had enough time to complete his action?

Your Honor, it is the position of the people that the taking of human life is the most serious issue to be addressed by this or any other tribunal. It is the people's position that a criminal judicial review is essential in a case riddled with ambiguities. A full and comprehensive review is possible only with the full investigatory process of a criminal trial. In a criminal trial, the court will have the opportunity to review evidence produced by discovery and have the added benefit of expert witnesses produced by the people to review the evidence submitted by Dr. Lister. It is possible Dr. Forrestal is innocent of criminal behavior. If so, a criminal trial will find him innocent. A man's life was taken. A child has lost his father and is now alone in this world. The people demand, when such suspicion is so readily apparent, that we take every measure to determine the killing of Jack York was justified under the laws of our state. The people demand a criminal trial.

Judge Rhinehope: The statues of the State of Kenton are based on the teachings of The Word. This book contains the ancient wisdom the foundation Elders have passed down to us for thousands of years. Our current laws are written by a small group of contemporary Elders, selected by the people, and based on a perceived need for a new law. Any new law must conform precisely to the teachings of The Word. In addition, all new statutes must be approved by the people in a referendum for societal need, and only then can the new law be chaptered and become the law of the land.

The Penal Code of the State of Kenton contains 570 statutes which permit the justified killing of another human being. All statues are approved by the people. Every aspect of our society is affected by the use of justifiable homicide. Every member of our society is acutely aware of the penalty of trespassing on another member of our community. Justifiable homicide is permitted for self-defense, the defense of our families, the elderly, the weak, and the feeble-minded.

Justifiable homicide is also permitted in commerce to ensure fair and proper exchange of goods and services, in our etiquette and customs, and in the protection of our property and reputations.

How does a society such as ours function when every adult member of society possesses the ultimate authority to take a life? The answer is that society, such as ours, functions extremely well.

We have no need for a police force or prisons.

We have little crime.

Commerce operates efficiently and fairly.

We live in a polite and respectful society.

How can this be? The Word teaches us that every individual in our society is inherently wise and just. This wisdom is not a function of education or wealth or perceived societal position.

Our society cherishes individual liberty, individual responsibility, and initiative. Our society also cherishes human life. The taking of human life must be deliberate. The Word teaches us the taking of human life must be tempered by every attempt of peaceful resolution. When differences arise, and the trespass is not applicable to arbitration or other reasonable alternatives, the citizens of our society may take another individual's life.

The taking of human life is the most serious responsibility citizens may undertake. If a life is taken, the homicide must be reviewed by a neutral fact finder to ensure the homicide is justifiable under the laws of our state. If an individual is determined to have committed unjustified homicide, that individual is banished or sentenced to death through careful due process.

The result of placing such authority and responsibility onto each adult member of our state is that we live in peace and harmony. Other states in our world, which legislate laws by decree, elected representatives, and dictators, or establish societal laws by religious leaders, are states that are inherently corrupt. The exponential growth of government, the loss of liberty, the burden of unfair taxes, and the meddling in commerce are but a few disadvantages of centralized control over individual freedom. Those states that invest in vast police forces to maintain peace have societies with far more crime than the State of Kenton. This is particularly true concerning the murder of the innocent citizens of those flawed states.

Our society does not function perfectly, but our system of governing works. Now, I must decide in the case before this court if the killing of Jack York was a justifiable homicide or if there is enough evidence to justify further adjudication of this homicide in criminal court.

It is the ruling of this court that the evidence presented today does not justify further review. Conrad Forrestal's actions were consistent with the highest standards of our society and within our state's laws and were not applicable to arbitration. This coroner's inquest finds no probability of criminality in the taking of Jack York's life. These proceedings are finished.

End of Proceedings

With the judge's verdict, the courtroom erupted into joyous hoots and hollers. Conrad turned and kissed his wife, who was seated behind him. The kiss was long and sweet. Then, while holding his wife tightly he whispered into Ellen's ear, "Please, no more secrets. Promise me?"

"I will never keep a secret from you again, Conrad. I

promise."

Conrad faced forward again and standing next to him with a big smile, was Charles Neill. With a strong grasp on Conrad's hand, People's Representative Neill stated, "Congratulations, Dr. Forrestal. Judge Rhinehope made the correct decision. I would have shot that monster myself. You did all of us a favor by removing that deviant from our state. Well, good luck and, well, straight-shooting."

Conrad, a bit surprised, returned, "Thank you and, well, keep your powder dry." He guessed that was the proper refrain.

Ellen turned to Mr. Bass, gave him a big hug, kissed him on his plump cheek, and said into his ear, "Seize the York property at the first opportunity and have the house burned down. I will be sending you a detailed message tonight concerning the child."

Mr. Bass stepped back and loudly stated, "You are very welcome. I am always at your services. You know that."

Ellen smiled, "You always make me happy, Mrs. Bass. I am so fortunate you are in my life."

Conrad and Ellen glowed with happiness and walked through the crowd, where there was much congratulating and handshaking. Timothy was standing by the door to the makeshift courtroom, and with a full smile, returned Conrad's pistol. "I replaced the spent shells for next time."

Conrad took his gun from Timothy's outstretched hand and said, "Thank you for taking care of me. I was lost when you brought me to Mr. Bass's office."

Timothy returned the handshake and said, "You are my hero, Dr. Forrestal," then stepped back so other members of the crowd could shake the doctor's hand and pat his back.

Susan James, a young girl of thirteen, ran up and grabbed Conrad's arm and yelled in a loud, very public voice, "I am going to name my first son after you!"

A startled Conrad could only reply, "Well, thank you."

A chorus of well-wishers broke into an impromptu song: *"Conrad shot Jack York dead, two to the body and one in the head."*

Ellen, hearing the crowd's ghastly tune, whispered, "This is getting strange. Let's excuse ourselves before they come up with a second line of chorus."

Conrad and Ellen hurried to their carriage, climbed aboard, and waved a farewell to the crowd. Conrad snapped the reins, and Demon took them home. Conrad and Ellen stabled the horse and carriage, clinging to each other and laughing like newlyweds while walking to their mansion by the sea. The couple, entering their home, were greeted by the house staff, realizing the advantageous verdict by their employers' happy demeanor. Jane spoke for the staff, "We are so happy everything will be all right, sir."

Conrad smiled back. "It is so good to be home. I am glad we are together again."

Ellen then inquired of Benjamin's whereabouts. Jane quickly responded, "The cook wheeled him outside to be with his horse. The corral was finished this morning, so we had the stable bring Fortune to be with the child."

Ellen expressed her thanks and rushed through the mansion and out to the backyard. She found Benjamin sitting in the middle of the new corral with his horse towering over him. Benjamin seemed happy, stroking the horse's face with his hand and whispering to his friend. Ellen, laughing and hugging her child, asked, "I hope you enjoy Fortune living with us for a while until you are back on your feet again?"

"I am so happy. Is father all right?" Benjamin asked, knowing more than he should have.

Conrad joined them, "Everything is simply fine. Your new brace and shoe should be here any day now, and you will be riding Fortune all over Kent County before you know it."

Benjamin looked at his mother and did not say a word.

Later that night, during dinner, Benjamin was quiet. When Conrad left the table to retrieve a pair of reading glasses, Ellen whispered to Benjamin, "Why are you so quiet? Tell your mother what's wrong."

Benjamin, with tears in his eyes, replied, "I am afraid. I

think Jonnie York will try and hurt me again now that father has killed his father. I do not want Fortune to be hurt again either. I am so afraid."

Conrad was outside the door when he heard his wife: "I promise that I will protect you. You will not be hurt by that boy again. You trust your mother, don't you?" Benjamin nodded and returned to eating the food specially prepared for him. Conrad felt a wave of sadness come over him, knowing he did not kill the child when he had the chance. He also felt a strange dread knowing that Ellen would do anything to protect her child.

~

Later that night, Ellen walked to her office, took the only key from her dress pocket, entered, and locked the door behind her. She waited a few minutes with her ear to the door, and when she was convinced no one was near, she approached her telegraph key and tapped the code. Seconds later, Mr. Bass sent his identifying code back to Ellen, so there would be no doubt Ellen's attorney was receiving the message. Ellen typed the following:

Meet me at the end of the long pier -Stop- Five-thirty tomorrow morning -Stop- Time is of the essence -Stop-

Mr. Bass understood completely.

Conrad returned to the hospital after dinner and returned home around 3:00 a.m. the next morning. He was in a deep sleep at 5:00 a.m. when Ellen slipped from their bed, dressed, and walked down to the service porch where she put on another layer of clothing. She then covered herself with an oversize coat and a large floppy hat she occasionally wore to garden, and left out the back door as quietly as possible. Hoping Fortune would not announce her presence, she walked through the row of bushes on the opposite side of the property and made her way to the beach.

Ellen walked nearly two miles down the beach before

passing through a group of small fishing boats, their crews preparing for another day. Keeping her face concealed, Ellen reached the boardwalk and continued another mile to the old, wooden pier. The pier had a dozen early morning fishermen hoping the tide would bring them luck and breakfast. The long, heavy planks of the pier vibrated with the sea's motion and music. At the very end of the pier, a large man covered in a huge overcoat leaned against the wooden railing, looking out to the vast Eastern Sea. He feigned an early morning fisherman, his head covered with a grey knit hat and a long fishing pole reaching into the sea. He would not, however, be catching fish in the morning mist. He had no hook on the line, only dead weight.

Ellen walked up to her lawyer and friend. Together they watched the sun rise from beneath the sea. Then she said it, her words muffled by the wind and waves so only her Mr. Bass could hear: "Kill the boy. Make it look like an accident. The assassin must not know the source of payment. Make it soon."

Then she turned and walked away.

~

Two weeks later, Conrad was reading the morning paper in the formal sitting room when he saw a small story of accidental drowning on page six. The article read:

Jonnie York was found dead Thursday by berth 17 near the steamship Mortilus from drowning. Witnesses were quoted saying Master York was seen after midnight consuming a large amount of hard liquor and smoking opium with an unidentified stranger at the Loose Lady Saloon about three blocks from the harbor. Jonnie York was seen leaving the saloon about two in the morning with the unidentified stranger. The crew aboard the Mortilus spotted Master York floating face down near the passenger ship's stern about six in the morning the same day. The coroner's inquest declared the drowning accidental due to inebriation. Jonnie York would have turned eighteen in a few weeks. Jonnie York had no known family. His father died nearly two weeks ago by legal homicide. There was speculation he was depressed and in mourning when he became intoxicated and fell into the sea. Jonnie will be buried in the pauper's cemetery at 9:00 a.m. on December 6, 1894.

Conrad folded the newspaper and placed it next to him. He passed the morning listening to the sound of the grandfather clock. Conrad knew his wife would do anything to protect her son, and he felt relief that the deviant offspring of the man he killed was no more among the living. He would never speak of Jonnie's death and his suspicions, and he would never speak of things he felt he must do. There are some secrets, he realized and accepted, that cannot be shared, even between lovers.

Conrad walked toward the Riverdale Cemetery about eight in the morning on December sixth. The sun was trapped in a tangle of dark clouds. A summer storm was coming, and the gulls were returning from the sea. Conrad's thoughts were on the young man he nearly killed who was now lying dead in his coffin. He walked through the cemetery gate facing the sea and up the hill to the final resting place of the indigent and the disavowed, passing numerous unmarked graves of forgotten souls. There, he came upon the men about to place Jonnie York beneath the soil. The coffin was suspended above the grave. James Pickering and the other gravedigger stood in silent respect with their hats removed, their faces drawn and sad. Of all who have known death and realized the fragility of life, none were more sensitive than those who dug the graves and buried the dead.

Mr. Maxwell had just finished reading from The Word when he looked up and, realizing Conrad's presence, smiled.

"I had a feeling you would come. Would you say a few words for this young man who is truly alone?"

Conrad stood at the end of the suspended coffin: "Today we place this troubled young man beneath the soil. May we all recognize the sad fate this child traveled in life. The impossible burden he carried by circumstances beyond his control and beyond his life experience to mitigate. How terrible to be a child with such a dark and heavy heart. The Word teaches us that all children are innocent and cannot commit a crime regardless of behavior or intent. We cherish the teaching of our fathers and accept this simple truth. So today I am compelled to ask divine providence to remove the weight from this child's heart and place his dark burden on me so that Jonnie York's heart may be as light as a feather and the Raven will have the strength to carry this child's spirit to heaven on Raven's wings."

The group echoed in unison, "On Raven's wings."

The Raven soared high above the world; his gaze fixed upon the curvature of the planet separating the soft blue horizon of life with the black coldness of space. The Raven then felt a familiar tug calling him back to the world. On this day, the Raven would be accompanied on his ascent to heaven.

Chapter 10
The Examination

Benjamin began his studies at the Advanced School and, with his necessary tutors, completed the required curriculum in record time and in good standing. But his few acquaintances at school seemed to withdraw in his presence, and his teachers were clearly uneasy and vacant when interacting with him. At first Benjamin rationalized that his youth or physical deformity were the cause of this estrangement. He discovered the real source of his alienation while visiting the hospital when, quite by chance, Benjamin overheard an impromptu meeting of the very exclusive doctors' wives group speculating why Ellen Forrestal was aloof and failed to participate in the many charitable activities they supported. Through the thin walls of his father's office Benjamin could clearly hear one of the women speculating as to the rumors that Ellen Forrestal was somehow extremely wealthy and was consumed with her many business activities. Why else would she be absent from the humanitarian functions the wives were expected to participate in. She was too busy for them. The frequent visits to her mansion by wealthy individuals and executives of large corporations also fueled their speculation that Ellen Forrestal was somehow more than just a doctor's wife.

Benjamin heard one woman very clearly, "Yes! I have been told she has some kind of business empire. There is always some kind of big shot going in and out of her mansion."

Another woman added, "With her wealth she could get away with murder and probably did." The group mumbled their acceptance of such a proposition.

Benjamin's mind began racing at such an idea. Did my

151

mother kill Jonnie York to protect me?

Benjamin rejected the thought. Jonnie York died by drowning. The newspaper unambiguously described the strange details of his death. Benjamin would not listen to such gossip. He left the office and went in search of his father. He would not mention what he heard. The very idea his mother would kill someone in a way not permitted by The Word was simply unfathomable.

The accusation that Benjamin's mother was a murderer did not stop with the hospital gossip. Benjamin, immersed with his studies, rarely visited Riverdale. When he did go into town, one of his parents would accompany him, and they would go to a fine restaurant or a clothing store. One warm afternoon, Benjamin decided to walk through town alone to visit with many of the town people he fondly remembered as a young child. This was difficult to do with his brace. Still, Benjamin was happy to see his old friends.

But the people of Riverdale had changed. No one in town looked directly at him unless forced by circumstance. Karl Werze managed Riversdale's grocery market and was, in many ways, the social center of the town. Karl was standing in the doorway of his store when he heard the familiar sound of thumping metal on wood. He turned to see a very happy Benjamin approaching. The grocer disappeared into his store. When Benjamin closed the distance to the doorway and entered the grocery Karl Werze had vanished into the backroom. How strange, Benjamin thought.

As he turned to continue down the street, he could hear pounding from Mike Musik, Riverdale's only blacksmith, fitting an iron rim onto a wooden wheel. Mr. Musik told stories to a younger Benjamin about the town before the harbor was constructed and how only a few people called Riverdale their home during those early years. The blacksmith looked up only once: "I am sorry, Benjamin. I really can't speak to you. I must live in this town." The blacksmith returned to his labors.

Mrs. Grey was the town baker. In years past she fed Benjamin pies and cookies when the child would visit. His mother was married to the town's only doctor, known for his charitable treatment to the poor. How else could Mrs. Grey show her gratitude? She would stuff young Benjamin with pastries and flatter his good looks. But not today. When Benjamin walked past the bakery, through his reflection on the glass, he could see Mrs. Grey standing a few feet behind her front window. Tears filled her eyes, and her hand covered her mouth to silence her sadness. She appeared to be in a state of forced isolation by the other members of the town. Benjamin looked through his reflection as this wonderful woman of his past turned and disappeared into the darkness of the store.

Benjamin continued down the street. This pattern of rude behavior repeated itself, and he heard the soft whispers of secrets all around him. The cadence of fellowship within Riverdale seemed shadowed by an eclipse from an unknown source. A kind word was never offered. He could see people running down the street seemingly to spread the word of his presence. Stores were closed, horse riders and carriage passengers looked past Benjamin and rarely gave him an acknowledging nod.

There was one exception to the cold disrespect. Mr. Madison, the president of Riverdale State Bank, saw Benjamin and called out from the top of the stairs at the entrance to the bank, "Benjamin, how are you? Wait, I wish to join you."

Mr. Madison was dressed in a most elegant black suit with a tall, matching hat and highly polished boots. His black ribbon tie contrasted with his pure white, silk shirt. His gold cufflinks glistened from the midday sun. He hopped down the stairs and warmly shook Benjamin's hand, "So good to see you. Are you enjoying your visit to the town today?"

"Mr. Madison, sir, no one will speak to me. It would seem I am a ghost. See the many people riding by horse and carriage? Only a few glances or acknowledgments have been directed at my presence and not one friendly greeting. No one will speak to me. I do not understand. What is wrong? What have I done?" Benjamin stared at the townspeople passing in front of him.

"Benjamin, please come to my office where we may speak of a cruel reality in which you have become entangled." Mr. Madison, holding Benjamin's arm, slowly climbed the stairs in front of the bank, opened the heavy brass doors, walked across the lobby of marble, brass, slate, and rich walnut, and entered the opulent office of the president of Riverdale's largest bank.

"Please, be seated," Mr. Madison motioned to a huge, black leather chair in front of his desk. Mr. Madison sat behind his desk and looked stoically at his young visitor and friend. "Benjamin, this town is made up of many good people. They all have an important role to play in our economy and culture. Your family is seen differently now from the time an impoverished, innocent, widowed mother, who lived above the butcher shop, married a county doctor. There is rumor that your mother killed Jonnie York. The consensus of the town is that your mother, in defiance of The Word, killed Jonnie York. He was a monster, but he was also a child and could not commit a crime. The town resents that such power resides in a single person that would make this abomination possible."

"My father?"

"He is cherished by the town's residents."

"Why do they resent me with these ridiculous thoughts?" Benjamin asked, fearing the answer.

"You are your mother's flesh and blood and she killed Jonnie York in an act of revenge to protect you. The shadow also falls on you. I am terribly sorry. The entire situation is unfair," Mr. Madison's voice trailed off while he turned to look through the large window in his office.

"I am ostracized because of a rumor? I thought that rumor was confined to the privileged hospital wives spreading that same garbage. This is insanity!" Benjamin felt angry and resentful.

"And, of course, your mother's perceived great wealth and power incites resentment. Benjamin, it would be best to remain in the company of more affluent and influential families in our community. You will always be accepted by the wealthy and powerful. You now reside in a more privileged class. Many of the people of Riverdale would resent your mother, and now you, for almost any reason. I am sorry you must carry this burden," Mr. Madison's voice diminished with every word.

"Did my mother kill Jonnie York?"

"I do not know."

～∞～

Benjamin would never completely accept the loss of his friends from the streets of Riverdale. He wanted to shout his discontent and confusion to the community. He knew that was not possible. A few months later, Mr. Madison's lesson as to why Benjamin lived on the rim of the world would be reinforced.

The day had just begun. Benjamin entered the livery barn to groom his horse before an early morning ride. The livery barn was empty. Benjamin walked over and opened the stable of his horse and began brushing the beautiful animal. Jim Johnson, the county water master, entered, followed by the stable master leading Mr. Johnson's horse. Benjamin could clearly hear Mr. Johnson's instructions for the care of his horse. While Benjamin quietly continued grooming, he heard these ugly words uttered: "That deformed Ellen Forrestal kid stables his horse here. Must give you the creeps knowing his mother is a murderer. One false move and you're dead!" Both men chuckled nervously. "Yeah, Ellen Forrestal killed York's kid and got away with it. Money, I tell you!"

Benjamin again felt the town's prejudice. Mr. Madison had warned him of the widespread belief of his mother's culpability, and these rumors had become part of the culture of Riverdale. Rage consumed Benjamin overhearing such pejoratives. With one motion, he dropped the brush and with little thought flung the stable door open with such force it smacked the adjacent stable with a loud crash. The two men froze in disbelief as Benjamin walked out of the stable, "Yes, and she will kill both of you if I ask her too. If I hear of any such talk from either of you . . . well, put your estates in order, gentlemen." Jim Johnson leapt into the saddle on his horse and rode away at great speed. Benjamin walked through the stable and pointed his finger directly at the stablemaster's face. The stablemaster backed against the gate and then bowed his head. Benjamin left the stables to begin his walk to the mansion. He repeated the same thought: *That was really stupid. That was the stupidest thing I ever did. I think it best not to tell mother. How stupid can you be?*

When Benjamin completed the Advanced School's requirements, he had a year and a half before he could enter the university in Londonderry. His mother insisted that he continue his education with the study of accounting, an important skill for his responsibilities to come. His father objected. Conrad insisted Benjamin should be allowed time off from his studies to enjoy his remaining boyhood. This was difficult for Ellen who feared Benjamin might become a dullard in the absence of continued education or, worse, that he might be hurt again by an unforgiving and dangerous world. A compromise was agreed upon. Benjamin would have at least four days a week free of studying. He would be required to continue his studies on the other three days.

On one of these days free from study Benjamin was riding through the outskirts of town when he came upon a boy that appeared to be around his age being bullied by a group of much larger and older boys. Benjamin was enraged by such a sight. He removed a small caliber pistol from the back of his belt, a gift from his mother on his sixteenth birthday. With a flash of his weapon the deviants scattered down the alley and over dirty broken fences. Benjamin took the boy home and cared for him. They became friends. His name was Petie, and for the first time in Benjamin's life he had a close friend. They shared their activities and their thoughts as they explored the world together. Benjamin could at last escape the strange world he was born into and do childish things. The opinions of others in the community toward his mother were forgotten. His tutors were no longer Benjamin's only link to the world. The moments that Benjamin and Petie would share in life, however, were fleeting. Petie died not long after they met, while riding one of Benjamin's horses. Benjamin was lost once again. His boyish world had ended.

With the loss of his dear friend, Benjamin learned to lessen his sorrow by channeling his energy into preparing for the examination to become a certified public accountant. Benjamin found solace and sanctuary in persistent concentration on mundane tax laws and bookkeeping techniques. What once was a three-days-a-week affair of academic torture while Petie walked the world became a welcomed relief from pain. With the increased concentration required to escape his emotions, and with significant help from his tutors, Benjamin completed his studies in months. Benjamin and his tutors were confident he had sufficiently assimilated the abstruse aspects of the Cunningham's Correspondent School of Accounting and would be successful in passing the Kenton State uniform certified public accountant examination and qualify to be a licensed certified public accountant.

So, early on a Monday morning in late September, as the sun's light crowded out the stars, Benjamin, at the age of seventeen, accompanied by his father, boarded the passenger steam train to Londonderry to arrive at the appointed time at the Brice Assembly Hall on the University of Londonderry campus for the biannual state examination. Benjamin spoke little as the train carried him on his journey toward professional, societal recognition.

Benjamin demonstrated no outward anxiety. He was centered and confident beyond his young age. He passed the time looking out the passenger car, captivated by the passing scenery made more interesting by the brilliant dawn. The powerful engine, with methodical precision, mastered the scalding steam within the boiler to compel the iron wheels down the tracks. With each stroke of the giant pistons, the distance closed between Benjamin and the most significant challenge to his young academic life. So, while the train labored against friction, waste, and slip, the bucolic beauty of green hills and expansive farms preoccupied Benjamin's thoughts. The source of abundant water so necessary for such successful food production on an industrial scale seemed obvious and intuitive to the young, bright student. He studied the distant mountain range on the edge of the fertile agricultural basin. He reasoned that the majestic mountain peaks collected the rain from the ascending clouds, creating vast freshwater rivers to irrigate thousands of acres of agriculture in the valley below. At that point, Benjamin began to consider what advantageous soil conditions must be present for large-scale food production and if soil supplements could be added to increase crop yield. Something with a nitrogen base, he reasoned, attempting to remember his lessons concerning plant physiology.

Benjamin was deep in thought about the agricultural landscape, serenaded by the iron wheels' hypnotic rhythm, when his reveries abruptly ended. Benjamin's father broke the spell, "Benjamin, I have a surprise for you when you have completed your examination. I am going to introduce you to one of the professors at the university who is a friend of mine and who shares many concerns about the nature of the world you have expressed to me on occasion. I think you will find the visit enjoyable."

After a short pause, Benjamin stated, "I think you are being a little mysterious, father. I love a good mystery, so I think I will enjoy meeting with your friend once this examination is behind me."

Benjamin's father responded, "I think you will find the visit . . . well, very special."

The train arrived on time, and the university was a short walk from the station. They easily located Brice Assembly Hall as it was one of the most prominent buildings on the campus. So, father and son made their way through a beautiful campus replete with traditional brick and tile buildings and crowded with ambitious students consumed with thoughts and energized with nascent knowledge, to the steps of the giant assembly hall. Before Benjamin entered the impressive building, a proud father placed his hand on his son's shoulder. Benjamin responded before his father spoke, "I know, father. I thank you and mother for the excellent education, and I will not disappoint either of you today."

Benjamin's father said with love in his voice, "I will always be proud of you. You are a special young man. You will accomplish great things in your life."

Benjamin put his hand against his father's heart as a silent gesture of love. He turned and walked up the many steps, unencumbered by the necessary steel supporting his mis-shaped leg, to the massive, brass-covered doors of Brice Hall, pulled them open, and disappeared into the examination forum.

Benjamin entered an enormous room with a ceiling nearly three stories high, and several oak desks pushed together to form a continuous table. Long columns of space between the grouped tables created a walkway permitting passage from the rear of the vast room to the front stage. Giant gas chandeliers hung from the ceiling, bathing the assembly hall in vibrant golden light. The side walls displayed dozens of large, intricate stained-glass windows permitting filtered sunlight to enter the hall. Many of the marvelous windows illustrated the timeline of Kenton's civilization progressing from the primitive hunter-gatherer period, followed by the development of early agriculture, and the writing of The Word by the first Elders. The final stained-glass window displayed the modern period of steamships and trains.

The test candidates were evenly spaced throughout the assembly hall by members of the accountant union to make cheating extremely difficult. The large room could comfortably seat a thousand individuals, but for today's examination a little more than a hundred individuals would be asked to demonstrate their accounting knowledge. One of the test administrators motioned to Benjamin to sit near the back of the room next to the stained-glass window depicting the

advancement of mathematics. A few more would-be accountants wandered into the hall. At precisely one o'clock in the
afternoon, a large sign was placed on the outside of the doors
proclaiming the examination had started, and there would no
more admission for the current testing cycle. The doors were
locked.

A nicely dressed, elderly man with a booming voice began the orientation for the prospective accountants: "Good
morning. My name is Roger Smith. I serve as a member on
the board of examiners for the certification of public accountants. I will be giving a brief summary of the examination and
the testing properties of today's exam. As the examination
instruments are being passed out during this orientation, no
candidate will open his or her testing document until the time
to begin the examination procedure is announced. The
uniform examination for the certification of public accountants serves the citizens of the State of Kenton by ensuring that
only qualified individuals are licensed as certified public
accountants. To qualify, the successful candidate must
complete the exam with a passing mark of ninety percent
within the period provided for testing. There will be two
opportunities to pass the CPA examination successfully per
year. A candidate for licensure may take the examination as
many times as necessary to pass the examination process. The
certified public accountant review is an essay examination. It
consists of four major areas of examination: audit and attesta-
tion, Kenton civil and commercial regulations, business
milieu and concepts, and financial accounting and reporting.
A candidate for licensure must complete the examination
within six hours. . . ."

Benjamin's mind began drifting as the monotonous orientation revealed no information that had not already been
provided by his tutors. One of Benjamin's tutors was a
member of the board of examiners for ten years before
accepting the lucrative position as Benjamin Walker's tutor.
His other tutor, a former university English professor, served
as Benjamin's writing coach to ensure Benjamin wrote clearly

and precisely. Benjamin was subjected to constant testing, evaluation, and instruction until his knowledge of the materials and his testing skills were honed to perfection. He had the opportunity to take a sample examination prepared by his tutors over eight times in the weeks preceding today's examination and demonstrated passing scores on his last four attempts. Each tutor was promised a considerable financial reward from Benjamin's mother if her son passed the certification process on his first attempt. Each tutor was extremely motivated to secure the bonus, the equivalent of two full years of a professor's salary, to supplement their already lucrative stipend. So, Benjamin's mind, thoroughly prepared, and somewhat bored, drifted from the examination milieu and orientation back to Kenton's vast agricultural area. His thoughts began to relive the visual experience of the fertile farmland he observed earlier. There was something about that experience that gnawed at his subconscious.

Benjamin began to visualize his mother's vast tract of land some miles west of Riverdale. Except for petroleum extraction and cattle grazing, the land had little value as farm property. Grain crops could be grown and easily shipped but were already overproduced and not lucrative. The area was far too distant to move fresh vegetables to the prosperous market of Londonderry and other large population centers without the shipment spoiling in hot freight cars during shipping. Suddenly, he imagined a freight car modified to store ice in the ceiling and floor, with double walls heavily insulated with wool and straw. Such an ice-cooled freight car with a white-painted roof to reflect the sun's rays might be able to preserve fresh vegetables for days before spoiling. Crops could be harvested and cleaned in the field and immediately placed into ice freight cars and sent to Londonderry for arrival within a few days in giant mobile iceboxes. Benjamin reasoned the vegetables would arrive at the market as fresh as produce grown in close proximity to Londonderry. Benjamin began to visualize how his theory could be tested when his thought experiment was interrupted by a loud thump of the thick examination booklet and writing tablet landing next to him by one the frantic examiners attempting to distribute the testing materials before orientation ended. A few minutes later, Roger Smith permitted the candidates to open the testing materials. Benjamin opened his examination booklet and peered down at the essay questions. The first question on the exam read:

Rothschild & Associates were engaged by the Kenton Stock Commission to audit the Kenton Cattle Company, a publicly traded company. Rothschild & Associates made several misstatements in the financial statement. When the flawed financial statement was published in the company's registration statement, the Kenton Cattle Company's stock value lost one-third of its prior assessed value. A private investor, Subject A, held a large portion of the Kenton Cattle Company stock purchased on the company's initial offering and was forced to sell the stock at a loss subject to a margin call. Recompense may be achieved under the following scenarios:
• Subject A may recover the financial loss from Rothschild & Associates under Section 11 of the Securities Act of 1855 if Subject A can prove, in binding arbitration, procedural malfeasance. Explain under what circumstances (fact pattern) and legal arguments Subject A must articulate to achieve recompense?
• Under what circumstances may Subject A use deadly force?

The first question seemed extremely familiar and straightforward to Benjamin. Benjamin took a few moments to read the other questions on the examination instrument. After reading the questions in the remaining sections, he immediately realized he had practiced writing answers to every problem presented in the exam, worded somewhat differently, many times before. Benjamin had a considerable advantage over the other candidates and demonstrated his prowess by completing the exam in three hours, well before any of the other individuals taking the test.

Benjamin emerged from Brice Hall and scanned the campus, searching for his father. The university was crowded with brick buildings, two and three stories high, and in between the buildings was a long commons area landscaped with trees, fountains, and grass-covered hills. He found his father sitting on a bench reading a newspaper by a large marble fountain in front of Brice Assembly Hall. Benjamin descended the steps, and crossed the wide walkway as fast as his steel brace would permit. As he approached, his father felt his son's presence and looked up to see a happy Benjamin running toward him with an ungainly gait.

"Father, I think I passed. The examination was not that difficult," Benjamin burst out with joy as he approached his father.

Benjamin's father stood and put his arms around his son and said, "Well, Benjamin, I am so happy you think you did so well. Judging by the time, you must have easily mastered the questions on the examination."

"Yes, father, I think so," Benjamin responded, smothered in his father's arms.

Benjamin's father stepped back and put his hand to his son's face for a few silent seconds, beaming with absolute pride, and said, "Your mother will be so happy. Benjamin, you are a wonderful son."

"I hope I will never disappoint you or mother," Benjamin returned.

Benjamin's father took out his pocket watch from his vest: "We have a few hours before my friend will be free to meet with us, so let us find something to eat. The university's food center is only a few minutes from here. You must be hungry, Benjamin."

"Yes, father, hungry and relieved. I can now relax before the next educational challenge mother requires of me."

Benjamin's father smiled, knowing his son was very insightful and accepting of his mother's obsession with his education. Father and son turned and disappeared into the disordered urgency of the scurrying crowds of students and faculty members. As usual, Benjamin began speaking of abstract and esoteric issues concerning the new revelation produced by his imaginative mind. His father was always interested in his son's observations and conclusions. He would ask probative questions to refine his son's arguments and clarify his premises. Today's topic concerned the transportation of fresh vegetables long distances without spoilage in modified train freight cars cooled by ice. His father was impressed by how a simple train ride could produce such an innovative concept. Neither father nor son preoccupied with discussion noticed the darkening sky, the strengthening wind, and the inevitable concealment of the sun. A storm was coming.

Ellen was alone as she watched the train leave the Riverdale station carrying her husband and son to Londonderry for the examination her son had prepared for all summer. She watched the engine erupt soot and steam as the train gathered speed and slowly disappeared, leaving Ellen to contend with a mother's anxiety of her child's ordeal in Londonderry. Ellen would resist such motherly indulges. She realized this was neither the time for nonchalance nor the time to be preoccupied with concerns about her son's success. She was compelled to complete her next mission to further her son's education, and this effort entailed a meeting Ellen had scheduled with a dear friend from her past across town in the industrial district. She turned from the train platform, and briskly walked to Conrad's black carriage, climbed aboard, and directed Demon to Kenton Boulevard in Riverdale's industrial section. She had arranged an early morning meeting with Jeffery Porter, a prosperous importer of Kuttor exotic handmade rugs and carpets. Jeffery Porter was the owner of one of the most successful wholesale companies in the State of Kenton.

Within the hour, Ellen arrived at one of Riverdale's most significant buildings strategically located a short distance from the harbor. The building, built with a corrugated metal exterior, was nearly three stories high and covered an entire city block. A huge painted sign on the building's side proudly proclaimed: The Porter Exotic Carpet Import Wholesale Company. Ellen brought her carriage to the business section of the large building, secured Demon, and entered the main entrance. The impressive lobby amazed Ellen. The spectacular room had an exceedingly high ceiling. From all the walls hung hundreds of imported rugs and carpets on removable racks that could easily be pulled from the wall and rotated so that prospective buyers could scrutinize the excellent workmanship of each handmade article. The floor of the immense room was covered with numerous carpets and rugs created by the artists of Kuttor. Ellen was amazed at the beauty of the rugs and, with little concern for cost, resolved to purchase several examples of these functional art forms to decorate her mansion after she finished her meeting. As Ellen pondered the intricate arabesque of several rugs, and the subtle colors of each design, a young, attractive, and well-dressed sales lady approached Mrs. Forrestal. "May I be of help?"

Ellen responded, "Yes, thank you. I have an appointment with Mr. Porter."

"Yes, Mrs. Forrestal, Mr. Porter, is expecting you. Please follow me and I will take you to his office."

The young lady guided Mrs. Forrestal through a labyrinth of offices and halls toward Jeffery Porter's massive office door with marble casing bordering the entrance. Jeffery Porter was chiseled boldly in the marble above the door. Mrs. Forrestal's escort gently knocked, and a voice emanated from within: "Yes, please come in." Ellen's escort stepped inside the office and announced Mrs. Forrestal's presence, holding the door for her to enter.

Mrs. Forrestal entered the enormous and opulent office of Jeffery Porter. Dark, imported wood from all over the world covered the walls. A stunning mural made of beautifully carved panels bordered each wall. The mural depicted the artists of Kuttor creating the world-renowned and much sought-after carpet treasures, that Jeffery Porter had made a fortune importing. The carved chronology illustrated the production of Kuttor's exotic carpets, beginning with the gathering of wool to the meticulous weaving by hand on giant looms. Magnificent crystal chandeliers hung from a hand-painted ceiling portraying fabled flying carpets of Kuttor carrying ancient magicians and mythical potentates through billowing clouds and endless rainbows. A vast, unobstructed window consumed one side of the office and overlooked the harbor commerce. Numerous horse-drawn wagons traversed a heavily trafficked gravel road, bringing rugs from Kuttor to the import warehouse, or to the waiting freighters to ship overseas. A stunning oak desk dominated the office center with several matching chairs sitting in front of the desk. A single magnificent carpet from Kuttor covered the floor.

Ellen, briefly mesmerized by the lavishness of Jeffery Porter's office, stood in stunned silence. She was brought back to the purpose of her mission by Jeffery Porter's voice, "Ellen, you have not aged in eighteen years, how have you been?"

Ellen focused on Jeffery Porter, a man she was quite close to many years ago. He was a striking man, taller than she remembered, with thick blonde hair, a carefully trimmed beard, and a pleasant smile that showcased perfectly white teeth. He was lean and fit. His eyes seemed different though—wiser, more worldly. He appeared quite prosperous in his luxurious clothes, and he too seemed to look years younger than his actual age. Ellen acknowledged her old friend's presence by placing her hand on Jeffery's cheek, "Jeffery, how have we allowed time to get away from us? I am so glad to see you looking so well. And, by the looks of things, doing well."

Jeffery paused briefly to gaze upon the beautiful face of a woman from his past, then broke the spell, "Life has come between us, Ellen, and thank you for your kind words. Please have a seat here in front of my desk so we can have a long conversation about all the things that have happened to us while we've been apart."

In the next hour, he spoke with Ellen of the various business successes and the happiness his large family had brought him over the years. Ellen spoke about Benjamin and how he had grown into a mature young man, and when the stories were told and the pleasantries completed, Jeffery asked, "Ellen, how may I be of service to you?"

Ellen smiled and began: "Jeffery, Benjamin is taking the exam to become a certified public accountant at the University of Londonderry. His tutors have promised me he will pass the exam. I am here to ask for a favor and offer a proposition. I would gladly pay my son's salary if you gave him some experience as an accountant. He will not be going to the university for a number of months. The accountant certification board requires a certified accountant to accumulate at least six months of real-world experience as a paid accountant to be permanently vested in his licensure after passing the examination. I would like to keep him at home as long as possible until he is ready to attend the university, and I was hoping you might give him some experience."

Jeffery looked surprised and was unsure of what he had heard.

"Ellen, your son is, what, sixteen or seventeen? And he is taking one of the most challenging exams given by any professional organization. Did I hear you right?"

Ellen nodded and said, "It would seem my son is a genius. He completed the advanced school much earlier than most students, and I initiated his studies in accounting because the university will not take him until he is eighteen. The university had a few problems with disgruntled minors killing their professors, and being minors—well, you understand, minors cannot commit crimes. A few always spoil it for the rest."

Jeffery responded, "I could see how some professors would require some restrictions on minors, but you are correct. All it takes is a few willful children and a few deaths, and things can get fouled up. I have always wondered why the creators of The Word leave children with so much behavioral freedom without criminal consequences. Well, I imagine the Elders, when they created The Word . . . I am sure they knew what they were doing."

"I suppose," Ellen returned, giving a slight shrug, having no real understanding of the underlying reasoning in the teachings of The Word, or of the identity or origins of the Elders. The populace merely accepted such things. Kenton was, after all, the most prosperous nation state in the world. The sacred writing of the The Word produced a society so completely practical, efficient, and fair that no one would question the veracity of the teachings contained within this, the most inviolate book ever conceived by the wisest of men.

Jeffery then became almost jovial responding to Ellen's proposition. "Ellen, I would love to help James Walker's son in any way I can. Please, I would be more than happy to pay for his salary as a full accountant and even give him an office and a competent secretary to assist him. If he manages to pass the exam, I will have him audit the company books. I have a few questions about our financial documentation, and I would like someone independent to review them. If my business were publicly owned, such an audit would be required annually. I am beginning to think such an annual review is a good idea. If he should fail on his first attempt, and almost everyone does, I will be glad to still give him some practical experience as a paid intern accountant to help him succeed with his next attempt at the exam. I believe those paid hours will also be counted for licensure vesting."

"That's wonderful. I cannot thank you enough. You are so generous," Ellen said, a little surprised by Jeffery's sudden generosity.

"Not at all," Jeffery began. "Let me tell you a story. A few years before you were married to James, I had a financial setback. Let me rephrase, I was insolvent. I was just starting this business. An opportunity arose to acquire a great deal of product from a gentleman in Kuttor who was dying and wanted to liquidate his large stock of rugs and carpets to provide some financial support for his family. Well, I borrowed every dime I could. I mortgaged the house, spent the kids' education fund, drained my life savings, parents' life savings, and sold everything else. I sailed to Kuttor, bought the man's carpets at a good price, made sure the product was correctly loaded on the freighter, and took a faster steamship home to prepare for the shipment to arrive. I had half of the product sold and doubled my money when I received word that the freighter, transporting my investment, floundered in a winter storm and sank. I could only afford to insure half the shipment, and the freight insurance claim could not be honored until lengthy litigation was completed to determine liability. The ship was registered in Kuttor and flew a Kuttor flag, and I learned the hard way to only ship with Kenton-registered ships, where these incidents are resolved quickly. No one wants to be shot. Well, I had just enough cash to make a salary for the three men who worked for me for about a week. One day, James appeared delivering my weekly winter coal supply, so I went out and told him of my lost shipment, and how I could not afford to pay for the coal. James smiled and said the children needed to be kept warm, and that our family should have hot water. He said not to worry about paying him back. A few days later, James returned with a box of groceries and continued to bring coal and food every week, keeping my family fed and warm for three months until the shipping insurance company was able to repay me for part of my loss. I could purchase some new product and start my business again. When I was a little ahead, I approached James and told him I wanted to pay him for all he provided to my family. James refused to be repaid. He said he hoped I would do the same for someone that needed help. If I did that, he would be paid in full. That was the kind of man James Walker was, and I never forgot what he taught me. I have tried my best to live up to his standards. I found the more I gave to others, the more I prospered. The Word clearly states the more we give, the more we will receive. So saith The Word."

Ellen returned, "So saith The Word."

Ellen's eyes were moist with tears hearing yet another story of James's generosity. "He was a wonderful man. We both failed him many years ago. What he did in life touched so many others, both in his life and after he was gone. Such a wonderful man."

"Yes, Ellen, he was a better person than both of us. I have my regrets. I am sure you feel the same. I would do anything for you and your son. Please, always remember that, Ellen." Jeffery was finished with his story.

A silent moment passed, then Jeffery asked, "Do you have a tintype of your son? "

Ellen grew still and reached into her skirt pocket, removing a small black-and-white metal photograph of her son taken a few months ago. "This is my son. He is a very handsome young man. He has worked hard, overcoming his handicap."

Jeffery carefully studied the photograph, "He is a very nice-looking young man, Ellen. He has your eyes. Are they green like yours? I can see a striking resemblance." Jeffery stared at the photograph for a long time. He slowly moved a tintype image from side to side, studying Benjamin's face and slowly lifted his head until his eyes met Ellen's.

Ellen replied then, "Jeffery, his eyes are not green. His eyes are a beautiful blue, like yours."

Jeffery was silent for a few moments, "How old, again, did you say your son is?"

Ellen reached across the gap between them and took Jeffery's hand, "Yes, he is your son. I am so sorry for not telling you before this. I knew I must tell you before you see him in person. He has your eyes and smile. I did not want you to wonder after you met him. We were both married so long ago, and I thought it best to go on with my life. I also did not want you to die. James would have honored his wedding vow. He loved me, and he would have been compelled. . . . Can you forgive me?"

Jeffery's eyes also welled with tears, and he placed his other hand on Ellen's shoulder, "This is why you disappeared from my life so long ago?"

"Yes," Ellen confirmed.

"The greatest shame I ever knew was touching the wife of the man who did so much for me when I was lost. Now this . . ." Jeffery reached up and touched Ellen's lips with the tip of his finger. "I have always loved you. I was never sure why you so completely vanished from my life until now. I am so sorry."

"Jeffery, the life you placed inside me was and is the greatest joy of my life. I would have loved having a life with you, but I could not bring myself to hurt James. He was such a wonderful man, and you were married as well. Please, try and understand."

"Ellen, I have always loved you. All I ask is your forgiveness for being so selfish. I had no right to touch you."

"You had every right," Ellen interrupted. "We were in love and fate drew us together, and a beautiful child was the result. I love that child more than life, and I do not blame you for my persistence in making our relationship intimate. I can only hope you will forgive me for keeping this secret from you. You had every right to know."

Ellen was now touching Jeffery's face, wiping a tear from his cheek as Jefferey responded, "I will keep what I have learned today as one more secret between us. When you disappeared from my life, I was saddened and lost. I am so glad you told me."

Jeffery stood, holding Ellen's hand. Then the couple embraced and kissed. A long kiss of lost love reunited. A quiet moment passed between them, and then Ellen stepped back.

They walked toward the office door, and Ellen asked, trying to normalize the moment, "One more thing, Jeffery. Could you put an advertisement in the local paper for the position? I would not want Benjamin to know I helped him get a job. You can understand."

Jeffery, trying to conceal his feelings and pretending the

intimate moment had passed, said, "I will place the ad tomorrow, and the advertisement should appear in Wednesday's newspaper. Please, before you leave, will you select a carpet from my showroom for your beautiful home, Ellen? The young lady you met in the showroom will help you make the arrangements. Just have her check with me if she has any questions. Please, take anything. I would be happy if you accept this small gift from me."

Ellen leaned over and kissed Jeffery's cheek, taking his hand, "Will you and your family honor us by coming to dinner next week, maybe Thursday evening about seven? You know the mansion."

Jeffery responded, opening the door, "I would love to, and please let us agree never to allow so much time to pass between us again."

"We must promise each other we will continue to be a part of each other's lives. I will always keep a place in my heart for you, so goodbye for now, and I will see you and your family in a few days."

Ellen turned and walked away, hoping she would not cry and reveal too much of herself. She was wrong to believe time would change who she was. Her emotions and attraction for Jeffery were undiminished.

⁓

Father and son arrived at the eatery on campus, which had hundreds of small tables covered with red and black checkered tablecloths and dozens of students, talking, debating, studying, flirting, and doing all the other things young students do between classes. A student working at the center scurried from table to table, passing out menus and taking orders while other unseen students in the kitchen were preparing the meals.

The eatery was large, capable of feeding four to five hundred students at one time. In many ways, the eatery served as a social center where students made new friends and found a welcome relief from the persistent lectures and long study

Unclaimed Son

hours. Father and son found a somewhat isolated table near a large window, and Benjamin scanned the room filled with animated students. He thought of a future time when his presence on the campus would not be as a visitor but as a student, gaining knowledge with each course completed. "Father, did you enjoy getting an education?"

"Yes, attending the university is a special time, and you will learn and grow so much, and one day you will use what you have learned here to accomplish many things in life, maybe great things," Benjamin's father stated as he looked out the window at the rolling hills and the school's brick buildings, remembering his time at the university.

"I hope I will be like you, father. Someone with the knowledge and skills to help people have a better life."

"I think you will change the world, Benjamin. I never get tired of saying that phrase. My faith in you is strong. I am not just speaking as an adoring father. I have known many people in my life, but only a few gifted individuals with the qualities you possess. I know this to be true," Conrad said in a hushed, thoughtful way.

Benjamin was happy to have such supporting parents, "I hope I will be able to live up to your expectations, father. Now . . . I am so excited about this notion of ice-cooled railroad cars. I have several ideas I want to share with you. So, please father, tell me what you think? Is such a thing possible?"

Father and son continued to speak of railroads and future university life for over an hour. When the late afternoon sun slipped closer to the western horizon, Benjamin's father reached into his vest pocket and pulled his watch out once again. "Benjamin, I still want you to see the university's library before we speak to my friend. Would you like that?"

"Yes, father," an attentive and excited son replied.

Father and son left the noise of the busy eatery and began their walk across the university campus to the library on the edge of the school grounds. Turbulence, produced by the changing weather, swayed the trees and shrubs, casting leaves and debris into the air and bringing a swirling commotion to accompany Benjamin and his father as they toured the campus.

The sun was low now, and shadows stretched across buildings and pathways. Most of the buildings were old and presented a uniform geometric and pragmatic architecture made from brick and tile. Each one contained classrooms, offices, research facilities, and dorms. Between the buildings were common green areas with trees, gardens, pathways, and benches. An occasional sculpture depicting celebrated educators and philosophers, cast in bronze with greenish-blue patina, decorated the many paths. One magnificent collection of bronze statues on the top of a nearby hill embodied the ancient Elders writing The Word. The metal sculptures were massive and imposing, and depicted the Elders dressed in ancient garb, crowded around a table in vigorous discussion. One Elder, referred to by the sacred document as the witness or scribe appeared to be writing down the verbal expressions of the other Elders on a scroll made of sewn lambskin. Students and faculty often sat on the benches placed near and around the enormous statues, reading from The Word or discussing and debating the philosophical and ethical implications of the marvelous teachings. The names of the Elders were unknown. The culture that produced such genius remained a mystery. The Word was silent about the society known as the golden age of knowledge, an ancient period that provided the intellectual and moral foundation of the modern world.

The university was built on rolling hills, and the many paths that flowed through campus were made from the same bricks as the surrounding buildings. Benjamin spoke of how excited he was about attending the university in less than a year. He confessed to his father that he was somewhat pensive about leaving home and taking classes with Kenton's brightest students. His father reassured him he would do fine, and his mother was prepared to hire the best tutors possible to ensure his success. His father also spoke of the difficult transition his mother would experience with his absence and admonished Benjamin to write to his mother often, so she would not worry about her only son. Promises were made and reassurances were given as they walked the half-mile from the campus center to the university library. The library was near several abandoned gold mines that tunneled into the nearby hills. A dense forest covered hundreds of acres just east of the campus. The last hill between the library and the rest of the university was steep. Benjamin struggled up the hill, and when he reached the top, he had an unobstructed view of the university library. Benjamin was startled at what he saw. The library was the most amazing structure—nothing like he would have imagined on a campus so replete with prosaic architecture.

"Father, how is such a thing possible? The building looks like something from another world. I do not understand what I am looking at!" Benjamin was stunned.

"You are looking at the future, son," Benjamin's father stated, remembering his reaction the first time he looked up at the unusual structure.

Chapter 11
The Supplicants

T
he library was uniquely futuristic. It was perfectly square with the base covering over a quarter of an acre and reaching fourteen stories into the sky. The library was constructed with steel I-beams bolted together and completely covered with dark-shading glass. The exposed bordering steel was a vibrant rust color. The entire structure was positioned on a succession of concentric concrete squares, forming a supporting base appearing as a sizable step-down pyramid. Water flowed from the top tier of the pyramid down each successive level, creating a beautiful waterfall effect and emptying into a square pool eighty feet below the base of the library. The water reflected the dramatic building and the darkening clouds. The library was dynamic and seemed alive with the motion and the sound of flowing water. Textured concrete walkways on all four sides of the building, about thirty feet wide, led to the entrances of the building. Dozens of students walked up and down the ramps carrying books and papers retrieved or returned from the immense repository of knowledge.

"Father, I didn't know such a structure could exist. It is so stunning and modern. How is such a building possible?" Benjamin stared at the enormous steel and glass library.

"The building is called a skyscraper because it is so tall that it touches the sky. The library is the first building made solely of steel, concrete, and glass. The steel gives the building immense strength, permitting the structure to reach such height. Until now, buildings were limited to only a few stories. The university developed many architectural engineering innovations to construct such a massive and unique structure. Benjamin, you are looking at the future of architecture. You will live to see entire cities containing hundreds of skyscrapers rising from the ground like trees in a giant forest of steel and glass."

Benjamin exclaimed, "So this is the library, the library of the University of Londonderry? Why was I not told about this?"

"You were lost in your studies while this thing was being built. Benjamin, you are looking at the largest building in the world, and this building contains the sum of human knowledge. Every book ever written, every journey article, and a copy of every printed newspaper, millions upon millions of words of every kind are contained in this, the greatest library the world has known. Scholars from every corner of the world come here to research. The growth of knowledge is expanding so fast the university is planning to construct an even larger library to complement this one. Truly, this is the most exciting time to be alive, and soon you will be able to study here for years and learn so very much before you graduate."

"Where does the water for the waterfalls come from? They must use thousands of gallons of water?"

"The water comes from a large stream that flows all year, high in the nearby hills. The water is trapped in large pipes and redirected underground to the base of the structure where copper pipes in the concrete base allow the water to emerge from the top step of the pyramid. The water continues down into the reflecting pool, where it's redirected to other fountains on campus before the water is reunited with the source downstream," Benjamin's father explained.

"Incredible, father. The whole thing is impossibly incredible . . ." Benjamin continued to repeat.

"And Benjamin, there is something else. I have arranged for us to visit the vault in the basement to see the State of Kenton's foundation document. The original is a five thousand years old manuscript of The Word, handwritten by the Elders. The book is written on lambskin using ancient dyes for ink. It is carefully preserved in a hermetically sealed room away from sunlight. The room's temperature and humidity are carefully controlled to ensure the longevity of the ancient manuscript. Every page of the manuscript has been photographed with a new kind of camera that uses nitrocellulose instead of sensitive metal. I promised mother I would buy you a copy of the facsimile of The Word as a congratulatory acknowledgement when you are certified as a public accountant."

A pensive Benjamin responded, "Nitrocellu . . . what? I have never heard of anything like this, and father, is it possible to read The Word in the original language?"

"Yes, Benjamin, the language has not changed from the beginning of written language."

"Father, are you suggesting our language has not evolved in five thousand years?" an incredulous Benjamin asked.

"Well, Benjamin, there are certainly more words in our vocabulary now, but the basic linguistic structure has remained the same. The vocabulary of The Word is made up of the same words we use today. The ancient text is very legible."

Benjamin grew still as he pondered this. "How is it possible the language has not changed in thousands of years?"

"Benjamin, I think many of your questions will be answered before this day is through. Show some patience, young man, and much will be revealed."

"Father, you are being—I love a good mystery," Benjamin stated once again as they continued their journey into the skyscraper.

Father and son walked the long, winding brick path down the last steep hill adjacent to the library. Conrad occasionally helped his son, as the steep hill tested Benjamin's skills to walk with his steel brace. Within a few minutes, they reached the edge of the reflecting pool. The immense concrete ramp before them, several hundred feet long, was designed with a gentle slope requiring only mild physical exertion to ascend regardless of the visitor's physical condition. The strong wind of the approaching storm sprayed mist from the pool into the air. Benjamin and his father, pulling up their coat collars to ward off the chill, began their long, gentle climb to the library entrance.

Benjamin could not contain his curiosity, "Father, how large is the library?"

"The building is fourteen stories tall, a little less than two hundred feet high. The library is a perfect cube, so each side of the library is exactly as wide as the building is tall. The structure has fifteen levels, counting the basement and the utility level on the top floor. The building is an experimental structure, a prototype for future buildings. This library uses a contraption called an elevator for the first time in a large building. Elevators are these small rooms capable of holding a dozen people, which can move up and down the height of the building, permitting access to all levels without requiring any physical exertion on the part of the transported passengers."

"See the windows, Benjamin? The windows cannot be opened, so fresh air must be pulled into the building using large fans at the top of the building. In the summer, cool air is pulled from a nearby abandoned mine using large, insulated concrete and copper pipes. In the winter, the fresh air is pulled into the building and warmed by a steam boiler in the basement. Cooling and warming the building is called air conditioning," Conrad explained, sounding much like a university docent conducting a tour. His father's busy arms and hands pointed and waved to aid his explanation.

"Father, how can the small rooms move up and down? Are there steam-driven gears in the building supplying the necessary energy?" Benjamin asked while father and son neared the entrance of the building in the middle of the cube.

Benjamin's father stopped his ascension and paused to reflect on how to answer Benjamin's question, "A few years ago, the university opened a new research department called the department of electrical engineering. I don't understand how the process works. The university has discovered how to generate electricity and use it to power electric motors and even to generate light using small glass globes. I simply do not know how it works, but many of those innovations are incorporated into this prototype. I know how strange this may sound. The gentleman you will be meeting and speaking to will give you a better idea of how it all works."

Benjamin considered his father's words, "The school has figured out how to make lightning, and control the energy of lightning to create artificial light and run engines. Is that what you are telling me?"

"That may be one way of saying what the engineers have been able to accomplish, but in a little while all your questions will be answered. Can you wait a little longer?" Conrad asked curtly, knowing his son's insatiable curiosity while these wondrous things were unfolding all around him.

"Yes, father. I know there is a reason you are sharing all this with me, so I will be quiet and allow things to unfold as you think best." Benjamin was increasingly aware his father's behavior seemed a little strange—secretive, stressed, evasive. At first, Benjamin dismissed his father's demeanor as an empathic gesture concerning the morning's examination. Yet, when he had finished the exam, he could feel a foreign uncertainty in his father. Something was going to happen, and he knew his father was preparing him.

Benjamin and Conrad reached the top of the ramp and approached the transparent double doors of the entrance. The doors were tall and wide, and constructed with thick glass and steel. Benjamin pulled on a clear, glass cylinder suspended between two brass pieces, which served as the handle, and opened the door with some effort. The first thing Benjamin experienced was a strange, white light emanating from within, and a blast of cold, dry air striking his face. Benjamin, with his father at his side, stepped inside the library and into the future.

Benjamin took several steps before astonishment overtook him. There was not a single thing that looked familiar inside the vast lobby. Benjamin felt he had stepped into a time machine sent a hundred years into the future. The eerie light from the ceiling suggested to young Benjamin the world may never know darkness again. The ceiling, three stories above, consisted of hundreds of square glass panels framed in dull, silver metal. Each panel of the ceiling radiated a white, diffused light considerably different than the light generated by gas lamps. The illumination evenly lit the lobby, creating a soft radiance and nearly eliminating shadows from the room.

A strange thump caused Benjamin to focus on a tall, concrete cylinder at least twelve feet in diameter in the middle of the room, reaching from the floor to ceiling, some fifty or sixty feet in front of him. A sizable, curved door could be seen slightly inset into the round structure. Above the door in large brass letters, the word ELEVATOR proclaimed the transportation machine's presence. He looked intently at the strange device. The muffled thump had come from inside the circular structure. The door began to slide to one side, and a young lady appeared behind the door in a strange-looking uniform. With skill and a great deal of effort, she pushed and pulled the door open. The curved door disappeared into the large cylinder, revealing a small metal room gleaming with chrome. The small group sequestered within focused their attention on the determined elevator operator. Only when the young lady gave permission did the group walk into the lobby. When the room was empty, the young lady looked around for other potential vertical travelers. Absent of new passengers, the impressive lady pulled the curved door shut. With a soft hum and vibration, the room was gone. The concrete cylinder was quiet.

The entire lobby was surrounded by glass, revealing the concrete waterfalls at the base of the building, the nearby tree-covered hills, and the darkening sky. A dark, salmon-colored wool carpet covered the lobby. A row of futuristic-looking chairs sat near the windows, each made with chrome steel forming curved legs, and the backs adorned with thick leather that matched the carpet. The outside glass walls, supported by a labyrinth of thin and thick steel supports, formed the perfect illusion of a windowless room.

A curved lobby desk adjacent to the central cylinder with the elevator bustled with library visitors. Several young women behind the desk gave directions and answered questions to the inquiring crowd. As Benjamin approached the counter, he noticed the young women wearing the same uniform as the elevator lady. A white blouse with a black ribbon tie, and a salmon-colored jacket edged with black trim. A small gleaming nameplate on each of the jackets conspicuously proclaimed the identity of each woman. Each woman wore a black hat resembling an upside-down pie plate. The woman's dresses, matching their jackets, were worn tight to their legs from the waist to just above the knee. The limited length revealed a significant amount of the ladies' naked legs. Benjamin was sure his mother would not approve of such scandalous fashion.

Benjamin and his father reached the curved lobby desk. Benjamin was staring at the young ladies' legs when one of the receptionists, identified by her badge as Linda, turned and asked Benjamin, "May I help you?"

Benjamin did not speak. The experience was too much to process. He stood speechless, his mind on overload. Benjamin's father broke his son's uncomfortable silence, "I am Dr. Forrestal, and I have an appointment with Dr. Hayek this early evening."

The young lady opened a large ledger of Dr. Hayek's appointments and found a note clipped to the top of the page. "Yes, Dr. Hayek has indicated he will meet with you at five o'clock this evening in the antiquarian lecture hall in the basement."

Benjamin's father retrieved his watch and responded, "Well, that will work out perfectly. My son and I were just on our way to the vault in the basement."

The receptionist then asked, "Do you have school identification?"

Conrad reached for his wallet and produced his alumni identification card. The receptionist looked at the identification, "Thank you, Dr. Forrestal. Will you please attach this visitor badge to your coat? Who is this young man next to you?"

"This is my son, Benjamin," Conrad stated proudly. "He

will be attending the university next year, and I wanted him to see the library before our meeting."

"Oh, that's nice," The receptionist stated robotically while retrieving and handing a visitor's pass to Benjamin.

A large sign on the wall just behind the lobby desk advised in bold letters:

PLEASE CHECK ALL FIREARMS AT THE LOBBY DESK.

"Do either one of you fine gentlemen possess a firearm on your person?" Father and son, without hesitation, reached behind their coats and retrieved their revolvers. The etiquette of the culture required that guns be unloaded before handing the firearms to the receptionist. Each weapon was carefully unloaded, the bullets stuffed into their pockets, and the firearms surrendered. The young woman smiled, accepted the guns, and returned a claim check, "May I help you with anything else?"

Benjamin blurted, "Why are you dressed like that? My mother wouldn't approve."

Another receptionist listening in on their conversation began laughing, "You're right. My mother would not approve of my uniform, either."

Then all the young ladies burst into laughter. Benjamin's father fought hard not to join the chorus. "Benjamin, these ladies are displaying futuristic fashion in keeping with the theme. Now come along to the basement, and you will be going back in time. Maybe you will feel better among the ancient manuscripts." Benjamin was still looking back at the reception desk as his father directed him across the room.

With some effort, Benjamin finally turned his attention to the direction he was being pulled. Adjacent to the elevator was a wall displaying hundreds of black and white photographs printed on paper, a chronicle of the library's construction. The photos began with a small group of dignitaries enacting the first symbolic effort: a minuscule shovel of dirt.

The next group of photographs depicted pouring the elaborate cement foundation, and the steel frame construction utilizing steam cranes lifting the massive I-beams into place. The last photographs in the sequence displayed the opening day ceremony just over a year before Benjamin's visit. Benjamin found the several hundred photographs fascinating. He slowed his pace to study the photographs until he felt his arm pulled along again toward the giant cylinder in the middle of the lobby.

"Benjamin, you will have plenty of time to study the library's construction after our discussion with Dr. Hayek, so please come along. I think you will find the elevator just as interesting."

Benjamin and his father approached the elevator. The metal door was polished, curved, and reflected a distorted image of the lobby. There were no visible hinges. Benjamin stood looking at the strange entrance when a low humming sound began to emanate from within the cylinder. The sound grew louder, and the floor began to vibrate, then ceased with a muffled thud. The door opened slowly, revealing a young lady dressed in the standard library uniform. A cluster of travelers stood behind her. She strained, as before, pulling and pushing the metal door into a thin crevice between the elevator room and the cylinder wall.

When the elevator room was completely open, the young lady stepped back and examined her effort. She pulled her ruffled jacket into propriety, put up her hand, and stated with authority, "Please do not enter or leave the elevator until the floors are aligned and level."

The lady walked back to the curved elevator side, and expertly adjusted the elevator position until the floor was perfectly even. When the feat was accomplished, the elevator operator announced, "It is now safe to exit the elevator room."

Benjamin and his father walked into the metal room, dodging the previous occupants escaping the small enclosure. The presence of the young lady was strangely comforting.

Like the ladies at the front desk, much of her legs were also bare. Benjamin tried not to look. The elevator operator grabbed a metal handle on the closed curved door and, with some effort, pulled the heavy door closed.

When the door was completely shut and locked, the disciplined operator stated, "Please do not go near the elevator opening until you are told it is safe to do so." It was very apparent the door was meant to secure the lobby from the elevator shaft. The small room remained opened and exposed the concrete lining of the elevator shaft. When the young lady was satisfied that all safety protocols had been scrupulously followed, the machinery was ready for transport.

The elevator operator put her hand on the control handle and asked, "What level would you like to be elevated too?"

Conrad answered, "We are going to the basement, please."

The elevator operator pulled the handle down, and with a vibrating drone, the elevator descended. Benjamin fell against the wall, compensating for a loss of balance—a reaction to the strange movement. The lobby door slowly floated upwards and disappeared above the elevator ceiling. The concrete lining of the elevator shaft flowed past the open door. After a brief period of time, the opening revealed the basement entrance at the floor of the elevator room, slowly ascending until the entrance and the elevator door aligned. A flick of the lady's wrist halted the elevator. The small room grew quiet.

The young lady stated, with a firm voice, "Please do not attempt to leave the elevator until I indicate it is safe to exit." Once again, the operator struggled to open the metal door to the basement floor. She grabbed a steel handle and leaned and pulled as hard as she could until the door opened a few feet. She continued her mission by pushing the door into the crevice. When she had completed her task, she straightened her ruffled jacket and returned to the control handle. She made some final adjustments, aligning the floor of the elevator with the basement floor.

When the door was aligned and safe, the elevator operator stated, "You may now exit the elevator."

Benjamin and his father walked into a glass hallway. On each side of the corridor behind glass walls, and illuminated by small bulbs descending from the ceiling, were antique books with scholarly annotations. A large sign on the door at the end of the hallway announced the rules to visitors:

- Please do not open the door until the elevator door has been shut.
- Please do not touch any of the antique books without wearing white gloves.
- No minors permitted beyond this door unless accompanied by a responsible parent or legal guardian.
- You will be under constant observation in this section of the library.
- If this entrance door is locked, the threshold of occupancy has been reached. You will be able to enter when the number of visitors is reduced.
- The antique collection of the University of London-derry is considered a state treasure. The theft or attempted theft or destruction or inappropriate handling of any book or any other object within the antique collection is punishable by death under Statutory section 43-2, section 8-d, Justifiable Homicide: Theft or Destruction of State Treasures.

Benjamin's father pushed through the glass door. Cool, dry air, and the musty smell of ancient manuscripts occupied the entry wall. The windowless basement seemed to go on for hundreds of feet in all directions. Benjamin and Conrad stepped into the vast library of antique manuscripts.

The basement contained bookshelves with thousands of leather-bound books. Benjamin looked up and was surprised to see a heavy steel grate just above his head instead of an ordinary ceiling. Several library personnel peered down and watched their every move. As they ventured into the collection, a member of the staff followed overhead. A row of small glass globes hung in a line between the steel bookcases holding the aged books. Each clear globe had a twisted wire emitting a soft glow and was held in place by thick black cords reaching up and disappearing through the metal grate. The sheer number of globes, numbering in the hundreds, provided sufficient light to facilitate the examination and reading of the book collection. The area occupied above the guards was dark. The bottom of their shoes and part of their legs were visible, illuminated by the lighted globes beneath their feet. Benjamin's attention shifted to the globes. His young mind struggled with the concept of artificial light generated by electricity.

A metal barrel at the end of each bookshelf contained hundreds of white cloth gloves. Above each barrel, a sign in large red letters bore another warning:

"Handling any book or manuscript in this collection without wearing white gloves is considered destruction of state treasure. Visitors must always wear white gloves. Be warned. Failure to heed this rule is punishable by death."

Benjamin and his father crowded around the first barrel containing dozens of white gloves of different sizes. When each hand was adequately covered, Benjamin stated, "I would hate to forget to wear gloves and pick up something in here and not be able to attend the university."

Conrad responded, "You are right. The library staff is deadly serious about the rules."

Father and son looked at each and started to laugh. Benjamin then repeated, "Yes, really deadly serious."

Benjamin's father stated, "We don't have time to explore all these ancient books at this visit. You will enjoy reading these books when you are studying at the university. I want to show you the vault before we meet with Dr. Hayek."

Benjamin's father directed Benjamin through the stacks of leather-covered books written hundreds of years ago. The sound of footsteps above them reminded the two that they were being continuously observed. After meandering the stacks, they found the vault enclosing the rare book repository. There was a large, printed sign above the entrance:

No admission without permission.

A heavy, chain-link fence surrounded the entire vault from floor to ceiling. The entrance was also made of chain-link and was locked. At the vault entrance sat a sentinel. He was an older, overweight gentleman with a disheveled appearance. His uncombed, white hair sailed in all directions. He was wearing the obligatory white gloves and a fine pair of wire spectacles. His countenance was ruddy, and he seemed to snort through a cauliflower nose while wholly absorbed in a large leather-bound book, *The Reign of the Fourth Estate and the Subjugation of the Individual: The Foundation of Totalitarian Rule.*

Conrad pulled his wallet from the inner pocket of his coat and took out a small, brass card with a series of stamped letters and numbers. The rotund guard, realizing a distinguished man and a young boy were standing in front of him, stood up, and carefully placed the book he was reading on a table next to him. Without saying a word, he took the brass card, walked over to a giant ledger, and searched for matching numbers and letters. A few minutes later, he returned with a small piece of rice paper in his hand and asked Benjamin's father for further identification. Dr. Forrestal produced several more documents. The elderly sentry scrutinized the documentations and asked Dr. Forrestal to recite his memorized code. Dr. Forrestal stated, "w-w-3-3-g-h-t." The sentry penned the code on the paper. After a pause, he took a key from his pocket and opened a steel box hanging on the wall just above the first ledger and retrieved a thick, grey volume of names and codes. He carefully examined the contents until he found a code matching the code just articulated. The sentry then popped the rice paper in his mouth and swallowed. The custodian of the sacred vault was satisfied. Dr. Forrestal had established his authenticity. He handed Benjamin's father his identifying documents. Without hesitation, the guard walked to the wired door, took out another key, and liberated the contents within. He said only, "You will be watched at all times."

Father and son walked into the room, and Benjamin asked, "How old are these books and scrolls?"

Benjamin's father replied, "The books and scrolls in this section are at least a thousand years old and many are much older. There are more than ten thousand precious books and scrolls in this section. Now Benjamin, let me show you the greatest of all the state treasures, the foundation document of our civilization, The Word, handwritten and five thousand years old."

Conrad held his son's hand as he quickly navigated a maze of bookshelves where ancient manuscripts waited for scholarly scrutiny. The air was thick with the musty scent of time. Some of the far more ancient tomes appeared more crudely bound with ill-trimmed pages, irregular and stained, protruding from leather bindings. Other books seemed to be collapsing and were held together by acid-free string wrapped around the deteriorating leather binding. As Benjamin and his father approached their destination, the appearance of the ancient manuscripts changed from leather-bound books to rolled up scrolls. Metallic footsteps from above shadowed their every move. Benjamin wondered if a misstep on his part might be perceived as a desecration of the ancient documents resulting in the swift blast of a heavy pistol from the all-seeing library guards. Benjamin dismissed the morbid thought when he realized that such an execution would undoubtedly adulterate many ancient manuscripts with his blood and skull fragments. No – such retribution for the desecration of the aged collection would be accomplished in a far cleaner manner somewhere outside the library. Benjamin found some solace knowing he would surely survive long enough for his mother to rescue him somehow.

Benjamin's father, in a hushed tone, stated, "Benjamin, this is it."

With a final turn at the end of a row of ancient scrolls, Benjamin came to a small, dimly lit area. A sizable, open steel door, supported by massive metallic hinges, paralleled the concrete walls. Above the entryway, a backlit sign cast an eerie glow proclaiming:

THE   FOUNDATION   MANUSCRIPT   OF CIVILIZATION: THE WORD

Placards of dire warnings and admonitions for misbehavior flanked the entrance. Educational materials were also prominently displayed detailing the room's contents. Benjamin was blind to various posters. He was not aware of anything but what was straight ahead of him. Conrad would serve as a guide and educator for the exhibit.

Benjamin was spellbound by the presence of the holy of holies, the actual manuscript of The Word. As he entered the display room, he observed a massive glass display case. The lighting was extremely dim with a line of small globes emitting faint yellow light. When his eyes adjusted to the darkness, he was able to see a glass mausoleum at least twenty feet long and five feet tall. The glass was several inches thick and quite formidable. The case protected the collection of large books covered with creamy lambskin. The ancient books sat on glass shelves. The spine of each book faced the observer and revealed an ancient numeric expression written in Progue. Each book was at least three feet tall and nine or ten inches thick. The book covers appeared to be constructed of several layers of lambskin pressed and glued together. On top of each book spine The Word was crudely penned. As Benjamin leaned closer, he saw four open volumes of The Word on the display's bottom shelf. Each book was opened to the title page and table of contents. Benjamin could easily read the ancient script summarizing the contents. He trembled reading each word written by the ancient educators, the Elders.

"Father, I didn't realize the book was made of so many

volumes," Benjamin exclaimed.

Conrad responded, "Benjamin, remember the Elder scribe was writing on lambskin, which is much thicker than paper. The printing press had not been invented. The Word is one book made up of twenty-seven individual volumes. Modern printing of The Word utilizes very thin paper and small print. The book of ancient wisdom is almost four inches thick in the most current publications. Most people also fail to realize that nearly a third of The Word is not printed in contemporary editions. These sections were inappropriately labeled the Apocrypha. Apocryphal means of questionable authenticity.

"As you know, The Word is five thousand years old. Several hundred years after the creation of The Word, in a period which modern scholars refer to as the dark ages, much of the civilization and culture of the Elders was inexplicably lost. It was during these dark times that a sect of skeptical scholars advocated the last third of The Word was false teachings propagated by heretics motivated to adulterate the Elders' teaching as hubris. The last third of The Word contained hundreds of pages filled with obtuse proverbs and unintelligible parables. The Apocrypha's real significance has only now been partially translated by modern scholars. As you become more familiar with these ancient texts, you will gain a better understanding of the many mysteries that you have been wondering about this world."

Benjamin turned and peered at his father in the dimly lit room, "What are you saying, father?

"All I am saying, Benjamin, is that you will learn a great deal at this university. That is why we are meeting with Dr. Hayek, to talk about furthering your education."

Benjamin responded, "All my life, I have studied The Word, and I had no idea about all of this. The entire thing seems so strange."

Benjamin leaned closer to the thick glass and began reading the chapter title of one of the open volumes aloud, *Volume 6, Chapter 4, The Origin of the Species: Natural Selection and the Evolution of the Human Mind.* The light was far too dim for Benjamin to read the small text under the title, but Benjamin was remarkably familiar with the content, having read this section several times. Moving down the glass case, Benjamin read the title page from the next text, *Volume 5, Chapter 2, The Heliocentric Planetary System and the Philosophical Implications of Non-Centricity.* Benjamin could not imagine how anyone thought our world was the center of the universe and the planetary system. Benjamin thought, how lost early humanity must have been before the enlightenment of the Elders. The next chapter he read, *Volume 8, Chapter 16, The Discontinuous Universe and the Effect of Observation on the Establishment of Reality.* Benjamin could never understand the ideas expressed in this chapter of The Word. Father and son had spent many hours discussing the physics of the subatomic scale. Benjamin was hopelessly lost with the concepts and resolved to understand the issue better when he attended the university. The last open chapter on display was by far the most practical and imminently relevant body of knowledge elucidated by the Elders. The chapter title page read, *Volume 1, Chapter 1, The Absolute Corruptive Nature of Centralized Government and the Rise of Individualism, the Necessity of Unconditional Liberty and Personal Responsibility.*

"Father," Benjamin began, "this chapter of The Word is the basis of our society in Kenton. I cannot imagine living in a society based on anything other than total freedom. We are lucky fate has brought us the teachings of the Elders to Kenton, and this wonderful state of being."

Conrad returned, "We are fortunate. The other states in this world have governments that hold their citizens directly or indirectly in disdain. We are fortunate, Benjamin, that we live in a free state."

Benjamin's father retrieved his watch and squinted to read the dial in the dim light. He put his watch directly under one of the faint glass globes above the display case and announced, "The time has come for you to meet Dr. Hayek, Benjamin."

Benjamin and his father left the exhibit. Conrad once again guided his son through dozens of metal bookcases and hundreds of ancient documents. Within a few minutes, they stood in front of a metal fire door in a dimly lit corner of the rare book collection. To Benjamin's surprise, his father pulled out a key attached to his gold watch chain and opened the door. The narrow hallway was completely dark. At the end of the hall, Benjamin could see a faint outline of another door. These gaps of light directed them toward their destination. Benjamin did not say a word as his father entered the corridor to lead him through the darkness. The door behind them was closed and locked, leaving them only the faint outline as guidance. They proceeded down the hall, feeling the wall with their hands.

Benjamin's father stopped when they reached the door and stated, "This is where we will speak to Dr. Hayek, in the auditorium on the other side of this door." With that said, Conrad opened the unlocked door to reveal a lecture hall with several hundred leather theater seats in a semicircle facing a slightly raised stage. A large desk was center stage and a huge blackboard behind the desk formed the backdrop facing the intended audience. The seating area was a few short steps from the stage. The rear seats in the lecture hall were located nearly twenty feet above the front row. Dozens of gas lights in three distinct rows illuminated the room. In stark contrast to the concrete walls of the rare book section of the library, the lecture hall was rich in polished mahogany and walnut woods.

Father and son entered the lecture hall at the top row. Benjamin looked down at the stage before him. A thin, studious man leaned against the wooden desk. He seemed lost in thought, patiently waiting for his guests to arrive. He appeared to be in his late forties or early fifties. He wore a dark suit with a dark vest and a crisp, white shirt. His tie was the style of a thin scarf hanging down the front of his shirt then disappearing under his vest. As Benjamin carefully descended the many steps, mindful not to misstep with his steel brace, he could see a pair of wire glasses over the intense eyes of the man he was about to meet. When Benjamin and Conrad reached the bottom of the stairs and approached the stage, the man presented a slight smile and began to walk toward them.

Conrad introduced Dr. Hayek to his son.

"Dr. Hayek, I am proud to introduce you to my son, Benjamin Walker. Benjamin, this is Dr. Hayek."

Dr. Hayek offered his hand and smiled, "Mr. Walker, I have heard a great deal about you from your father. I am happy to meet you. We have much to speak of."

Benjamin quickly removed his white gloves, grasped the professor's hand, and said, "I am glad to meet you, sir. My father has been a little mysterious about this meeting, and my father is usually a very deliberate man, so I must confess I am a little apprehensive."

"Indeed, Mr. Walker. Please, will both of you have a seat so we may begin our discussion?" Dr. Hayek motioned toward the front row seats. He waited until his guests sat, then began to speak of things that would change Benjamin's life.

"Well, Mr. Walker, may I begin by congratulating you. It would seem you passed your certified public accountant exam with a perfect score," Dr. Hayek stated while turning to retrieve Benjamin's essay exam booklet from the desk. "Roger Smith asked me to secure your permission to publish your answers so future candidates will have a better understanding of what kind of standards the exam board expects from potential accountants."

Benjamin attempted to comprehend what Dr. Hayek had said. "Sir, did you just say I passed the exam? That's wonderful! What a relief. Of course, he may use my examination answers any way he wishes. I am so relieved. My mother had high expectations of me. How was the exam evaluated so fast?"

"Well, Mr. Walker, I asked Roger Smith if the board of examiners would grade your examination after completing the testing procedures. The excellent results of your efforts have a bearing on the conversation we are about to have concerning your future. You must be proud of your achievement," Dr. Hayek stated without emotion.

"Mother hired the best tutors. My mother is very desirous of a successful education for me," Benjamin explained.

"Indeed, Mr. Walker, it would seem so," Dr. Hayek responded. "Before we begin our conversation, there is the matter of the blood oath of confidentiality concerning the issues we will discuss today. I must secure this from you before we continue."

"I do not understand. For what purpose would I need to enter into such a solemn agreement? Besides, I am a minor and legally unable to enter such a contract," Benjamin said, relying on his newly acquired knowledge obtained while preparing for his just-completed examination. He was realizing this was not going to be a simple orientation meeting for a future university student.

Benjamin's father reached over and put his hand on his son's arm, "Benjamin, all of this will make sense in a few minutes. I am asking you to trust me on this. I am prepared to sign an emancipation of a minor petition for the Kent family court so you will become a minor having the same legal rights and responsibilities as an adult. I have already prepared the document to be notarized."

A bewildered Benjamin looked at his father, "Does mother know about all of this? Does she approve?"

"Your mother knows nothing about any of this. She believes the reason for your visit to the university was solely to pass the accountant exam and tour the university. Benjamin, I know you, and I know you will want to know what Dr. Hayek is about to reveal. I ask that you sign and accept your emancipation from childhood and sign the blood oath."

"Well, father, more mysterious. And you know I love a good mystery. I think . . ." Benjamin hesitated. He felt as if he stood before a precipice and was being asked to take a leap of faith. "I will do anything you ask of me. I trust you completely, you know that" Benjamin stated, knowing his father always had his best interest in mind.

Dr. Hayek continued, "Benjamin, what we will talk about must be kept in the strictest confidence. I must insist you must accept the gravity of the commitment I am asking of you."

Dr. Hayek walked across the auditorium floor to a door at the side of the room. Opening the door, Dr. Hayek spoke to someone in the next room, then a middle-aged woman entered the auditorium and walked to the stage. She was dressed in conservative attire and carried a clumsy, black attaché case. She was there for business. Dr. Hayek accompanied Mrs. Higgs to the desk.

She presented an emotionless glare toward the audience of two and stated, "My name is Mrs. Higgs, and I am a certified notary and an officer of the Superior Court of Kent. I understand, Dr. Forrestal, you require a witness for the purpose of emancipating your son. If this is correct, please step forward to have the emancipation document you have completed reviewed and notarized."

Dr. Forrestal stood, walked to the stage, and placed the emancipation document on the desk. Mrs. Higgs carefully reviewed the document and then stated in monotone, "Dr. Forrestal, by affixing your signature on the emancipation document, your son will be legally an adult with all the responsibilities and privileges of that legal status. Do you wish to emancipate your son at this time?"

Conrad stated, "Yes, I do."

Mrs. Higgs then, in a terse voice, "Does Master Walker have the means to provide for food, clothing, and shelter, a source of income?"

Dr. Forrestal returned, "My son is qualified to seek gainful employment, having completed the examination for certified public accountants, and a blood oath signed by an adult is required for future employment. In addition, a banking account in Benjamin Walker's name has been opened at the Londonderry Commerce Bank with an account balance of two-hundred-thousand dollars. He has the maturity to manage the essential affairs of life."

Mrs. Higgs looked at Benjamin sitting a few feet away and asked, "Very well. Benjamin Walker, do you accept this change in legal status?"

Benjamin was surprised by his father's statement and, with some difficulty, he quietly responded, "I do."

"Dr. Forrestal, will you please affix your signature on the document here?" Mrs. Higgs requested, pointing at the appropriate location for Dr. Forrestal to sign.

Dr. Forrestal signed the document, and Mrs. Higgs pulled a notary stamp from her black case and embossed the superior court seal on the document. Mrs. Higgs completed the procedure by pulling a grey ledger from her case and requesting that Dr. Forrestal once again affix his signature at the appropriate place in the ledger. After Dr. Forrestal's signature, Mrs. Higgs signed and dated the ledger.

Mrs. Higgs then addressed Dr. Forrestal, "This document of the emancipation of Benjamin Walker will be recorded at the court's convenience with the county of records no later than thirty court days from this date. Mr. Walker, your legal status, currently, is that of an adult. Dr. Hayek, I understand you have a blood oath for Mr. Walker to sign?"

Dr. Hayek placed a promissory note of confidentiality in triplicate for Benjamin Walker's signature on the desk in front of Mrs. Higgs. Mrs. Higgs reviewed the documents and looked up at Benjamin, "Mr. Walker, Dr. Hayek has presented for notarization a blood oath requiring your signature, which stipulates upon becoming a signatory party to a contract of confidentiality with the organization represented by Dr. Hayek . . ." Mrs. Higgs paused briefly before continuing. "Mr. Walker, you will forfeit your life if you should breach confidentiality directly, indirectly, or implied, concerning any information provided to you in the verbal or written discourse Dr. Hayek will initiate with you today."

Mrs. Higgs paused, then restated, "This includes any communication conveyed by Dr. Hayek or his associates of the said organization should deem necessary to you in verbal or in written discourse. This blood oath, when entered, is irreparable and will exist in effect in perpetuity. This is a solemn agreement of the highest order, and I say again, is irrevocable for now and all future time. Benjamin Walker, you must enter into the said agreement with sufficient due diligence required for such an ominous resolution of breach. Mr. Walker, what say you to this contract?"

Benjamin took a deep breath, wondering, What say I? What am I getting into? I have a few thousand questions. What information? What organization and what associates? He stood up, walked to the desk so he could view the document, looked down, and asked only, "Where do I sign?" He was putting his complete trust in his father's judgment.

Mrs. Higgs motioned to the proper location, and Benjamin Walker affixed his signature on the line indicated on all three contracts. Mrs. Higgs requested his signature in her notary ledger book, and upon completion, Mrs. Higgs signed her name in the ledger and wrote the date. She then embossed the superior court seal to the three contracts and placed one document into her black case. Mrs. Higgs handed one copy to Dr. Hayek and one to Benjamin.

She then stated, "The terms of this contract of confidentiality are now in effect. This contract of confidentiality will be recorded at the convenience of the court with the county of Kent public records no later than thirty court days from this date." She paused for a few seconds and looked at Benjamin, "I hope you never talk in your sleep."

Benjamin jokingly responded, "I will never marry."

Mrs. Higgs responded without emotion, "I think that would be best."

With that, Mrs. Higgs turned and exited. Benjamin's father put his arm around his son and said, "All of this will make sense in a few moments."

Benjamin replied while father and son returned to their seats, "I know, father, you have a good reason for all of this. I will always trust you with my life. You know that."

Dr. Hayek walked to the center stage in front of the desk

and looked down at Benjamin, "Mr. Walker, please forgive me for all the dramatics. I cannot stress the importance of absolute secrecy concerning the subject matter and the nature of the organization we will be discussing. If you should divulge any information I am about to share with you, you will be killed. The bylaws of this organization will require . . ." Dr. Hayek stared straight into Benjamin's eyes, "Your father, who sponsored you, will have the responsibility of taking your life or will forfeit his. Of course, the taking of your life would fall to another member, perhaps the responsibility would fall to me, and I will not hesitate. I would extinguish your life at the first opportunity. Benjamin, you must decide now. Do you wish to continue?"

Benjamin turned and looked to his father with the countenance of a fearful child. His father gave a determined nod. Benjamin turned from his father and peered at Dr. Hayek, held his breath, and sternly proclaimed, "I am my father's son. My life is his."

"Very well," Dr. Hayek stated firmly. "Mr. Walker, your father, and the membership committee have nominated you and have agreed to admit you into the Order of the Supplicants. This order is made up of several thousand exceptional individuals representing many diverse fields of knowledge and expertise. The Supplicants are scientists, philosophers, educators, linguists, mathematicians, and now, after you have accepted our offer, the youngest CPA in the history of Kenton. The Order of the Supplicants is dedicated to unraveling knowledge and seeking the truth in all things. We humbly seek the answers for the most basic of questions: who we are, why we are placed here, and what must we do to fulfill our biological and ethical imperative.

"Forgive me, Mr. Walker, being tedious with the obvious. Still, I want to remind you of a few basic facts that you may not have thought about for a while."

Dr. Hayek walked to the wall gas valve and decreased the light in the auditorium and pulled down a reflective sheet from above the stage. A magic lantern sat in the center of the stage on a small table. Dr. Hayek lit a kerosene lamp inside the lantern and a bright circle of light projected onto the screen. Dr. Hayek slipped a glass slide into the projector. On the slide was a hand-painted artist's rendition of the geographic locations of the five independent states of Deseret. Dr. Hayek walked to the screen with a long cue pointer and began his lesson: "These are the five individual states on our planet: the far northern state is Patagonia, the next state is Krem, next Liberty, then, of course, our state, Kenton, and on the extreme south, Kuttor. All five states have the exact square mileage, all five states have equal access to the Eastern Sea, and as near as we can tell all five states have equal amounts of natural resources. The exception is Kenton, now that we have begun the colonization of Newhopeland. I think you would agree the basic similarity of these five states geographically, possessing exactly the same availability of natural resources is too great to be a coincidence. Does it not seem somewhat contrived?"

Dr. Hayek continued his lesson by removing the glass slide of the states of Deseret, and replaced it with another, an artist's rendition of the solar system. "Mr. Walker, I am sure you are familiar with this drawing of the four planets of the inner solar system. The first two planets nearest the sun have no importance to our discussion today."

Dr. Hayek pointed his cue at the third planet from the sun, "This, Mr. Walker, this is the subject of our interest today. Oceania, a world mostly covered by water, and the large moon, Mortilus, orbiting it."

Dr. Hayek moved the cue to the next planet, fourth from the sun and bright red, "This is our world, Deseret. Mr. Walker, our planet is a desert world, and appropriately called Deseret. Please keep these basic facts in mind. Oceania, the third planet from the sun and the nearest planet to our world – Deseret."

Dr. Hayek briefly stared at the projection of the two worlds towering above him before turning the gas valve open and brightening the room. The magic lantern was turned off and the cue stick put away. The time had come for Benjamin's lessons. "Mr. Walker, this is the end of your childhood. From your earliest memories, you were taught that five thousand years ago, in a golden age of knowledge and enlightenment, a small group of the wisest of men, the Elders, perhaps on a beautiful spring day beneath a golden sun, stood around a table dictating to a scribe the pinnacle of human knowledge concerning science, ethics, and government. Their effort was the foundation document of our civilization, The Word. Years after The Word was written, humanity fell into disrepair, and so began the age of darkness, requiring our fathers and our father's fathers, and all the others before them to crawl back from the abyss. Eighteen hundred and ninety-five years ago, near a small hamlet named Kenton, forty miles from the Eastern Sea, the founders of our state, using the wisdom from The Word, created the most sophisticated organized state in the world dedicated to the proposition that society cannot be successful without absolute freedom for every citizen of the state. So began our modern calendar, and so began the State of Kenton."

Dr. Hayek paused to collect his thoughts before proceeding, "Mr. Walker, you must prepare yourself for a different perspective. I will be direct. There was never an age of enlightenment or a collection of wise scholars memorializing the evolved wisdom of earlier generations. Mr. Walker, the creation of The Word by ancient wise men is a myth. There was never an age of enlightenment. There are no ruins of ancient cities. No evidence of an early civilization in this world. The sophisticated concepts found in The Word concerning the creation of the universe, the laws that keep the planets in their orbit and all the other knowledge, both worldly and philosophical, did not originate on this planet.

"Mr. Walker everything you know, the language you speak, the ethics you follow, the tenets of your society all originated from our neighboring planet Oceania and were brought to Deseret over six thousand years ago by a spacefaring race of beings that colonized this world and populated the planet with all the various forms of life, including, at some point, us. Early in human history, thousands of years before the five states of Deseret were organized, five unique tribes of humans were placed in different geographical areas of the world to evolve into modern societies. We now know our progenitors from Oceania gave each of these early tribes a unique language and written foundation documents. Kenton had the honor to receive The Word, the foundation document of our society. Our tribe would form the State of Kenton based on the teaching within The Word. Each of the other literate states would evolve an intrinsically unique set of defining creeds based on their foundation documents. The exception, of course, was Patagonia, which has no written language and remains, even today, a primitive hunter-gatherer tribal culture."

Benjamin sat in cold silence. How could anyone accept what he was being told? What he was experiencing had a dream-like quality. How he wished to be home studying or riding his horse—how much simpler the world would seem. If he accepted what he was being told, his world had come to an end. Benjamin turned to his father.

"Father, I am frightened."

Dr. Hayek paused and looked at Dr. Forrestal, "Dr. Forrestal?"

"Give my son a moment. This is a great deal to comprehend."

Benjamin realized he was going through shock. He felt cold and clammy. His deformed leg began twitching and tapping a soft rap on the oak floor, creating an audible metallic rattle. Benjamin took a full moment to gather his faculties, and with a deep breath, Benjamin, in the calmest and steadiest voice he could muster, "Dr. Hayek, this is my fate."

"Very well, Mr. Walker, the lesson will continue. Please feel free to stop me at any time if you should need to ask a question. I realize this is a bit much. Try and understand how difficult this would be for the general population without proper preparation. We will spend some time on the issue of societal exposure at a future time. As a member of the order, your views on this topic will be considered." Dr. Hayek was concerned this discussion was premature for the order's newest member.

Benjamin responded, struggling to contain his fears, "How could you have come to such an extraordinary conclusion of otherworldly involvement?"

Dr. Hayek began, "The answer to that question is somewhat complex. Mr. Walker, your father, has indicated to me you have been aware of the paradox that coal and petroleum exist on this planet where there is no evidence of life on Deseret earlier than six thousand years. The entire planet has been explored, and ice core samples have been taken at the poles with the same results. The conclusion is inescapable. Life appeared for the first time on Deseret six thousand years ago, wholly evolved. The Word explains in detail how the evolution of life occurs. The evolution of complex life forms takes millions of years of natural selection. The only evidence of Deseret's ancient life is large amounts of coal and petroleum deposits, which require millions of years to form from vast amounts of biomass. Geologists and chemists from this university have been studying coal beds for years and came to the startling conclusion: the coal and petroleum did not originate on this planet. These vast quarries containing fossil fuel deposits were dug with sophisticated machinery and deliberately buried on this planet between fifteen to sixteen thousand years ago. You may, of course, read the confidential reports and conclusions generated by the geological research teams at your convenience."

Benjamin responded, "Deliberately buried. Why Oceania?"

Dr. Hayek continued, "Yes. Why Oceania? There are some obvious reasons why Oceania would be our first choice of otherworldly involvement and has been the focus of our interest for a great deal of time. Oceania is the closest planet to Deseret in our planetary system. The planet has an atmosphere similar to ours. Oceania undergoes seasonal shifts of color, which suggest an abundance of plant life. Every two years, when the planet is at opposition—that is when Oceania is the closest to Deseret in orbit—astronomers using the Porter 40-inch refractor telescope have produced photographic evidence of very straight, artificial lines crossing some of the more significant landmasses, suggesting roads or canals. Photographs have also been taken during the dark phase of Oceania, revealing a number of these lines are illuminated with what appears to be some form of artificial light. These lines culminate in a large cluster of lights which we think may well be large cities."

Dr. Hayek walked over to the desk, picked up a folder marked "Confidential" containing photographs of Oceania, walked over to Benjamin, and handed him the photographic evidence.

Benjamin and his father studied the telescopic images of Oceania.

"Dr. Hayek, these photographs seem to show something like vast road systems outlined in lights and illuminated cities. Why have I never heard of these discoveries? I have studied a great deal about our planetary system. I don't even recall any speculation of advanced life on Oceania," Benjamin asked, mesmerized by the images of Oceania.

"The Order of the Supplicants suppressed this photographic evidence of intelligent life on Oceania. Of course, the astronomers involved in this research were members of the order. A few of those astronomers attempted to disseminate these findings hidden from the scientific community and, as a result, they were put to death," Dr. Hayek answered Benjamin in a cold, objective manner.

Dr. Hayek continued, "The sister planet orbiting Oceania, Mortalis, the dead world, also reveals some startling evidence of an advanced civilization. For over forty years, astronomers at Porter have taken a series of photographs of Mortalis. In the area labeled the grey field, in the third quadrant designated 3-B, there appears to be a large, open-pit mining operation of some sort in the shape of a vast square excavation."

Dr. Hayek retrieved another folder from the desk, also marked "Confidential," and again handed the evidence to Benjamin and his father. Dr. Hayek pointed to the region of interest.

"If you start your examination with the photograph designated 1828 Opposition, and then compare the next photograph designated 1830 Opposition, you will see the square region has grown about ten percent in size. Now comparing the photographic records with the following three oppositions, you will see the amazing growth of the excavation. The astronomers at Porter estimate the area is approximately two thousand square miles. The advanced technology exhibited on Mortalis would be the same kind of technological sophistication necessary to place large coal and oil deposits in our world."

Benjamin stared at the photographs, spellbound and consumed with awe and trepidation. Dr. Hayek said, returning to the desk on the stage, "There is something else, Mr. Walker. We have reason to believe we are under constant observation by these beings."

Benjamin looked at Dr. Hayek with a bit of angst, "What makes you think that?"

"Several small objects have been discovered in a near-perfect circular orbit about a thousand miles from our planet's surface. For many years, the prevailing scientific opinion was that these objects were meteors or small asteroids captured by the gravity of our planet, and their near-perfect circular orbits were just random coincidence. Several years ago, astronomers at the Porter observatory, using a wide-field camera, were methodically photographing the entire night sky in preparation for a comprehensive star catalogue. While photographing the night sky, the astronomers discovered three satellites over the equator that remained in the same location without moving. Their orbit precisely matched the rotation of Deseret."

Dr. Hayek walked to the blackboard and drew a large circle representing Deseret and three small circles representing the satellites. Dr. Hayek drew a straight line to each satellite, forming a perfect equilateral triangle. "Mr. Walker, these three satellites are in perfect orbit over the equator to remain stationary in the sky, are in exactly the same orbit, and are evenly spaced. This cannot be an accident of nature. These satellites orbiting our planet demonstrate intelligent intent. We have hypothesized, based on information we have obtained from encrypted information concealed within The Word, that these synchronized satellites appear to be relay satellites orbiting and observing Deseret. We believe the satellites use electricity or, more precisely, electromagnetic energy, to communicate with one another and send information back to Oceania. When the time is right, you will learn more about electromagnetic energy. This is not the time. I think it would be a fair assumption we are under constant observation."

Benjamin managed to respond, trying to appear in control of his emotions, "Now, I understand how disconcerting these observations would be to the people in Kenton. We have no real understanding of Oceania. What you are saying is truly frightening. But what do you mean by encrypted information?"

"Mr. Walker, we will speak of secret codes in time. Be patient," Dr. Hayek pressed. "There is something else, Mr. Walker, you need to realize. Our yearly calendar was created for us by the authors of The Word and matches the yearly orbit of Oceania around the sun, not Deseret. Our months equals one orbit of Mortalis around Oceania. Our day is the same as Oceania, twenty-four hours, but our orbit requires two of Oceania's years to complete one orbit around our star. Using Oceania's orbit as a reference for our calendar year is integral to the alternating period of the summer and winter seasons we experience from year to year. We believe the authors of The Word selected this temporal measure for our calendar year in order to draw our attention to their world."

Benjamin returned, "We just accepted our calendar like everything else. We trusted the wisdom of the Elders. I don't know what to think."

Dr. Hayek crossed his arms and leaned back on his heels, proclaimed in a loud firm voice, "What to think? Mr. Walker, you are free and expected to think critically. I am not here to stir your childish fears. Knowledge is power, and you have been invited to join us so you may use your unique intellect to facilitate our understanding of all things mysterious and difficult. Mr. Walker, are you ready for the next revelation?"

"My mind is open, Dr. Hayek," Benjamin returned.

"Very well, Mr. Walker, let us continue." Dr. Hayek began the next chapter in Benjamin's education, "Let us turn our attention to the other four literate states on Deseret . Each autonomous state has a unique foundational document. We know from our archaeological research and historical records that each state on the planet originated at the same time, approximately two hundred years in the past. Each of these states with written foundation documents have unique creeds and governance paradigms, and a unique mythos as to the origin of those documents. Mr. Walker, consider the ethos of each state.

"Kuttor, a repressive theocracy ruled by religious fanatics based supposedly on the written teachings of the Xue or The Way Giver. The teaching of their holy book proclaims that human existence is to surrender the self to the mystical obedience to the god-head Row."

"The state of Krem, a totalitarian regime based on the writings of Songy, extols the belief that individualism is nonexistent. The central purpose of Krem's government is to control every aspect of every member of that state. The role of each subject is to exist and function for the benefit of the collective.

"The next organized state is the Democratic Republic of Liberty, a cynical sham democracy where corrupt politicians are purchased and bribed by corporate elites and special interests and largess is distributed to a dependent populace while productive members of society are subjected to ruinous taxation and fiscal uncertainty. This government is allegedly based on the Freedom Papers and a constitution written by rebellious patriots that deposed monarchical rule.

"Only in the State of Kenton, based on the teaching of The Word can we find a truly free society. In Kenton, the central government is nonexistent. The economy is based on free-market principles, and individuals are empowered with absolute liberty, even in matters of life and death. The teachings of The Word are the foundation of a society that promulgates absolute freedom, innovation, and prosperity.

"The state of Patagonia, without literacy, has remained a primitive hunter-gatherer culture.

"Mr. Walker, why would an advanced civilization from another world create such diverse forms of governance at the same time on Deseret?"

Benjamin was careful with his response: "Dr. Hayek, might we assume this is some form of experiment on a planetary scale to determine the most advantageous society, with the state of Patagonia, without a written language, representing the control for comparison?"

"Well, Mr. Walker, at one time, a number of individuals in the order promoted such a hypothesis," Dr. Hayek continued. "After further translation and evaluation of a hidden code within The Word, we have determined the diverse societies of this world were created as an object lesson for our edification. Kenton is the most successful, prosperous, and technologically advanced civilization in the world—the preferred choice of the enlightened, a way of life that promotes self-actualization and human progress. How many millennia of societal evolutions must have occurred on Oceania before that ancient civilization realized the most advantageous society is one that values individual freedom above all else and recognizes the inherent wisdom and profound sense of justice within each human being? The Word gives us a clear warning of the inimical nature of centralized governance regardless of the manifest form. This is the pronounced lesson given to us from the true Elders from another world. The other forms of government on this planet are the road to serfdom. In time, all the various nations in our world will be absorbed into Kenton by choice. By this process, a one-world society will evolve in a most stable and accepting manner.

"Please speak to me of secret codes," Benjamin asked, trying to assimilate what he was learning.

Dr. Hayek continued, "Ten decades ago, a group of linguistic scholars from the university studied the syntax and diction of the writings of The Word. Those scholars discovered in the word choice and sentence structure a hidden language. The Word contained an encrypted second book—a book within a book. The first message discovered was a simple repeating sentence. The sentence was detected by drawing a diagonal line from the top right corner of the first page to the bottom left corner. The letters the lines passed through spelled a simple repeating sentence, "look within." The inhabitants of Oceania were talking to us using an encrypted code embedded in the text of the first book given to us at the beginning of our civilization. Cryptographers and mathematicians from the university began the long process of deciphering the code. The encryption was initially simple to solve, but the decryption of the code grew more difficult as the cryptographers extracted increasingly more amounts of knowledge. Realizing the societal implications, a decision was made not to release their findings directly. These first scholars were the founding members of the Order of Supplicants."

"What knowledge?" an anxious Benjamin asked.

"The preamble of the deciphered code went into great detail. The beings of Oceania created the five states of Deseret for our edification so that we might realize an accelerated social evolution," Dr. Hayek answered, pausing for a moment in thought, and then continued. "In addition, The Word contains an amazing amount of scientific information. This very library, this fantastic architectural achievement, the largest building in the world made with advanced metallurgy and sophisticated engineering, was derived from information obtained from the hidden code. The creation of electric motors and electric generators, all our newly acquired under-standing of electromagnetic energy was taught to the order, and thus to the world, from the efforts of cryptographers continuously decrypting the hidden knowledge from within The Word. The decrypted code also contained hundreds of futuristic images. The unique interior of the lobby of this library, and even the staff uniforms, was obtained from The Word. Mr. Walker, The Word contains entirely new technol-ogies and new fields of science previously unknown to our civilization. In time, much more will be revealed to you as you continue to participate in the order's activity."

Benjamin contemplated the revelations Dr. Hayek had shared.

Dr. Hayek continued, "Something else I will share with you tonight, Mr. Walker. The decrypted code was clear. The construction of this library was our first message to the inhabitants of Oceania. The creation of this library will proclaim our first few steps in a much greater journey. Oceania will know we have awoken."

Benjamin reached over and took his father's hand, "Did you know, father?"

"Yes, what you have learned tonight and much more," Conrad answered. "Now your tutors are from another world. This is your first day of school."

Benjamin asked, "What do you expect from Oceania when they receive this message made of steel and glass, and how will all this new knowledge from The Word be revealed to the world?"

"Mr. Walker, to your first question, we are simply not sure what to expect from the authors of The Word. We don't know what, if any, their response will be. To the latter question: we must be cautious how we conduct ourselves sharing what we have discovered. The mental hygiene of the citizens of our state, and those of other states on Deseret, must be taken into consideration. We don't know—I mean, we must be careful not to undermine the ethos of the world without proper preparation and education. Without thorough conditioning, we may cause the world to slip into chaos, disarray, disorientation, even violence. We are not sure."

For the first time, Dr. Hayek seemed to lose his professorial demeanor. His expression became lost within his thoughts. His gaze was distant, and his voice trailed off into a whisper. For the first time, Benjamin felt the burden of the order and realized why the blood oath was so necessary.

"Dr. Hayek," Benjamin spoke in a hushed tone. "Is the Raven real? I mean, does The Word teach us all we believe in is just a myth? The afterlife, a heart so pure as to be light as the feather, so that we—"

"Benjamin," Dr. Hayek interrupted, "The true Elders from our sister world who taught us so much of the universe, the intricacies of the atom, the geometry of the stars and the meaning of freedom, also revealed to us the Raven. The Raven is the physical manifestation of the divine in our world—the bridge between the Creator of the universe and us. The Raven is real, and so is the divine force that sets all things in motion. Benjamin, the Raven is real. So saith The Word."

"So saith The Word," father and son repeated.

Benjamin was greatly relieved hearing the professor's words. This was the first comforting thought all evening. Conrad looked at his watch, then interrupted.

"Benjamin, we must bring this discussion to an end. The hour is upon us, and we will miss the train if we do not leave soon. Dr. Hayek, I must thank you and the order for giving so much trust to my son and me, and I sincerely appreciate the honor the order has bestowed on my son. I am sure he will not disappoint and will spend the rest of his life constructively participating with members of the organization."

"Yes," Benjamin continued, "I am deeply moved and honored by the confidence conferred to me by the Order of the Supplicants, and I pledge my life to be a meaningful and active member."

Dr. Hayek nodded with approval.

"Mr. Walker, when the time is right, much more of the

organization and the knowledge gained from the beings from Oceania will be shared. You were provided more information than most new members of the order out of deference for your father. He believes in you, and so do I. When the time is right, you will be contacted with a time and place for our next meeting, where you will be introduced to several other members of the Supplicants. They will share with you some of their findings revealed by The Word. Until then, please excuse me."

Benjamin asked one last question, "What do the beings on Oceania look like?"

Dr. Hayek peered at Benjamin, then stated, "In time . . . in time."

With that, Dr. Hayek walked over to Benjamin, who stood and offered his hand. Benjamin took Dr. Hayek's hand, and two men, without words, communicated a bond between them. Dr. Hayek shook Dr. Forrestal's hand, returned the photographs to their large yellow envelopes, and walked away, disappearing through the oak doors on the side of the stage. Benjamin and his father were alone in the lecture hall with only the hiss of the gas lights invading the silence.

"Father," Benjamin questioned, "if we believe in the inherent wisdom of each individual, are we not hypocrites by the order's secret nature?"

Benjamin's father paused, then stated, "Other members of the Order have voiced similar concerns. In time, I think you will join that chorus within the organization. The Order as a whole, at this time, believes Kenton must maintain intellectual and technological superiority to ensure the social stability of the world. Until we are wise enough to proceed with the revelations from Oceania openly, we will reveal the newly obtained knowledge from The Word by the theater of epiphany from individual 'genius,' carefully chosen by the Order. Selected men and women of Kenton will seemingly rise above all others with magnificent science, medical, and technological inspiration, changing the world so all will benefit. A few of us will know the truth. Benjamin, you will know the truth."

Conrad placed his arm around his son, "The hour is late, and we have a long way to travel. You have a journey before you in this world. Be patient and allow the events of your life to unfold as they should. Gain wisdom with experience. In time, you will know what to do. If, in time, you think societal exposure of this secret is necessary, persuade the others in the Order that the time is right to share the truth with the world. For now, you are the student. Stay quiet and keep your mind open."

"Yes, father. I will follow your guidance," Benjamin responded, respectful of his father.

Father and son walked from the lecture hall and up a flight of stairs to the now-quiet lobby. Stopping at the lobby desk, they retrieved their guns and proceeded to the door leading to the outside world. When they reached the massive glass, Benjamin and his father passed over the library's threshold, and slowly descended the long incline surrounded by the movement of water. Reaching the base, Benjamin stopped for a moment to look up at the now darkened, cloudless sky.

The short storm had passed, and the stars were brilliant against the black mantle of the evening sky. Benjamin studied the planetary plane. Just above the horizon, a blue planet reigned unique among the stars. Benjamin gazed at the mystery, turned, looked at his father, and took his hand. Together, they continued home.

Chapter 12
Tale of the Talisman

enjamin awoke from a deep sleep. He had
dreamed of other worlds. His room glowed from
the soft morning light filtering through sheer
cotton window curtains. The cool ocean breeze
penetrated his room with the crisp, clean smell
of the Eastern Sea. His conscious mind struggled
to master the new day against his fading drowsiness. Then,
rising from his bed, Benjamin bathed, dressed, and attached
his metal brace and prosthesis and opened the swaying curtain
to capture the ocean view from his bedroom window. Below,
on the sea's edge, a rebellious adolescent girl rode a Kenton
walking horse in a shallow tide. Her long, yellow hair danced
in the gentle wind, her exposed arms and legs darkened by the
sun. Benjamin could see her clearly, laughing and talking to
her horse, then—quite unexpectedly—as if she could feel his
presence, she turned and looked directly at Benjamin. Although Benjamin was not sure, she seemed to smile, then she
raised her hand to wave a morning greeting. Benjamin
returned the gesture, and the girl continued down the beach,
fading from his sight by distance and perspective. How
beautiful the young girl, Benjamin thought, how magnificent
the striding horse, bred for perfect conformation by guided
intent.

Benjamin's reflections of the remarkable horse brought a
disquieting thought. His memory carried him back to last
evening to the library lecture hall and the revelations Dr.
Hayek shared with him—how humanity and all life was
established with guided intent by spacefaring beings from
Oceania.

His mind began to entertain several disturbing possibilities. What if humanity on Deseret was bred specifically for
the unique environment of this world? How different might

the progenitors be? The vast oceans of Oceania may be the source of intelligent life from that distant world. Aquatic intelligence and form so unique and different, only the most disciplined and agile mind would not be overwhelmed with prejudice and repulsion—the true Elders possessing tentacles, gills, scales, and fins—how disconcerting the mental image. His young mind railed against such a possibility, and he was determined to suppress such abhorrent and needless speculations. Benjamin resolved to concentrate on the real challenge of understanding the gift of advanced knowledge from Oceania and, by such effort, achieve the mental maturity and wisdom necessary to solve any cultural and anatomical conflict. Benjamin, with that thought, turned from his bedroom window. He passed through the door of his room and walked down the hallway of the second floor to the stairs in the hope of finding his mother waiting patiently for him.

Benjamin carefully managed the stairs with his brace. Halfway down the descent, he paused, realizing the oak floor in the formal sitting room was newly covered by an exquisite, handcrafted carpet, undoubtedly created by a gifted artist of Kuttor. As he continued down, he was struck by the intricate patterns of vines, flowers, and clouds, more like a fine painting than a woven pattern. The artist also wove numerous examples of winged seraphim descending from heaven, conveying ancient scrolls of moral guidance and divine wisdom to the prophet Xue. The magical skills of the weaver created the illusion of angels floating above the carpet. The genius of the carpet captivated Benjamin. The coincidence of his newly obtained knowledge of otherworldly influences was not lost on him. The beautiful carpet covered the entire floor of the formal sitting room, enhanced by the soft glow of morning light from the large bay windows at the front of the house. The carpet's delicate colors and hues complemented the grand piano's polished woods and the adjacent harpsichord. The pale marble mantel of the fireplace reflected the soft tones of the carpet, adding a warm quality to the stone centerpiece. Upon reaching the sitting room, Benjamin could not resist releasing his brace's locked metal knee joint to kneel and touch the tight weave and knots of the fantastic piece of art. Continuing to the dining room, Benjamin was once again surprised by another exotic carpet from Kuttor covering the entire floor of the room. It was just as magnificent as the one in the sitting room.

The joyful sound of his mother interrupted Benjamin's concentration: "Benjamin, my wonderful boy!"

Benjamin saw his mother at the dining room table drinking a glass of red wine, undoubtedly containing hydrate of lithia, and reviewing piles of financial reports from her varied business endeavors. The nascent sunlight created an aura of true splendor all around her and her vibrant black hair reflected the light from the dining room windows. Her green eyes glowed magically, and her pale skin was as flawless as delicate porcelain. As his mother rose and raced toward him, Benjamin thought she was the most beautiful woman in the world. He felt elated as they embraced. He loved his mother: the unbroken source of nurture and substance from the moment of his conception, a constant source of strength and support that would never leave him. Ellen held her son tightly and pressed her lips against his face. She was proud of her son. Only a feigned request for air by the gleeful new accountant permitted sufficient reason to temper her motherly enthusiasm.

"Mother, please," Benjamin pleaded. "Accountants need air to live!"

Ellen stepped back, releasing her son. "Benjamin, your father told me this morning you passed the examination with a perfect score, and the accountant organization requested your permission to publish your answers so others may realize the high standards required for success."

"Yes, mother. Father arranged for his friend, Dr. Hayek, to provide the results of my examination during our talk. I am so happy and relieved I did not disappoint you or father."

Taking her son's hand, she responded in delight, "Please sit with me in the dining room, and I will have breakfast prepared for you while you tell me all about your adventures at university."

Benjamin's mother pulled on the long ribbon ascending through the ceiling in the dining room, ringing a bell in the kitchen and notifying the downstairs maid. Benjamin chose to sit across from his mother. Just as Benjamin reached his chair, the attractive, substitute maid entered the dining room: "Yes, Madam?"

Benjamin's mother, preoccupied with carefully gathering, sorting, and placing financial files aside before sitting, responded with a scowl and nodded her head in Benjamin's direction.

The maid turned her attention to Benjamin, "Yes, master Benjamin?"

Benjamin's mother curtly responded, "Sara, you will refer to my son as Mr. Walker. Do you understand?"

Slightly stunned by the unexpected admonition, she responded, "Sorry, Madam," and turned to Benjamin. "Mr. Walker, how may I be of service to you?"

Benjamin responded, "Sara, I would like a breakfast of one pheasant breast, two scrambled goose eggs, veal steak, medium well, and mashed potatoes." Benjamin hesitated a moment, then continued, "Also, a pitcher of cold lemon phosphate."

"Yes, Mr. Walker," Sara responded contritely.

Benjamin warmly returned, "Thank you, Sara. You are looking most attractive today."

Sara, visibly shaken, replied: "Thank you, Mr. Walker," before rushing into the kitchen.

Benjamin's mother briefly waited until the maid left the room, "Now Benjamin, remember what we talked about." Benjamin's mother was genuinely concerned about hiring a young maid substitute during Martha's absence. Ellen instructed the downstairs maid never to be alone with Benjamin and to maintain the most proper relationship with her son. She warned her son that any form of fraternizing between himself and the servant would result in the maid's immediate dismissal. Benjamin, in a most serious manner . . . "Yes, mother, I guess this means the engagement is off." Benjamin started to laugh as his mother tried to contain herself, realizing her clever son had manipulated her. Benjamin's mother lost her composure and laughed at the irony of such a ridiculous idea.

When composure returned, Benjamin's mother requested, "Tell me about the accountant examination. Did you find the test difficult at all?"

"The tutors you selected for me did an excellent job. The essay questions on the test were remarkably similar to those I practiced writing many times during the summer. The examination was given in a large auditorium with magnificent stained-glass windows depicting Kenton's history and the rise of our society. About a hundred other individuals were attempting to pass the test, and I was the first to finish. I think the test took me about two hours. Sometimes the slowest runner finishes first, right mother?" Benjamin said, sadly looking down at the table.

Benjamin's mother leaned and reached across the table as her son grasped her hand: "You are an exceptional man, Benjamin Walker. You will accomplish great things. Remember this, we all have strengths and weaknesses. Your unique strengths make you special indeed . . . very special."

"Thank you, mother," Benjamin responded. "I have never wholly accepted my deformity. I feel so ugly at times. I wonder if a woman will ever want to be seen with me. My leg is hideous."

Benjamin's mother squeezed his hand harder and whispered, "The right woman will love you for who you are. Please trust me on this. Be yourself, do your best, and one day someone special will enter your life. The right woman will not even notice your leg. She will see only you."

Benjamin nodded and gave his mother a slight smile, "Thank you for your confidence and guidance. I do so love you."

Benjamin's mother returned, "I love you, too," then released his hand.

Ellen continued: "Now tell me about this emancipation thing. I mean, I agree with your father's decision. I was just a little surprised he did not mention it sooner. I think you should be considered an adult being an accountant and everything. You should have your own money to manage. Two hundred thousand dollars should help you with your education expenses. At our first opportunity, we will have to go to Londonderry and select an appropriate mansion for you near the campus and hire competent servants."

"Well, mother, I am sure he did not want to say anything before I demonstrated a successful examination. As you know, I am required to be an adult before I can enter a blood oath, and a blood oath is required before I can be hired as a certified public accountant. I am also required to have six months of paid experience before I am fully vested in my licensure. I was fortunate father was so thoughtful to expedite my career. If I had not become an emancipated minor, I would have had to wait over three months before being hired. Such a delay would prevent my entrance to the university by another semester and being vested is something I wanted to accomplish as soon as possible."

Benjamin did not feel he was lying to his mother, just omitting part of the truth.

Benjamin's mother responded, "I believe he made the right decision. Speaking of expediting your vocation, Ralph Jordan, the editor of the Riverdale Voice, sent a runner over this morning to let you know the Porter Import Company is placing an advertisement for a new accountant position in the newspaper tomorrow. I spoke to Ralph last week about how you were going to be taking the state accountant examination, and he wanted you to have the advantage of interviewing for the position first. Wasn't that nice of him?"

Benjamin immediately realized his mother's involvement.

"Wow, mother, what fate. I passed my exam and became an emancipated minor only yesterday, and the very next morning a job opportunity mysteriously appears. Speaking of strange occurrences, and this is a truly astounding coincidence, expensive Kuttor carpets suddenly appeared in our home from the very import company that needs an accountant, hmmm. . . . My only question, and please forgive my cynicism, are you paying for my salary as well?"

Benjamin's mother softly responded, "No, I would never do anything like that. Jeffery Porter, the company owner, is a good friend of mine, and I spoke to him about hiring you to gain some experience. He told me he was considering hiring an accountant to review his books. He would be happy to give you the required experience before you start attending classes. I just wanted you to think you obtained the job without my involvement. Please don't be angry with me."

"Thank you, mother. I appreciate everything you two have done for me. I would have been disappointed if you didn't arrange my next educational experience. I will ride over to the import company after I finish breakfast. Thank you for providing the job opportunity."

Benjamin was deeply moved by his mother's actions, as always.

Ellen continued, "Benjamin, your father told me I should ask you about an idea you had about transporting vegetables long distances. Tell me of your notion."

"Yes, mother, I have an idea that came to me on the way to Londonderry last morning. I was watching all the farms passing by the train window, and I started thinking about the land we own west of town and how we can't grow perishable crops on a commercial scale on the land because of spoilage during transport to distant markets. Then I started thinking we might modify a railroad boxcar with insulation, like wool or straw, and install compartments for ice in the ceiling and floor and paint the exterior roof of the boxcar white to reflect heat—"

"Yes, of course! What an elegant idea, Benjamin," she excitedly stated.

"There's more," Benjamin continued. "Vegetables could be harvested, cleaned, sorted, and boxed in the fields, then placed on racks in the cold boxcar for immediate shipment. I am not sure how far we can ship different types of farm and range perishables, but I think we could experiment with a modified boxcar and test the feasibility. What do you think?"

She stared for a second at her son, then pulled a blank paper from her stack of reports, picked up a fountain pen, and began sketching a depiction of her son's idea. After a moment of vigorous drawing, she turned the illustration around and showed her son, "Is this what you had in mind?"

Benjamin studied the sketch. "Yes, double walls with insulation and ice stored in the ceiling and under the floor. That's it!"

Benjamin's mother continued to stare at the drawing. Then, a magical creative synergy began.

"Benjamin, tell me what you think of this. Instead of modifying existing boxcars, we could use flatcars and place a modified container on the flatbeds with several containers on each flatbed. A railroad crane could remove the containers during the long winter months so a flat car would not be tied up. Benjamin, think of this: Newhopeland is growing fast with homes and industrial development but relies entirely on the Kenton mainland to provide food supplies. We could have cranes at the harbor lift the containers from railroad flatcars directly onto ships, and upon arrival at distant ports cranes could again transfer the containers onto flatcars. This change could revolutionize shipping, and individual boxes of fruits and vegetables would not need to be unloaded box by box— Benjamin, I love your idea."

Benjamin continued, "Let's take this thing to the next logical step. We could make containers for dry goods as well. Manufacturers could rent a container from the railroads, and when the containers are full of product, the railroad could pick up the containers, then unload the containers at the market or the harbor on . . . container . . . ships. Yes!" Benjamin's voice grew louder, "Ships could be explicitly modified for the transportation of containers in the cargo holds and on the deck. Containers could be stacked on each other inside the ship and on the deck. Containers would be sealed so no one would have contact with the product from the point of origin to the distribution. Think of the efficiency, and the preservation of products from breakage and theft. I think this has a million possibilities."

Benjamin's mother continued, "Shipping containers will revolutionize transportation. An idea like this will change the world."

"Really, mother? Do you think so?"

"Yes, Benjamin, this is genius. Now let's develop a plan of action," she replied. "First we have Gilbert Design and Engineering on retainer and under a blood oath of confidentiality. We will begin to design the containers and cranes. We will quietly begin acquiring farmland and property suitable for citrus orchards in the south near Kuttor. I also have an opportunity to buy the controlling interest in the railroad, and this has just given me the reason I was looking for. I will purchase it as soon as possible. Benjamin, you are indeed an amazing son. I will tell you when our initial meeting with Gilbert Design will be, and I will insist on a meeting in the evening so as not to interfere with your accounting position. I am excited and I am so proud of you."

"I am so happy you liked and contributed to my idea. I hope we will make a lot of money," Benjamin replied.

Benjamin's mother nodded while looking down at the drawing, and then slowly raised her head. She looked directly at her son and stated confidently, "We always make money."

The discussion came to an end when Sara entered the dining room with Benjamin's breakfast on a large plate and a full pitcher of lemon phosphate. She carefully placed the meal on the table in front of Benjamin. She removed utensils and a napkin from her apron, placing them in the correct order on both sides of the breakfast plate: "Mr. Walker, will there be anything else?"

Benjamin looked at his mother to be sure she was looking and said, "Yes, Sara, a large, chilled tumbler. Thank you." At that point, Benjamin gave Sara an exaggerated wink, causing the flustered maid to turn and leave the dining room quickly.

Benjamin's mother, with a smile on her face and shaking her head, scolded, "Just stop it. You are going to drive that poor girl crazy."

"Sorry, mother."

Benjamin looked down at his breakfast while carefully cutting his veal steak before placing a forkful into his mouth.

After a few minutes of frantic eating to satiate his hunger, Benjamin paused, looked up at his mother, and said, "I must share what I saw at the fantastic university library."

Benjamin passed through the ornate iron gate in front of his sizable two-story mansion and began the short walk to the livery stable at the end of the block and around the corner. He wore his finest black silk-wool suit with delicate red pinstriping, a white dress shirt, and gold cuff links. His tall, black boots shined to a gloss, and his head bore a black homburg fedora shaped from felted beaver fur. Despite his pronounced limp, he presented the striving appearance of accomplishment and wealth. A simple brick path defined his short journey. To his left, a long, white picket fence in front of the opulent ocean-side homes lined the walkway, and to his right, a cobblestone road, Ocean Front Boulevard. The boulevard was alive with the commotion of daily traffic, members of the upper class: gentlemen on horse or buggy politely tipped their hats, ladies in elegant carriages provided a slight smile and nod. Benjamin responded with the proper salutation and a tip of his hat.

Benjamin knew his first day of work would be unique. He had not forgotten what his father had taught: be open and thoughtful to every learning experience and endeavor in life. Benjamin's father had patiently instructed him that, regardless of his academic accomplishments, he would remain a student in many ways—the wisest of men never stop learning. Benjamin fully realized the challenge before him. He would mature, acquiring knowledge in the real world in a professional and measured manner. His next goal: become an exceptional accountant. He would strive to apply the theory and tools he had learned, tempered by real-world experience, to become an outstanding certified public accountant. A good accounting student did not guarantee a good accountant. He resolved to be persistently receptive, to continue to learn as much as possible, and to try extremely hard not to disappoint his employer.

The homes nearest the stables were more modest bungalows—mostly white with ash blue trim. The homes were monotonously similar, individualized only by the unique gardens reflecting each occupant's taste and sense of beauty. The spaces between the houses revealed the nearby sea. The ever-moving, soft-whispering waves radiated the rising sun. The soft, warm sand on the ocean's edge provided an inviting setting for leisure on warm days and formed a demarcation between the sea and the many homes on Ocean Front Boulevard.

Turning the corner, Benjamin was confronted by a stray black gelding peacefully feeding on the tall green grass by the road's edge, most likely an escaped tenant from the stable. Benjamin carefully approached the freed horse and gently patted its neck, spoke a few soft words, placed his hand beneath the horse's jaw, and guided the animal back. When Benjamin entered the stable, he surprised the new stable master, Ralph, who was busy cleaning a stall. The stable master jumped from his task, grabbed a nearby rope, and quickly secured the horse, leading the animal to a nearby stall.

"Thanks, Benjamin," the stable master said. "That horse is a magician—third time this week."

"Yes," Benjamin replied. "Some are."

"Do you wish for me to saddle your horse?" the stable master asked.

"The dress saddle and bridle on Fortune, and my chaps, please," Benjamin stated, carefully watching his steps among the piles of manure. He walked over to his horse's stall and greeted Fortune with a friendly pat on the neck, "How's my beautiful horse today?"

Ralph had disappeared behind the stables and returned with the saddle, bridle, and chaps from the locked storage room. Benjamin lifted the chaps lying across the saddle and began securing them around his waist and legs while Ralph made Fortune ready. The chaps ensured the cleanliness of Benjamin's suit pants. Horse sweat leaves a pungent odor on unprotected clothing. After preparing Fortune for riding, Benjamin placed his good leg in the stirrup and, holding the pommel, lifted his braced leg carefully over the horse. Once Benjamin situated himself in the saddle, he released the knee lock on his brace, permitting his leg to bend. Then, with his hand, he lifted and guided his booted prosthesis into the modified stirrup and positioned his knee. Benjamin was able to ride his horse with the same skill and agility as any capable rider.

Benjamin looked back at the stable master: "I will not be back until late. I am going over to the industrial sector of town."

With that said, Benjamin gave Fortune a gentle nudge with his heel. "Let's go, Fortune," he commanded. Fortune commenced a quick trot, taking Benjamin away from the stable and in the direction of his future employment.

Benjamin headed up Kenton Boulevard in the direction of the Porter carpet import company. Kenton Boulevard ran along the harbor, and the harbor teemed with the energy of maritime trade. The wooden docks moored numerous seafaring crafts, both wooden sailing vessels and much larger iron steamships. A multitude of dock workers hurrying to maintain schedules dictated by the crush of commerce loaded and unloaded the vessels and ships. Benjamin could see dozens of freighters silhouetted against the distant horizon, waiting to be moored or sailing away. The sailing vessel's cargo originating from Kenton was bound for the many seaports all around the Eastern Sea.

The Porter Exotic Carpet Import and Wholesale Company warehouse sign on the building's side could be seen from several blocks away. The enormous, corrugated building stood over three stories high, and Benjamin felt excitement as he closed the distance between himself and his future job. Upon arriving, Benjamin rode Fortune to the company's stables on the building's side and carefully dismounted.

Benjamin entered the stable door and was greeted by the stable master: "Hey, don't bring that thing in here—employees stable—don't you know!" The man confronting Benjamin was an utterly disgusting little man, filthy and unshaven. His stench was quite alarming, even in a livery barn full of horses and manure.

Benjamin stated with calculated pretension as he descended from his horse, "I am an employee. I am Mr. Walker and will be stabling my horse." With that said, Benjamin opened his coat, took out his wallet, and removed a twenty-dollar banknote, "I am willing to pay you twenty dollars a week to care for my horse. Are you interested?"

The stable master stared at the banknote and nodded his acceptance, "Yeah, I'll give your horse special attention."

The stable master began to reach for the note, and Benjamin pulled back, "This is what I expect in return. My horse will have his saddle and bridle removed upon arrival. The horse will be curried, and his hoofs will be cleaned and polished. His shoes will be inspected for wear or compromised nailing. After a thorough brushing, his tail and mane will be braided Kenton style. Place him in the largest stable. The stable will be clean with clean straw. During the day, when my horse soils his stall, the manure will be immediately removed from his stall, and the stall will be cleaned and fresh straw added. The horse will be grained one cup three times a day and receive a half a bale of fresh hay daily. When I arrive in the morning, you will greet me outside the stable. In the evening, you will bring the horse to me as well. When the end of the workday approaches, the horse will be thoroughly inspected for cleanliness. Also, I expect the saddle to be oiled and the silver polished every day. The bridle should be polished as well. The horse should be saddled and ready to ride before I arrive at the stable in the evening. Stable master, what do you make a month . . . fifteen, twenty dollars?"

The stable master replied, "Twenty dollars . . . yeah."

"Well, stable master, you will be making an additional eighty dollars a month. Do you understand my expectations?" Benjamin asked.

"Yes, sir," the stable master returned, continuing to reach for the banknote.

Benjamin finished his instruction while removing his chaps and placing them across the saddle on his horse. "I may, during the day, unexpectedly drop by to inspect my horse, and if my instructions are not followed, you will not be paid for the week. Also, I will have you terminated from your position and provide the next stable master the same opportunity to earn the salary I have offered you. Do we understand each other?"

"Yes, sir, you are more than generous. I will not disappoint. . . . No, sir." To the stable master, the bonus payment was a small fortune.

Benjamin then released the banknote into the stable master's filthy grasp while turning to leave. "And, stable master, if I work late, you work late. I do not want my horse left alone. Clear?"

The stable master responded, "Yes, sir, I will not disappoint. What is that thing's name?"

Benjamin walked out of the stable, giving his back to the stable master, "You don't need to know that thing's name, and I also expect you to bathe and shave daily from now on." With that said, Benjamin disappeared around the corner and did not hear the contrite stable master's final "Yes, sir."

Benjamin walked into the immense showroom and removed his fedora, as was the custom. He was amazed by the many carpets and tapestries that adorned the walls and covered the large showroom floor. The carpets were stunning, and their presence created the same ambiance as an elegant art gallery replete with beautiful paintings and marbled statues. However, these expressions of human thought were not created from the gentle mixing of colored oils or the shaping of stone; these artistic expressions, these carpets, were the synthesis of the weaving of genius with woolen threads into an intricate tapestry of unique artistry. While admiring the haunting beauty, Benjamin recalled a simple child's poem from The Word about a great war in heaven whispered to him as a baby in his mother's arms; he could hear her words as if she were present.

Then the stars began to fall, like rotting tapestry in ancient hall.
Angelic legions now misty ghosts, fallen rampart of Heavenly hosts,
Blacken angel of Raven's wing, the sword of light he will bring.
Craven Darkness shall then descend, as heaven's light begins again.

Benjamin then observed across the room something which seemed almost miraculous. On the back wall, under a large brass plaque engraved "Master Artist Collection," hung an astounding treasure of carpets. These carpets were not folded into one another with iron rods to view one at a time. These carpets were displayed in full view, hung like paintings upon a museum wall. Eight carpets in all, each created to cover the floor of a large formal sitting room and each seemingly alive. With each step taken by the young accountant, the images woven into the carpets seemed to move, creating the illusion of an outward-looking window. Each carpet was a portal to an unknown world, flourishing with animated life: unfurling vines, delicate blossoms, birds leaping from branches and flying through the air. Clouds would drift across the skies, darken, and begin to rain. With the slightest movement of Benjamin's body, each carpet's woven artistry displayed a unique image, in splendid animation, of a different theme of nature. One exceptional carpet revealed a pride of lions chasing an antelope on a vast unknown savanna. With each movement of Benjamin's body, the lions became energized with life. They could be seen overtaking the sacrifice, and with sharpened claws and teeth, rending the poor creature apart in gory mutilation. Benjamin stood awestruck.

Jeffery Porter watched his son from across the room—a son he never knew. What a handsome young man, he thought. Benjamin's expensive silk-wool suit and highly polished boots presented the air of a man of confidence and excellent taste. He stood tall with a slight build and thick blond hair. His physical appearance was the same as Jeffery's at Benjamin's age. Even his bright, nickel-plated brace seemed to add a mystery to this precocious accountant as he stood firm and capable as any man could appear to be.

Now the time had come for Jeffery to meet his unclaimed son. Jeffery felt a strange agony as he walked across the showroom toward his newest employee. He would cross this showroom a dozen times a day in haste, but this traversal was the longest. His mind became consumed with intangibles, then questions: Will I show a revealing expression of a bond between father and son, never disclosed until this desperate moment? Will he realize his true father's presence? What would be the unintended consequences of such a revelation . . . a maelstrom of pain from an indiscretion so long ago?

"I possess a secret between lovers that must not be shared," he softly said to himself. "To do so would cause my world and the world of others to tumble into disarray. I must act my part of his employer and do nothing more."

Jeffery Porter walked up and stood next to Benjamin Walker. Benjamin, mesmerized by the movement contained within the carpets, slowly moved his head back and forth and up and down without being aware of his employer's presence. Jeffery Porter broke the silence, "Magnificent, are they not?"

Benjamin, still preoccupied, unconsciously responded, "Magic."

"Benjamin Walker, I presume," Jeffery Porter began his introduction.

Benjamin slowly acquired a sense of awareness of Jeffery Porter's presence as he turned to face his new employer:

"Yes, sir, I am so sorry. These pieces of art simply spellbound me. I am Benjamin Walker, and I am grateful for this opportunity, sir," he stated while reaching out his hand.

"Your mother has spoken well of you. It would seem you are a very impressive young man accomplishing much in such a short time," Jeffery spoke in a somewhat detached manner.

"Well, mothers tend to say that sort of thing about their sons. I hope I will not disappoint," Benjamin returned, then stated, "Mother told me of the little secret between the two of you. I am grateful to be here of course."

Jeffery Porter was an accomplished man of commerce. With his sense for business and cunning intellect, he created the most successful import company in the world, yet Benjamin's statement made him feel like a leaf trapped in a whirlwind, his knees felt weak, and his strength started to fade. He knows! Jeffery thought. The implications were overwhelming. He did not say a word. He simply stared at the son he dared not claim as his own.

Benjamin, somewhat confused by Jeffery Porter's void demeanor, continued, "About putting an advertisement in the newspaper for the accounting position so I might believe I obtained the position without motherly involvement. I confronted her, knowing my mother is obsessive about furthering my educational experience, and she admitted she spoke to you. I am very appreciative of the opportunity to serve you, sir."

Jeffery Porter took a reflective few seconds and responded, "Your mother and I are good friends. I welcome you to my company." Jeffery Porter, quickly changing the subject, continued: "These few carpets you have been looking at are quite impressive, wouldn't you agree?"

Benjamin returned his gaze to the mysteries upon the wall. "Yes, sir. How is such a thing possible? I have never seen moving pictures before this day. How is such a thing possible?"

"Benjamin," Jeffery began to explain while pointing at the carpets around the showroom, "all the carpets in this showroom were created by apprentice artists except for the carpets on the wall in front of you that were weaved by the masters. A typical weaver begins to learn his craft at the age of fifteen. If the child demonstrates talent, he will be allowed to continue instruction in the carpet weaving art under the guidance of a master carpet weaver. A typical apprenticeship requires thirty years of instruction. Only the best of those artists become master carpet weavers and are allowed to learn the secrets of motus vivus, which, when translated from the language of Kuttor, means 'living motion.' A typical master will make two, maybe three carpets using the techniques of motus vivus in his lifetime. The secret of motus vivus is in the complexity of weave and the tying of the knots. On each thread of wool appears many fine threads of colored weaving containing several different images. Each image is weaved at a slightly different angle to the other images, so when the observer moves his angle of observation, a different image appears. The images are integrated into a logical sequence, creating an illusion of a moving scene of nature. How they accomplish this remains a closely guarded secret."

"How many images are contained in a carpet to create such a smooth, fluid motion picture?" Benjamin asked, slowly walking back and forth to energize the artist's creations.

"Thousands of images all precisely spaced and angled. The entire process is extremely time-consuming, and many master artists have gone insane and committed suicide before completing a motus vivus carpet. In the event of the death of a master artist before the completion of his carpet, the weaver is wrapped in his unfinished carpet and cremated so his spirit may complete his unfinished weaving in the afterlife. This belief is a very important facet of the culture of Kuttor," Jeffery answered.

"These works of art must be worth a fortune. Who can afford such things, Mr. Porter?" Benjamin asked, turning to look at his new employer.

"The least expensive carpet on this wall will obtain one

hundred thousand dollars, and the most expensive, 'The Lion's Pride,' will bring a half-million dollars," Jeffery explained. "These art pieces will be purchased mostly by art museums and several individuals in the State of Liberty who can afford to collect this type of woven art. The wealth of that society tends to accumulate among the corrupt political and corporate class."

"Of course," Benjamin responded. "Can these carpets be used as carpets?"

"Yes, these carpets are as practical as any of the woven carpets in this showroom." Jeffery Porter lowered his voice and said, "Now I will show you a master carpet no one dares to walk on."

He pulled a small, brass key from his pocket: "Follow me across the showroom, and I will share with you something only a few people have witnessed. I expect the same level of confidentiality pertaining to this matter as I expect concerning all the business matters of this company."

Benjamin agreed: "Yes, Mr. Porter, I am ethically and le-gally bound not to reveal any lawful aspects of this compa-ny's proceedings without the express permission of my employer or the company's governing board."

Jeffery smiled when he heard the young accountant's pe-dantic response, and said, "Okay then . . . walk with me. Those carpets conceal the door for which this key is made on the far wall." Jeffery pointed and began to walk in the direc-tion of a true mystery. Benjamin's first real lesson on his first day of employment would be as disquieting as the knowledge of the supplicants he received evening last.

In a far corner of the showroom, a large rack of tapestries and carpets were moved away from the wall by Jeffery to reveal a dark walnut door. With a glance to ensure privacy, Jeffery opened the door to a darkened room. The room was completely dark except for small pilot flames in each of the four gas lamps hanging by chains from the tall ceiling.

Taking Benjamin's arm, Jeffery directed him a few feet into the room and shut and locked the door. "Benjamin, do not be frightened and don't move while I turn up the gas lights."

Benjamin stood peering into the darkness, listening to his employer fumble in the dark, attempting to find the wall's gas valve. Seeing only the dim pilot flames near the ceiling, Benjamin instantly realized the great distance between the gas lamps, indicating he was standing in a vast room. He heard an increasing hissing sound as the volume of gas increased to the ceiling lamps. His eyes quickly adjusted as the room was revealed, illuminated by the gas lamps' warm glow. The room was windowless, and the walls covered with rich walnut paneling. A few feet from him, lying on an oak floor made from planks, was an enormous square carpet hundreds of square feet in volume with a blood-red trim on all four edges nearly a foot wide. In the center of the carpet and dominating the eerie room was an ominous woven image of a giant raven perched on a branch of an ancient oak. The raven's body was in a profile to Benjamin, but the raven's head was turned directly at the young accountant. The raven's intimidating, dark eyes seemed as menacing as a sharp rapier thrust in Benjamin's direction. The raven's curved black bill and plumage appeared as real and vibrant as any living animal trapped in a giant square cage with invisible bars. Benjamin was afraid to move and bring the bird to life. This raven was far too real to be a simple rendition of artistic effort, this dark creature had a palpable spirituality, foreign to the inanimate.

Jeffery Porter gave a stern admonition to his new employee. "Now listen carefully to experience the true mystery of the carpet. Do not go any nearer to the carpet than you are now. Do not touch the carpet. I want you to begin to walk slowly around the carpet, clockwise. You must speak quietly. Each side of the carpet is one hundred feet in length, and each side will take thirty or forty paces, you must not stop once you begin. I want you to begin . . . now."

Benjamin did not question, he simply turned and took a step with his unencumbered leg. His attention always focused on the raven. With his first few steps, the giant bird came alive, his piercing dark eyes glistened with a menacing awareness of Benjamin's presence. The raven's head turned to follow while the bird's plumage bristled and flowed, energized by the muscles straining to maintain balance on a shifting oak branch swayed by the wind. The raven's blackened beak opened to reveal a black tongue and mouth. His wings began to unfold as the creature crouched as if to pounce. As Benjamin rounded the first corner, the bird lunged into flight.

Benjamin instinctively stopped and crouched to shield from danger, an action that evoked Jeffery Porter's loud reprimand: "Don't stop. . . . The raven is an illusion. It can't hurt you!"

Once again, Benjamin began his halting sojourn, carefully manipulating his braced leg not to slip on the hard, polished oak floor. The raven was now in full flight, the branch and tree seemed to glide away, and with every pulse of the raven's wings, the distance between Benjamin and the raven seemed to close, Benjamin's manifest fear was turning to terror. The impossible was becoming real. This animal seemed to be stalking him. With each articulation of the bird's great wings, Benjamin felt the air stir in the room, caressing his face and hair with horror. Benjamin reached the midpoint of the first side when the raven's beak widened and a deep rumbling sound began emanating from within the animal; the soft rumble grew to consume the room with a deafening screech.

Benjamin, holding his hands against his ears, now moved as fast as he could as the adrenalin burned through his veins and arteries, his eyes frozen on the growing beast. With every step, the bird adjusted its flight to match Benjamin's desperate movements and continued to appear larger. The bird's plumage exhibited the reflected highlights from an unseen sun, causing an eerie purplish cast to ripple down the raven's body and a greenish gloss to pulsate along his wings. Benjamin tried to escape. The room now swirled with great tumult, gaslight swaying, wind roaring, Jeffery Porter screaming unheard commands, and still, the bird grew closer, larger.

The wings of the creature now touched each edge of the carpet, and as Benjamin reached the second corner of the carpet, he could clearly see his reflection in the bird's black, shining eyes. The raven opened his great blackened beak and released a hot stinking blast of putrid air rising deep from within. Benjamin gagged on his own vomit as his body recoiled from the dreadful stench, and he now staggered around the third corner of what was surely a sorcerer's carpet. Benjamin could no longer look at the avian demon that shadowed his every move. Benjamin's only thought was escape.

Midpoint of the third carpet side, Benjamin's brace caught on the protruding edge of a loose board, causing him to fall. As he fell, his body twisted, and when he landed on the polished floor, his momentum pushed him within inches of the carpet, his right arm and hand falling into the hellish design of the raven's world. Benjamin's eyes focused on the monster's beak as the raven stretched out its neck to grab Benjamin's right arm to pull him, undoubtedly, into the carpet and a painful death. With tremendous effort, Benjamin pulled his arm from the raven's grasp, but not fast enough to be spared the razor-sharp edge of the bird's beak, ripping a deep gash on top of his hand and causing blood to gush down his arm and onto the floor. An incision so deep it revealed pallid bones between the fold of torn flesh. Benjamin righted himself with a superhuman effort. He glanced at his adversary—only the raven's head and body could be seen. The raven's wings and claws stretched beyond the edge of the carpet. The room now spun with commotion, the wind pressed down on Benjamin's shoulders, impeding his escape. The gas lamps whirled in circles, casting eerie shadows and confusing flickers from failing flames. The boards of the floor and wall seemed to pulse and clamor. The room shook with a deep rumble of a death rattle; the world was coming to an end. Benjamin reached the fourth and final corner of the carpet, and as he turned, he observed a perplexed Jeffery Porter speaking words that he could not hear. He took one final glance at the raven. The raven was so close that only its terrible head could be seen. Benjamin could see his panicked image reflected in the raven's dark pupil growing ever larger; he could smell the raven's hot breath; he could feel and hear the flapping of the raven's wings, and with one final cry, the monster's wings brushed against Benjamin's soul.

When he reached the midpoint of the carpet where this macabre adventure began, the room became silent, the wind ceased, the gas lamps went still. The carpet was completely black as the raven's eye occupied the entire area of the carpet except for the blood color trim. Benjamin stared at his reflection in the deep, dark, glossy pool, stepped back, and collapsed into unconsciousness.

"Benjamin . . . Benjamin," Jeffery Porter repeatedly called out, attempting to revive his newest employee as he cradled Benjamin's head and shoulders on his right arm, carefully pouring a small stream of water on Benjamin's pale face.

After a few minutes, Benjamin began to stir. His eyes began to flicker, and a string of unintelligible words were mumbled, followed by a deafening scream of a young man in terror. His panicked cry seemed to bring Benjamin back to consciousness and an awareness of his surroundings. Looking up, Benjamin saw a kneeling Jeffery Porter, and beside him a nicely dressed older lady and two men dressed as laborers. Employer and employees stared down at him with concerned expressions on their faces.

Jeffery asked the two workmen to leave and then asked, "Benjamin, how are you feeling?"

Benjamin, attempting to sit up, said, "What happened?"

"After you walked around the motus vivus raven carpet, you fainted," Jeffery Porter answered. "I had you brought to my office, and we have been trying to wake you for the last ten minutes or so. How are you feeling now? Can we get you something?"

Now sitting upright on the leather couch where he had been placed, Benjamin answered, "I don't know what happened. I remember beginning to walk around the carpet, and I saw the raven leap toward me, and I dropped to the floor because it seemed so real. . . . The animal seemed so real, and I remember you telling me that I should not be afraid because it was an illusion, and then I woke up here."

"You cannot tell me anything else? I mean, do you recall walking completely around the carpet?" Jeffery Porter asked.

"No, I can't recall anything. I feel very anxious—persistently anxious. I mean, something happened. I can feel it, but I don't know what it was. I feel so cold, and my right hand has a sharp pain as if my hand were badly cut, but I see no wound. My hand appears unharmed. My behavior is so shameful. I must make apologies."

Benjamin began to realize this was not proper behavior for a new employee on the first day of employment. "Sir, I am not prone to this sort of thing. I cannot remember a time when I fainted this way before. Please forgive me."

"Benjamin, please," Jeffery Porter insisted, "You have not done anything inappropriate. This has been a stressful week for you, and perhaps you were a bit dehydrated. In any case, what is important now is how you are feeling. We can arrange a carriage to take you to the hospital," a concerned Jeffery Porter added while handing Benjamin the glass of water.

Benjamin drank some water and unconsciously wiped the excess from his face with his hand and arm. He asked, "Tell me what happened—please tell me everything that happened in that room."

Jeffery sat down beside Benjamin. "There is really nothing to tell. You walked completely around the carpet, and you spoke of how beautiful and alive the raven appeared. You asked many questions about how it was possible to weave and tie such a carpet, and when you finished walking around the carpet, you stopped and seemed to stare for a moment at the carpet, then you fainted. Until you collapsed, nothing unusual happened."

"I just can't explain the strange, disquieting feeling I have. I am sure you are right. . . . I might have been dehydrated," Benjamin stated as he began to stand, acknowledging the lady in his presence by offering his hand in respect.

"Please excuse me, madam. I did not mean to be rude. I am Benjamin Walker."

"I am Mrs. Cromwell. I am Mr. Porter's personal assistant," she replied, responding to Benjamin's gesture with a smile and taking and shaking his somewhat wet hand. She asked, "Do you feel well enough to complete some paperwork today, or would you like to wait until tomorrow?"

"I am feeling much better now. I am ready to complete any preliminaries required today."

Benjamin was lying. He felt something terrible had happened. But he could not remember.

"Very well, then. Please come sit in front of my desk, and we will complete the necessary paperwork."

Jeffery pointed in the direction of a pair of leather-covered chairs sitting in front of his oak desk and assisted Benjamin to one of the chairs. "Mrs. Cromwell is a notary, so this won't take long."

Benjamin sat quietly while Mrs. Cromwell took several copies of a blood oath from a drawer in Jeffery Porter's desk and placed them in front of Benjamin for review. While examining the oaths, Benjamin removed a copy of his notarized declaration of the Emancipation of a Minor, handing the copy to Mrs. Cromwell. She carefully cut a coupon from the bottom of the document, stamped the coupon with her seal, and then glued it to a page in her notary book before returning Benjamin's proof of emancipation. She then signed the page and returned the book to Benjamin to secure his signature and date. At that point, Benjamin signed the Blood Oath of Confidentiality and Fiduciary Fidelity and returned the copies to Mrs. Cromwell. She placed her notary stamp on the documents and again signed her notary book. Then she indicated the location for Benjamin's signature. With the book signed, she thanked Benjamin and turned to Jeffery Porter: "I will be in my office if you require anything of me."

"Thank you, Mrs. Cromwell," Jeffery stated, his attention turned back toward a somewhat distant Benjamin. "Well,

Benjamin, your mother tells me you require six months of paid experience as a full-time accountant to be vested in your licensure. I think this will work out fine for my needs. I will pay you at an entry-level accountant rate of eighty dollars a month. Tomorrow, I will show you your workstation and your assignments."

Jeffery Porter reached over his desk to select a small piece of paper. He picked up his gold pen, wrote a series of numbers carefully down on the paper, turned, and handed the piece of paper to his new employee. "This is the combination to the company's vault. Please memorize this combination and destroy the paper."

"Yes, sir," Benjamin stated, glancing at the numbers and carefully folding the paper and placing it in his vest pocket.

At that point, Jeffery Porter reached into his vest pocket and took out a large brass key and gave it to Benjamin while returning to his chair. "This is the master key for the building. You will have unfettered access to the entire operation with this."

"I will be most responsible, sir," Benjamin stated while placing the key in the same pocket he had previously put the paper with the combination.

"Are there any issues you wish to clear up before tomorrow?"

Benjamin thoughtfully responded, "Sir, you are very generous. I will do my best. Thank you for this opportunity." After a brief pause of reflection, Benjamin quietly asked, "May I ask you about the raven carpet? I think it is one of the most amazing things I have ever seen. There must be a story about it."

Jeffery nodded, "Well, there is a tale, and I will share it with you, but please keep this confidential."

Benjamin replied, "Of course."

Jeffery took a moment to reflect, sat back on his chair, and began. "Several years ago, I was in Drenen, the largest port in Kuttor, looking for product. I purchase most of my carpet inventory from the Kuttor Export Guild, but I also like to search for carpets owned by individuals. Occasionally, I find a family heirloom, for example. These carpets can be quite old and valuable. Well, my teamster and I were driving a one-ton wagon down this crowded road in the center of Drenen's main market, and a dirty little boy came running up to the wagon screaming that a man wanted to sell me a very rare carpet. Now I hear this kind of thing two or three times every trip I take to Kuttor, and once in a while, I make a find. So, I asked the teamster to care for the horses, and I followed this child to a narrow back alley. The boy pointed down the alley, and I gave him a silver coin, and he ran off. I started walking down this alley, which was more like a narrow walkway, and after a few hundred feet, this strange elderly man with haunting eyes and dressed in white linen steps out of a doorway, smiles, and states to my surprise, 'Mr. Porter, I am so pleased to meet you. My name is Gabriel, and I think I have something that will interest you.'

"So, I asked him how he knows my name and without answering, he gestures for me to follow him into this brick building. He leads me into a large room, almost completely dark, with a couple dozen burning candles for light. In the middle of the room is this large, rolled-up carpet bound with leather straps, and he tells me not to untie the straps. I can tell by the weaves and knot pattern on the back of the carpet this was an unusual and ancient carpet. So, I am excited, but I attempted to appear emotionally discrete.

"Benjamin, you should know I have heard a million magic carpet stories, usually right before I am told how much I am going to have to pay for the product, so I prepare myself for the obligatory presale tale. Many times, these stories are about some form of sorcerer or secret society of something." Jeffery continued. "So, I was thinking, here we go; then Gabriel starts his saga of the history of the carpet. He tells me the carpet was a motus vivus and woven by a master carpet weaver named Yornell, who lived ten decades ago. He labored on the carpet for over fifty years, and the carpet was only one third finished when Yornell died. As was the custom, he was wrapped in the unfinished carpet and cremated. Well, the story goes, before he died Yornell was familiar with rumors of a secret society in Kenton called the Gnostics. This secret society was disseminating unknown knowledge of the universe through carefully selected philosophers and learned men of Kenton. This knowledge would transform Kenton into a state of great material wealth and sacrilegious beliefs. Yornell feared such material wealth and the freedom of Kenton would seduce the people of Kuttor and in time destroy his country and the sacred beliefs of his religion would be lost. This was Yornell's greatest fear, and he vowed to destroy the Gnostics by releasing a powerful curse upon the world.

"I remember Gabriel's tone became very ominous as he completed his tale. Gabriel explained, 'Yornell was so outraged by the possible truth of these rumors, he wove a curse into the carpet that would change fate by destroying the Gnostics. If a Gnostic looks upon the carpet, the Gnostic will be cursed. The Gnostic, and every member of their family, would die a terrible death, forcing their silence so their knowledge and beliefs would be forever lost. The curse would preserve Yornell's mythology forever.' I must admit this tale was very original. Gabriel told me Yornell planned to make a carpet so incredible that every learned man and woman in the world would seek the carpet out. The carpet would become a true wonder of the ages. This astonishing carpet would ensnare every Gnostic. Gabriel explained Yornell was able to accomplish this achievement by completing his carpet with sanctified wool from the afterlife and by weaving his very spirit into the carpet. Yornell's soul is the carpet. Yornell martyred his eternal life to preserve the ancient, sacred beliefs of his culture. Yornell believed this consecration of the carpet by his soul would create a most formidable talisman with the power to attract and destroy the heretical Gnostics."

Benjamin interrupted, "Sorry, sir, what is a talisman?"

"Well, a talisman is an object—in this case, the raven carpet—and it has magical properties. The magical properties protect someone or a group of people from evil. The conse-cration of the carpet derives this carpet's great magical power from Yornell's soul. From Yornell's perspective, the carpet is a talisman. He believed the talisman would save the world from the knowledge of the Gnostics, and his religious beliefs would be saved from desecration," Jeffery briefly explained.

Benjamin quietly stated, "Thank you, sir. I am sorry for interrupting the story."

Jeffery Porter replied, "That's quite all right, Benjamin—please interrupt me any time you have a question. Let's see now, oh—then Gabriel explained to me, Yornell weaved his carpet to appear as a beautiful raven flying to each witness who walked around the carpet. He selected the raven because of our beliefs, and he knew how irresistible such imagery would be to our culture. The vast majority would see the carpet as an artistic masterpiece, but to the Gnostics, the real nature of the carpet is a desecration of the Raven and a trap. Yornell believed the Raven is heresy, a profane form of idolatry. When a Gnostic gazes upon the carpet, the talisman, the raven in the carpet, will appear as a monster, and this apparition will reach out and touch the Gnostic's soul. Each Gnostic who has gazed upon the carpet will then possess a corrupted soul and go slowly insane, doomed to remain silent. Their loved ones would share the same fate. They would experience some form of a dreadful malady. The Gnostics who have beheld the carpet will not remember the awful experience so as not to warn the other Gnostics. In time, every Gnostic in the world would be cursed, and their knowledge lost forever. Gabriel was able to obtain the carpet, somehow, and when the time was right, directed me to the location of the carpet. Gabriel then told me I was the one who would bring the carpet to Kenton, where the carpet must be destroyed by fire or all humanity would be lost. He said the destruction of the carpet would require some kind of great human sacrifice of one who believed in the Raven. He said something about some kind of human connection that was required in all of this because Yornell had been a human or something. Of course, all of this is frankly ridiculous.

"Gabriel told me the carpet was mine to take with only one condition. I had to give my solemn word, pledged on Raven's wings, not to look upon the carpet until the carpet was in Kenton. So, I gave Gabriel my promise and followed his request. As I was studying the intricate detail on the back of the carpet, Gabriel simply disappeared. I turned to ask a question, and he was gone. When I returned to Kenton, I opened the carpet, and I found a true wonder. I think Gabriel was most likely disturbed and his story is groundless. Still, he gave me a true miracle to share with the world. Of course, I have no intention to burn the carpet. On the contrary, I am intent on preserving this extraordinary treasure for now and future generations to come."

Jeffery Porter smiled and jokingly said, "Benjamin, if you are one of those Gnostics, that may explain what happened to you today. Do you possess any secret knowledge that will change the world or belong to a secret organization or anything?"

Benjamin sat in cold silence. He forced himself not to reveal the slightest gesture of discontent or apprehension with Jeffery Porter's tale of secret knowledge and corrupted souls. He was terrified, and with all the strength and courage he could muster, with all the self-control he could manage, he calmly replied, "I am just an accountant."

Jeffery Porter continued, "Well, whatever the truth is behind the carpet, there can be little doubt the thing is a fantastic piece of art. It is a true inexplicable mystery and a miracle without equal. Sometimes I think this carpet must have been made in the afterlife."

After a slight pause, Benjamin asked in a somewhat hushed tone. "May I purchase the carpet? My mother has many philanthropic endeavors, and I am sure she would be interested in donating this masterpiece to a museum so the world would have access to this miracle," Benjamin lied.

Jeffery Porter was confused by the request. "Benjamin, the carpet is priceless. I know your family would want to share the carpet with the world, and I share the same senti-ment. I have already decided to have the carpet on display when the new University of Londonderry library is complete in a few years. The carpet will be in a secure place with the other treasures of Kenton, and scholars and students from all over the world will be able to view it and study the genius of this unique piece of art. Until that time, we must keep the carpet a secret to ensure its safety. The carpet would sell for millions in Liberty. I seek no gain; this carpet belongs to the world."

Benjamin feigned a simple response, "I think that is a wonderful idea. I understand why mother holds you in such high esteem. I think I will learn a great deal from you before I leave to complete my education."

"Thank you for your kind words." Then Jeffery Porter spontaneously declared, "I wish you could have been more in my life before now. I am looking forward to working with you."

Benjamin was somewhat surprised by Jeffery's odd com-ment, but politely replied, "I do as well. We have time now to come to know each other better. If it is permitted, I will take my leave."

Benjamin straightened his braced leg and locked his knee into place. He used the chair to right himself and walked over to the leather couch, secured his black fedora, held his hat by his side, turned to look at Jeffery Porter, and said, "Sir, if there is nothing else required of me today, I will not take any more of your time. I will be prompt tomorrow morning. Thank you again for this opportunity. I did so very much enjoy you taking the time to show me your beautiful carpets and sharing with me the strange tale of the raven carpet. Goodbye for now."

Benjamin then turned and disappeared into the hallway. The sound of his metal brace lingered as he walked away.

Jeffery Porter sat in his quiet office. He looked out onto the harbor. Tears filled his eyes.

～

Benjamin entered the emergency entrance to the Riverdale Hospital, walking as fast as his leg permitted. He did not notice the numerous greetings from nurses and doctors as he hurried down the hall, passing many closed doors to specialized wards. His mind was obsessed with the strange experience at the import business and the tale of talisman. The appearance of Jack Church, the hospital administrator, caused Benjamin to stop abruptly and ask, "Mr. Church, do you know where I might find my father?"

Jack responded, "Well, hello, Benjamin, how are you this afternoon?"

Benjamin, with a strain in his voice, returned, "Fine, thank you. Do you know where I might find my father?"

"I believe you may find him in his office. Is there something wrong?" Jack asked, sensing anxiety in the young man's voice.

Benjamin simply said, "Thank you," ignoring the question.

A few moments later, Benjamin arrived at his father's office and frantically knocked on the heavy oak door until he heard a familiar voice, "Yes, come in."

Benjamin entered the office and, somewhat out of breath, quickly stated, "Father, I have something important to discuss with you. May we speak here without being overheard? Can you spare a few minutes?"

Benjamin's father was pleasantly surprised to see his son, and said reassuringly, "Of course we can have a private conversation. I always have time to speak with my son."

Benjamin walked over to the chair in front of the cluttered oak desk, released his knee joint, and sat down. Benjamin's father stood, brought a chair around to the front of his desk, placed it next to his son, sat down, took his son's hand, and asked, "Benjamin, what is troubling you?"

"Father, what I am about to tell you I just signed a blood oath of confidentiality not to divulge with anyone, but this is an exigent situation. What I have learned today has a bearing on the information shared with me last night. May I share this confidence with you?" Benjamin asked stridently.

Benjamin's father rose from his chair, walked over, and locked his office door. Returning to his son, he sat down and whispered, "Keep your voice low, and your confidence will be protected."

"Father, did you know mother secured employment for me as an accountant at Jeffery Porter's import business?" Benjamin asked in a soft, strained voice.

"Yes, I knew," his father replied.

"I rode over to meet Mr. Porter to secure the position as soon as mother spoke of it. Mr. Porter was most gracious, and he took considerable time to show me his beautiful carpets and tapestries." Benjamin then asked, "Are you aware of carpets known as motus vivus?"

"Yes, your mother has spoken about such things . . . carpets with moving images activated by the movement of the observer. Such a thing is difficult to understand. I hope to view this artistic mystery at the first opportunity," Benjamin's father whispered, somewhat confused by the question.

Benjamin leaned closer, "Mr. Porter permitted me to witness a huge motus vivus he keeps in a secret room just off the main showroom. Apparently, only a few people know the carpet exists. The carpet was a square a hundred feet on each side, and the woven artistry depicted an enormous raven standing on an oak tree branch. Mr. Porter told me to walk around the carpet clockwise, and as soon I began to walk, the bird came to life, as real as any living raven. I turned the first corner of the carpet, and within a few steps, the raven leapt from the branch, and the illusion of this imposing animal lunging in my direction was so real it caused me to instinctively crouch. I heard Mr. Porter clearly say the illusion was harmless, and before I could rise from my kneeling position, I blacked out and returned to consciousness lying on a couch in Mr. Porter's office. He told me I was unconscious for several minutes."

Benjamin's father quickly stood and expressed concern by this revelation. "Benjamin, how did you feel after you returned to consciousness—any weakness in your limbs or impairment of your vision?" Benjamin's father reached over and put his left hand on Benjamin's forehead and pulled down the bottom edge of his right eye to assess the color under the fold of skin.

"Please, I am fine. Now you must listen to what I am telling you . . . " Benjamin stated while removing his father's hand.

"Are you sure?" he asked with concern.

"Now listen and please sit down," Benjamin continued. "I asked Mr. Porter what happened, and he told me I walked around the carpet expressing my amazement at the artistry of the carpet, and when I completely circled the carpet, I stopped and seemed to stare at the image for a moment, then collapsed. Father, I don't remember anything after Mr. Porter told me the carpet was harmless."

"Are you sure?"

"Yes, now listen." Benjamin's speech was becoming pressured as he continued. "When I was feeling revived, I asked Mr. Porter if he would tell me more about the carpet. This is important, pay attention," Benjamin commanded his father. "Mr. Porter explained he was given the carpet from a man named Gabriel in Drenen. Gabriel told him the carpet was the creation of a master weaver named Yornell, who died before he could complete it. In life, Yornell had somehow gained knowledge of a powerful secret order that would modernize the world. Yornell feared as Kenton became more modern and wealthier that the people of Kuttor would be seduced by such affluence and reject the teaching of the sacred prophets. The order was called the Gnostics.

"Yornell so loved the teachings of his religion, he devised a scheme to destroy the Gnostics. Yornell created the raven carpet using sacred wool from the afterlife. Yornell also martyred his eternal life by weaving his soul into the carpet, which consecrated the carpet, turning it into a powerful talisman that would trap and destroy the Gnostics and their family when a member of the secret order gazed at the image. The Gnostics would be cursed to die a terrible death before they could share their knowledge with the world. They would not recall anything unusual after experiencing the carpet's curse, so other members could not be warned.

"Gabriel then took the carpet to Drenen so the carpet could be given to Mr. Porter, who was destined to bring the carpet to Kenton where the carpet was supposed to be destroyed by fire, saving the Gnostics from the terrible curse. Mr. Porter thinks the tale is a canard and plans to display the raven carpet in the new university library so everyone on Deseret may view it. Father, the coincidence is too great to be chance. Do you believe me?"

Benjamin's father took a reflective moment before he carefully responded, "Benjamin, I love you and deeply respect you. You know that I do, don't you, son?"

"Yes," Benjamin stated.

"Benjamin, I think you were right when you said the tale of the raven carpet was a coincidence, and I think Mr. Porter was right when he said the tale was a canard. I have never heard of the order of the Gnostics, and I don't believe a man can create a talisman by weaving his soul into a carpet. Benjamin, how could the secret of the carpet be kept if everyone with secret knowledge fainted when they looked at the thing? I mean, wouldn't that make people in the order suspicious if only the members of the order had the same reaction? Benjamin, sometimes when a person is under a great deal of pressure, their mind will seek an escape by shutting down. I think that is why you blacked out. The amazing piece of art you described was a breaking point."

Benjamin interrupted, "Father, please. . . . "

"Benjamin, now let me finish," he asserted.

"Yes, sir," Benjamin acquiesced.

Benjamin's father continued, "Benjamin, look what you have been through. Only yesterday you completed one of the most difficult professional examinations in Kenton. Then, on the same day, you became an emancipated minor and were initiated into the Supplicants and learned the true Elders were from Oceania. The very next day, you were employed for the first time in your life and as a professional accountant. Benjamin, that is simply too much for the young mind to take in such a short time. I think you need a few days of rest before you begin working for Mr. Porter. I will send a note to Mr. Porter explaining you are suffering from a mild case of stomach flu, and you need a few days to recover. He will understand."

Now this time, Benjamin took a few thoughtful moments to respond assertively to his father. "Father, we need a moment of clarity, so please listen to me."

"Of course, Benjamin," he responded respectively.

"I was not stressed out by the accountant examination—to the contrary. Do you know why? Because I had an advantage over everyone else taking the examination. I was given the questions worded somewhat differently before the test and practiced taking the exam all summer before taking the actual test. Mother had hired tutors who helped develop and write the examination, and they were guaranteed a substantial bonus if I passed the examination on my first attempt. Father, the circumstances of my examination preparation were conducive to my success.

"Furthermore," Benjamin continued, "I was not stressed over being emancipated a few months before I turned eighteen. Emancipation did not change my life. Oh, did I mention receiving two hundred thousand dollars? Wow, what a burden to be rich. As for the Elders' true origin and their influence on our world, I found the entire thing amazing and benevolent to our lives. I was privileged to be offered membership into such a wonderful organization with the world's finest minds—an organization dedicated to systematically improving humanity. Such an association does not burden me; in fact, I am honored.

"Now for my first real job, I know my mother asked her friend to help me out. Mr. Porter did not treat me as a new employee. He took a great deal of time to show me his carpets, even the secret one. He treated me more like family than someone looking for a job. Mr. Porter also told me he wished he'd been in my life more before now. What was that all about?

"Father, I love you and mother, and I sincerely appreciate the obvious advantages both of you have given me, but I am not naïve. What I have achieved is a direct result of fate giving me such wonderful and caring parents. I am not stressed. I am frightened because of what happened to me in Mr. Porter's secret room. I don't know if every Supplicant would have the same reaction I did, but I know this: they will not know the history of that carpet and the potential of their imminent demise. I think my fainting may not be the norm. I still feel an icy presence deep within me, a violation of some sort. Please try and understand what I am trying to tell you. This is important. There is something in that warehouse that presents a danger to us all. I know this to be true. I think revealing this dark harbinger to you is my fate and perhaps the most important thing I will ever do. This is a clarion call. Please hear me."

Benjamin's father was much moved by his only child and reached over and placed his hand on the side of his son's head: "Benjamin, I am immensely proud of you. Please don't ever self-deprecate. Yes, you have had advantages, but you are very bright, and you have flourished with your circumstances and have become an incredibly wise and accomplished young man. A lesser man, almost all men, would not have done as well. If you tell me there is a danger, I believe you. Forgive me for doubting you. Tell me what you expect from me."

"I want you to promise me two things. Even if you have doubts, I want you to promise me you will never look upon that raven carpet under any circumstances, and the second thing you must agree to, if something should happen to me, if I change in some inexplicable way, if my life becomes a nightmare and I cannot fulfill my responsibilities as a Supplicant. If I am cursed, please recognize that I am trapped and held hostage to something evil. You must do everything in your power to destroy that carpet with fire. Destroy that thing before it enters the world. If this is my fate, then accept your fate and fulfill the prophecy of Gabriel. If I am correct about this, you will realize when the time is right."

Benjamin's father stood up, closed the space between father and son, kneeled in front of Benjamin and put his hands on his son's shoulders. "On Raven's wings, I solemnly promise to do what you ask of me. If what you fear comes to pass, and my son is taken from me, I will not fail you."

Chapter 13
Attestation

J effery Porter sat at his large, hand-carved oak
desk. The morning hours of most workdays involved
written correspondence concerning the many facets
of his import company. The subject of Jeffery
Porter's last letter of the morning pertained to the
replacement of product:

Riverdale, November 8, 1895

Dear Sir,
Please accept our order for shipping by the first vessel that
leaves Drennen, bound for Riverdale, the annexed named
articles of exotic carpets of various patterns, and best quality.
Designated by proper numerical indicator born from catalog
ZY-1276 of your most recent publication concerning such
offerings; for the amount of which we shall be pleased to
honor your draft at thirty days sight, at your convenience to
draw on us, with prompt acceptance and recompense. Having
secured by past transaction of a similar nature, we beg leave
to ask your favor in whatever method your kind consideration
may confer; and pledge our honors, as merchants and gentlemen, for the strict obedience of your commands.
We remain your respectful servants,
Jeffery
Porter and Company

Abdei Almasi, Proprietor
Drenen

Jeffery Porter was placing his gold fountain pen on the

brass and marble pen holder when he heard a knock on his office door. "Yes, please come in," he declared.

Much to Jeffery Porter's delight, Benjamin Walker entered his office at precisely eight o'clock in the morning. "I am so glad you were able to attend your employment this morning. I was worried you might be ill," a concerned Jeffery Porter expressed while standing, walking to Benjamin, and extending his hand.

"Thank you, sir; I am feeling proper for my duties," Benjamin returned, shaking his new employer's hand.

"Please sit with me, and we will discuss your duties. I am so happy you have offered your expertise to my business endeavor."

Jeffery Porter motioned Benjamin to the two leather chairs in front of his desk. Benjamin sat in one of the chairs, and to his surprise, Jeffery Porter sat next to him instead of taking the proper place behind his desk. Once again, Benjamin felt he was being treated more like a member of the family. Benjamin assumed his employer's relationship with his mother was a factor in his preferential treatment.

Jeffery began, "Benjamin, I need you to conduct a confidential audit of my business interests for the last three years. I do not think anything is wrong. In fact my business is thriving, and as near as I can tell, everything seems to be in order. I have two excellent certified public accountants, both accurate and industrious, and both have provided faithful service for years. Jack Prince, my senior accountant, has been with the company for fifteen years and has modernized our bookkeeping procedure. I have the highest esteem for his loyalty and efforts. Paul Harris has been an excellent and trustworthy employee for eight years. As you would expect, the division of labor has been in such a manner to ensure accuracy and trustworthiness, each gentleman's accounting must be consistent with the other. Any errors in documentation or necessary calculations are quickly ascertained by the other; both sets of books must tally with one another. Also, any effort to defraud would require complicity and such collusion is unlikely."

"Yes, sir," Benjamin replied. "Seems like an excellent system."

He continued, "Yes, I think everything is most proper."

Benjamin tried to be as delicate as possible: "Mr. Porter, something is bothering you. Forgive me for my presumption, but why do I feel a faint sense of doubt in your admiration of your accounting staff?"

"Your frankness is appreciated," Jeffery Porter stated. "I want you to conduct a confidential audit. I do not want you to discuss any aspect of the audit with anyone. All your communications must be limited to Mrs. Cromwell and me as to the nature of your relationship with this enterprise or any findings of fault concerning the accounting. You will work in a private office, and Mrs. Cromwell will assist you. If you inform me my bookkeeping is sound, I will accept your conclusion and proceed as usual. If there is a problem . . . well, we will deal with it."

"Yes, sir," Benjamin replied. "May I ask the nature of the suspected problem?"

"I feel terrible about this, and I must admit I am reluctant to elaborate, but I doubt Mr. Prince's veracity. There is nothing tangible in my suspicions. I do not want to cast aspersions on an exemplary employee. But I think he is lying to me. When I look at him, he appears to be laughing at me, not overtly, I just sense it. How terrible is that? I mean, he has not given me cause whatsoever. I wish him no harm and I don't want him to be offended by my unsubstantiated concerns," Jeffery Porter explained in a most contrite manner.

"Sir, you have built a most impressive company using acumen, both tangible and instinctual. I pledge my best effort to resolve any uncertainties you may have concerning the bookkeeping of this company," Benjamin tried to reassure his employer.

"Thank you, Benjamin," Porter said while rising from his chair. "I will show you your workstation. I must say again: please do not initiate any contact with the other employees except for Mrs. Cromwell or myself. Mrs. Cromwell is at your disposal if you need assistance. Please walk with me."

Jeffery led his new accountant out of his office and down a long hallway to a small door. Opening the door revealed a long stairway illuminated by a gas lamp two stories above the threshold.

"When I designed this building, I originally planned to have my office up here. I found myself running up and down these stairs a hundred times a day. So, I moved my office downstairs—much more practical. Please forgive the stairs, will you be able to manage?"

"Yes, sir," Benjamin answered without hesitation.

The stairway was narrow, and Mr. Porter patiently walked ahead of the new accountant, very conscious of Benjamin's difficulties. The stairs led to a massive office on the second floor, a good twenty feet across, and running the building's length. On both sides of the room floor-to-ceiling windows revealed the showroom below on one side and the vast warehouse on the other. The warehouse was replete with scores of workmen carefully wrapping and storing carpets in proper locations and removing carpets from storage, then inspecting and preparing them for shipment. Large hand cranes and pulleys balanced carpets as they ascended and descended in proper order, altogether a dramatic image of effort and industry. A long banister ran the length of the room on both sides to prevent a viewer from accidentally falling through the glass. Such a fall would most likely culminate in death, so great the distance. The ceiling had four large sky-lights, two sloping north and two sloping, south bathing the room in sunlight. On the north side of the room, perpendicu-lar to the glass walls, was a large oak desk with a brass gas table lamp placed on the front corner of the desk near the wall. The gas lamp with a hand-blown glass shade produced a faint flicker from the perpetual pilot light. A long, black, rubber hose descended from the base of the lamp, down the side of the desk, running along the floor, to a brass gas valve emerging from the wall beneath the window. The lamp provided sufficient lighting for the long, tedious hours of bookkeeping scrutiny required of the young accountant. Next to and in line with the oak desk was a long oak library table, a small walking space separating the two. The table also had a lamp with a hose running to a valve on the floor. Three large piles of books, ledgers, and journals representing the last three years of the company's financial activities were neatly stacked on the library table and ready for the audit.

Jeffery Porter raised his hand in the direction of the desk and table: "Well, Benjamin, here is your workstation. I hope you will not get lonely up here. If you need anything, please don't hesitate to notify Mrs. Cromwell or me."

Benjamin smiled at Jeffery, "Sir, please have no concern. I shall begin my review at once."

Jeffery put his hand on Benjamin's shoulder. "I have complete faith in your ability. I will be back at 11:30. I know of a great eatery a short distance from here. We can take my carriage. Until then, I will leave you to your efforts."

"Thank you, sir; I would very much enjoy having lunch with you," Benjamin returned, somewhat perplexed by his employer's continued pleasantness.

Benjamin waited a moment, listening to the sound of his employer descending the narrow stairs. When the sound grew faint then silent, Benjamin walked over to the large window overlooking the extensive showroom and stared at the wall covered with tapestries and carpets that concealed the secret room: the focus of all his fears. He felt a driving force to destroy the monster behind the door, but this was not the time. The thought of destroying the raven carpet was his persistent companion in the coming days and nights. He would repress such feelings for now; this was a time for accounting. The time for slaying monsters would come soon enough.

Benjamin turned and walked up to the pile of records containing the complete fiscal year 1894. Just by looking at the labels of the many journals and books in the pile, Benjamin realized the accountants were using the archaic and complex system of double-entry bookkeeping. The most extensive book in the pile was the day book. This was the most important book in the accounting records. The day book was a concise daily history of every transaction that had transpired in the company. The next book Benjamin noticed was the journal containing a list of debtors and creditors specifying the amounts of each account; it was a derivative of the day book and conveyed a detailed financial history of suppliers and patrons.

The ledger contained a numeric description of all the account activities of the debtors and creditors. The financial records for the import company also included the cash book, invoice book, sales book, commission sales book, account sale book, letter book, account current book, bill book, receipt book, checkbook, book of expenses, and many more documents, bills, folders, and records. Benjamin was ready. An expert had trained him in accounting, and he was confident he would not fail at ascertaining the fiscal integrity of the company.

Two days after successfully passing his uniform certified public accountant examination to earn his certificate, Benjamin Walker began the onerous task of auditing one of the world's largest wholesale businesses. Benjamin's daily activities would be repetitive and predictable.

At eight o'clock in the morning, he would arrive at work. He would greet Mrs. Cromwell and Jeffery Porter with the appropriate pleasantries, ascend the stairs to his office, and begin reviewing the company books. Without exception at 11:30 every day Jeffery Porter would climb the stairs and retrieve Benjamin from his labors. Jeffery Porter would select a restaurant. Both men would spend a leisurely lunch, usually several hours in length, discussing their life stories and various beliefs and values with each other. After a few weeks, Benjamin's employer insisted Benjamin call him by his first name, and Benjamin slowly accepted Jeffery as a friend, he was becoming more than just an employer. Jeffery repeatedly told Benjamin he would always have a job with the company, and Benjamin would thank him for his kind offers. Jeffery had no idea Benjamin was independently wealthy and had no desire to seek employment outside his family's business. Benjamin's talents would be necessary elsewhere. Still, Benjamin hoped they would remain friends after his tenure.

At the end of the fourth week, Benjamin completed the audit for the last three fiscal years. The bookkeeping appeared perfect. Not a single miscalculation or inappropriate entry, everything tallied, every cent was accounted for. At this point, most accountants would have been satisfied the company's books appeared in proper order. However, Benjamin respected Jeffery Porter's judgment and his high esteem for his employer would not allow him to accept the audit results. If Jeffery Porter sensed something was wrong, Benjamin would continue his investigation until he found the source of his employer's intuition. Benjamin sat back in his chair and wondered if it was possible he might have missed something. He stood up and walked around his desk, staring out the large window into the warehouse. He watched a score of workmen moving expensive products. After some time, he came to a realization. The existing and past inventory is a critical aspect of bookkeeping, and he assumed the inventory entries in the day book were accurate. What if the actual inventory was inconsistent with the tallies in the books? A single carpet could be worth thousands of dollars. He concluded the actual inventory must also be scrutinized.

The system employed by the company was thorough in keeping track of the valuable inventory. Every carpet entering or leaving the warehouse was carefully documented by the warehouse foreman. One of the accountants had to attest to the accuracy of the foreman's documentation before the product description and disposition were entered into the day book. Outright theft may have involved a conspiracy between the warehouse foremen and the accountants—possibly the shippers whose documentation would also have to be modified. The young accountant had not compared the warehouse and shipping records with the recently reviewed books.

Benjamin resolved to review the records pertaining to the inventory for anything suspicious or inconsistent. He would begin with the letter book looking for inconsistency between the correspondence concerning the selling and ordering of carpets and the company's books and inventory.

Benjamin reviewed hundreds of correspondences for 1894 and the two years prior. He mostly studied letters of intent to purchase carpet of a given description and cost. A few of the letters pertained to requesting refunds for the returned carpet product related to a lack of customer satisfaction concerning the color or pattern of the carpet. Every carpet was unique, and samples and catalogs could be inaccurate portraying an unseen purchase. While reviewing the many letters, Benjamin stumbled on a strange inconsistency—an inconsistency which was the thread that would unravel the source of Jeffery Porter's concern.

The Arabesque Exotic Carpet Company of Liberty was the largest retailer of exotic carpets in the world. Arabesque purchased more than a half a million dollars' worth of carpet from Jeffery Porter in the fiscal year 1894. The sales were represented in the many letters sent by the company for the purchase of product over the year. There were twelve letters indicating thirty-eight carpets were being returned. In all but four letters, Arabesque requested a credit be given to their account for the returned carpets; this made perfect sense considering the volume of product being purchased by the company. Four letters from the same company requested a direct refund by cheque. The repayments represented a relatively small amount of money: $3,028. One correspondence read:

Portsmith, Liberty June 16, 1894

Dear Sir,
We sincerely regret our recent purchase of the annexed named articles of exotic carpets that were found unsatisfactory by the prospective buyer; this is not a condemnation of

high quality of the product or reflection of the integrity and esteem we place in your establishment and management; on the contrary, the failure of sale was our inability to anticipate our client's preferences in such matters. We humbly request a return by cheque of the amount advanced for the said items after the arrival of merchandise and proper inspection by your staff.

    Having a significant history of commerce between our establishments, we beg to leave to ask favors in whatever form your thoughtfulness will confer. As merchants and gentlemen, we pledge our honor to accept your actions and pledge our continued loyalty to the beneficial relationship between our organizations.

We remain your obedient servants,
Arabesque and Company

Jeffery Porter, Proprietor
Riverdale, Kenton.

    Benjamin thought this a most peculiar request. Why would Arabesque request a refund for such a small amount of money? Why were there four letters requesting a refund instead of the usual resolution? Accountant Paul Harris indicated in the day book the returned carpets had been placed back into the warehouse inventory. Benjamin then secured the canceled cheques from the processed cheque folder. The cheques were properly made out to the Arabesque carpet retailer and bore the stamp of the Arabesque Company's endorsement on the back. Almost immediately, Benjamin realized a problem. The cheques had been processed through the Bank of Londonderry, and Arabesque used the Reserve Bank of Portsmith in Liberty for all the company's banking transactions. The cheques had been penned and signed by Paul Harris. Paul Harris had entered a debit in the journal and ledger books. Paul Harris had documented the refund and the return of the carpets to the inventory in the day book.

Benjamin placed the four processed cheques in front of him on the table. He removed a magnifying glass from his desk and examined the Arabesque company stamp endorsing each cheque. The endorsements appeared authentic. Benjamin then noticed something peculiar. The "Pay to the Order" space revealed the Arabesque Retail Carpet Company as the receiver of the payment. The printed line beneath the receiver's identity appeared normal and continuous until after the last word "Company" of the payee name. At that point, the line, which continued to the edge of the cheque, had a series of gaps and spaces. At first Benjamin thought the small flaws represented nothing more than imperfections in the printing of the cheque. When he compared all four cheques, he found similar gaps and spaces in the line but in entirely different locations on each cheque. The lines did not match. The gaps in the line were not a printing error. Benjamin recoiled with realization. At that moment, Benjamin understood. Benjamin thought, Paul Harris is a thief, and this is an error in the execution of an otherwise perfect crime! . . . This simple, innocuous inconsistency is the fatal flaw in his deception. Benjamin had to be sure. Undoubtedly both accountants were involved, and what to do next weighed on him like no other event he had experienced in his short professional life.

Benjamin would not say a word until he gathered his evidence, so he set into motion a plan that would demonstrate culpability or his own flawed reasoning. Benjamin wrote a confidential note to the warehouse foreman asking him to review his records and locate the "returned" carpets identified in the four correspondences. The note contained the inventory number and the description of the returned carpets as indicated by Paul Harris' entries in the day book, the very same inventory numbers on the reimbursement cheques signed by Paul Harris. Benjamin then penned a confidential note to the senior accountant of the Arabesque Carpet Company:

Riverdale, February 12, 1895

Dear Sir,

My responsibility as a confidential certified public accountant is to attest to the fidelity of the current accountants employed by the Porter Exotic Carpet Import Company; scrutiny requires the unpleasant, though necessary task of informing you of possible fraud. An intentional deception made for personal gain at the expense of my employer, which may have occurred using the good name of your business institution. If true, the dastardly scheme involved the felonious deception of reimbursement by cheque of the product allegedly returned to this company by your fine and honorable business enterprise. Your company management's upright character is not in question in any form; on the contrary, your company's excellent reputation is noteworthy.

Annexed to this correspondence is a list of four carpets with a brief description and inventory numbers purchased by your company that were allegedly returned for reimbursement by cheque in the year 1894. The corresponding cheque numbers, dates, and amounts are also specified on the attached tally and were all processed through the Bank of Londonderry. I humbly request information as to the disposition of these mentioned articles of product, as reflected by your records.   Time is of the essence.

I cannot stress the confidential and ominous nature of this investigation. If proven and accepted as factual to the satisfaction of the County Auditor-Controller of Kent, such malfeasance is a capital offense. Furthermore, if the individuals in question are, in fact, innocent, my intent is not to besmirch otherwise competent accountants.

As a certified public accountant, I beg to ask favors in whatever form your kindness will confer them; and pledge my honor, as an accountant and gentleman, to utilize such favors to protect and enhance our profession. Ever mindful of our responsibility to conduct ourselves as a proper servant to those who entrust our profession with their fortunes.

I remain your obedient servant,
Benjamin Walker, CPA

| Certified Public Accountant |
| Arabesque Carpet Company
Portsmith, Liberty |

Benjamin placed the letter in an envelope and addressed the letter to the senior accountant at the Arabesque Company.

Benjamin then descended the long stairway and walked to Mrs. Cromwell's office and gently knocked on the door.

"Please come in," Mrs. Cromwell's pleasant voice passed through the door.

Benjamin walked into Mrs. Cromwell's office with a somber countenance. Mrs. Cromwell respectively stood, "Yes, Mr. Walker; how may I be of service to you?"

Benjamin began his request for assistance.

"Mrs. Cromwell, I have a list of four carpets allegedly returned to our company in the fiscal year 1894. In the most confidential fashion, I am requesting the warehouse foreman to determine if these carpets are currently in the company's inventory and, if absent, to prepare a written report as to the disposition of these items."

Mrs. Cromwell immediately sat down and began writing down Benjamin's instructions.

Benjamin continued, "In addition, I have prepared an urgent correspondence to the Arabesque Company to be sent by Quick Express rider service. Please facilitate this at your first opportunity. I cannot stress enough the importance of receiving a reply to my letter as soon as possible. When the reply arrives, please bring the correspondence to my attention."

Mrs. Cromwell briefly looked up, somewhat surprised. "Yes, sir," she responded before looking down at her notes and continuing to write.

Benjamin continued his requests: "I also require a few supplies from the local apothecary and food market. I will need the following items: two fresh eggs, a lemon, a small paintbrush, two small glass bowls, a quart of distilled water, an eyedropper, a glass pharmacist swizzle stick, a graduated pint chemist beaker, and an empty perfume atomizer. Please have the runner obtain these items and have them placed on my desk by tomorrow morning."

Benjamin's final words, "And Mrs. Cromwell, my instructions are to be held in strict confidence except for Mr. Porter. Do you have any questions?"

"No, sir," Mrs. Cromwell responded. "I will give the note to the warehouse foreman immediately and will send the runner to the Quick Express stables this afternoon."

"No, Mrs. Cromwell, you may send the runner to retrieve my supplies; I want you to deliver the letter to the Quick Express stables. I do not want to trust this letter to the boy. The issues contained in the correspondence are of a grave nature," Benjamin ordered in an uncharacteristically harsh tone.

"Yes sir, I will deliver your instructions to the foreman and secure my carriage and hurry to the Quick Express within the hour," Mrs. Cromwell responded politely.

"Thank you, Mrs. Cromwell," Benjamin stated while leaving the office.

Benjamin slowly ascended the narrow stairs and returned to the solitude of his office. He walked over to the pile of accounting books for 1893. He secured the process cheque folder for that year and carefully reviewed the canceled cheques. Once again, four cheques of reimbursement for returned carpets were found to the Arabesque Company and processed through the Bank of Londonderry for the year 1893, representing the sum of $3,137. In the previous fiscal year, 1892, Benjamin found five cheques for reimbursement to the Arabesque Company, representing $2,943. This cheque collection was also aberrant to the standard accounting method of operation concerning returned carpets from the Arabesque Company. Paul Harris penned all the cheques. Benjamin then located the relevant entries in the day book and placed the corresponding processed cheques on the notation page to act as bookmarks. Paul Harris wrote all the day book entries. Benjamin carefully bundled the cheques for the 1894 into an envelope with the corresponding letters allegedly from the Arabesque Company requesting a refund. He then placed the envelope in the 1894 day book and took the book down to the company's large vault in Mrs. Cromwell's office and secured his evidence.

Benjamin returned to his office and watched from above as Mrs. Cromwell walked through the busy warehouse. When the warehouse foreman was located, a brief conversation ensued and concluded with Mrs. Cromwell handing the note to the foreman. While Mrs. Cromwell was leaving, the foreman could be seen studying the note. Several moments later, the foreman began his task of complying with his instructions. First, the warehouse foreman appeared to be looking into his files to determine the carpets disposition as recorded by his inventory records. The warehouse foreman then began his search of the warehouse inventory for the carpets referenced. The foreman did not understand why these particular carpets needed to be located, but he tried his best to comply. Benjamin watched him for three hours. At the end of the workday, all the laborers and office staff prepared to return home, not the foreman. He continued his quest for another eight hours, covertly observed by Benjamin through the glass walls of his now darkened office. At one o'clock the next morning, a very tired and frustrated foreman ceased his search. He was confident he could provide an accurate written statement concerning his findings to the management. Not one of the carpets on the list could be located in the company's inventory. Benjamin watched the tired man as he sat down at his desk with a kerosene lamp, the only remaining light source in the warehouse, to pen his findings. When his note was finished he took his findings to the main office and placed the note on Mrs. Cromwell's desk. When the foreman left and locked the building, Benjamin walked down the narrow stairway, entered Mrs. Cromwell's office, and read the document authored by the foreman:

Mrs. Cromwell,

After a thorough review of the company's inventory by ledger and actual, I have concluded none of the carpets described on the opposite side of this paper can be found in the warehouse. My records show all the listed products were sold to the Arabesque company in the fiscal years 1892, 1893, and 1894 have not been returned. I am at your service for further instruction.

Dave Perkins, Warehouse Foreman

Dated February 13, 1895

Benjamin took the foreman's written statement, walked over to the iron safe in Mrs. Cromwell's office, dialed the correct combination, and opened the safe. He folded the written statement and placed the document on top of the 1894 day book containing the suspect cheques. He closed the heavy iron door and spun the combination, locking the vault. Benjamin locked Mrs. Cromwell's office door with his master key and continued through the darkened showroom illuminated only by the faint light of the chandeliers' pilot flames. He tried not to look toward the secret room, and for a brief second, he thought he heard a strange sound emanating from that dark place. Benjamin's awkward gait quickened as he crossed the showroom. He welcomed the sight of the large main entrance door, which would permit his escape from the warehouse and his haunting fears of things unknown. He hurriedly unlocked the door, crossed the threshold, turned, and secured the door with his key. Both fatigued and relieved to be beneath the stars, Benjamin slowly walked to the stable next to the corrugated building and found an exhausted stable master holding the reins of Fortune. The man and the horse had been waiting eight hours for Benjamin's return. Without saying a word, Benjamin secured the reins, mounted his horse, and rode into the night.

Chapter 14
Rage and Regret

Benjamin arrived early and opened the door to the carpet showroom with his master key. He was tired and had slept little the night before. He knew this was not going to be a typical workday and was very pensive concerning the events to come.

He navigated through the showroom, entered Mrs. Cromwell's office, opened the safe, and secured the evidence. Benjamin carefully ascended the stairs and entered his office. Far below, he could see the warehouse workers queuing up in front of the time clock to have their work cards stamped before resuming their efforts.

Benjamin placed the evidence on his desk and began moving the accounting books for 1893 and 1892 to the far end of the library table. When the end of the library table nearest his desk was clear, Benjamin placed the day book for 1894 on the open space. He opened the envelope and began sorting the four suspect cheques by date and placing them back into the envelope. He had to again convince himself what he realized the day before was correct. The fate of two men's lives was a heavy burden for the youngest accountant in Kenton's history, and the ramifications of what he had set in motion were overwhelming.

Benjamin thought of the recent times, when his only concern was pleasing his parents and his tutors. Today, he would accuse two men of capital crimes, and, just for a moment, he wished he could return to his recent serenity. At that point, Benjamin began sorting the corresponding letters allegedly from the Arabesque Company requesting refunds for the returned product. Once again, he tried to reassure himself.

Benjamin placed the warehouse foreman's written findings next to the correspondence. He sat down, placed his feet up on his desk, crossed his arms, and tried thinking of happier times when he was just a child, when everyone expected him to be just a child, not a child attempting to act the part of an adult—an adult with so much responsibility. Everything was happening so fast. He tried to center himself and not be preoccupied with the intangibles of future events. His eyes slowly closed. In those quiet moments alone, his mind slipped into a merciful sleep. He dreamt of a horse on a beach with a beautiful young rider and faraway worlds. Thirty minutes later, Benjamin was roused by a young boy's voice, the runner, "Sir, I have the things you asked for."

Benjamin opened his eyes and saw a young boy, twelve or thirteen years of age, holding two large paper sacks. Benjamin sat up and removed his feet from the desk. "Yes, please place the sacks on my desk and wait a moment." Benjamin removed the contents of the paper sacks and inventoried the items. When he was satisfied that the young man had been obedient to his demands, he removed a five-dollar banknote from his coat and handed the note to a very surprised boy.

"Thank you," Benjamin said with a sleepy expression while motioning the boy away. He watched the runner disappear down the stairs, removed the empty sacks from his desk, placed his feet back on the desk, closed his eyes, and once again slipped into sleep.

"Benjamin, Benjamin, wake up," the friendly voice of Jeffery Porter asked while gently touching Benjamin's shoulder.

Benjamin slowly regained his wits and apologized, "I am so sorry, sir. This is not my normal demeanor. I did not sleep well last night. Please forgive me."

"Benjamin, you are one of my hardest workers, and the time clock showed you unlocked the iron safe at 1:15 in the morning. I have no concern whatsoever as to the effort of your activities. I think something has happened. Mrs. Cromwell explained the assignments to me that you have given her, and I have a response from the Arabesque Company to the correspondence you sent to them yesterday. The letter just arrived by Quick Express. Benjamin, do you wish to speak to me about your findings? I am most interested in your discovery."

Benjamin stood and found his employer a chair. "Yes, sir. I think I have revealed the source of your concern. If I am right, I have indeed found a deliberate fraud while reviewing the company's books for the last fiscal year."

These words saddened Jeffery Porter. He sat motionless staring at Benjamin, took a breath, and broke the silence, "Please continue."

Benjamin began explaining his findings: "The bookkeeping for fiscal year 1894 was flawless, all accounts, both debits and credits tallied correctly. All discount and interest calculations were precise, as were all the other calculations concerning payroll and related activities. The day book gave a clear and concise history of every transaction of your business. The continuity between the day book and journal and ledger documentation was also accurate and cogent. In my opinion, the weakest link is in the documentation of actual existing inventory in the warehouse, as recorded in the accounting books. The system currently relies on one of your accountants to accurately monitor and record all incoming and outgoing products in the warehouse and to scrutinize the documentation of the product by the warehouse foreman. Of course, the warehouse foreman does not review the day book and all ancillary entries in the many journals and ledgers. This is the weakest link in your accounting system. No one scrutinized the accountant's accuracy. This lack of accounting is the flaw I thought might be exploited."

"Did you find something to do with the inventory?" Jeffery asked.

"Yes," Benjamin returned, "I believe the fraud has occurred in the inventory, and I believe I can prove it."

"Go on, please," Jeffery Porter said with a tone of trepidation in his voice.

"I began reviewing the correspondence concerning the purchase and return of the product, and I found a strange inconsistency."

Benjamin reached over and selected one of the correspondences for the fiscal year 1894.

Jeffery Porter took a moment to read the letter and then looked up, "I have never seen this letter, and the Arabesque Company has never asked for a cheque refund. That company has been consistently asking for a credit against future purchases for the returned product."

"That is correct. Several letters indicate the return of the product, and always Arabesque requests a credit against future purchases except on four occasions in that fiscal year," Benjamin agreed and continued. "I then reviewed the day book entries by Paul Harris concerning those carpets returned by Arabesque for reimbursements. The day book entries claimed the carpets were returned to inventory. I also examined the corresponding cheques, penned by Paul Harris, your company allegedly utilized to refund Arabesque." Benjamin then secured one of the canceled cheques from the envelope allegedly processed by the Arabesque Company.

Benjamin's employer studied the cheque and stated, "The cheque was processed through the Bank of Londonderry. Arabesque uses the Reserve Bank of Liberty for all of the company's business activities."

"That is correct," Benjamin responded.

"The cheque is endorsed by the Arabesque Company," Jeffery stated, looking at the back of the cheque.

"Do you think so," Benjamin returned, "just because the cheque has the Arabesque stamp?"

"Do you think the stamp is a forgery?" queried Jeffery.

"I do," answered Benjamin.

"What else?" Jeffery Porter asked.

"I sent a note to the warehouse foreman to determine if the four carpets in question are currently in your company's inventory and what the records indicate regarding the carpets' disposition," Benjamin stated while handing the foreman's note describing his efforts and findings.

Once again, Benjamin's employer studied the evidence,

Unclaimed Son

"So the carpets are not in our inventory, and the foreman's records indicate the carpets were sold to Arabesque and never returned."

"That is correct," Benjamin replied. "I wrote to the senior accountant at the Arabesque Company requesting information concerning the disposition of the four carpets." Benjamin held up the Arabesque correspondence, "And this is their response."

Jeffery Porter looked at the unopened envelope and quietly said, "Please read it to me."

Benjamin carefully tore the end of the sealed envelope, unfolded the response, and said, "The Senior Accountant at Arabesque has responded to my request for information. The letter is notarized."

Benjamin took a deep breath and read the letter to Jeffery.

Liberty, February 12, 1896

Dear Colleague, I deeply regret that my duty to you requires the unpleasant task of verifying your concerns of significant errors in your client's records pertaining to the alleged reimbursement of funds directed to the Arabesque Company for the return of products. Permit me to be concise:

Concerning your queries as to the disposition of the four carpets allegedly returned to your client's company for a monetary refund. The Arabesque Company records reveal,

1.Carpet # 2567-8 is currently located in our stock.

2.Carpet # 4891-8 is currently located in our stock.

3.Carpet # 4788-2 was sold on December 17, 1893, to Mr. and Mrs. J.B. Pierce of Liberty.

4.Carpet # 7488-2 was sold on June 14, 1894, to the Majestic Hotel of Liberty.

The policy of the Arabesque Company is to request credit for returned products against future purchases. This policy has been strictly followed without exception.

The Arabesque Company exclusively utilizes the services of the Reserved Bank of Liberty for all banking interests.

I must commend you on your sterling representation of your client's financial interest. I hold your efforts as honorable and consistent with the highest standards of our profession. If I may be of any further aid concerning your endeavors to render your client's accounts accurate and whole, I pledge my abilities and time at your service.

I remain your obedient servant,
Walter Marsh, SA., CPA

Benjamin Walker, CPA
Riverdale.
Witnessed: Joyce Roberts, Notary Public #698773

"I find your efforts in this matter honorable and professional as well," Jeffery Porter said while Benjamin handed the letter to his employer for further review.

"Thank you, sir," Benjamin returned.

After further reviewing the letter, Jeffery Porter walked over to the desk and opened the envelope containing the remaining cheques bearing Arabesque endorsement. He studied the cheques, flipping the cheque over several times. "How were they able to cash these cheques? No bank of repute would honor these cheques unless the funds were directed to the Arabesque Company. How did they do it?"

Benjamin simply stated, "These cheques were adulterated to appear as two-party cheques allegedly signed over to Jack Prince by the Arabesque Company as a draft for services."

"I don't understand. These cheques indicate a reimbursement to Arabesque," Jeffery Porter stated.

"Yes," Benjamin replied. "The first indication of impropriety I noticed was small breaks in the printed line under the

Arabesque Company name on the cheque," Benjamin stated, handing a cheque to Jeffery Porter.

"The line on the cheque has been adulterated by an unseen chemical agent. Let me show you." Benjamin stood and selected a lemon sitting in one of the glass bowls on his desk. Pulling a small pocket knife from his trousers, Benjamin cut the lemon in two and squeezed the lemon juice into a calibrated beaker. Benjamin then diluted the lemon juice with four parts of distilled water. After mixing, he used his eyedropper to place the fluid into the open atomizer. Benjamin selected one of the chicken eggs, broke the shell, and carefully allowed the egg white to flow into an empty bowl. Benjamin placed the yoke and shells in an empty paper sack.

Next, Benjamin turned the valve up on his desk's gas table lamp. He put his hand over the round hole in the glass shade. He moved his hand up and down until he determined the correct distance for the right temperature. At that point, Benjamin took the alleged refund cheques from his employer, placed one cheque on the middle of his desk, and carefully sprayed the diluted lemon juice onto the cheque. He waved it up and down in the warm draft of air rising from the gas lamp.

"Come closer and watch the cheque," Benjamin said.

Jeffery Porter stood and watched as almost immediately the name Jack Prince appeared next to Arabesque Company with a slash separating the two payees. When the name had darkened, Benjamin took a small brush and lightly painted it with albumen. "This will fix Mr. Prince's name so that the name won't fade," Benjamin explained to an amazed Jeffery Porter.

Benjamin repeated the procedure on the back of the cheque, clearly revealing the cheque was endorsed by Jack Prince. After preserving the signature of Jack Prince's endorsement with albumen, Benjamin handed the evidence to Jeffery Porter and sat down to answer his employee's questions.

"I don't understand!" Jeffery Porter exclaimed.

"A schoolboy's trick . . . invisible ink," Benjamin explained. "Paul Harris secured a blank cheque using the proper measures. He filled out the cheque to the Arabesque Company for the supposed return of the product. Paul Harris further adulterated the cheque by applying a counterfeit Arabesque endorsement seal on the back of the cheque. Before the cheque was cashed at the Bank of Londonderry, Jack Prince signed the front and back of the cheque, creating the appearance of a two-party cheque. His signature matches the breaks in the line when the letters of his signature occasionally cross the cheque line. The signature on the cheque also matches his writing in the numerous entries in the company's account books. His bank in Londonderry accepts two-party cheques. He added his name next to the original payee's name with invisible ink and endorsed the back with invisible ink. He cashed the cheque at his bank, and after a few hours, his name faded and disappeared. When the canceled cheque was returned to your company, only the original payee and counterfeit stamp remained. They used a schoolboy's trick to steal money from you, sir."

"How could you have possibly known this?" Jeffery asked.

"I was a schoolboy not long ago . . . " Benjamin responded with a smile.

"Jack was laughing at me. I could feel it," Jeffery Porter groaned, looking into his memories.

"Yes," Benjamin confirmed.

"Both accountants were involved!" Jeffery Porter responded rhetorically.

"Yes," Benjamin confirmed.

"Why?" Benjamin's employer asked.

"Well, they doubled their salaries, and they were somewhat smart about it by stealing a relatively small amount of money. I have identified approximately the same amount of money stolen from you in the years 1892 and 1893. This small amount of money and a few small carpets missing in such a large inventory and huge turnover may have gone undetected for years . . . it probably has," Benjamin explained.

"They would risk losing their lives for a few dollars?" Jeffery Porter asked.

"Why do people do immoral things? Why do people commit adultery or anything else immoral and destructive? I guess they think they will get away with it. I am sure it is a form of self-deception," Benjamin responded.

The statement struck Jeffery Porter. He realized his many flaws in that moment, and after a pause, he stated, "I don't want them killed. Not for a few dollars."

"The law is noticeably clear on this issue. You may commute their death sentence with permission of the chief arbitrator representing the Accountant Guild. Also, as the accountant who indicted the accused, I, too, must agree with the commutation. All I ask is that both accountants must write a letter to the Certified Public Accountant Professional Association requesting their license to be revoked on the grounds of fraud and theft while performing their duties," Benjamin responded.

"I absolutely agree," Jeffery Porter stated, "I will send Mrs. Cromwell to the County Auditor-Controller's office and request a hearing as soon as possible on this matter."

~

Benjamin and his employer spent their time that morning reviewing the evidence and planning the best methods for securing replacement accountants after Harris and Prince were removed. Within the hour, both men heard many feet ascending the stairs to Benjamin's office. As they turned, they were surprised to see Robert Kaiser, the senior accountant from the Kent Auditor-Controller's office. He was an elderly man with years of experience. He was tall and thin, and he wore a long, black dress coat partially covering a crisp white dress shirt with brass buttons and gold cufflinks, the collar secured at his neck with a black ribbon tie. His boots were tall, stopping just below his knee, conveying a most beautiful black sheen. He carried a large, black leather briefcase at his side containing the necessary documents for the inquest to come. His countenance bore years of a driven life, and his eyes appeared as deep blue radiating beacons in the night. His pace was deliberate, and he seemed to carefully study the composition of those waiting in the room.

Following the senior accountant was Miss Taylor, a most attractive and innocent lady in her early twenties. Her unsophisticated appearance belied the fact she possessed an exceedingly high aptitude for stenography and was deeply respected for her transcription abilities. She seemed to struggle with the heavy stenograph machine but sought no relief from her burden. Mrs. Cromwell came next, bringing with her the company's new and substantial Stellar Typewriter, with appropriate typing and carbon paper. She also carried a large file under her right arm containing critical contracts the accused had entered as a condition of their employment.

"Mr. Kaiser, I am so happy you were available on such short notice. I would like you to meet my confidential accountant responsible for reviewing my books," Jeffery Porter said, offering his hand.

While shaking Jeffery Porter's hand, Mr. Kaiser focused on the young accountant. "Please tell me you are a licensed accountant."

"Yes, sir," Benjamin proudly responded. "My name is Benjamin Walker, and I am a certified public accountant."

"I heard about you. You are some kind of a phenom or something. What are you—fourteen or fifteen?"

"Seventeen, sir," Benjamin stated.

"Do you think you are old enough to put a man to death, if necessary?" Mr. Kaiser asked with an air of condescension.

"Sir, I hope it will not come to that," Benjamin responded.

Mr. Kaiser walked over and shook Benjamin's hand, and with a gruff look said, "I hope so, too."

Benjamin motioned where Mr. Kaiser was to sit by walking over and politely pulling the chair from beneath the library table. He pulled out a chair for Mrs. Cromwell as well, and she sat next to Mr. Kaiser with her typewriter.

Mr. Kaiser introduced his stenographer, pointing his hand in her direction, "Miss Taylor will be the recorder for these proceedings."

With that said, Jeffery Porter secured a chair for Miss Taylor and thanked her for her presence while she assembled her stenograph machine by pulling the lid off the device and unfolding its legs. Benjamin surrendered his desk chair to Jeffery Porter and positioned himself next to the showroom window about ten feet from Mr. Kaiser. The latter would act the part of arbitrator, representing the Certified Public Accounting Professional Organization. This was the standard position for the participants in this type of proceeding.

Mr. Kaiser opened his black briefcase and took out a heavy, well-worn piece of paper. "I am required to read the following to the plaintiffs in this proceeding, so bear with me while I place the instructions of this meeting into the record. I will answer your questions when this preliminary is completed. Miss Taylor, are you ready?"

Miss Taylor responded with a somewhat flat affect, "Yes, Chief Arbitrator."

"I am Robert Kaiser, the senior accountant for the Auditor-Controller's office in Kenton, and I will act as Arbitrator for this proceeding. I have been empowered by the Certified Public Accountant Professional Organization in Kenton to conduct an evidentiary hearing and, if necessary, a trial to determine the guilt or innocence of accused certified public accountants in the State of Kenton who may have committed malfeasance while performing their function. Today's date is February 13, 1896. This hearing is taking place at the Porter Exotic Carpet Import and Wholesale Company. This hearing has been convened at the request of Jeffery Porter, who is in attendance and owner of said company, to determine if the accountants employed by Mr. Porter have willfully, without right or mistake, conspired with premeditation to systematically and methodically commit a fraud against the financial interest of Mr. Porter for the purpose of self-gain. Further-

Day K Altair

more, Jeffery Porter accuses the accountants in question of having conducted their nefarious acts with the explicit intent to conceal such activities by falsifying the accounting books of their employer's company. These crimes, if proven beyond a reasonable doubt, are capital offenses.

"The accusation of fraud and ill-will has been brought to this proceeding by Mr. Porter's confidential accountant, Benjamin Walker, CPA, who is in attendance," the Chief Arbitrator continued. "The certified public accountants accused of these acts are. . . ." Arbitrator Kaiser looked up from his script and turned to Mrs. Cromwell. Mrs. Cromwell quickly wrote both men's names and titles down on a piece of paper and gave the paper to Chief Arbitrator, who then identified the accused. "Senior accountant Jack Prince, CPA and Paul Harris, CPA, both employed by Jeffery Porter at his company in the role of accountants. Other individuals in attendance are Helen Taylor, stenographer, and Ruth Cromwell, Jeffery Porter's assistant. This proceeding has two distinct parts. The first part is an evidentiary hearing to determine if there is sufficient evidence that a crime has been committed. If the evidence demonstrates a substantial likelihood of a crime, the accused will be asked to join the parties present to hear the indictment against them and be advised of the next phase of the proceeding: the trial. The accused will be given a complete explanation of the trial and their rights, and of the accusations against them. Those accused may plead innocent and ask for legal representation before participating in the trial. If such a request is made, the trial would be postponed to a future date. The trial will utilize the formal rules of evidence and be held at the Advanced School Auditorium of Kent. The accused will be warned that failure to appear at the trial will be considered an admission of guilt, and a bounty will be placed on their head of five hundred dollars for proof of death. Such proof of death will consist of, but not limited to, the body or head of the deceased accused. This postmortem evidence must be presented to the Auditor-Controller's office for verification no later than fourteen days

280

after death to ensure proper identification lest corruption vanquishes the accused.

"By the statutes of Kenton, this preliminary hearing is required to be conducted by an Arbitrator chosen by the Certified Public Accountant Professional Organization concerning accusation of malpractice or wrongdoing by members of that honorable association. This is true for all professional organizations in Kenton, may it be attorneys, civil engineers, physicians, or other professions. Our society requires the responsibility for determining fault and rendering judgment against a professional must be adjudicated by members of their professional association. If a person or persons accused were to become excessively belligerent or threatening to the participants of the hearing, or if the accused attempted to flee the hearing, the certified public accountant representing Jeffery Porter is required by law to terminate the accused. In the event the accused are found guilty, in a future formal trial with legal representation present, the certified public accountant representing Jeffery Porter is required to terminate the guilty individuals unless the victim of the crime, in this case Jeffery Porter, asks for the adjudicated guilty accountant or accountants' sentence to be commuted to a lesser penalty. The conditions for commutation must be approved by the victim's certified public accountant and the certified public accountant from the Auditor-Controller's office. The accused may also confess to the crime without a trial and ask for mercy in the form of a commutation. The penalty for willful theft and adulteration of accounting records by a certified public accountant is death. May Providence and his messenger, the sacred Raven, guide us and give us wisdom to determine the truth, and the grace to forgive those who have trespassed against us."

The Chief Arbitrator looked up and stated while returning his written instructions to his briefcase, "At this time, I will take questions concerning this proceeding."

The room was deafly quiet as the participants considered the ominous meaning of the words just spoken.

"Okay, let's continue," Mr. Kaiser stated, looking at Jeffery Porter then Benjamin. "At this time, I will review the blood oath of confidentiality and fidelity signed by the accused accountants as a condition of employment."

Mrs. Cromwell handed the Chief Arbitrator the contracts from her file. After a careful review, the Chief Arbitrator stated, "I will submit the blood oath for Jack Prince and Paul Harris are in order and both individuals have legally sworn an oath of death if their conduct is determined by trial to be felonious in the commission of their professional employment. Okay, let us proceed. Mr. Walker, you may present a narrative of the discovery of facts that have led you to believe the accountants in question have conducted felonious actions, fraud, against their employer, Jeffery Porter. Please be succinct."

Taking a deep breath, Benjamin walked several steps closer. As a student, Benjamin had spent many hours studying and rehearsing for this moment when he would be required to present a case against another member of his profession. He remembered what his teachers had taught him, and he was prepared to act his part in the proceedings he set into motion. At this moment, Benjamin was not encumbered by physical infirmity or youth; he was as strong and confident as any man carrying such a burden. He looked directly at the Chief Arbitrator, paused briefly to gather his thoughts, and began. "Thank you, Chief Arbitrator Kaiser. I am Benjamin Walker, CPA, and I hereby indict Jack Prince and Paul Harris of felonious malfeasance."

The tribunal grew very still after Benjamin uttered those words. He continued, "I have been hired by Jeffery Porter to conduct a confidential audit of the accounting books for his company for the fiscal years 1894, 1893, and 1892. While I examined the books for 1894, I discovered evidence which led me to believe malfeasance in the form of fraud, and manipulation of company accounting records to conceal fraud, on the part of the two accountants employed by Jeffery Porter. These actions appear to be in direct violation of the statutes of Kenton, the code of conduct of Certified Public Accountant Professional Organization and in violation of the very blood oath each accountant signed. The accused is Jack Prince, CPA, senior accountant, and Paul Harris, CPA. My conclusion is based on the following discoveries.

"The accounting practices of Jeffery Porter's company appeared precise and well-ordered except, in my opinion, when reconciling the actual company inventory of product with the books. The accounting procedure relied on only one accountant, Paul Harris, to accurately and truthfully document the removing and the return of product in the day book without further scrutiny. To determine if there were any suspicious anomalies in this practice, I initiated a review of the correspondence concerning the return of product. My review of the letters of correspondence from the Arabesque retail company of Liberty indeed revealed a series of suspicious circumstances."

Benjamin walked closer to the desk where the evidence was neatly sorted. He took out one of the cheques from the envelope and placed it next to appropriate correspondences.

"I discovered four letters from the Arabesque Company requesting a monetary refund four separate times during the year 1894. This was inconsistent with the normal operational methodology of the Arabesque Company. It is standard practice for Arabesque to request a credit against future sales when carpets are returned. The Book of Correspondence contains twenty-six letters from the Arabesque Company pertaining to the return of product, all but four requested a credit against future sales. The four letters requesting monetary refund had the value of . . ." Benjamin hesitated while looking at his notes scribbled in the margin of the letter he purposely selected. "Three thousand thirty-six dollars, compared to the other twenty-two letters requesting credit against future purchases of well over twenty thousand dollars. The inventory numbers for the returned carpets in the letters requesting monetary refunds . . ." he again hesitated while checking his notes, "are number 2567-8, number 4891-8, number 4788-2, and number 7488-2." Benjamin, at that point, handed the four letters requesting monetary refund to the Chief Arbitrator.

Arbitrator Kaiser examined the letter and stated, "Mr. Walker has submitted for my review four correspondences requesting monetary refund from the Arabesque Company for returned product and the inventory numbers indicated on the letters are consistent with Mr. Walker's previous statement. Please continue Mr. Walker."

"Thank you, Chief Arbitrator." Benjamin next moved to the cheque he had selected sitting on the desk. "I reviewed the four cheques representing the refund to the Arabesque Company penned by Paul Harris. Each cheque clearly indicates the returned carpet's corresponding inventory number consistent with the letters requesting a monetary refund. In addition, I noticed the cheque had been processed through the Bank of Londonderry. This is significant because the Porter Wholesale Company records indicate the Arabesque Company exclusively uses the Reserve Bank of Liberty. I would like to submit one of the cheques into evidence at this time."

The Chief Arbitrator received the cheque from Benjamin. "Mr. Walker has submitted for my review one of the four processed cheques, dated July 1, 1894, for reimbursement of returned product with carpet inventory number 7488-2 noted on the cheque. This cheque and inventory number for product correspond to the letter dated June 14, 1894, originating from the Arabesque Retail Carpet Company for the purpose of refund. The inventory numbers on the submitted cheque are consistent with the letter requesting a refund. Mr. Walker, may I ask why you do not submit the other three cheques for review at this time?"

"I am prepared to present the other cheques momentarily in relationship with other corroborating evidence if the Chief Arbitrator will permit some latitude in the sequencing of evidential presentation," Benjamin responded.

"Of course, please proceed as intended," the Chief Arbitrator agreed.

"Thank you, Chief Arbitrator," Benjamin continued. "To ascertain the carpet's disposition as reflected by the warehouse records, I requested Dave Perkins, the warehouse foreman, to review his records of the carpets in question. He responded in writing dated early this morning. His written statement indicated that 'the warehouse records state the carpets in question were shipped to the Arabesque Company and were not returned to inventory. A review of the existing warehouse inventory also did not reveal the presence of the carpets under question.' I would like to submit for review to the Chief Arbitrator the handwritten note by Dave Perkins."

Benjamin selected the foreman's note among the other pieces of evidence on the desk and handed the document to the Chief Arbitrator.

"Thank you, Mr. Walker. Mr. Walker has submitted to me for review a note written by Dave Perkins, and the note is consistent with Mr. Walker's description of the note's content. If necessary, is Mr. Perkins available to testify?"

"Yes, Chief Arbitrator," Benjamin responded.

"Very well. Continue, Mr. Walker," Arbitrator Kaiser stated.

"Thank you, Chief Arbitrator," Benjamin continued. "Yesterday, I wrote the Arabesque Company's Senior Accountant, Walter Marsh, requesting information concerning the disposition of the four carpets in question. The returning correspondence states two of the carpets in question are currently in the Arabesque inventory. Two have been sold. The identified purchases are exhibited in the correspondence. Senior accountant Marsh also states the policy of Arabesque Company is to request a credit. There have been no exceptions to this policy. In addition, the senior accountant reports the Arabesque Company only utilizes the Reserve Bank of Liberty for all banking transactions. I would like to submit this correspondence to the Chief Arbitrator for review."

Benjamin handed the letter to the Chief Arbitrator. After he reviewed the document, Mr. Kaiser stated, "I have been given for review a notarized letter from the senior accountant at the Arabesque Company, and the information in the correspondence is consistent with the statement made by Mr. Walker."

Chief Arbitrator Kaiser looked up from the letter and picked up one of the cheques, saying, "Please tell me you have evidence with a direct nexus to these cheques being cashed by the two accountants under indictment."

"Yes, Chief Arbitrator," Benjamin stated with confidence, "I do."

Benjamin retrieved one of the cheques penned by Paul Harris from three remaining cheques not submitted to the Chief Arbitrator and approached the jurist. Holding the cheque in his hand, he pointed to the line under the payee's name. "Chief Arbitrator Kaiser, I submit for your review one of the processed cheques. Please focus your attention to the small gaps and spaces in the line after the word 'Company' on the payee underline."

Chief Arbitrator, after a brief moment of scrutiny, stated, "Let the record show Mr. Walker has submitted for my review one of the processed cheques, and the line beneath the payee's identity and after the last word of the payee's name has a number of breaks and spaces in the line. Please continue, Mr. Walker."

"Thank you, Chief Arbitrator," Benjamin continued. "The spaces and gaps in the line are the result of writing over the line by Jack Prince when he added his name as he cashed the cheque as a two-party cheque. If the Chief Arbitrator will step over to the desk lamp, I will demonstrate."

Jeffery Porter stood and pushed his chair into the desk. He stepped back to allow Chief Arbitrator Kaiser to position himself next to the gas lamp. Benjamin, on the opposite side of the desk, turned the gas valve to increase the gas and said, "Chief Arbitrator, I am now going to spray a fine mist of diluted lemon juice on the face of the cheque and place the cheque over the warm air."

Almost instantly, after the cheque was exposed to the gas lamp's rising heat, Jack Prince's name appeared on the payee line. "Jack Prince used disappearing ink to sign his name, thus creating a two-party cheque. After a few hours, his name disappeared, and only the Arabesque Company name appeared on the payee line."

Benjamin repeated the process on the cheque's back, revealing that Jack Prince had also endorsed the cheque under the Arabesque stamp. "I will apply a thin coating of albumin to fix the signatures, preventing them from disappearing. This cheque is the second cheque I have demonstrated containing Jack Prince's name on both the payee line and back of the cheque. I have held two undeveloped cheques in reserve for the trial."

Chief Arbitrator Kaiser reached over, took the cheque from Benjamin, and studied it while flicking the cheque front to back several times. At that point, he looked at the stenographer and stated, "Mr. Walker has submitted for review a cheque penned by Paul Harris allegedly for a refund to the Arabesque Company. When Mr. Walker applied a mist of lemon juice to the front and back of the cheque and then applied heat using the gas lamp, Jack Prince's name appeared on both the payee line and under the endorsement stamp of the Arabesque Company, causing the cheque to become a two-party cheque with Jack Prince the recipient of payment. Mr. Walker, do you have any additional evidence to present to this proceeding?"

"Yes, Chief Arbitrator. Paul Harris exclusively had access to the day book for the purpose of documentation of inventory. He was the only one that could have falsified the inventory records dealing with the returned products. Paul Harris's signature is affixed in the day book, affirming the carpets in question were returned to inventory."

"Anything else, Mr. Walker?" the Chief Arbitrator asked somberly.

"No, Chief Arbitrator Kaiser. I respectively request at this time consensus from the Honorable Chief Arbitrator as to my indictment of Jack Prince and Paul Harris for felonious acts against my client, Jeffery Porter, and I pray the Honorable

Chief Arbitrator will establish a time and place for a capital trial. I pledge my respect and obedience as to the findings and verdict of the Chief Arbitrator pertaining to the accused individuals."

Benjamin responded with the appropriate and necessary concluding remarks required for this kind of proceeding. He stood straight and tall, looking directly at the Chief Arbitrator. He had learned his lessons well, and despite his youthful age, his representation was adept and hopefully persuasive.

The Chief Arbitrator returned to his chair, paused, then stated in a strong, firm voice, "I have reviewed the evidence provided by Jeffery Porter's confidential accountant, Mr. Walker. Mr. Walker has placed Jack Prince and Paul Harris under indictment for fraud and falsification of accounting records—a commission of a crime while performing their duties as certified public accountants. This Arbitrator concurs with Mr. Walker's indictment by clear and convincing evidence. Jack Prince and Paul Harris stand indicted. We will now proceed with the next phase of the hearing explaining the crimes of indictment and the right to be represented by legal counsel to the accused."

Mrs. Cromwell leaned closer to the Chief Arbitrator and softly stated, "I will gather Jack Prince and Paul Harris to these proceedings if so ordered."

"I so order, Mrs. Cromwell," the Chief Arbitrator responded.

Mrs. Cromwell walked around the end of the library table and, with a quick pace, disappeared down the narrow staircase. Benjamin resumed his proper distance near the showroom windows and looked to his employer. Jeffery Porter nodded his head in the affirmative and accordingly communicated his approval. The room grew quiet; only the soft noise of the warehouse far below managed to reach the room. The quiescent milieu was about to end.

Because of his location in the room, Benjamin was the first to hear the footsteps coming up the stairs. He knew the men he had indicted only by their works and faults. If he had passed Jack Prince and Paul Harris on the street, he would not have recognized them. The anonymity of those accused was about to end. Mrs. Cromwell was the first to enter the room. She crossed the room in haste and resumed her seat. Two men followed her. The first to enter the room, Benjamin assumed, was Jack Prince. An older man in his fifties, thin, tall, and well-dressed in a black suit and white dress shirt. His grey hair was cut short, and his face appeared intense, hidden somewhat behind gold spectacles. Jack Prince seemed to be scanning the room, attempting to comprehend his circumstance. As he passed, the older man seemed to glare at Benjamin, and Benjamin felt his body recoil with the man's closeness. Just a few steps behind him, a younger man entered, disheveled without a coat and wearing an ink-stained white shirt, cuffs rolled up, and collar open. His hair long, dark brown, and uncombed. Mr. Harris seemed more passive, looking around with palpable trepidation.

Two empty chairs sat near the warehouse window next to the stenographer, and as the men drew near, Jeffery Porter stood, motioned toward the chairs, and stated, "Mr. Harris and Mr. Prince, please bring those empty chairs and sit down in front of Chief Arbitrator Kaiser."

The older man asked with a harsh tone, "What is this all about—what is the meaning of all this?"

Jeffery Porter responded, "Please grab a chair and sit down. This is important."

The two men followed their employer's direction and sat about five feet in front of the library table facing the Chief Arbitrator and Mrs. Cromwell. Looking directly at the two indicted accountants, Chief Arbitrator Kaiser began, "Jack Prince and Paul Harris, you have been indicted for professional malfeasance. Specifically, fraud and the falsification of accounting books for the purpose of concealing fraud. I am Chief Arbitrator Kaiser, the purpose of this proceeding—"

Jack jumped up, knocking the chair to the floor with a loud bang. His face seemed contorted with fear, his mouth gaping as if he were attempting to scream. He turned and ran down the long length of the office in an attempt to escape his fate. He knew too well he had been caught, and the penalty for his crime was death.

Benjamin watched the terrified man attempting to escape. He stood, reached beneath his coat and pulled a heavy caliber revolver from his belt at the small of his back. Benjamin pushed his leg brace against the wall, carefully aimed his revolver, and pulled back on the hammer. He took a breath and held it, waiting for Jack Prince to clear the warehouse windows. When his target was only a few feet from the stairs, Benjamin squeezed the trigger. The detonation of the revolver in the enclosed office was truly deafening. The heavy lead bullet snapped across the short distance, striking the fleeing accountant in the base of his head. The terrible pressure of the bullet breaching the skull and passing through the brain caused the indicted accountant's head to burst, flinging skull, skin, and grey matter into the air and forming a blood-red cloud. Jack Prince was dead before his mangled body hit the floor. The office grew still. A misty cloud of burnt gunpowder softly swirled, forming an aerial display that went unnoticed by those in the room.

Paul Harris let out a soft whimper, then a moan as he witnessed his own possible fate. Miss Taylor, frozen in disbelief, pulled her legs tight against her body as she formed a fetal position, balancing awkwardly on her chair. Mrs. Cromwell slowly stood up, turned, and walked over to the corner of the office, stooped down, and vomited. Jeffery Porter and Chief Arbitrator Kaiser watched the body fall from life in stoic silence, both men instantly and instinctively accepted the necessity of Jack Prince's death. Still, to see a man die only a few feet in front of them formed an indelible image. Benjamin stared at Jack Prince's corpse. He watched as a river of red blood and urine escaped the lifeless remains. He observed the liquid from the corpse slowly flow to the wall a few feet away, and then form a mixed pool of body fluid. The smell of urine, blood, and feces invaded the office air, replacing the fading cloud of smoke.

Benjamin felt an immense wave of rage consume his very essence. He pivoted toward Paul Harris, whose attention now shifted from his dead colleague to the man holding the gun. Benjamin's countenance, sanguine and contorted, confessed his inner anger. The swollen capillaries in his eyes caused a scarlet sclera to complement his knotted eyebrows and wrinkled forehead. The young, physically impaired accountant now waved his gun in the direction of Paul Harris while he took several quick halting steps closer to the horrified surviving accountant.

When the space between the two accountants was only a few inches of separation, Paul Harris fell from his chair and attempted to crawl away from his fate. Benjamin reached down and grabbed the frightened man by his shirt and yanked him back onto the chair with his left hand while continuing to point his menacing revolver toward Paul Harris's head. "Now sit here and tell these witnesses what you and Jack Prince did. Tell them now and tell them the truth or by Raven's wing I will spray your brains all over this room!"

Jeffery Porter and Chief Arbitrator Kaiser sat motionless in stunned silence, expecting to see another death before their eyes. Paul Harris screamed, "Yes . . . yes, I will tell you everything . . . I beg you, please don't kill me."

The Chief Arbitrator held up his hand, "Stop."

Paul Harris froze.

"Miss Taylor, are you ready to record Mr. Harris's statement?"

Miss Taylor, shaken and pale, slowly uncurled her legs until her feet touched the floor and placed her hands on the keyboard. "Yes, Chief Arbitrator," she whispered.

Chief Arbitrator Kaiser stated, "Let the record show that when Jack Prince realized the nature of this proceeding and attempted to escape, as required by statute, Mr. Walker killed him by a pistol shot. As the only indicted survivor, Mr. Harris would like to make a statement of culpability concerning the fraudulent actions of both Jack Prince and himself. Mr. Harris, we are ready for your statement. Mr. Harris has

indicated he is willing to waive his rights to legal representation and trial, correct Mr. Harris?"

Benjamin pushed his gun in the direction of Paul Harris's
head. Still staring at Benjamin, Paul Harris shook his head in
the affirmative and stuttered, "Yeah . . . ye . . . yes."

Benjamin, still glaring in rage, took several steps back and
placed his gun in his belt and crossed his arms, his eyes
frozen on the surviving accountant.

Paul Harris could barely speak, "Jack Prince and I. . . . "

"Speak up, man! We have to hear this clearly to record
your statement," Chief Arbitrator admonished.

Paul Harris continued, "Jack said we wouldn't get caught.
He said he embezzled small amounts of funds for years. He
said if we didn't get greedy and took small amounts of money
from the company, and controlled the books, and hid what we
took . . . I mean, I think he did a lot of things wrong. I don't
know all of it. I only know about writing false refund letters
from customers and then falsely documenting in the day book
that the carpet had been returned. That's what I did. I entered
into the day book the carpets had 'been returned.' I wrote the
refund cheque, used a counterfeit endorsement stamp, and
Jack Prince took the made-up cheque to his bank in Londonderry where he made it a two-party cheque. I think he bribed
someone to—anyway, Jack used disappearing ink, so his
name faded away. For the last few years, ah, we used the
Arabesque Company to fake the cheques. Before that, it was
other companies. It went on for years. . . ."

"How much money was taken from Mr. Porter's Company?" the Chief Arbitrator asked.

"Between three and four thousand dollars each year. Jack
would take care of all that . . . between three and four thousand dollars for the eight years I was employed," a contrite
Paul Harris responded.

The Chief Arbitrator leaned closer to the indicted accountant: "Now this is particularly important. I want you to
be truthful, absolutely. What you tell us now may very well
have a bearing on you coming out of this alive. Do you

understand?"

Benjamin took a few steps away from the showroom window and toward the indicted accountant. Paul Harris snapped to attention, turned, and looked at the menacing approach of Benjamin Walker and yelped, "Yes . . . yes, I promise—on Raven's wing, I will tell the truth. Don't let him hurt me."

Chief Arbitrator Kaiser looked over at Miss Taylor and promptly stated, "Please have, 'Don't let him hurt me' stricken from the record. Now, Mr. Harris, we want the entire truth."

"Yes Sir—he never told me, but I think sometimes he stole carpets from the inventories, small stuff. He hinted he had someone in the warehouse working with him. A laborer, I think. Someone inconspicuous. I think some minor carpets were stolen. I don't know anything more. I only know what I was involved in . . . that's all I know," the frightened accountant stated, carefully watching Benjamin Walker from the corner of his eye.

Chief Arbitrator Kaiser harshly asked, "Were any of these thefts recent? Is his accomplice still working in the warehouse?"

Paul Harris responded, "I think so . . . I don't know who it is . . . I swear, I just don't know."

"Do you have anything else to say before I pass sentence?" the Chief Arbitrator asked.

"Please, Mr. Porter, I have a wife and three children, and I am their only source of sustenance. Please spare my life and commute my sentence—please, I will do anything you ask."

Chief Arbitrator Kaiser looked directly at Paul Harris and stated, "Having stated clearly that you have committed capital crimes and all the evidence presented at this proceeding corroborates your admission of guilt, I am compelled to sentence you to death. Benjamin Walker, Certified Public Accountant, will determine the time and place of your execution as required by law. Mr. Porter, at this time, do you wish to commute Paul Harris's sentence of death?"

"I do," Jeffery Porter firmly stated, much to the relief of

Paul Harris.

"Mr. Porter, please specify the conditional requirement for the commutation of Mr. Harris's death sentence," Chief Arbitrator Kaiser requested, turning and looking at Jeffery Porter. "And Mrs. Cromwell, are you feeling well enough to type out the conditions so all participants to this proceeding will obtain a signed copy of those specifications required by Jeffery Porter?"

Leaning against the back wall of the office behind the Chief Arbitrator with her head down, Mrs. Cromwell was trying not to faint. Her pale complexion defied her response, "Yes, Chief Arbitrator."

"Very well, please type and make duplicates of Mr. Porter's condition for the commutation of Paul Harris," the Chief Arbitrator asked while turning and helping Mrs. Cromwell to her seat.

Mrs. Cromwell took four pieces of paper and three pieces of carbon paper and placed them into the Stellar Typewriter. She typed on the top of the paper, "Conditions of the Commutation of Paul Harris's Death Sentence. February 13, 1896." She then stated, "I am ready, Mr. Porter."

Mr. Porter began, "Condition 1): Mr. Paul Harris will immediately pen his resignation to the Certified Public Professional Organization, clearly stating he has committed fraud and falsified accounting records to hide fraudulent acts. The written resignation must be to the satisfaction of Benjamin Walker, CPA, and must be accomplished no later than seventy-two hours from the conclusion of this proceeding. In addition, copies of this resignation letter will be delivered to Jeffery Porter, Benjamin Walker, and the Chief Arbitrator for Kent County for their records.

"Condition 2): Mr. Harris will remain employed by Jeffery Porter as a warehouse laborer class III, in good order, with all wages and benefits bestowed by that position with the exception that ten percent of his income will be garnished and returned to Jeffery Porter as reparation until the monies unlawfully obtained for the fiscal year 1894 have been

restored. Mr. Harris, at that point, may seek gainful employment elsewhere or continue his employment in that position at
the Porter Exotic Carpet Import Company, if his work ethic
warrants continued employment.

"Mr. Walker," Jeffery Porter asked, looking at his confidential accountant, "Do you wish to specify additional
conditions?"

"Yes, Mr. Porter, I have a condition," Benjamin returned.

"Condition 3): Mr. Harris will thoroughly clean my office
of all remains of his former co-conspirator after Jack Prince's
body has been removed, as well as anything else necessary to
restore my office to cleanliness and good order. This will be
accomplished by the beginning of the next workday."

Chief Arbitrator Kaiser and Jeffery Porter looked at each
other and tried not to smile, "Seems right," Jeffery Porter said
to Chief Arbitrator.

The Chief Arbitrator agreed, "Sure does."

The Chief Arbitrator waited a few moments as a nauseous
Mrs. Cromwell completed the transcript of the conditions.
Indicating she had finished, she looked at the Chief Arbitrator
and said, "I am ready. Please continue."

The Chief Arbitrator completed the conditions of commutation by stating, "Jeffery Porter, as recipient of Paul Harris's
felonious acts, you are hereby appointed sole warden of said
articles of commutation and shall monitor compliance of the
guilty and report any failure of compliance to Benjamin
Walker, CPA, for the purpose of the summary execution of
Paul Harris, without appeal. The execution of the guilty party
will be by the hands of Benjamin Walker, CPA, or if not
available, a licensed public bounty hunter. May Divine
Providence give us the strength, wisdom, and resolve to
enforce justice."

Chief Arbitrator Kaiser turned to Mrs. Cromwell and patiently waited for her to complete her typing. Upon completion, Mrs. Cromwell removed the papers from her typewriter,
separated the sheets of paper from the carbon paper, and
handed the typed papers to the Chief Arbitrator.

The Chief Arbitrator carefully read the articles of commutation from death. When he was satisfied that the typed statement accurately reflected the comments of the contributors, he passed the remaining copies to Benjamin, Jeffery Porter, and Paul Harris. After several minutes, when the parties of the proceeding had completed their review of the commutation conditions, Chief Arbitrator Kaiser stated, "Are we in agreement the conditions for commutation have been accurately transcribed?"

Jeffery Porter and Benjamin Walker in unison answered, "Yes, Chief Arbitrator."

The Chief Arbitrator then repeated the question, "Paul Harris, does the document before you accurately reflect your understanding of the articles of commutation expressed in these proceedings?"

Paul Harris whispered, "Yes, Chief Arbitrator." He bowed his head in shame.

The Chief Arbitrator, at that point, ordered the typed document and the three carbon copies circulated among the parties, and when all had affixed their names, the Chief Arbitrator ordered Mrs. Cromwell to notarize the documents. When Mrs. Cromwell had recorded the necessary information in her book, affixing her notary seal, the Chief Justice gave the typed copy to Jeffery Porter and carbon copies to Paul Harris and Benjamin. He kept one copy for his files.

The Chief Arbitrator looked directly at Paul Harris and said, "You have been given an opportunity to complete your natural life after committing a capital crime. Please conduct yourself with high morals and good order. May the Raven always watch over you. This proceeding is closed."

Paul Harris sat shamefully quiet, staring at the document permitting him to live and now defining his life, he managed a soft, "I will do my best, sir."

Mrs. Cromwell gathered her things, and, trying not to look at the body of the former employee by concentrating on her feet, slipped past the others, and went down the staircase in a desperate attempt to find sanctuary in the fresh air. Miss

Taylor followed close behind.

Jeffery Porter offered Mr. Kaiser his hand, which was quickly shaken. Before pleasantries could be expressed, Mr. Kaiser turned in the direction of Benjamin Walker. He approached the young accountant with hand extended, and when Benjamin raised his hand to acknowledge the gesture, he was met with a loud "Congratulations!"

The Chief Arbitrator grasped Benjamin's hand with both hands and said, "Mr. Walker, you are genuinely a phenom. I have witnessed many accountants defend an indictment, yet I have witnessed few accountants with such a forceful argument. How you conducted yourself in this proceeding was exceptional, and you're not a bad shot either. When you are vested, I want you to become part of the County Arbitration Panel for certified public accountants. I think you will make an excellent jurist."

Benjamin was somewhat bewildered by the Chief Arbitrator's offer, and could only say, "I have so much to learn—I mean, thank you. I am not sure I am qualified."

"Let me assure you: you are qualified. I am a good judge of these things. You could clerk for me, and I would be honored to instruct you. Please consider my offer. I rarely make such an offer, so please think about it. I will be expecting you in a few months. Good-bye for now."

The Chief Arbitrator turned, walked across the office, and, paying no attention to the corpse, disappeared down the stairs.

Jeffery Porter, having overheard the Chief Arbitrator, said, "I guess the Chief Arbitrator doesn't realize you're going to work for me."

Benjamin's expression was equivocal. The sound of heavy footsteps on the stairs directed both Benjamin's and Jeffery Porter's attention.

Suddenly the smiling face of Oboe Jackson appeared as he reached the top of the stairs. "Dave Perkins heard the shot and saw the blast down below in the warehouse. He knew what had happened, and he had sent a runner to the firehouse.

One of the two accountants was dead or wounded. Either way, the fire wagon was needed." With a smirk of delight, Oboe leaned down by the body and stated, "Looks like someone got caught with his hand in the cookie jar."

With that tasteless comment, Oboe chuckled and looked up to see Benjamin Walker standing with Jeffery Porter across the room.

"Benjamin!" Oboe hurried to greet the young accountant. "I heard you passed the accountant exam and you were working for Mr. Porter," he said, reaching the young man. "Is this your work?"

Benjamin said, "Yep, guess so."

"Well, you got him with a headshot. Nice going." Oboe continued, "Sure stunk the place up. You have your father's eye, that's for sure. He's a great shot too, I recall."

Benjamin and Jeffery Porter did not really understand the levity, but they accepted the gallows humor was somehow part of the job. Before either man could say anything, the other firemen arrived with a stretcher. One man from the fire brigade burst out, "Whew, we got a stinker here. Let's get him to the icehouse."

The three men watched the firemen gather their lifeless burden and descend the stairs. Oboe, at that point, turned to Benjamin and said, "Well, congratulations on becoming an accountant. We are all proud of you."

Benjamin thanked him, and with that said, Oboe sprinted away, disappearing down the stairs.

Jeffery Porter took Benjamin's arm and walked his employee to the stairs. He leaned closer to his young confidential accountant, "You have done very well today. I want you to go home now. This has been a stressful day. I will make sure your office is put in good order. I want you to get some rest. Tomorrow we'll begin rebuilding the accounting office, but now I want you to go home."

"But sir, you have no one to do the accounting, and there is so much to do!"

Benjamin was interrupted with a stern, "Benjamin, go

home, I need you well rested. That's an order."

Benjamin smiled, "Thank you, sir, I am exhausted. I will see you in the morning." With that said, Benjamin carefully descended the stairs.

Jeffery turned to the last remaining person in the large office, a very emotionally distraught former accountant. Jeffery grabbed a nearby chair and sat down in front. "Paul, I want you to know I completely forgive you. The Word teaches us to forgive those who have trespassed. We all have failings. Your mistake was terrible, but now you have been washed clean. You have paid a terrible price for what you have done, but our new relationship begins today."

"How will I face my family?" Paul Harris asked, not able to control the tears from escaping.

"You will tell them the truth, they will forgive you, and life will go on," Jeffery responded.

"I am so ashamed!" Paul exclaimed.

Jeffery interrupted, "As well you should be, but this is the time for new beginnings, so listen to what I am going to tell you. I will send up three caretakers to help you with cleaning and returning this office to good order. You have lost your professional standing, and I cannot imagine how painful such a loss must be, that alone is a terrible punishment. However, you will have employment with me so you and your family will not suffer from impoverishment, and if the ten percent reparation is unmanageable, well, I am sure we can work things out."

"Walker will kill me if I deviate from the conditions of commutation," a desperate Paul whispered as if he feared he would be overheard.

"Benjamin Walker is your indictor and executioner, but I am your warden, and Benjamin can only take your life at my direction. There is only one exception. If you should take my life, he will not hesitate to kill you, and there will be no due process. This is the law from The Word. I will speak today with Dave Perkins. I want you to assist him with the warehouse inventory records. He asked me several times to find him some help. As you can imagine, the warehouse is very demanding, and your help with the inventory books will be a great relief to him. This task is a better match for your talents than lifting carpets all day. I will tell him I expect him and the other workers to treat you like any other worker, and if there is any manifest condescension or judgment, I will not approve."

"How can you trust me with such matters when I have stolen from you?" Paul asked while looking at his employer.

"I can trust you because you will swear on Raven's wing you will never betray me again. Will you do that for me?" Jefferey Porter asked.

Paul Harris did not hesitate, "I so swear on Raven's wing I will never betray you. I so solemnly promise as the Raven is my witness. Let my heart be so heavy, the Raven cannot carry me from this world to next, and the path to heaven barred to me forever should I betray you again."

"Then it is done, and you are my trusted employee. One day, someone will trespass against you, Paul. I want you to remember this day and forgive him as I have forgiven you," Jeffery said.

"I will never forget this day," a very appreciative employee responded.

"Enough of this then. I have a particularly important assignment that only you and I will know about," Jefferey Porter stated.

"Anything I might help you with!" responded Paul.

"Okay then. I need you to find out who is the thief Jack Prince was working with," Jeffery Porter continued. "I want you to be discreet but alert. I think he will be approaching you in time, considering your new position tracking and documenting the inventory. He will assume you can be corrupted. We deal with treasures. I have suspected for some time there is some leakage of product and you will help me stop it. Can I count on you?"

"Thank you, sir, for your trust," Paul continued. "You are most gracious. I will do anything I can to help you."

Jeffery Porter put both his hands on Paul's shoulders and said, "To a new beginning then. Now, let us get this office in good order."

A grateful employee responded, "Thank you, sir."

Jeffery Porter sat in his darkening office at the end of a terrible day. He offered a prayer for Jack Prince's deliverance.

Benjamin opened the ornately carved oak door to the mansion he called home. He was greeted in the foyer by Martha, the downstairs maid.

"Good afternoon, Mr. Walker. May I take your coat and hat?" A very preoccupied Benjamin passed her without comment.

Benjamin turned and scanned the dining room, then the formal sitting room, and when he could not locate his father, he turned to the previously ignored maid and asked, "Martha, is my father home, where may I find him?"

Martha walked out of the foyer and into the formal sitting room, pointing in the direction of the back porch. "Dr. Forrestal is visiting the sea, sir. I think he is sitting on the stone bench. Yes, that's where you will find the Doctor—by the sea."

Without saying a word, Benjamin passed through the formal room with a hurried, unsteady gait. He passed through the lavish room containing the opulent marble fireplace, the fine musical instruments, and walls covered with antique oil paintings depicting ancient battles and beautiful scenes of nature. He passed through the servant's hall containing the many boots, coats, and tools required for outside activity and flung the back door open, searching the beach for his father. As fast as his leg would allow, Benjamin hurried past the now empty horse corral, and up a sandy rise sprouting clumps of long green seagrass. When he reached the top of the mound, he could see the ocean's edge and, a few hundred feet from the moving waves of the Eastern Sea, he could see his father wrapped in his heavy wool overcoat wearing his beaver-skin black hat. His father seemed to be staring at the endless horizon or the passing of some unknown freighter, unaware of his child's resolve to reach him. Benjamin called out for his father's attention without success. The sky carried scores of crying gulls, creating an impenetrable wall of shrieking noise. Benjamin leaned into the brisk wind's dense wall and struggled to resist the entrapping sand grabbing at his bulky brace. The burden of the day's events compelled him to seek his father's guidance and comfort.

Benjamin fought to close the distance between himself and his father, and only when he was quite close did the temperament of the Eastern Sea yield to the needful son. Sensing his son's presence, Benjamin's father rose and lovingly embraced him.

Benjamin was able to release his tormented discontent, "Oh, Father, I killed a man today. I shot him and stole his life. How can I live with such a thing? Help me, for I feel utterly lost."

"Why did you feel the need to take a man's life, Benjamin? Sit with me and tell me what happened," the concerned father said.

"I indicted a man who was a thief, and the Chief Arbitrator concurred, and when he was brought forward and was informed of his indictment, he tried to escape so—"

"You killed him as you should have," Benjamin's father interrupted.

"Yes, I shot him in the head, and I was consumed with what seemed like absolute rage. Father, I was blind with hate, and I came within a breath of killing the other thief. I nearly killed him simply because he was sitting there. He was afraid, I could see the fear in his eyes, yet I could only see his death for that one moment. I am so ashamed," a perplexed Benjamin confessed.

"Benjamin, listen closely. You were consumed with rage because this thief put you in the position to kill him. You were compelled by law to take his life. This is the terrible reality of our way of life. You are the most gracious and loving son a father could imagine. You love people. You seek them out to help them, to comfort them. How terrible you were forced to take a man's life! You were angry because mindless greed put you in such a position. You must learn to endure the great contradiction of being compassionate and vigilant in such matters concerning life and death. You must try and understand this and forgive yourself for what was required of you," Conrad explained with great care.

Now near tears, Benjamin asked, "Why should a society like ours be consumed with death, a society with hundreds of laws requiring the killing of so many? I studied hundreds of hours preparing for my examination, learning the many circumstances I would be required to kill a dishonest accountant, or advise my client of his requirement to take life. How can this be the most advanced, the most sophisticated society? How can all of this be the culmination of the finest minds in the universe? Did the Elders from Oceania truly mean to place this burden on us? Surely there must be a better way. I mean, this man stole only a few dollars—a few dollars—and tried to run away, and I executed him. How can we accept the The Word when those teachings are full of death?"

"Benjamin, listen," his father implored. "Kenton is a state of absolute liberty. We have no police force to control us, no prisons to hold us against our will, and, most importantly, no centralized government requiring us to pay homage or dominate with corrupt laws created by corrupt politicians. We believe all centralized government is intrinsically evil and submission to such authority is the road to serfdom. Our society flourishes because we are free to pursue our self-interest, without limits, save the injury to another. We are all free to seek happiness in whatever form we please, limited only by our gifts, efforts, and ethics. Great freedom requires great responsibility. Every individual in our society is compelled to ensure the good order of Kenton. We have created a system of laws which require us to take life when a deviant from civility threatens our way of life. We are both the shepherd and the flock. This is the great realization those otherworldly Elders learned through countless millennia of societal evolution. We believe the vast majority of individuals that comprise our society are inherently fair, wise, and moral. We require no central government to maintain a civil society. Benjamin, never permit any government to have authority over you."

"Father, must a liberated society be based on an ethic which requires taking life to maintain order?" Benjamin asked, struggling with such a concept.

"I absolutely believe so," Benjamin's father stated.

"People wrong one another all the time because of a mis-understanding. So many things are a matter of interpretation and perspectives," Benjamin interrupted.

"And so, the Elders from Oceania taught us that, whenever possible, such disputes between individuals must be resolved through binding arbitration. A single man or woman may challenge their neighbor or the mightiest corporation, and both are considered equal under the law. To become an arbitrator is the most sacred responsibility a society can bestow on an individual. They must attempt to be absolutely fair. They must be extensively educated in the law as well as the vast body of decisions made by other arbitrators over the years. The Word teaches us this type of dispute resolution system is as rational and fair as the human condition will allow. All arbitrators must be scrupulous, or they too will face death. All parties in an arbitration process must adhere to the arbitrator's decision, or they will face death. Ours is not a perfect system, but it works, and the system is continuously evolving and improving." Benjamin's father paused.

"Some crimes are not subject to binding arbitrations. You killed that monster for violating mother," Benjamin stated.

"As I should."

"Father, I understand the logic of all of this. It is still dif-ficult to accept now that I have the actual experience of taking a man's life. I feel terrible. Indescribably dreadful. Will taking the life of another come easier with experience?"

Benjamin softly asked while leaning into his father so he might be heard.

The loving father gathered Benjamin into his arms, holding his son tight, and whispered, "No, it never will."

～

The rain had fallen all night, cleaning the air and painting the town of Riverdale with the crisp, clean gift of renewal. The trees and flowers, now free from the grime and dirt, lining the streets in the west end of town were brilliant with colors. The west end of town did not have the advantage of cobblestone roads. The long line of bungalows on the streets were well maintained but modest. Tall street gas lamps were present but scarce, only two per block—barely enough to spare the streets from the darkness of the long winter nights to come. Benjamin rarely visited this end of town as he was fated a different circle of friends and acquaintances of his parents' choosing. The west end residents were the families of miners, wheelwrights, ironsmiths, and now one deceased accountant.

The people of the west end did not know Benjamin, but they knew of him, and he was consumed with trepidation as Fortune carried him down Tsuga Street to the former home of Jack Prince and a bereaved family of a man he had killed just a few days before. The house was obvious and easy to locate. Benjamin directed Fortune to the home with a large number of horses and carriages representing the many gathered there to console the grieving, for this was the day Jack Prince was buried in the cold, wet soil of the Riverdale Cemetery. After the graveside eulogies had been spoken and The Word read for guidance and comfort, the mourners returned to Mrs. Prince's and her daughters' home to comfort them. As he approached the house, Benjamin could see a woman carrying a platter of food into the home. Men were grouped near the front doorway on the porch, most likely speaking of fond memories of a happier time.

Benjamin maneuvered Fortune close to the wood plank

walkway one house down from his destination. If he dismounted in the muddy street, his brace would be impossible to clean without removing, and Benjamin would never be so thoughtless as to track mud into the home of Martha Prince. So, he carefully stepped down on the wooden sidewalk, tied his horse to the metal and wood hitching post, and began what would surely be an exceedingly long walk. Benjamin carefully ascended the faded concrete steps to the front porch while tapping his heart, as was the custom. The men grouped there did not seem to notice his presence. As he stepped inside the doorway, he was surprised by the lavish interior that belied the bungalow's modest exterior. The furniture was exquisitely made from the finest hand-carved walnut and cherry wood. An immense grandfather clock measured time with the swing of a golden pendulum, and the many glass and oak cabinets displayed extensive collections of hand-painted china and fine silverware. A stunning inlay whist table sat near the large front window surrounded by beautiful red leather chairs. The walls displayed several fine oil paintings with gold inlay frames, and in the middle of the formal room was a large, expensive carpet from Kuttor. Benjamin estimated the value of such carpet to be well over two thousand dollars. Clearly, this garish display of wealth was a tribute to Jack Prince's consummate skill as a thief.

Benjamin began to remove his hat when a large man with a bearded face and wearing a black overcoat grabbed his arm, "You don't belong here, cripple!"

Benjamin glared—such poor etiquette was considered worthy of the revolver, yet Benjamin just pulled his arm away, and before anything was said between the two men, Martha Prince diffused the tussle. "Please let the young man come forward."

Benjamin turned to see Martha Prince and her two daughters, Helen and Jane, sitting on what appeared to be a very costly red leather couch. The entire room of somber people was now focused on the young man with a brace and withered leg. Benjamin carefully walked across the formal sitting room with polished oak floors while tapping his heart. He stopped directly in front of Mrs. Prince and her two daughters, released his brace so he could bend his leg, and knelt in front of Jack Prince's survivors.

While the entire room of mourners watched spellbound, Benjamin softly spoke his condolences, "Mrs. Prince, Helen, and Jane, I am so very sorry for your loss."

Mrs. Prince had been crying and despondent for hours, as were her daughters, yet this kind gesture by the man who took her husband's life struck her as thoughtful and kind. Martha realized how difficult it must have been for Benjamin to come to her home at this time under these awful circumstances. After hearing Benjamin's kind words, Mrs. Prince leaned over to Benjamin and offered her hand. Benjamin responded, grasping her hand, and she followed by placing her other hand on Benjamin's hand, "Mr. Walker, I must know. Did my husband steal money from Mr. Porter?"

Benjamin was not expecting the question, and all he could say was, "Yes."

"Did he try to run away?" she continued.

"Yes," Benjamin responded softly.

"Then you did the right thing, and I accept your kind words," Mrs. Prince said while standing and taking Benjamin's arm to help him stand.

"I hold no ill-will for your actions. This is the way of the world. You did what you had to do, and I accept this terrible fate. Please go now in peace, Mr. Walker."

"Thank you, Mrs. Prince," he returned while squeezing her hand one last time. Benjamin reached into his coat pocket and handed her a small manila hemp envelope. Nothing else was said between them. They would never speak again. She watched the young man who killed her husband stand, turn, and walk across the room, through the door, and down the steps.

Mrs. Prince sat there a moment thinking about what had just happened when Helen asked, "What is in the envelope, Mother?"

Mrs. Prince opened the envelope and showed both of her daughters the cheque made out in her name for ten thousand dollars.

Chapter 15
Elisabeth Zurich

Three months had passed since the killing of Jack Prince. Benjamin sat reading in his office as a cascade of shadows from the late afternoon passed through the clear casements above him and crept across his office floor, gradually stealing the light of day. He was reading an article concerning a new way of computing compound interest using a base five number system in the Annals of Modern Book-Keeping when he heard heavy footsteps coming up the stairs. As he looked to the stairs at the other end of his office, he prepared himself for another supervisor or manager seeking advice or directions from the Porter Import Company's now-acting director. Jeffery Porter had sailed to Drenen to purchase products and asked Benjamin to manage his company during his planned three-week absence. Benjamin considered this a great honor, and he pledged his best effort.

Benjamin, somewhat overwhelmed by his responsibilities, would stand and walk over to each window that defined his office. From this vantage above he could observe the intricate parts of the business functioning like gears of a fine watch.

There was so much for him to learn before feeling qualified to hold such a prominent position. However, Jeffery Porter had insisted, so Benjamin reluctantly accepted. The footsteps grew louder. He watched as the visitor climbing the stairs rose above the floor into the afternoon light and was pleasantly surprised and relieved to see his father beaming with happiness. Benjamin's father had not found the time to visit him at his employment before now. Benjamin turned and walked as fast as his braced leg would permit and embraced his father.

"Father, I am so glad you are here. I hope you can stay awhile. Nothing is happening right now. I need relief from the stress of things. I am trying to get through the day by losing myself reading articles from a truly dreary journal on accounting I found in one of the accountant offices downstairs. I have so much to share with you. Please come and sit at my desk so we can talk."

Benjamin's father held his son's hand as they walked to the large desk. When they were situated, Benjamin's father said, "Your office is huge. I can't believe anyone in Kenton has an office like this."

"This was going to be Jeffery Porter's office when he built this warehouse, but he found it impractical, so he selected another location in the building for his office. After that, this room was seldom used except for conferences and things like that. When I was hired, I had to work in a secluded area, so this room was perfect for my confidential work. Mr. Porter told me I could use his office in his absence, but I thought that was a bit presumptuous. You know what I mean?" Benjamin responded.

"I think Jeffery Porter has a great deal of respect for your judgment to give you so much responsibility. I am so immensely proud of you," Benjamin's father stated.

"Well, don't be beguiled by the perception. See that hose thing on the wall next to you with the brass cone?" Benjamin pointed at the wall behind his father, "with that whistle hanging next to it?"

"You have a ship's voice pipe installed," Benjamin's father stated, glancing at the strange-looking device.

"That's right, and that hose thing goes right down to Mrs. Cromwell's office, Jeffery Porter's personal assistant. She really is the one running this operation. A supervisor or a manager will come up here and ask a question, and I will always say, 'I will need to give some thought to that, please come back in an hour or so.' When they leave, I blow that whistle into the voice pipe and Mrs. Cromwell will answer back. I ask her what I should say or do, she tells me, and when the individual returns, I give them my 'expert' advice. My adept skill as a 'captain of industry' is entirely dependent on a highly intelligent lady in another part of the building. This whole thing is smoke and mirrors, the perception lacks substance," Benjamin said with a self-deprecating laugh.

"Benjamin, I know you, and I know why Jeffery Porter placed you in charge of his business. I will never understand why you are so hard on yourself. There is a little more going on than you just blowing a whistle into a long rubber hose," Benjamin's father said, shaking his head.

"Well, father, I do supervise the new accountant that Jeffery and I selected, and we are redesigning the accounting books to make them more sensible and easier to audit. I guess I am doing stuff like that," Benjamin admitted.

Benjamin's father nodded his head, knowing his son's true abilities and intellect.

"Father, I did make one independent decision which may protect my client's investment when the time comes. I quadrupled Mr. Porter's fire insurance. He is now fully covered if this place should burn down," Benjamin explained with a very somber tone. He held up his hand, stood up, took a piece of paper from his desk, walked over, and plugged the voice tube to ensure the continuing conversation with his father would be private.

Benjamin returned to his seat and said, "We can speak freely now, father, so go ahead with your thoughts."

"Benjamin, are you still concerned about that strange carpet and what you experienced when you first started working for Jeffery Porter? You have not spoken of it since you came to the hospital and told me about your fears nearly four months ago," a genuinely concerned father stated.

"Come with me to the window and look down on the showroom," Benjamin stated while standing. Father and son walked around the desk and over to the long window. Benjamin leaned against the glass and pointed in the direction of Jeffery's secret room. "Do you see that group of exotic carpets and tapestries pressed against the wall?"

"Yes, I see them," he acknowledged.

"That's where you will find the monster. Please do not

forget what I told you. I can still feel that thing's awful presence within me. I have never lost the feeling of being violated and I live with it every day. I just cannot shake it. I just cannot find the strength within me to destroy the thing. I am somehow controlled by the curse. You do still remember our conversation?" Benjamin asked, turning and staring into his father's eyes.

"I remember everything," Conrad said, putting his hand on his son's shoulder.

Benjamin reached into his pocket, pulled out a key on a gold chain, and put the chain over his father's head. "Father, I have made a copy of the master key to this warehouse. Keep it close and keep your promise never to look upon the monster. Please be careful, the monster will try and pull you into the carpet when it realizes your intentions."

Benjamin's father pulled his collar away from his neck and slid the key beneath his shirt, hiding it from the world, "I will keep my promise, Benjamin, as the Raven is my witness."

"I try not to obsess about the carpet because I fear you will begin to think I am becoming insane or something," Benjamin explained.

"I have complete faith in you, Benjamin. You must believe me. I would never think you are losing your mind. You are one of the most rational individuals I have ever known. I will do everything you've asked of me if it comes to that."

"You will know when the time is right, you will know," Benjamin said softly. "The Supplicants are the hope for the world's future. They will change everything. I am sure many lives will be saved and enriched with the knowledge obtained from Oceania and shared with the world."

"A Supplicant has already saved someone I love dearly," Benjamin's father said, smiling.

Benjamin looked at his father, confused, then realized to whom his father was referring to, "Doctor Lister is a Supplicant?"

"He seemed almost miraculous with his advanced

knowledge of pathogens and aseptic procedures and so many other advanced medical interventions when he first started practicing medicine at the Riverdale Hospital. Without his advanced medical knowledge, you would have died," Benjamin's father stated.

"I thought that might be the case. Before Dr. Hayek told me about otherworldly involvement with our planet, I always thought how mysterious it was that one man could have done so much to change our understanding of medicine. After that meeting, many things began to make sense. Did Dr. Lister sponsor you so you could become a Supplicant?" Benjamin asked, realizing the answer.

"Yes," Benjamin's father explained. "One day, I sat down with Dr. Lister and asked him how he could be so knowledgeable about so many innovative things in medicine. I told him he was a brilliant man. Still, his continual introduction of revolutionary medical knowledge seemed increasingly improbable. That is when he told me his knowledge was from the future, a future that had already happened. He said others were becoming increasingly suspicious of his continual breakthroughs, and, obviously, there was a need for another 'genius' doctor. He recommended me for membership in the Order of the Supplicants, and, when accepted, I was told everything about Oceania and the gifts from that civilization. We now know so much more about the circulatory system, the treatment of various forms of physiological shock, anesthesia, pathogens, blood transfusion, antibiotics, and the other things from another time and place. A hundred years of medical knowledge given to us in just a few years, and Benjamin, something else, something important pertaining to mental hygiene. The cryptographers have just translated information concerning an entirely new class of drugs to treat mental illness based on a chemical compound called Phenothiazine. The antipsychotic properties of this new class of drugs will revolutionize the treatment of mental illness. Your mother has agreed to build a modern mental hygiene institute adjacent to the Riverdale Hospital. In a few years, patients from all over the world will come to Riverdale to realize the benefits from this new class of antipsychotic drugs capable of relieving so many lost souls."

"Father, we live in the most marvelous of times and nothing must stop the Elders' intent from Oceania. Their knowledge must survive," Benjamin stated, looking down at the secret room. "If we can accept the presence of angels, then surely, we must believe in the possibility of monsters!"

"I believe only in my son's wisdom, and I will not forget what you have asked of me," Benjamin's father responded.

"Now, I will take you down to the showroom and show you the master collection of Motus Vitus carpets. When you look upon them, you will see a true mystery, so try to understand. What I can remember of the monster in that room is hundreds of times more powerful and more dramatic and much more real. I think it may help you with any unbelief you may have," Benjamin explained as he led his father in the direction of the stairs.

As they walked, Benjamin's father reassured his son, "Please always remember I have absolute faith in you. Absolute faith. If it becomes necessary, I will burn this entire harbor down, all of it."

"Thank you, father."

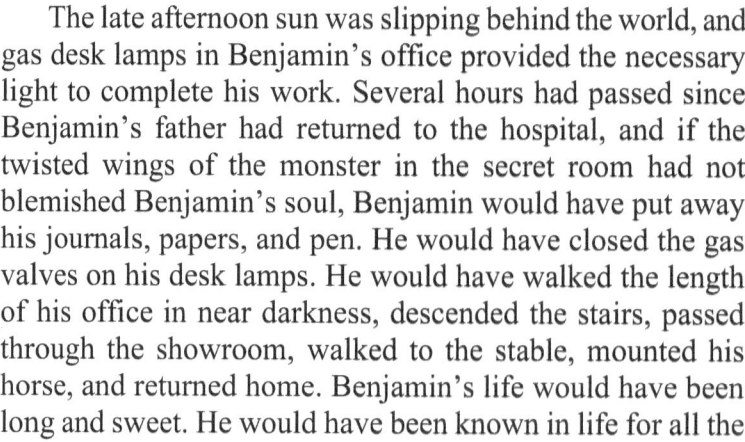

The late afternoon sun was slipping behind the world, and gas desk lamps in Benjamin's office provided the necessary light to complete his work. Several hours had passed since Benjamin's father had returned to the hospital, and if the twisted wings of the monster in the secret room had not blemished Benjamin's soul, Benjamin would have put away his journals, papers, and pen. He would have closed the gas valves on his desk lamps. He would have walked the length of his office in near darkness, descended the stairs, passed through the showroom, walked to the stable, mounted his horse, and returned home. Benjamin's life would have been long and sweet. He would have been known in life for all the great things he accomplished, the knowledge he shared with the world, the vast wealth he amassed, and the charity he showed. He would have met and fallen in love with a most beautiful and intelligent woman, married, and raised gifted children who loved him. His family would have mourned when he was taken from this life and would have carried that terrible burden of loving loss until they too passed. In a future time, when the people of Deseret spoke of Benjamin's life, their voices would have been hushed with reverence. Such would have been the stature of this remarkable man. Yet all these things were not to be. A dark shadow had crossed his path.

Benjamin put his pen down and was about to turn the gas down on the lamps when he once again heard footsteps coming up the stairway into his office. The gas lamps' glare blinded him from seeing across the room, forcing him to block the light with his hand to see the approaching figure. The outline of the person seemed familiar, a tall silhouette of a woman with long, dark hair. A sense of joy consumed him, as he believed his mother was near. He stood, darted past his desk, and when the light was behind him, the image of the woman was fully illuminated.

Benjamin was shocked to see an image of a beautiful young woman with dark raven hair, porcelain white skin, and stunning green eyes. She was not Benjamin's mother, but she could have been his mother's younger twin. Benjamin stared at the young woman in silence. Her manner of dress was remarkable, and unlike anything his mother would have ever worn. Her blouse was a soft white satin with several of the buttons unfastened from her neck down in a most revealing manner. Her skirt was tight about her legs, the length of which stopped several inches above her knees. Her shoes were tipped forward by small pedestals beneath her heels. Her futuristic style of dress resembled the fashion of the young women in the university library.

He stood there in silence until the woman broke in, "Are you Benjamin Walker?"

"You look just like my mother," the young accountant spontaneously announced without thought. Benjamin could not believe the first thing out of his mouth was such a bizarre statement.

The young woman laughed and responded, "I am going to accept that as a compliment . . . I think."

Benjamin tried to recover, "Oh, yes, you are very nice looking, and you are much younger than my mother, of course. It's just I was surprised by the similarity. You both have long black hair, green eyes, and beautiful white skin, I mean yes! I am complimenting you. Well, uh, yes, I am. My mother would not wear such a short dress. I mean, she is much older than you, of course . . . very nice dress!"

Benjamin stopped himself from talking, aware of his odd behavior. He just stood there with his eyes closed, hoping for the moment to pass.

"Well, thank you. I am glad you approve of my appearance. All the young women at the university are wearing their dresses short this year. The young ladies working in the university library started the trend and, soon after that, all the dressmakers around campus started selling them. My name is Elisabeth Zurich, and I work in the catalog department," Elisabeth said while extending her hand to Benjamin.

Benjamin took her hand awkwardly, "Well, please sit down." While releasing her hand, he quickly retreated to the security of his chair behind his desk.

Much to Benjamin's surprise, the young woman did not

sit on one of the numerous chairs near his desk. Instead, she walked around Benjamin's desk and remained standing. Leaning against the desk, she asked, "All the ladies in the catalog room talk about you. You killed Jack Prince for stealing money from Mr. Porter. Shot him in the head. We all want to know—what's it like to kill a man?"

At that moment, Benjamin no longer felt any sense of intimidation or awkwardness toward this beautiful woman. Those feelings passed. Clearly, the young woman standing in front of him was naïve and foolish.

"I felt terrible, simply awful. Now, if this is what you are here to talk about, well, I wish you would go. What did you think I would feel?" At that point, Benjamin stood up, pushed his chair under his desk, walked around the startled young woman, and began turning the gas valves down.

"I am so sorry. I am not from Kenton. I have never met anyone who killed someone. The culture is so different from the other countries on Deseret. People in the rest of the world think of Kenton as a death culture. I mean, you can kill people, and it's legal and everything, so I thought somehow you would feel good about killing a thief. I am just trying to understand." Elisabeth paused, and then continued, "I was thoughtless. How foolish I was for trivializing the taking of a man's life; of course, it must have been terrible. I am so sorry—please do not be angry. I just didn't think before I spoke."

"I had to look his wife and daughters in the face and give my condolences for taking away her husband and their father. I took their very way of life from them. I never want to hurt another person as long as I live, not like that. It is simply too much. I hope fate spares me from doing anything like that ever again."

Benjamin found the conversation distasteful and wanted to leave, "This is not a death culture. This is a society based on absolute liberty. We have no central government or police force or prisons. We would rather die than be subordinate to the state. In Kenton, we are responsible for our actions, and we all must ensure the stability of our society. There are rules, Miss Zurich. How long have you been in my country? I seriously doubt 'the ladies' in the catalog room said anything like what you just said."

"You are correct. No one spoke of death, only about how you must be an exceptional person. Please don't be upset. Can we begin again, Sir? Please?" Elisabeth was upset.

Benjamin stopped for a second and gave some thought to the young woman's words, "Yes, I still have some problems with the whole thing. It is not your fault. It was a terrible experience."

Benjamin walked around his desk and returned to his chair. Elisabeth put both hands on the edge of Benjamin's desk and lifted herself onto his desk. She crossed her exposed legs and tried to smile. Once again, she did not realize how inappropriate her behavior was. Benjamin did not complain. "Everyone is talking about how smart you are. The girls in the catalog room said you must be an accountant detective or something for figuring out how the accountants were stealing from Mr. Porter."

Benjamin thought about the concept of being a detective, "A bookkeeping detective . . . well, I guess, in a way, an accountant is a kind of a detective doing an audit. I never thought about it like that. What do you do, Elisabeth? How long have you worked for Mr. Porter?"

"I am working here between semesters. I am attending the university, and my father arranged for me to work for Mr. Porter to better understand the wholesale aspects of the carpet business. I am from Kuttor, and my father is an important business leader in my country's export guild. So, I had the opportunity to receive my education outside the country. Someday, I will become a member of my father's business and help my country sell its products to the world. Exporting carpets is one of the few ways my country can obtain hard currency. My father is very influential with the Locks, the ruling religious leaders. He had to get special permission for me to leave the country and be educated, especially being a woman and everything," Elisabeth explained nervously.

"You speak the language so well. I am extremely impressed and envious of your bilingual skills!" Benjamin's tone was becoming much more cordial.

"My father employed servants who spoke the language of Kenton. The ability to speak different languages allowed me to be educated in countries with different . . . let's say, traditions from Kuttor," Elisabeth said. "I had three years of finishing school in Liberty before I started at the university. I will be a sophomore next semester."

"You have been to the university? That is great! I plan to start next semester when I have satisfied my work experience requirement for my accountant licensure. Please forgive my next question, I know you are not from this country and everything, but the question you asked about killing Jack Prince, the way you put it—your tone—was offensive. After being in this country for over a year, you still do not quite understand our society, do you?"

"I have been in some kind of a cultural shock since I arrived. When I was in Liberty, we were taught Kenton was some kind of a death culture. A lawless country where people killed each other all the time and the poor starve to death. They had me convinced I would not be safe here, and I should stay in Liberty where the state would ensure my health and safety. My teachers said Liberty was so much more progressive because women and men are considered equal, and the poor and the ill were taken care of. They had me thinking Kenton was under the control of organized crime or something and many people were homeless."

Elisabeth continued, "My father never said anything like that about Kenton. My father told me the University of Londonderry is the finest school in the world. So against my teachers' advice, I came here. What I have experienced in Kenton is considerably different than what I expected. I am very aware of the death laws, but Jack Prince was the first death I heard about. I mean, this country is prosperous and safe. I have not seen or heard anything about any crime taking place. The people here are very polite – well, everyone except for some spoiled children. I do find it strange that everyone carries a gun on them, even my teachers at school. I think this country is much more progressive than Liberty. Why did they lie to me?" Elisabeth asked.

"Your teachers in Liberty failed to tell you about the large number of people that emigrate to Kenton from Liberty each year, and that banishment from Kenton is considered worse than going to prison. Your teachers were in denial, and they teach propaganda about Kenton attempting to reduce the defections from that desperate state. If they could, they would build a wall between our two countries to keep the people of Liberty captive. In time, I think the absorption of Liberty into Kenton is inevitable as more and more individuals leave. Did you take any history courses or comparative government classes in your freshman year at the university? Have you taken a class in the teaching contained in The Word?" Benjamin asked.

"No, all my coursework was language-oriented; basic language skills, literature, poetry, and such. I was attempting to improve my language skills before taking subjects that would require comprehensive language skills to understand. Because I was a foreign student, I received an orientation from the university staff about Kenton's laws and culture. I was told to be very polite, not to touch anyone or defame anyone, and of course, not to steal from or intentionally harm anyone. I could be potentially shot because everyone is required to enforce the law, and the law permits deadly force. It sounded frightening, but I've found everyone genuinely lovely to be around, and as I said, I have not heard of any crimes taking place. Still, I found it strange and maybe a little frightening. So many people carry guns, and guns are not permitted in Kuttor or Liberty. I guess you know that."

"The basic rule to live by in Kenton is not to do anything to anyone you would not want someone to do to you. Of course, it is always good to do good things for people and not expect reciprocity, I mean, always expect them to return good deeds. I think that would be a bit much, even for Kenton," Benjamin smiled.

Elisabeth sat quietly for a moment, translating and thinking about Benjamin's lesson of local traditions. She then turned and looked directly at Benjamin: "Why is Kenton such a prosperous and peaceful country? I mean, you have no government. How can it possibly work?"

"Miss Zurich, volumes have been written attempting to answer that question. I have thought about it my entire life. There is not a simple answer. Clearly, The Word teaches us individual liberty is the essential aspect of a free and prosperous society. In Kenton, we are open to pursuing self-interest as long as we don't violate others' liberty. We are taught never to surrender our freedom to the state or to any authority for that matter. The freedom to pursue self-interest is the key, to strive to protect the rights of others. Yes, to pursue self-interest is the essence of Kenton and the source of our freedom. So saith The Word."

"So saith The Word," Elisabeth returned, remembering her university orientation.

"Thank you, Miss Zurich—now that was most respectful. I hope you will come to know the wisdom of The Word as I have throughout my life. I am still learning."

"I hope so too," Elisabeth softly returned and then asked, "Why do you think Liberty is such a failed state—as it's obvious you do?"

"In time, the government became corrupted as all central governments do."

"Benjamin, why didn't the people of Liberty rebel?" Elisabeth asked.

"They do, Miss Zurich. They escape to Kenton."

"There must be some form of central government which will promote freedom for the governed?" Elisabeth asked.

Benjamin's countenance was emotionless, "No. When the state is given power to govern, the state will collect power and manipulate the populous to gain even more power until the state devolves into a totalitarian state. Such a thing is inevitable, the only question is how long and what process it will take. The obvious lesson of history is that only the individual citizen can guarantee his or her rights. Centralized government and centralized power must be eternally resisted."

"I guess you feel pretty strongly about all of this," Elisabeth cautiously stated, knowing she was in sensitive territory.

"I do," Benjamin forcibly replied.

"How can you be so sure?" Elisabeth pressed.

"Well, for one thing, the Elders who wrote The Word were clear concerning the danger of central government. Miss Zurich, I ask you to compare Kenton with the other countries on Deseret. What do you see?" Benjamin asked.

"Kenton seems wonderful. I just cannot understand how such a society can exist without a government. Kenton has laws; how were they made without government?"

Benjamin reflected again on how to explain, "Yes, we have laws created to apply to Kenton's entire state. The creation of national laws in Kenton is considerably different from the fallible governmental methods used in Liberty. In Kenton, we have the Council of Elders that formulate proposed laws to be ratified by the people."

"What?" Elisabeth asked.

"A direct vote of the people on law or some other issue is called a plebiscite. Kenton's process to create a national law is a little complicated, but the process is exactly what you would expect in a country fearful of a central government." Benjamin took a breath and continued, "Kenton has a Council of Elders made up of one Elder, or representative, from each of Kenton's five counties. The Elders are selected by each county's residents to serve a two-year term with the opportunity to be reelected to a second term. Two terms are the maximum time an Elder can serve, and there is no exception. If a citizen of the county aspires to become an Elder, they must submit to an examination of their knowledge of The Word and existing laws. The Council of Elders secretly creates ten questions for each new term designed to reveal each candidate's knowledge of The Word. On a given date and time in each county, those who wish to participate in the exam gather at a designated location. Serving on the Council of Elders is the most prestigious role any individual may hold in our society. It is the greatest of honors to deliberate as a modern Elder. There are many applicants. The contenders' answers are published in newspapers and posted in prominent locations throughout their county, and each resident of the county has the opportunity to review the answers. The candidates for the council also tour their county and give speeches and debate. After six months of discussion and debate, the next representative Elder for each county is selected by the majority vote of that county."

"Can anyone ask to be considered?" Elisabeth asked.

"Any adult resident of the county can take the examination," Benjamin stated.

"Can women become Elders?" Elisabeth queried.

"You're not in Kuttor, Miss Zurich," Benjamin responded.

"Of course, please go on," Miss Zurich requested.

"Within thirty days of the beginning of each two-year term, anyone or any organization can submit proposed national laws," Benjamin continued. "The Council of Elders review the proposed laws, and several of the proposed laws are selected by the Elders by a majority vote of the Council. The Council reviews and rewrites the proposed laws to be consistent with the teaching of The Word. Submission of the proposed laws for review and comments by Kenton's citizens is the next step. Any individual or organization in Kenton can submit arguments for changes in the proposed law. The Elders consider the revisions and then submit the final draft on the people's proposed laws for review at the end of the first year of their term. The people of Kenton have nine months to review, discuss, and debate the proposed laws, then on Legislation Day, every adult in Kenton has the right to vote by secret ballot, and if they agree on the proposed law, the law will be chaptered.

"The law must pass by at least two-thirds of the votes cast. Obviously, very few proposed laws become actual laws. Removal of existing laws utilizes the same process. Also, the corruption of a serving Elder will result in death if such deception is established by indictment and trial. The responsibility for a deviant Elder execution falls to the replacement Elder. This manner of creating national laws is dictated by The Word."

"Have any Elders ever been executed for corruption?" Elisabeth probed.

"A long time ago, maybe. No one recently."

"Sounds like a form of centralized government to me," Elisabeth stated.

Benjamin thought about her statement for a second and responded, "Maybe government with a real small 'g.'"

"What about county or city government?" Elisabeth asked. "They exist, don't they?"

"Yes, Kenton permits local government. County governments are responsible for county projects such as ensuring the community has a safe water supply, sewers system, roads, firemen, street lighting, schools, courts, projects of collaboration between counties, and the collection of county taxes. Local political positions are closely monitored and deviant behavior is dealt with harshly.

"You have given me so much to think about, Mr. Walker. It is hard to understand. The culture of Kenton, your very way of life, depends on the good judgment of people enforcing and ensuring the rules of your society," Elisabeth stated quietly. "If people are inherently good and wise, a government, in any form of government, should be acceptable if good people make up the government, yet you believe central government is always dangerous. Surely good people can make good government."

Benjamin paused, remembering what his father once told him, "When individuals assume power over others, they change. It is our nature. Power corrupts, and people mistake the honor to govern as an excuse to rule. The Word teaches us that the human mind, the human ego is incapable of the objectivity necessary to separate the self from the responsibility to have power over others. It is just a matter of time before a governing individual is subject to the delusion of superiority. We will never, we must never trust the state to guarantee security or liberty. We must rely only on ourselves. One of the early founders of Liberty said, 'if people were angels, there would be no need for a central government.' The Word teaches us we should expect and require people to act like angels, so we will never require a central government. We have faith in the individual. We genuinely fear the corrosive effect of power on individuals. We believe that human rights are not bestowed by the state but inevitably vanquished by the state. Those who are not 'angels' among us are put to death. I know it sounds terrible, but we have a system, it is far from perfect, but it works."

"Death angels—you are talking about people becoming death angels and putting people to death, Mr. Walker. Is that not a form of power over others, and such power will corrupt as well?"

"There are rules, Miss Zurich. Every life taken is carefully reviewed by an independent objective authority set up by the county, usually a coroner's inquest, to ensure the laws authorizing the taking of life are carefully followed. In my situation, I indicted and was regretfully compelled to take the life of Jack Prince who attempted to escape. That was my responsibility. At the time of the deviant's death, my actions were reviewed by the Chief Arbitrator chosen to review my indictment against Jack Prince. There are rules and reviews. Miss Zurich, do you see this scar on my face?"

Benjamin pointed at his cheek.

"Well, I was stabbed in the face by a deviant child who had a long history of hurting children. In Kenton, no child under eighteen can be indicted or charged with a crime. This sort of thing is usually resolved between responsible parents. When the father of the deviant child was confronted by the father of the child who was injured, the deviant child's father would physically attack him. One of the fathers whose child was violated was beaten so badly, he lost an eye. In Kenton, this terrible man should have been put to death by one of the attacked men. If they were unable to kill the man, someone else should have taken on the responsibility. No one did. So, the deviant child continued to harm other children. One day, I was attacked, and my brace was stolen miles from town. I nearly died. My mother found me and saved me, and when she confronted the boy's father, she too was attacked and violated, so my father killed that man."

"Why didn't one of the other fathers kill him?" Elisabeth asked.

"They were weak, Miss Zurich, and children suffered. My mother suffered. I suffered." Benjamin explained.

"Does the child still live in Riverdale?"

"No."

Elisabeth knew the answer to her next question: "Where is he now?"

Benjamin stated with no regret, "Dead."

A quiet moment passed until Elisabeth responded, "Yes, seems right. Perhaps I will have a better understanding of Kenton after I have lived here a while longer. I did so enjoy your explanation. You kind of sounded like one of my professors when you explained this to me," Elisabeth said, leaning into Benjamin.

"I know I can be pedantic at times—please forgive me," Benjamin responded.

"Pa-dan-tic?" Elisabeth was not familiar with the word.

"Dull," Benjamin explained.

Elisabeth pulled back and, with a somewhat sharp tone stated, "Not at all. Why would you say something like that? Do you think me dim-witted?"

"No, of course not. I just meant I can go on sometimes," Benjamin explained.

"When I say I enjoy something, I mean it. If I found you boring, I would have excused myself. I am a student, and you can teach me many things about your society, and I am sure I can teach you a few things if you give me a chance," Elisabeth continued.

"Of course," Benjamin stated.

Elisabeth stood up, straightened her skirt, turned and looked directly at Benjamin, "I am starving. We should go and get something to eat, and I can teach you about the society where I was raised."

Now, this was somewhat unexpected, and Benjamin sat there inhibited. He had never been with a woman alone in society, and his hesitation was purely innocent.

Elisabeth broke the awkward silence, "Oh, I am sorry. I am being a bit forward. I am still learning the customs and everything. I realize it is not appropriate for you to be seen with me in public without an escort because you are pledged or married."

Benjamin carefully considered her statement before responding to this beautiful woman, "Miss Zurich, I am not pledged to anyone. I would like very much to take you to dinner."

Benjamin stood, pushed his chair beneath his desk, carefully walked around Elisabeth to the front of his desk, and turned down the gas lamp. The room grew dark as Elisabeth walked around the desk and stood next to him in the darkness. "Mr. Walker, if I take your hand, you won't shoot me or anything? I am not sure of my way in the dark."

Benjamin reached down and, after a few fumbling attempts, grasped Elisabeth's hand. He felt a pleasant tingling run through his hand and arm as they touched. He slowly helped her across the long, dark office. A faint glow of the gas lamps on the lower floor revealed the stairs. Benjamin placed Elisabeth's hand on the railing and stepped back to allow his new acquaintance to descend to the lower floor.

Elisabeth paused, "Mr. Walker, will you please address me as Elisabeth? I mean, at least while we are away from work?"

Benjamin smiled in the darkness, "I would like that, Elisabeth, and please call me Benjamin."

With that said, Elisabeth descended the stairs. Benjamin followed, and upon reaching the ground floor, Elisabeth turned: "Benjamin, will you give me a moment to get my coat?"

"Of course."

Elisabeth disappeared down the hall, and Benjamin walked into the showroom. The caretakers were carefully cleaning the floors and carpets, and when he heard Elisabeth approaching from the shadows, he was again surprised by the vision. She was wearing the most beautiful black coat trimmed in brilliant crimson. The coat was full length with a hood pulled over her head. The fabric seemed almost alive with a subtle fluid motion, which complemented her soft white skin and brilliant green eyes.

"Elisabeth, your coat is simply beautiful. I have never seen such a wonderful coat."

"Thank you. My father had it woven for me by a master weaver as a going-away present. I am not sure how it was made, but it is soft and supple, unlike a heavy carpet. My father said there was no other coat like it in the world, and when I wear the coat, I should remember him. I hope you will meet my father. I think you would like him," Elisabeth said softly.

"I would very much enjoy meeting your father," Benjamin returned.

Elisabeth bent down and took off her pedestal shoes and placed them in one of the pockets in her coat. She then removed a pair of leather slippers from another pocket and put them on her feet.

"These pedestal shoes are terrible to walk in," she explained while again taking Benjamin's hand.

The young couple walked across the showroom to the main door and stepped into the cold night, continuing to Benjamin's horse by the stable master. Benjamin uncharacteristically thanked the stable master and waited until he disappeared into the stable. Then he turned to Elisabeth and said, "Where are we going? The nearest diner is nearly a mile from here. Do you have a carriage?"

"No, I am sorry, Benjamin, I walk to work," Elisabeth stated.

"I am afraid I can't walk that far with this stupid brace."

"That's okay. I will ride behind you on your horse if that's okay with you."

Benjamin attempted to envision how she could sit on a horse with the dress she was wearing.

Elisabeth said, "It will be okay . . . go ahead and mount the horse."

Benjamin put the foot of his good leg into the stirrup and lifted himself onto the saddle. He released the joint on his brace and guided his braced foot into the stirrup and turned to see a genuinely novel sight. Elisabeth was hitching up her dress around her waist, revealing her stockings' tops, and strange-looking stocking fasteners, and her white private under apparel. "I know, not very ladylike. Now let me use your stirrup, and with a little help, I will ride behind you. Will your horse be okay?"

Benjamin slipped his foot out of the stirrup, "We'll see. This is a first for us. I think he will be fine."

With both the horse and Benjamin studying her every move, Elisabeth put her foot into the stirrup and reached for Benjamin's arm, and with his help, she lifted herself and came to rest behind Benjamin. She quickly removed her foot from the stirrup to permit Benjamin to keep control of the horse. Fortune danced around, adjusting to the unfamiliar weight while Benjamin softly commanded him to be still. Elisabeth put both arms around Benjamin's waist and held on as tight as she could with her head resting on Benjamin's shoulder, and when the horse calmed, there was once again a moment of silence.

Benjamin spoke first, "I guess we are really getting to know each other."

Elisabeth expressed a slight giggle while she covered her legs with her coat and returned to grasping Benjamin's waist. "I am ready, but not too fast."

"Let's go, Fortune."

⌒

Thirty minutes had passed when Benjamin brought Fortune to a stop. Elisabeth looked up from Benjamin's shoulder and was amazed at the destination Benjamin chose for dinner. The large, illuminated marquee on the two-story opulent building proclaimed the Commerce Eatery and Tavern. Benjamin had taken his new friend to the most exclusive restaurant in Riverdale.

"Are we eating here?" Elisabeth asked, surprised and confused.

"Yes," replied Benjamin. "Now let me help you off."

Benjamin slipped his foot from the stirrup, and Elisabeth replaced his foot with hers. While Benjamin held her arm, Elisabeth descended to the ground and quickly pulled her dress down while nervously looking about. Fortune once again danced around, unaccustomed to the shifting weight. When Benjamin brought the horse under control, he also dismounted and tied his horse to a cast iron statue of a servant holding a golden ring. Elisabeth quickly walked up to the window but could not see into the interior through the heavy red and gold drapes that provided privacy for the guests inside. The light from the bright gas streetlamp reflected off the young woman, so her diffused image appeared in the front window's wavy glass.

Elisabeth took the opportunity to comb her long, black hair. Pulling a small comb from her coat, Elisabeth gazed into the ghostly translucent reflection. She carefully stroked her hair until it was shining and in good order. She then quickly retrieved her pedestal shoes from her coat and replaced the leather slippers, straightened her skirt one last time, fluffed up her coat, and unconsciously ran her hand over her hair while taking a deep breath. "I had no idea we were going to a place like this. Have you eaten here before?"

Benjamin walked up to his new friend and offered his arm, "A few times."

Elisabeth accepted his arm, and Benjamin opened the door into a world of wealth and power she had never experienced before. The couple stepped into an immense dining room containing several dozen round tables occupied by the financial, business, and legal elite of Kent County. The soft rumble of many conversations became increasingly quiet as the many dining guests' attention was drawn to the handsome young couple. Every adult in the dining room knew Benjamin Walker, but this stunning young woman with an unusual black and red coat and a scandalously short dress was a stranger. Stranger still, this younger woman could have been a younger twin of Benjamin's mother. This would be the topic of many discussions and gossip for weeks to come by Kent's power brokers. In a few days, Benjamin's mother would become aware her son was no longer hers alone.

Benjamin recognized many of the individuals gathered there. Mary Rinehart, the chairperson of Consolidated Mining, was the first friendly face he recognized. Mary Rinehart smiled with approval when Benjamin looked her way. Benjamin acknowledged with a nod, Robert Wayne, the President of the Lawyer's Association, and his family, and the gesture was returned. The ritual of acknowledgment of friends and acquaintances continued as Benjamin scanned the room of the rich and powerful, acknowledging each with handshakes, greetings, and facial expressions. He was the son of the most respected and affluent couple in Kenton. This upper echelon of society had watched Benjamin grow into a man. His licensure as an accountant at such a young age and his recent execution of a thief had fostered his stature in the community. The "royalty" of Kent were increasingly becoming his peers. His presence among them that evening with a beautiful woman seemed the most appropriate continuation of his maturity.

Elisabeth gazed upon the assembly of richly dressed men, women, and children. A fantastic variety of lavish food and wine garnished every table. Beautiful collections of silver dining ware, crystal goblets, and fine china plates glimmered across the room. Each table was graced with a white satin tablecloth. Every citizen in the room was dressed in the finest of clothing. Men in elegant dark suits and white dress shirts and women in all manner of elaborate dress which in many ways seemed progressive, even practical. Elisabeth quickly realized, by the way the women were sitting, their dresses did not require a hooped underskirt or corset. This was in stark contrast to the formal wear of the ladies of Liberty. Some women in the restaurant wore taut velvet coats of blues and reds, and other women wore practical frock coats and tapestry lined jackets of red and brilliant blues or combinations of red and black. Many gowns appeared layered with beautiful silks and velvets and flowed loosely to the floor. Many of the women also wore elaborate silk hats with plumes of feathers of rare and exotic birds. All the fine ladies were covered entirely from their necks to their ankles, as such was the proper appearance of a high society woman participating in a formal dinner.

As Elisabeth continued to look about the large dining room, she observed four enormous gas crystal chandeliers hanging from a tall copper-covered ceiling. The immense room walls apparently covered with dark walnut paneling, and every piece of railing, metal door casing, knobs, and hinges plated with gold and shining from the light of the gas lamps. On one wall of the dining room hung a giant, cast-iron representation of the Raven with wings spread, beak open, and eyes glaring. The venerated corvid centered on a polished copper background. On the other side of the large eatery in an adjacent room, a large oak and mahogany copper-covered bar with gold rails and red leather seats invited unescorted men and women to meet and relax over drinks as they shared their day's adventures. A beautiful blonde barmaid in a revealing crimson dress served the bar guests and offered polite conversation. A seamless mirror covered the wall behind the bar reflecting the entire room and creating an illusion that the room was twice as large. The blank oak floor was highly polished and oddly covered with sawdust that clung to the hems of the many elegant dresses and dusted the shoes and boots of the dining guests. Elisabeth was spellbound by the milieu and would have remained so if the trance had not broken.

A tall, formally dressed maître d' standing behind a tall walnut pedestal most politely asked, "Mr. Walker and guest, do you wish your private dining room this evening?"

"Yes, thank you, Robert," Benjamin politely responded.

The young couple followed the maître d's lead as he navigated the many tables between the restaurant entrance and an elegant staircase near the rear of the dining room, ascending to the most exclusive area of the commerce building.

Elisabeth attempted to look nonchalant as she held her escort's arm and traversed the quiet room. Several older women appeared to scowl while scrutinizing her exposed legs, but most of the guests simply smiled and nodded as the young couple went past their tables. On several occasions, Elisabeth would consciously pull her coat together in a vain attempt at modesty. She may have been the first to wear such a daring dress in such refined company, but she would not be the last. Kenton was changing, and ladies' fashion was very much emblematic of the many new things to come.

The maître d' began ascending the stairs ever conscious of Benjamin's limitations. Elisabeth still grasped Benjamin's arm as the young accountant held to the stairs' gold-plated rail taking slow labored steps. After several moments, Elisabeth and Benjamin reached the entrance to the private dining room. Benjamin pushed the heavy, gilded door open and reached for the inside wall in the darkened room. Trying not to fumble, he found and turned the gas valve to the elaborate chandelier hanging in the center of a fabulous dining room. One large table covered with a pure white silk cloth sat beneath the imposing gilded chandelier. Three intricately carved walnut chairs upholstered with luxurious red leather sat at equal distance around the table. The dining table had nine crystal goblets and numerous silver eating utensils rolled in silk napkins with silver rings. The table was prepared to serve three individuals. Three walls were covered with the cream-colored shimmering satin fabric and trimmed with richly polished walnut. The ceiling was gilded metal, and a glass wall facing the dining room below was made of a single pane of glass. A gilded walnut handrail attached to the floor in front of the glass ensured safety. Unlike the main dining room's sawdust-covered oak floor, the private dining room had a custom, wall-to-wall, handwoven carpet from Kuttor displaying the most intricate arabesque. In the center of the wall opposite the wall of glass was a large and elaborate image of the Raven carved from a single piece of clear dark walnut placed in the center of a highly polished golden plate, which reflected the soft glow of the gas chandelier. Several extra chairs sat against the wall beneath the Raven. The room was quiet except for the soft hiss of the gas chandelier.

Robert walked over to the table and pulled out one of the chairs for Elisabeth and helped her remove her coat. When Elisabeth was seated, the maître d' began removing the extra chair and place setting. At the same time, Elisabeth looked down below at the main dining room. "Benjamin, can they see us up here?"

"They know we are here. I am not sure what the people downstairs can see. I have never eaten down there," Benjamin answered while adjusting his braced leg after sitting across from Elisabeth.

When the maître d' had placed the extra chair with the other chairs beneath the Raven and the extra place setting on a small buffet in the corner of the room, he turned and asked, "May I be of any further service before I summon your servers?"

"No, thank you, Robert," Benjamin replied.

When the maître d' had left the room, Elisabeth in a soft distressed voice, confessed, "Benjamin, I have only three dollars. I really can't afford this!"

Benjamin sat quietly, staring at his guest, trying to understand why she would have said such a strange thing, "Elisabeth, you don't have to pay for anything. I do not have to pay for anything either. My mother owns this place."

"Your mother owns this restaurant?" a surprised Elisabeth asked.

With that query, Benjamin explained, "Yes, she owns several restaurants in Riverdale, Londonderry, and Newhopeland. So, don't worry about anything, just enjoy yourself. Have you had a formal meal in Kenton since you started school in this country?"

"No . . . what's going to happen?"

"Well, I will try and explain as we get going. Just keep in mind this is all for fun, so just relax and go with it," Benjamin reassured her.

Elisabeth took a deep breath, sat up straight, smiled at Benjamin, and said, "All right, let's do it!"

Benjamin smiled and said, "I think you will enjoy the dinner."

"So how long has your family been in the restaurant business?" asked a curious Elisabeth.

"That's kind of a funny question. My mother owns a lot of different businesses."

A confused Elisabeth turned and looked directly at Benjamin, "What kind of other business does your mother own?"

"Well, she just purchased the controlling interest in the Kenton Railway Company. She has a lot of real estate, mining, and petroleum companies, agricultural and cattle companies, Eastern Sea Shipping Company, and other stuff like that. You don't know who my mother is, do you?" Benjamin said proudly.

Elisabeth felt a strange chill flow through her body as she very carefully asked the logical question, "Who is your mother, Benjamin?"

"My biological father was James Walker. He died the day I was born, and I bear his name," Benjamin continued. "My mother remarried Conrad Forrestal. My mother is Ellen Forrestal."

"Ellen Forrestal!" Elisabeth screamed, causing Benjamin

to jump at the unexpected shriek. "Your mother is the richest woman in the world! I have been reading about your mother in the newspaper's business section for months—ever since she revealed her vast holdings. Benjamin, your mother is Ellen Forrestal!"

"I don't think she is the richest woman in the world. Yeah, the paper was on to her. She kept her business secret for years. My mother does have a lot of business interests. I don't think she is the richest woman in the world." Benjamin paused for a second to reflect on Elisabeth's statement and then continued, "I mean, is that what the newspaper says?"

"Yes! You don't know that?" Elisabeth questioned.

"I haven't been reading the newspapers. The whole thing was kept secret from the world." How strange there are stories written about my mother in the newspaper, Benjamin thought.

An excited Elisabeth declared, "Benjamin, when you are buying up all the publicly owned companies globally, people will know who you are."

"I have been so busy preparing for my accountant exam and my job working for Mr. Porter," Benjamin told her. "I guess I kind of lost touch with the world. I mean, everything seems to be moving so fast. Do you mind if my family is rich?"

Elisabeth shook her head, "No, I am glad I didn't know. I would have been much too inhibited to go up and talk to you. I mean, I just would have never considered talking to you."

"Really. Well, I am glad this was a surprise," declared Benjamin.

A tall waiter entered the room with two menus and handed one to both Elisabeth and Benjamin. Elisabeth began reading in silence while turning the pages. The waiter stated, "I am Ronald, and I will be your server this evening. May I bring you something to drink while you are considering your meal?"

Elisabeth looked over her menu at Benjamin, tilted her head, widened her eyes, and stared leaning slightly forward toward Benjamin.

"Why yes," Benjamin stated, looking across the table at Elisabeth, "Please bring us a red and white wine from my mother's wine cellar and a pitcher of lemon phosphate."

"Very good," the waiter replied.

After the waiter left the room, Elisabeth asked, "Why are we drinking three different things, and what is lemon phosphate?"

"Well, everything served in a formal dinner is served in threes. So we will be served three drinks, three entries, three soups, three salads, three types of vegetables, and three different kinds of dessert, . . . and as for lemon phosphate, all I can say is it is my favorite drink."

"Why threes?" Asked Elisabeth.

Benjamin pondered Elisabeth's question and responded, "I am not sure why. This has always been how formal dinner is done. Everything in threes."

"Well, all right," Elisabeth said, reading while turning the pages of the menu. "All the restaurants I have ever eaten at, you would order by just giving the number of the meal you wanted to eat. This thing has pages for every part of the meal. I think I will let you order for both of us."

Benjamin smiled, "I will. This way, you can tell me what you think of my favorite foods."

Elisabeth laughed and said, "That's why all the tables downstairs had so much food. Are you expected to eat all of it? I mean, I couldn't do that."

Benjamin shook his head, "No, just eat what you want. You're not expected to eat all of it. Just sample and eat what you like."

Two waitresses entered the room. One was pushing a small cart with two pitchers of lemon phosphate, two bottles of red wine, and two bottles of white wine. Each waitress selected a bottle of red wine. One waitress served Elisabeth, and one served Benjamin. Next, the white wine was served, and the practice was repeated for the lemon phosphate. One of the waitresses pushed the cart to one side. Without saying a

word, both waitresses turned and left the room.

"Now, why were we served wine out of different bottles? I mean, that is really strange," Elisabeth asked, placing her elbow on the table, and resting her chin on her hand, and staring at the three full crystal goblets set in front of her.

"In Kenton, it is customary at formal dinners to be served out of different wine bottles. During the meal, we will be served out of different bowls of food. Even the meat dishes will come from different animals. Unless you are married or going to be married or a member of the immediate family, it is considered much too intimate to be served out of the same bottle or bowl of food," Benjamin explained without expression.

"Too intimate! What? Why? Benjamin, what a strange idea. How can it be intimate drinking out of the same bottle of wine? I mean, it's not like we are taking swigs out of the same bottle and passing the bottle around the table. Please explain this custom," Elisabeth wanted to be polite and nonjudgmental, so she tried not to laugh.

Benjamin once again tried to come up with a rational explanation for the custom, "I think it is just some kind of symbolic thing. Like when the bride and groom exchange gifts during the wedding sealing. If you and I were to eat out of the same bowl or drink from the same bottle of wine, we would be telling the world we are intimate and plan to marry."

"You mean sexually intimate? Who is going to know in a private dining room how we eat our food? I mean, will the servers gossip?" Ellen asked.

"Yes," Benjamin stated. "If we drank out of the same bottle of wine, we would be saying we are having sex, and the servers are not supposed to talk about what we say or do in the room. I don't know why these things are the way they are. Why—do you want to eat from the same bowl or something?"

"In Kuttor, when we eat dinner, we all eat out of the same bowl. I mean the very same bowl," Elisabeth continued her explanation. "The family and guests lay on big pillows, and the meal is served in a large copper bowl called a Ritarbe. On each side of the Ritarbe is a different part of the meal. Usually, the meat is lamb or chicken, and the vegetables are turnips or potatoes, sometimes rice. There is always some form of cheese and bread as well. Everyone just uses their hands and takes some of each food and eats directly out of the Ritarbe. We are expected to eat all the food to be polite, which is easy because there is usually not that much food. Our culture seems to be opposite of yours when it comes to eating."

"Well, let's break some rules and eat from the same bowls," Benjamin said, laughing. "You are correct, of course. It is a strange custom. I wonder how long before it gets back to my mother."

"I don't want you to get in trouble, and I think I may have already caused some problems for you wearing this attire to this place, so let's follow the rules tonight," Elisabeth requested with a worried look on her face.

"Of course, you are right again, and I would not be very respectful of you if we broke that rule anyway . . . I wasn't thinking."

"Thank you, Benjamin, I didn't think of it like that. I mean, it would be like kissing and telling!" Elisabeth said while laughing at the thought of how you ate a meal with someone could suggest you were having sex.

The waiter entered the room and asked, "May I have the selection you have chosen?"

Benjamin replied, "Yes, I will be selecting for the young lady as well."

"Very well," the waiter stated, pulling a small tablet and pencil from his apron.

Benjamin began, "The soups will be oyster, fish, and fried beans. The salads: potato, Kenton, and a sea salad. The meat dishes will be pheasant, goose, and prime rib. The vegetables will be wild rice, sweet potatoes, and mashed potatoes. The bread will be rye, sourdough, and bleached flour. The desserts will be vanilla ice cream, cherry pie, and chocolate cake. We will start with soup and salad. After that, please bring the rest except for the desserts, of course."

"Very well," the waiter said as he turned and motioned for the musicians to enter the room.

Four properly dressed young ladies entered the room, carrying string musical instruments: two violins, a viola, and cello. The string quartet walked over under the Raven, sat down using the extra chairs, and prepared their musical instruments.

"Benjamin," Elisabeth stated while looking at the four musicians. "What's this all about?"

"Musical entertainment during dinner," he responded.

"What?" exclaimed Elisabeth.

"There is not supposed to be any talking during the meal. Talking suggests the meal is boring or unpalatable, so the musicians entertain us."

"No!" Elisabeth exclaimed. "I want to get to know you, and I want to be able to talk to you, so please break this rule. Besides, everyone was talking during dinner when we came into this place, so why should we be different?"

Benjamin asked for Ronald's attention by tapping his knife against a goblet. The waiter turned and asked, "Yes, sir?"

Benjamin leaned closer to the waiter, "Send the musicians away for now."

"Yes, sir." Ronald walked over to the four young ladies and whispered something inaudible. At that point, the four young ladies stood and walked out of the room in single file.

"Thank you, Benjamin," Elisabeth stated relieved. "What a strange idea."

"Now, while we are waiting, I think I will try your lemon phosphate," Elisabeth said, reaching over and picking up the goblet containing the yellow liquid. Elisabeth brought the goblet to her lips, took a mouthful of the lemon phosphate, then instantly puckered up with a distressed expression. Her eyes bulged, and her cheeks expanded as if she were about to spray her dinner companion with his favorite drink. She was saved from that embarrassment by grabbing one of the cloth napkins to block her mouth while forcing herself to swallow the foul-tasting liquid. The silver ring napkin holder flew into the air, striking the large-paned window, producing a deafening thud, causing several of the diners below to stop eating, look up and wonder. The quick placement of the goblet on the table proved to be unstable. The crystal glass tumbled over, spilling and splattering the yellow liquid all over the tablecloth.

Elisabeth screamed, "No!" as she unsuccessfully reached for the goblet in a desperate attempt to save the tablecloth.

A contrite Elisabeth looked at the mess before her and said, "I am so sorry I had such a strong reaction to your drink and ruined this beautiful tablecloth."

Benjamin was briefly stunned by Elisabeth's reaction to the drink and stated, "Don't worry about that for a second. I am so sorry you didn't like it."

At that point, Benjamin picked up his knife again and struck one of his goblets, causing the almost immediate appearance of Ronald, who entered the room and apologized for the mess, "I am so sorry, Miss. Did your beautiful gown get soiled?"

"No," Elisabeth replied, looking at the frantic waiter.

"Thank goodness," Ronald said as he turned and summoned the staff to correct the situation.

"Don't worry, Elisabeth. The staff will clean it up. Was the lemon phosphate too strong?" Benjamin asked with concern in his voice.

"Benjamin, please don't be angry, but that phosphate stuff tasted like liquid dirt with lemon flavoring."

"Well, I didn't know," Benjamin replied.

"It must be an acquired taste?" Elisabeth said with a slight grimace.

"I guess. I have been drinking it all my life. I am sorry. I didn't mean to poison you at our first dinner!"

Elisabeth laughed, "Well, I hope you're not planning on poisoning me anytime soon."

"Well, the evening has just begun, let's see how it goes!" Benjamin jokingly returned, causing Elisabeth to laugh again.

Suddenly the room was a flurry of servants. Two of the servants each pushed a cart, one empty and the other contained a new tablecloth and appropriate replacement place settings. The servant with the empty cart began pulling goblets, all the silverware, napkins, and plates from the table. Next, the tablecloth was carefully removed ensuring the soiled cloth did not touch Elisabeth or Benjamin in any way and placed on top the cart with the removed utensils and glasses.

While one of the waitresses removed the cart with the distressed tablecloth, the other waitresses wiped the table with a damp cloth and placed a fresh silk tablecloth on the table from the other cart and continued her activity by replacing the goblets, silverware, and napkins for each guest. A third servant appeared with a bowl of warm water and a washcloth, knelt next to Elisabeth and began washing the hands of Benjamin's very startled dinner guest. After the waitresses left the room, Ronald then poured the red and white wine, careful not to confuse which bottle of wine was appropriate for each guest. When he reached for the lemon phosphate pitcher, Benjamin stated, "Ronald, I think we will have mineral water instead of the phosphate."

"Very well, Mr. Walker," Ronald replied while leaving the room to secure Benjamin's request.

"The waitress washed my hands! Can you believe that?" an incredibly surprised Elisabeth exclaimed. "She washed my hands!"

Benjamin laughingly responded, "Imagine what she would have done if you had spilled the phosphate soda on your dress."

"No, you are joking, aren't you," Elisabeth said, shaking her head and squinting her eyes at the implication.

"I don't know. Let's try it."

"Absolutely not," Elisabeth began to laugh at such an idea, causing Benjamin to also burst into laughter.

After a moment, Elisabeth said, "I hope they will be able to get the stains out of the silk. The tablecloth is so beautiful."

"It will be thrown away. Tablecloths are never used twice. I guess that's another custom. It is considered improper to use a tablecloth twice. It is considered as eating off dirty dishes to use a tablecloth twice, even if it has been cleaned."

Elisabeth shook her head while looking at the refreshed table. "This is so strange. Kenton is such an affluent culture. I hope they will use the glasses and silverware again. If not, may I take them home with me?"

Benjamin laughed again, "No, the dining utensils will still be used. Kenton is not that affluent—not yet anyway!"

With that said, Ronald returned, holding two bottles of mineral water followed by two waitresses, each pushing their cart. As Ronald poured the appropriate mineral water for each guest, the two waitresses positioned themselves at each end of the table, so one of the waitresses served only Benjamin and the other Elisabeth. Each waitress began placing soup bowls and salad plates in front of the specific guest they served. Then, each waitress served the appropriate soup in each bowl and the salad on each plate. The two waitresses worked in perfect unison and began serving each guest at the same time. Their movements were hypnotizing!

Elisabeth sat and watched each server's synchronized movement, and as the waitresses left the room, Elisabeth said, "They must practice."

"I hope you like the different salads and soups. If not, this place has plenty of tablecloths," said Benjamin.

With great caution, Elisabeth sampled each soup and salad and proclaimed, "Wonderful! Everything tastes fantastic."

"I am glad you like it!" Benjamin said.

For a few minutes, the room was quiet while Benjamin and Elisabeth focused on consuming their favorite soups and salads. Benjamin broke the silence: "Now tell me what it is like to live in Kuttor? I know so little about your country."

Elisabeth's expression of contentment vanished, "Kuttor is awful. It is a truly dreadful place. Every part of the culture is obsessed with religion. The Locks, the religious leaders, run every aspect of life, and the Lentics are the thought police who ensure everyone acts and speaks according to the demands of the Locks. In the language of Kuttor, Lentic means the infallible because it is believed they are guided by God and cannot make a mistake. The Lentics are the judge and jury of our society.

"Our country is dirt poor. Most of the men there are farmers or raise herds of sheep, and most families live in shacks made of baked mud and straw. Every man is required to pray at least ten times a day at prescribed times. Of course, the amazing artisans of Kuttor are permitted to create their wonders, but everything they make is owned by the state, mainly for export. My family is the exception because of my father's export business. Still, we are not considered affluent by Kenton standards. Women in Kuttor are property. The Locks dictate that women are intrinsically evil because they can control men with their sexuality. When girls reach puberty, they are married. All marriage is arranged after every female child is born. After marriage, the young girl is considered the property of her husband. Women are not allowed to be educated and must be completely covered from the top of their heads to their feet when they are permitted to leave their homes, which is seldom. The woman's role in Kuttor is to serve her husband and make and care for babies. Oh, get this—if a woman is born with blue or green eyes, she is considered extra evil and must also cover her eyes when in public. Some female babies who are so born have their eyes removed by their fathers because potential husbands are afraid that the woman will make a poor wife. Some women are disfigured in other terrible ways, so they won't enjoy sex in order to ensure they will be faithful to their husbands. I could go on all night. Let's just say Kuttor is a society of ignorance and superstition. Benjamin, I will never go back there. I would die before returning. I have seen the world, I am educated, and I would never submit to such cruelty."

Benjamin stunned with Elisabeth's words, and after a

brief pause, asked, "How did you escape?"

"My father was educated and spoke the language of Kenton and Liberty, so he could sell the artisans' efforts, especially the carpets, as his father did before him. He has a great deal of influence with the Locks, and more importantly, he bribes them. It took a great deal of money to allow me to be educated in a foreign land. So few people are bilingual in Kuttor. The hope is I will be able to continue in my father's business when I have completed my education. I don't know what I will do if they attempt to force me to return. I think I would try and hide in Newhopeland or something. I do not think it will come to that. My father has a great deal of influence. I know he will protect me. I just know..." Elisabeth's voice tapered off as she reached to fill her spoon with soup.

Benjamin sat in silence, and when the time was right, he said, "I hope everything will work out. Many people immigrate to Kenton to escape persecution, Elisabeth."

"I am sorry I didn't mean to be so gloomy. My father has always protected me, and I am sure I will have a long and productive life helping my father in his export business. The Locks can always be bought off. They love their wine, rich foods, and prostitutes. I have been given the great gift of awareness, and for that, I will always be grateful to my father. I know he would do anything to keep me free." Elisabeth explained with an uplifting tone.

Just as Elisabeth completed her explanation, two waitresses entered the room and served from their carts full of food.

Elisabeth immediately attacked the various meat dishes. "Benjamin, the meats are wonderful. I love the prime rib."

"I think the prime rib is my favorite as well."

Elisabeth sampled every vegetable and every type of bread, and after a few minutes, she looked up at Benjamin as he sampled some goose meat and said, "This is wonderful. Thank you for this experience."

"I am glad you are having a good time, Elisabeth. What is your favorite vegetable?" asked Benjamin.

"Potatoes with butter, and I love the sourdough with but-ter. I have never had a meal like this," she said, reaching for some red wine.

"And the wine?" Benjamin asked.

Elisabeth replied, "Love the red, not so much the white."

The couple continued to eat and talk about the meal for the next hour. When the young couple had nearly finished eating, Ronald entered the room. He scanned both Elisabeth and Benjamin and asked, "May I be of any further service at this time?"

Elisabeth was just finishing all three meat dishes when she sat back in her chair and said, "Benjamin, if I eat any more, I won't have room for dessert."

"Ronald, please remove the food and bring us our des-serts," he requested.

Ronald turned to the open door and raised his hand, and both waitresses quickly removed the remaining food and dishes from the table. Elisabeth cleaned her palate with some mineral water and, with one hand on her stomach said, "I am ready for dessert."

The two waitresses returned each with a cart of desserts. Elisabeth could not believe her eyes as she was served a quarter of a cherry pie, an enormous piece of chocolate cake, and a quart of ice cream in a clear crystal bowl, "You have to be joking. How can I eat all of this and live?"

Benjamin looked up with chocolate on his face and said, "Remember, you don't. Just enjoy what you want."

The young couple continued to eat and talk until they could eat no more. Elisabeth wiped her face and motioned to Benjamin and said in a teasing manner, "You have cake and ice cream all over your face."

Benjamin wiped his face and took a mineral water swal-low and said, "I digress into immaturity when I eat dessert. Did you enjoy your dinner?"

"Very much," Elisabeth said with a smile. "I am really enjoying myself, but I must go home now. I must do some washing before I go to bed, and we both must work tomorrow."

Without thinking, Benjamin said, "You can come in a few hours late tomorrow if you like, and I can send a carriage around to take you to work."

Elisabeth's expression turned cold, "What you just said was wrong and even offensive. You absolutely cannot treat me differently than any other employee, and we just met, sending a carriage to take me to work is too much, too soon."

Benjamin was shocked by Elisabeth's sharp tone and sat in silence, "I am sorry. You're right of course. I can't treat you any differently at work. My immaturity is obvious about all of this, and the carriage thing might make you feel . . ."

"Obligated," Elisabeth finished Benjamin's sentence.

"Of course," Benjamin said, feeling terrible he made such a mistake.

"Benjamin, I like you. I enjoy being with you. I know you are innocent. You must let things take their course and not try too hard. Your world of wealth and influence is a bit much, but remember, I like you for the person you are." She then managed a slight smirk and continued, "That would be true if your mother were only the second or third richest person in the world." Elisabeth completed her lesson with a joke so not to spoil the evening and distance herself from her new friend.

Elisabeth's gesture returned relief to Benjamin, "I am glad you feel like you can tell me what you are thinking. I think that is important. I will try to be a bit more circumspect."

"Let's agree we will always be open with each other. That is the basis of good friendship," Elisabeth said, holding up her glass of mineral water.

Benjamin held up his glass and said, "To friendship."

Benjamin tapped on one of his glasses after the couple toasted, and Ronald appeared, "Yes, sir."

"Elisabeth and I are ready to take our leave, Ronald," Benjamin said.

Ronald immediately produced a list of charges for the meal, and Benjamin signed the itemized list after writing down a large gratuity for the servants and the musicians. While Benjamin was signing the dinner bill, Ronald was assisting Elisabeth with her chair and coat. Benjamin stood, locked his brace, and thanked Ronald, "Please tell our servers and chefs how pleased we are with their service—and Ronald, thank you as well."

Ronald made a slight bowing gesture and said, "Thank you, sir. I am so happy you are pleased with us," Ronald walked over to the door and held the door open for the young couple.

Elisabeth took Benjamin's arm, and the young couple walked from the room and descended stairs. Many of the previous guests were no longer present, and the young couple ignored the late-arriving dinner guests. Their focus was strictly on each other. Benjamin opened the front door for Elisabeth, who continued to embrace his arm. The evening was much colder now, and Benjamin quickly mounted his horse. Elisabeth once again hiked her dressed, and with Benjamin's help, she mounted Fortune, covered her legs with her coat, and said, "Your horse is so warm."

"Which way to your home, Elisabeth?" Benjamin asked while backing Fortune away from the metal hitching servant and turning his horse into the street. "Are you cold?"

Elisabeth replied, "Between my coat and your horse, I am doing well. I think I am over one block and east a bit . . . I hope that's right."

Benjamin looked up and down the block. Several men bundled in heavy coats walked out of what appeared to be an alleyway a half a block up the street. "I think we can get to the next block by passing through the alley over there."

Elisabeth, holding tightly to Benjamin's waist while peeking over his shoulder, replied, "I am pretty sure I am one block over and a few miles down the block from work."

"We'll give this alley a try. If it goes through, I can get you out of the cold air sooner than going around the entire block."

Benjamin directed Fortune down the street. Arriving at

the entrance to the alley, Benjamin could see the next street over. To his surprise, halfway down the passageway, the alley was well lit with a series of gas lamps attached to one of the buildings. The dark entrance to the alley seemed somewhat frightening to Elisabeth, and for the first time, she felt some comfort knowing Benjamin was carrying his gun.

"I can see the next street, and there seems to be good lighting a little way down the alley, so I think we will cross here," Benjamin stated as he entered.

The alley was narrower than a typical city street but wide enough to permit wagon delivery. The alley was very dark at first, and Benjamin once again saw several men coming out of the building's side under the gas lamps up ahead. The men turned and walked in the same direction as the couple. As Benjamin and Elisabeth approached the row of lights, the alley became increasingly visible. The brick structure of the building could be seen. Some buildings had wooden waste barrels sitting beside closed doors, and the many windows that faced the alley were dark as a testament to the late hour. After several more minutes, the couple was near the row of gas lamps, and at that point Benjamin realized that beneath every gas lamp was a large window with low light emanating from within the building. Benjamin counted a dozen such windows, and each window had a door nearby.

"Benjamin, what are all those windows for?" Elisabeth asked, looking over Benjamin's shoulder, trying to get a better look.

"I don't know. I have never been down this way before. I think I can see someone standing in the first window we are approaching," Benjamin answered.

Benjamin rode Fortune up to the first window, and to the young couple's amazement, a woman was standing near the window in a long robe in a parlor setting. She appeared to be a young woman in her late teens or early twenties. She had long blond hair, somewhat mussed, and her cosmetics seemed oddly exaggerated. Her eye shadow was very dark. Her obviously fake eyelashes were extremely long, and her lips painted a crimson red. She became clearly visible as she approached the window. Without warning, the young woman opened her robe, revealing her naked body. After several seconds, the young woman slid her robe completely off and slowly spun around. After displaying every side of her beautiful figure, she walked up to the window and placed her lips on the glass, causing some of her lip coloring to remain when she stepped back. She then began to make kissing gestures toward her audience while motioning the couple to enter the door next to the window. Benjamin and Elisabeth froze in total shock at the unexpected sight. Without saying a word, Benjamin continued down the alley to the next window. This window revealed an extremely obese woman wearing only leather apparel. She stood in a small dark room with chains descending from the ceiling and handcuffs dangling from a large brass headboard of a disheveled, filthy bed covered with blood-stained bedding. Her body was a tidal wave of fat, with huge sagging sides, arms, and legs. Her huge drooping breasts were barely covered by thin, black leather straps flattening each orb's width, causing the top and bottom of the restricted globes to overflow, resembling a great cascade of pale, thick lard. She, too, slowly turned around, leaning side to side, as her considerable backside eclipsed the room. Divided by a thin strip of leather nestled in her deep crack, her jiggling dimpled derriere created the bizarre appearance of two blind polar bears attempting to mate.

When the rotund woman completed the display of her unique aspect and was facing the young couple again, she too pointed at the door next to her window. Elisabeth gazed at the bizarre sight and began to laugh uncontrollably! She held on to Benjamin's waist as tight as she could, fearing she might fall off the horse while laughing so hard. Benjamin was truly frightened. The strange grotesqueness of this slowly twirling fat woman surrounded by a freakish room of shadows and filth was too reminiscent of another freakish nightmare recently visited upon him. The serenade of unexplained laughter from his companion only added to the surreal experience. An overwhelming fear enveloped him, and the vapors of some unknown evil malady swirled within him.

Benjamin pointed his horse toward the approaching street. The gentle touch of his heels on Fortune's flanks commanded the horse to commence a mild jog. As Benjamin passed each window, he realized each displayed a different woman exhibiting various forms of indecency and depravity. Several of the windows had their drapes closed, and one window abruptly opened, and a man in a heavy coat walked out of the door. Benjamin finally realized his circumstance. The horse's quickened pace brought Benjamin and Elisabeth through the alley and onto the street on the next block. Elisabeth continued to laugh so hard she nearly passed out.

"I am so sorry. I think I brought you to a brothel!" a most embarrassed Benjamin explained.

Elisabeth took a moment to control herself and then responded: "Benjamin, that was the funniest thing I have ever seen. Did you see that fat lady with the leather underwear? You are so full of surprises."

"I think I surprise myself sometimes. I really did not mean to bring you to a brothel. I was aware brothels existed. I just didn't think we would be visiting one tonight."

"I enjoyed it, Benjamin," Elisabeth responded.

"I hope you weren't offended?" Benjamin replied.

Elisabeth stated, "Not at all! It was fun."

A relieved and happy Benjamin directed his horse down the street while Elisabeth laughed and giggled for the next several blocks. The street was in one of Riverdale's poorest areas, and the couple passed many simple homes and rooming houses which lodged the unfortunate. Students seeking low rent while continuing their studies at the local trade school also sought the inexpensive rent. Many of the homes had windows with curtains tightly drawn and illuminated softly from within by kerosene lamplight and fireplaces. The homes burning wood and coal for heat had chimneys releasing black smoke into the cold evening air blocking the stars directly overhead and filling the air with the scent of combustion. Benjamin had not traveled this cobblestone street, and the lack of streetlamps and the darkness of the cold night concealed the run-down condition.

Several blocks later, Elisabeth lifted her arm and pointed: "Benjamin, the bright yellow house is where I am living."

Benjamin unconsciously navigated his horse to the wooden hitching rail in front of the rooming house and helped Elisabeth dismount. He followed and secured his horse and walked Elisabeth to the front door.

"I would let you come in, but my landlady has strict rules about having male visitors after dark," Elisabeth said, looking into Benjamin's eyes. "I enjoyed the dinner and, strangely, the visit to the brothel."

"Well, maybe we can just skip the dinner next time," Benjamin teased.

"Next time, I am taking you to dinner," Elisabeth said before leaning over and giving Benjamin a kiss on his cheek. "I had a perfect time. I will see you tomorrow, so bye for now."

She then opened the plain wooden door and disappeared into the darkness of the house.

Chapter 16
A Mother's Instinct

Everything had changed. Benjamin's world had taken on another dimension. He sat staring across his office at the stairs where he first saw Elisabeth. There were no more thoughts of secret rooms or an inevitable dark fate. As a young man with feelings for a young woman, Benjamin was experiencing life as he should, like all the young men who had come before him. He fought the urge to walk across the room and down the stairs to the hallway, which led to the catalog department and the woman that consumed his every thought. Elisabeth was correct about appearing to favor her. She was his employee, and until the return of Jeffery Porter, they must act the part of employer and supervisor. His mind, however, was not on the mundane world of accounting and management. His thoughts were on the image of a beautiful woman laughing across a dinner table, kissing his cheek as she said goodnight, the warm feeling of her body next to his as she held his waist as they rode through town. These and a thousand other impressions skipped across his mind like a flat stone across a calm lake. His workday slowly faded away.

Earlier in the day, Benjamin met for several hours with the new accountants as they explained the many innovations to the company's bookkeeping practice. He did not hear a word they said. Benjamin strolled through the warehouse checking inventory numbers with the warehouse records, but his scrutiny was worthless. He unconsciously went through the motions of the many tasks required of him. Time slowed. The length of his workday seemed eternal. The lunch break brought an opportunity to walk outside the building and perhaps create a chance encounter with Elisabeth, but he resisted such an obvious and clumsy tactic. Benjamin sat at his desk and waited and obsessed within himself. She clearly said, "I will see you tomorrow." I hope I did not misunderstand, Benjamin thought. Perhaps it was merely a manner of speaking without any real form of commitment? Maybe she was not planning on returning to my office? At the end of the workday, she may have been thinking I would seek her out at her workstation or even outside the livery stable. I hope she is at work today. What if she caught a chill from the cold night air and became ill? Or after some consideration of me, she concluded I am too immature or my crippled leg too unsightly to form a relationship and would simply avoid me as her means of telling me she was no longer interested. Benjamin became increasingly fatigued as he considered all the possible outcomes about Elisabeth Zurich into the early evening.

Nearly thirty minutes after the end of the workday, as the world grew increasingly dark, Benjamin heard footsteps coming up the stairs. He leaped to his feet and walked around his desk so the desk lamps' glare would not block the source of the approaching footsteps. He felt his heart begin to pound in anticipation as Elisabeth emerged from the spiral staircase's shadows. She was wearing her beautiful black and red coat and had replaced her pedestal shoes with her leather slippers.

She skipped across his office and greeted Benjamin with a kiss on the cheek and tight hug, "I have been thinking of you all day. You feel so good. I am sorry I took so long. I thought Mrs. Cromwell would never leave."

"I am so glad to see you as well. I was afraid I misunderstood about dinner tonight," Benjamin stated as he embraced Elisabeth and smelled her pleasant scent.

"I am taking you to dinner, Mr. Walker, and I still have only three dollars, so where I am taking you will not be exactly the same kind of place you took me last night," she stated with a laugh.

Benjamin stepped back. "I am sure it will be lovely."

"Lovely is probably not the word I would have chosen, but I think you will like the food, and there will be a lot of it, and it will be cheap," Elisabeth returned.

"Give me a moment to shut down my lamp," Benjamin said as he turned to secure his desk lamp, and then the couple took each other's arms to begin their evening adventure.

Benjamin and Elisabeth stepped out of the warehouse into the cold night. With their arms still entwined, the couple turned in the direction of the company's stable and the patiently waiting stable master holding Fortune's reins.

Before arriving at the stable, Elisabeth stated, "We will not need your horse until after dinner. The place I am taking you is just around the corner, so it is an easy walk."

Benjamin approached the stable master and said, "We are walking to dinner, so it will be several more hours before I am ready for my horse."

The stable master replied, "Yes, Sir. Your horse will be prepared and ready for you when you return."

Elisabeth directed Benjamin to cross the cobblestone street, and halfway across, she looked back at the stable master returning Benjamin's horse to his stall. "He sure gives you great service. I mean, he remains with your horse and everything until you return."

"He is well compensated," Benjamin returned.

"Oh, of course," Elisabeth stated.

The young couple continued, and upon reaching the sidewalk of oak planks on the other side of the street, Elisabeth said, "Where I am taking you is on the pier at the end of the row of boat shops. Do you know the place?"

"I have never been on the pier," Benjamin responded, just as they reached a row of small marine shops.

At the very end of the pier was a small eatery with a sizable, unintelligible sign fastened to the corrugated metal roof. "There it is, at the end of that row of shops. What do you think?"

"I didn't know it existed. Do you eat there often?" Benjamin asked, trying to keep pace with his companion.

"Mostly for lunch. I especially like the food, and it is cheap. Mostly sailors eat there. I hope you like the place,"

Elisabeth continued with slight apprehension in her voice.
"Don't worry about that. What is the place called?" Benjamin said, attempting to reassure her.

Elisabeth looked at Benjamin and said, "It's called the Sea Grotto."

A confused Benjamin replied, "Sea Guano?"

Elisabeth thought for a second, translating Benjamin's response, and began to laugh. "Stop it! grotto, not guano."

Benjamin laughed. "My mistake."

The couple continued toward the row of small shops located on the pier. Upon reaching the shops, Benjamin attempted to peer through the dirty, salt-stained windows of each storefront. Some of the mysterious shops had their windows boarded up or painted over, concealing their interiors. The purpose of many of the shops was also difficult to ascertain in the darkness. The identifying signs, affixed to each shop, were severely neglected, and many only intelligible in bright sunlight.

Benjamin surmised that all the shops must specialize in the various paraphernalia required by men who labored at sea. Benjamin noticed the first shop he could peer into specialized in clothing—heavy coats and pants made from wool, hats to shield the sun on the unshaded sea, and boots made of rubber and greased leather. The next shop had a hand-painted sign across the door, "Marine Engine Repair," and appeared to have every manner of tools, parts, and bolts necessary to repair machinery found onboard a steam-powered vessel.

The adjacent shop, called The Fisherman, was well-stocked with fishing nets and poles, and other equipment necessary to catch fish, crabs, and lobsters. All the shops were dark and enigmatic. Benjamin resolved to return and spend a leisurely day exploring every shop and answering the many questions that consumed his thoughts.

"Hey, are you still with me?" Elisabeth asked, looking at a blank expression on Benjamin's face while his mind processed the many new sights of the pier.

"I was just thinking about how I would like very much to

bring you back to the pier during the day. Wouldn't it be fun to explore all these wonderful little shops for treasures and such?" Benjamin asked.

Elisabeth answered, "Yes, that would be lovely. I have not paid that much attention. I think it would be fun to explore these places. Who knows what we might find?"

She took a deep breath and said, "Here we are, the last shop in the row. Perhaps the last shack in the row would be more accurate. I hope you like this place. Like I said, it is a little different from where we ate last night."

Elisabeth expressed a nervous giggle as she unconsciously tightened her grip on Benjamin's arm to ensure he would not bolt into the night at his first sight of the eatery's interior. She pushed the door open, and Benjamin uttered a small gasp as he gazed upon the unique scene. The eatery was lit by several kerosene lamps placed around the outer walls and hanging by chains above the bar, creating a room of sharp contrasts and eerie shadows. A door, slightly ajar behind the bar, emitted slight whiffs of slowly floating grey smoke from a wood burning stove hidden in an unseen kitchen, drawn by convection to the warmth of the hanging lamps and disappearing into the glare of the flame. The three outside walls, made of salt-stained glass and weathered wood supports, revealed the endless sea and a couple of fishing boats slowly bobbing up and down. In the center of the room was a three-sided bar made from what appeared to be old cargo cover planks. On the side of the bar near the entrance were five tall empty stools covered with torn and stained leather, inviting the tired sailor to rest and eat.

On the side of the bar opposite the kitchen with their backs to the sea, two remarkably interesting sailors sat together with large bowls of food. Large mugs of dark lagers with creamy froths sat within arm's reach. The sailors seemed to be in an agitated discussion, but when the young couple entered the room, they stopped abruptly. Benjamin surmised the sailors deemed their presence some form of trespassing by wayward interlopers. Both men were clothed in heavy wool coats of dark blue. Upon their heads rested tired and mangled caps with large forward bills. It was their faces that were most striking to the young accountant. Each one bore the countenance of an anguished life at sea. Aged by sun and salt-laden wind and waves, these men had faces of deep crevasses and thickened skin. Their eyes were reddened, puffy, and dark, and their yellow teeth missing and broken. Each man's beard and hair of grey and white, Benjamin concluded, was colored by the stress of navigating tremendous storms and perilous, fog-shrouded seas. Men such as these were the survivors of an ancient trade that the young accountant could never fully appreciate or understand, so different their world and experience. Yet Benjamin's acumen required veneration for each man's fate. He fully realized the world could not exist without those who sailed and strived upon the sea. He nodded with respect when he passed the sailors as he would have acknowledged a chairman of a great railroad or a wealthy merchant, for The Word had so adamantly taught Benjamin that all men and women are equal and necessary.

The two sailors watched suspiciously as the young couple walked by and spoke not a word, their eyes following the couple's every move. A third sailor sat on the bar opposite the entrance, but unlike his alert peers, this man's face rested on the bar next to a spilled bowl of food and numerous empty mugs. The excessively strong drink had robed his consciousness. His sailor's cap had fallen onto the bar, revealing a bald head covered with dark patches of pigment and lesions from an unforgiving sun. His arms sprawled across the bar with filthy sleeves, stained with food and unknown debris. One of his hands unconsciously reached across the bar and held tight on the inner edge, defying gravity that was attempting to bring him to the floor. He would remain undisturbed until the morning cook woke him, preparing the eatery for the onslaught of hungry sailors seeking an early morning meal.

Next to the windows on the three outside walls sat several small tables covered with stained oilcloth and accompanying mismatched chairs. Elisabeth held Benjamin back before they sat and said, "Just a minute. Let me wipe the table and chair down before we sit."

A pile of old newspapers sat on the table next to the window. The soiled papers served as makeshift napkins. Elisabeth grabbed several sheets, crumpled them, and began wiping the table and chairs down from the spills and stains from previous meals.

Then, while tossing the soiled newspapers on the floor, said, "I think it's safe now."

Benjamin assisted Elisabeth to her seat, and sat down opposite her with the window showing the end of the pier behind her. Through the salt-stained windows, he could see several more sailing vessels moored on each side of the pier, and at the very far end of the pier, two large gas beacons stood sentinel, assisting sailors to locate the pier from far out at sea. Benjamin noticed the eatery floor was the same wooden pier planks as outside the building. The exposed wood frame of the shack secured the walls of rough-hewn planks. Tin can lid tops speckled the walls covering missing knotholes, the lids secured by bent, rusty nails. Before Benjamin could say a word, the sound of a door hitting the wall caused the young accountant to turn and see the cook coming from the kitchen holding a huge bowl of food and a spoon in each hand. The cook was fat and filthy. A long day of preparing food had stained his apron. He was bald and unshaven, with heavy jowls and dripping fat clinging from his face. To Benjamin, the man seemed not to have a neck, his head floating above his shoulders. The cook's shirt rode up his enormous white belly, exposing a jiggling, hairy midriff, creating a dinning milieu as appetizing as a squashed cat beneath an ore wagon. The cook lifted a section of the bar with one of his arms and continued to the couple's table. He tossed the bowls in front of each of his patrons, causing the liquid to slosh over the rim of the bowls and onto the table.

"Beers?" the cook asked in a gruff voice.

Elisabeth responded with a sarcastic reply, "Yes, please. That would be just exquisite."

The cook wallowed back to the kitchen, showing a generous portion of his upper buttocks, a result of his drooping and ill-fitting pants. Benjamin could hardly keep from bursting into laughter.

"We don't get a choice from the menu?"

Elisabeth was also trying not to laugh, "What menu? This place only serves one thing: grout."

Benjamin stared at the thick white liquid in the bowl.

"I thought grout was the white stuff between tiles."

"That too! Just try it. This stuff is wonderful."

With some trepidation, Benjamin picked up his spoon, and before he could explore the sea porridge, he heard Elisabeth say, "Wait until we get our beers."

A few seconds later, the cook returned with two large mugs of a dark beer, which he placed in front of the young couple and said, "That will be a buck."

Elisabeth reached into one of her coat pockets and handed a silver coin to the cook, and without saying a word, the sea chef returned to the kitchen. Elisabeth took out a handkerchief from her coat, dipped it into her beer, and reached over and took Benjamin's spoon, and thoroughly wiped his eating utensil and handed it back to him. She then repeated the sanitizing process with her spoon, smiled, and said, "Go for it."

The time for bravery was upon him. With a determined look on his face, Benjamin stuck his spoon deep into the white paste and brought forth a heaping pile of dripping deceased critters from the sea. Placing the heaping spoon into his mouth, he was pleasantly surprised by the thick chowder's wonderful flavor. "It tastes like clam chowder but more. What is it?"

"Well, it has a ton of clams but also potatoes and different kinds of fish. Grout and the beer are the only food they serve, but the grout changes every day. I do not know all the things put in it. Just enjoy," Elisabeth said while beginning to place a large spoonful of grout into her mouth.

"I have often wondered why there were so few cats

around the harbor," Benjamin joked.

"If you find a tail of some unknown creature in your mouth, just spit it on the floor. That's what I always do," she retorted.

Benjamin laughed so hard some of the thick grout escaped his mouth and only by a quick grab of nearby newspaper prevented him from showering his new friend with the partially chewed white paste.

He next took a swallow of beer, and his eyes opened wide. "This beer is wonderful. It reminds me of dark bread, but it is a liquid. I really like it."

"Have you had a beer before?" Elisabeth asked just before taking a large gulp from her mug.

"No, this is the first time, and I think it is delicious. I think I like this better than wine!"

"This kind of beer has a high alcohol level, so you've been warned," said Elisabeth.

The young couple continued to eat grout and drink beer for a few minutes without talking until Benjamin noticed both of their mugs were nearly empty. "Can you afford another round of beer?"

With her mouth full of grout, Elisabeth nodded, and without hesitating, Benjamin turned and yelled, "Two more beers over here."

The two sailors sitting at the bar jumped at the slightly intoxicated young accountant's loud shriek, and almost instantly, the corpulent cook reappeared carrying two large mugs of beer. Without expression, he set the mugs on the table and demanded fifty cents.

Elisabeth handed him a fifty-cent piece retrieved from her coat and gave the rotund cook a wink as a tip. The cook did not respond and returned to his wood-burning stove and perpetual pot of grout continuously evolving into a culinary triumph as new ingredients were periodically added to the cauldron. This ritual continued throughout the night and into the next day.

In less than an hour, Elisabeth and Benjamin had consumed as much grout as possible and drank the final dregs of beers. With silly smiles, they looked at each other for several moments. Elisabeth spoke first, "Well, did you like your dining experience?"

Benjamin responded, "Very much. You are full of surprises. I am so happy that fate has caused our life paths to cross. I think you will teach me things I have never known."

"I think you will take me places I have never been," Elisabeth returned.

"I think I want you to be part of my life. I am attracted to you, Elisabeth. I do so enjoy being with you," a soft-spoken Benjamin confessed.

"You frighten me. I am so attracted to you," Elisabeth said, unable to look directly at the man she was falling in love with. "You feel . . . right. I have never had such strong feelings and nothing like this so fast. It is as if I knew you in another life or we were drawn together by some unknown magic."

"I have always been self-conscious of my braced leg. Does it bother you much?" Benjamin asked.

Elisabeth looked directly into Benjamin's eyes. "If my leg were bound with metal or if I were missing an arm or eye, would you have shunned me when I walked into your office? Would you have still gone to dinner with me?"

"I do not think that would have made any difference," Benjamin stated without hesitation.

"You have your answer. We all have flaws. It is what makes us human," Elisabeth said as her eyes returned to the sea.

"What flaw could you possibly have?" asked Benjamin.

"My circumstance, Benjamin. The uncertainty of my life. My life outside of Kuttor is dependent on my father's relationship with the religious leaders. If something should happen and I was forced to return, I would kill myself. I mean, I would be put into an impossible position because they could threaten my family if I failed to return. Uncertainty, Benjamin, is my flaw. I have been able to live and study outside my country for years. I have no reason to believe I will not continue to study and help my father with his business outside my country in the future. Still, such a thing is inconsistent with the fundamental teachings of our religious belief and the very nature of my society. I was pledged from birth to marry the first-born son of a family I do not even know. I would be nothing more than chattel for the rest of my life. What if that family should protest my absence? What if my father's relationship with the Locks somehow changed? I would rather die than return. My greatest flaw is uncertainty. Do you still want to get involved with me, knowing my situation? I can never promise you certainty. This thing will always be a cloud over our relationship," Elisabeth confessed, looking at her empty mug.

"Well, you are now involved with one of the most powerful families in the world. You did not know that before we met," Benjamin stated. "You are safer now. My mother would buy your entire country to keep you safe if I asked her to."

"Benjamin, on Raven's wing, I swear all I knew about you is what the ladies in the catalog department spoke of—that you were a brilliant young man who killed a thief and who Jeffery Porter placed in charge of his business in his absence. I wanted to meet you because I was curious. I became interested in you because you were so intelligent and because of something intangible. I was drawn to you. I did not realize who you were until you told me about your mother. You must believe me. I would never expect to use your family's wealth to free me from any obligations placed on me," Elisabeth pleaded, realizing the implications of Benjamin's statements.

"Elisabeth, I believe you. I did not mean to suggest you were using me. I am saying fate has brought us together, and I would not allow anything to harm you. I say this because you are my friend. Forgive me if I gave another impression. Life is full of uncertainties. Tomorrow any of us could be struck down by some unseen force. The only certain thing in life is uncertainty," Benjamin responded, reaching across the table and taking Elisabeth's hand.

Elisabeth whispered, leaning closer to the young accountant, "Benjamin, I hope I did not spoil anything between us. I felt you should know before we go any further. What I feel for you is so strong, but you should know who and what I am."

"Thank you for telling me your concerns. You have not spoiled anything. How about a few more beers?" Benjamin exclaimed to reassure his new friend.

Elisabeth smiled and squeezed Benjamin's hand, then called out, "Two more beers over here."

The couple continued talking and drinking for another hour, and when the time was right, Benjamin said, "It is getting late. I should take you home."

Elisabeth smiled and said, "I think we should walk to the beach and get some air before we attempt to ride your horse."

Benjamin stood and felt the effects of the beer as he struggled to maintain his balance. "I think that's a good idea. This beer is rather strong."

Elisabeth laughed and took Benjamin's hand, and the couple walked out of the eatery. "I know a way to the beach from here," Elisabeth explained, guiding an intoxicated Benjamin back toward the large warehouse the couple passed earlier. "There are some steps over here to the beach."

Benjamin followed Elisabeth's lead, and the couple carefully descended the wooden steps to the beach, each holding the railing and trying not to stumble in the dark. Upon reaching the final step, Elisabeth thoughtfully asked, "Can you walk across the sand?"

"No problem," Benjamin responded as he stepped onto the beach.

"I really have to pee," an uninhibited, intoxicated Elisabeth announced, releasing Benjamin's hand, and disappearing under the pier.

Benjamin was relieved. His bladder was full as well. He took a few unsteady steps toward the sea, unzipped his pants, and relieved himself as quickly as possible before his date returned. A few minutes passed. Elisabeth returned, giggling, "Now that was truly not very ladylike."

"Thank you for taking the initiative. I was about to die," Benjamin confessed.

"Well, there is a bench over there. Can we sit for a while before we go back?" Elisabeth asked.

"I would like that," Benjamin said, taking Elisabeth's arm and walking to the wooden bench facing the sea, which was barely visible under the dim stars.

The couple sat down, leaned into each other, wrapping their bodies together. Neither spoke. Elisabeth stared out to sea. She then turned to look into Benjamin's eyes, leaned closer, and kissed Benjamin on the lips. A long, sweet first kiss. She pressed harder while her tongue slipped into Benjamin's mouth. Their tongues touched and pushed hard together, swirling, pressing deeper. Nascent passion consumed Benjamin. He had never experienced such intimacy. He was increasingly aroused as Elisabeth pressed harder, thrusting her tongue deeper into Benjamin's throat.

Elisabeth pulled back and whispered, "Touch me."

Before Benjamin could respond, Elisabeth placed his hand on her breast. Benjamin pressed his hand against her firm breast, his fingers swirled and softly pinched her hardened nipples hidden beneath her blouse. Elisabeth, with her eyes closed, gasped, and arched her back at Benjamin's touch. Elisabeth stood and pulled her dress up to her waist in one sweeping motion, exposing her stocking-covered legs. Without hesitating, Elisabeth straddled Benjamin's lap. Benjamin gently returned one of his hands to her breast. He placed his other hand on her leg. While the couple continued to kiss deeply, Benjamin moved his hand up Elisabeth's leg. He felt Elisabeth's silky stocking, then her firm thigh. His hand moving, reaching her now-wet undergarments. His finger instinctively stroked between her legs. Continuing to kiss Benjamin, Elisabeth slowly rose up and down, pressing her body harder against Benjamin. Her movement increased in speed. Suddenly, Elisabeth pulled her face away, arched her back, her body stiffened with tension and pleasure. She tilted her face to the sky and released a very audible groan.

Elisabeth grew still. She turned to Benjamin, drew closer, and quietly whispered in his ear, "That was wonderful."

Benjamin knew something had happened. He pulled his wet fingers back. His breathing slowed. His arousal diminished. He held Elisabeth tightly. Benjamin timidly confessed, "That was my first kiss."

Elisabeth was surprised and perplexed. "Well. . . . That is a surprise. You excite me so much. Can you hold on a little longer?"

"How much longer?" a frustrated Benjamin asked without hesitation.

"It won't be long. You excite me so much," Elisabeth repeated. "In fact, if we do not leave soon, we are going to complete what we started and get naked on this cold dark beach . . . well, we should find a better place."

Elisabeth could feel the excitement returning as she stood up and pulled her dress down and wrapped herself in her coat to help to ward off the cold night and her desires before sitting back on the bench.

"I am excited as well. What a wonderful experience," Benjamin responded.

"I could tell. I was sitting on your lap," Elisabeth said, laughing and placing her hand on Benjamin's leg. She realized his lap was soaked with her intimate fluids. "Oh, Benjamin, I am so sorry I have ruined your pants."

Benjamin was not sure what Elisabeth was talking about but decided this was not the time to reveal the depth of his innocence. "That's fine. I understand."

"Tomorrow is Saturday, and we will have all day to be together, and I have a suspicion we can find a proper place to make love. Will that be all right with you?" Elisabeth asked.

"Yes, tomorrow then. We will continue this tomorrow," Benjamin said softly. "I am so happy you have become part of my life."

"I am as well," Elisabeth returned, touching Benjamin's

lips with one of her fingers.

⸎

Benjamin quietly opened the door to his home by the sea. His mother greeted him. She had been patiently waiting in the formal sitting room. "Benjamin, I am so happy to see you," she said, receiving him with a tight hug. "Come sit with me so we may talk."

"Yes, Mother," Benjamin replied as he walked with her to the sofa.

Mother and son sat next to each other, and Ellen began, "I spoke to Alice Harper, who spoke to Edith Russell, who said she saw you at our restaurant last night with a beautiful young woman in a very short dress. Have you made a new friend? Would you mind telling me about her?"

"No, not at all," Benjamin began. "Her name is Elisabeth Zurich, and she is from Kuttor. She will be a sophomore next semester at the university in Londonderry, and she is from a very influential and wealthy family. She was raised with bilingual servants, so Elisabeth learned our language. She went to finishing school in Liberty for three years before continuing her education at the university, and Mother, many of the girls at the university are starting to wear short dresses. Please do not be harsh with her—short skirts are the new fashion."

"She is older than you," Ellen stated, audibly concerned.

"Mother, everyone is always older than I am. I mean, think about it," Benjamin answered.

"True. What business is her father involved with?"

Benjamin explained, "He is one of the largest exporters of Kuttor carpets, and he is something like the chairman of the Kuttor Export Guild, which is an esteemed position in Kuttor. Her father arranged for her to work for Mr. Porter between semesters, so she will have some real-world experience when she graduates from the university. I think you will like her. She looks a lot like you. I mean, a younger you. She is so bright and funny, and I like her."

"Her father must be very influential to be permitted to have his daughter study outside the country. I understand they have stringent rules regarding how women are to be treated and the role they have in their culture," Benjamin's mother stated, still worried.

"I think she has had many advantages because her father is so influential, including being educated to continue his business when she completes her education. His business brings a great deal of hard currency to an impoverished country, so he has been given a great deal of latitude pertaining to his family."

"How did you meet her?" Ellen pressed.

"She works in the catalog department, and we just started talking one day. Last night I asked her if she would like to go to dinner, and she said yes, so we went to our restaurant. She didn't know who I was until I told her you were my mother," a smiling Benjamin explained.

"How did that come up?" Ellen inquired.

"Elisabeth had no idea where we were going, and when we were seated, she whispered she had only three dollars, and she could not afford to split the dinner bill. I told her my mother owned the restaurant, and one thing led to another until she realized who you were," Benjamin told his mother. "Elisabeth became extremely excited because she had been reading the newspaper's business section about how you are buying up many publicly-owned companies. She said she read you were the richest woman in the world. Is that true mother—are you?"

"I really do not know. I know your idea about shipping containers is working out. We may be one of the richest families in Kenton. I really do not know. Being the richest— that recognition is not important, Benjamin. Every business we own, we do our best to provide a product or service people will want so we can make a profit. That's what counts," stated his mother.

"I am so glad I could help the family business," Benjamin said with some pride in his voice.

"You were with Elisabeth tonight?" Ellen asked, knowing the answer.

"Yes, she took me to a little eatery on the pier near Jeffery Porter's warehouse. We ate grout and drank beer, and it was wonderful. It cost her nearly her entire three dollars. We had three mugs of beer each, and I love the taste of beer. Mother, I am going to take you and father there for grout and beer next week!" Benjamin proclaimed.

Ellen laughed and said, "All right, I think that will be enjoyable. I would like to meet your new friend. Would it be possible to bring her here for dinner tomorrow night?"

Benjamin's face lit up at the idea, "Oh, yes, Mother! I will ask her tomorrow when I see her. I want you to meet her. I really like her, and I know you will too."

Benjamin stood and continued with somewhat pressured speech.

"I am excited about tomorrow. I have to get up early to purchase a carriage and proper horse before I meet with her, so with that, I will say good night."

"Good night, Benjamin. I am happy for you," Benjamin's mother said, realizing her son was growing up. "And Benjamin, be sure and have the maid clean your suit. Elisabeth's scent is very strong."

"Yes, Mother," Benjamin responded, turning and heading toward the stairs, wondering if his mother somehow knew about the other part of his evening.

～

On Saturday, Elisabeth awoke from a restless sleep. The young couple had planned the night before to spend Saturday together. Elisabeth knew this was a special day, and she had less than five hours to prepare. Her mission this morning was to make herself as beautiful as possible. She obsessed about her appearance and hoped Benjamin would find her most appealing. So, early on that Saturday morning, in her twenty-third year of life, Elisabeth leaped from her bed and began implementing a strategy to win over Benjamin's heart.

She began by bathing. She removed and tossed her night-shirt over her shoulder. The nightshirt floated through the air and disappeared under her bed. She filled the iron bathtub in her private room with hot water and opened a small window to release a gathering cloud of steam before stepping into the bathwater. A cool breeze from the window swirled around her as she picked up a bar of bacon grease and lye soap and began rubbing the bar against her body. Elisabeth spent almost an hour carefully cleaning herself.

With that undertaking accomplished, Elisabeth leaned over the edge of the tub and picked up a straight razor from the tile floor. Testing the edge with her thumb, Elisabeth realized the razor was much too dull for her next delicate task. She hoisted herself out of the tub, all the while holding the straight razor and dripping the soapy water in all directions. Elisabeth steadied herself on the porcelain sink and slid her bare feet across the cold, wet floor. Leaning against the side of the sink, she reached for the heavy leather strap attached to the wall and skillfully honed the razor's edge.

Ever mindful of her precarious situation, she slowly re-turned to the tub. Stepping over the edge once again, Elisa-beth sat down on the corner of the hard tub. Her feet and ankles disappeared into the creamy, soapy water. She lathered her legs and underarms, and with the remnants of the shrink-ing bar of soap, proceeded with the skill of a surgeon to remove the dark hair from her body. Staring down at the only remaining hair below her neck, and with little thought, she quickly lathered her feminine hair and shaved her pubic area the best she could. She stood and grabbed a large towel, dried thoroughly, and with a puff, covered her body in a blizzard of talcum powder. Waves of white floated into the air, coating the nearby sink and tile floor.

Wrapped in the towel, Elisabeth spent a moment gazing into her crowded closet. After deliberating about what to wear, she selected a pearl-white, silk skirt and spent several hours raising the hem so her legs would be more exposed. She was sure this alteration would make her more appealing to her new friend. Elisabeth made a choker and a hair ribbon from a pile of dark green silk fragments tucked into the corner of one of her drawers.

Before dressing, she meticulously applied her cosmetics. She stood naked in front of a full-length mirror, beaming with anticipation. Elisabeth sat down on the bench near the smaller mirror on her dresser and began with a small amount of rouge, made from talcum and red safflower pigment, to her cheeks. Her flawless, pure-white skin created the perfect foundation for the artificial blush.

She then pressed red safflower pigment mixed with soft wax onto her lips to exaggerate her mouth's natural color. Elisabeth carefully applied a fine mixture of ground charcoal dust and green mineral pigment to each of her eyelids to accent her beautiful green eyes. She used a small brush with brief strokes to perfect the lovely effect. She held her breath with each stroke, carefully avoiding infecting her eyes with the decorative powder so as not to spoil her efforts with blood-stained eyes. Securing a pair of scissors, Elisabeth carefully trimmed her bangs that covered her forehead. She leaned closer to the mirror and stared a moment at her face, considering one more enhancement. Against all of her girl-friends' advice, Elisabeth walked to her tall dresser and retrieved a small vial of clear liquid with an eyedropper. Elisabeth held her head back and patiently placed several drops of Belladonna into each eye. The room brightened instantly. "Success!" she whispered.

Her attention was once again drawn to the full-length mirror. Elisabeth studied her naked body, contemplating further alluring improvements. Inspired by a growing sexual tension, she smeared her finger with wax and red safflower pigment and carefully placed the bright mixture on her nipples. Stimulated by her anticipated encounter with Benjamin, Elisabeth dipped her finger once again into the pigment and outlined the opening of her most feminine private part. While sitting, she put her legs into a pink garter belt, securing the garment to her waist with a small, brass buckle. Elisabeth covered each leg with a silk stocking and secured them with the belt's hanging straps. She grabbed her hairbrush and stroked her long, raven-black hair to lustrous effect and with a length of green ribbon, she pulled her hair back, exposing her ears. Elisabeth chose a sheer-white, silk blouse from her closet, and without a proper bodice to cover her breast, slipped into the tight blouse using the white bone buttons to secure the front. She hesitated a moment. What if the bright sun makes the blouse too revealing? she thought to herself, and with a slight smile, continued. She decided she would skip her bottom undergarments as well. She was sure, considering her feelings and expectations, she would not be dressed for long. She stepped into her shortened white skirt and fastened a row of bone buttons on her right side and secured a green silk belt around her waist. She grabbed a pale, light-green chiffon overlay hastily placed on a nearby chair several nights before and covered her revealing blouse.

"That's better," Elisabeth sighed. She pirouetted one last time in front of the mirror. Elisabeth unconsciously retrieved her red-and-black coat and her green pedestal shoes and walked out her sleep room door. Just outside was a small table with a crystal bowl filled with yellow candy. As she walked by, Elisabeth clutched a handful of the lemon drops to sweeten her breath. Her cheeks bulged as she jammed her mouth full of the sweet confections. Elisabeth was elated. She slurped and skipped down the long hallway to the front door and her next adventure.

Elisabeth looked up and down the hardened dirt street from the porch in front of her rooming house. The thoroughfare was alive with heavy traffic. Several well-dressed men sat upon manicured horses and proudly trotted past the rooming house. Carriages clattered, transporting families to and from the harbor. Benjamin had said he would arrive before noon. Elisabeth was anxious and hoped he might be early. Memories of the night before consumed her thoughts. The intensity of her feelings were so strong she was frightened. She had never experienced such sexual tension and pleasure in any previous relationship. Elisabeth found herself in an entangling web of love and desire.

"It is still early in the day," she told herself and prayed Benjamin would be along soon. She tried to contain the pain of anticipation by turning from the street and leaning against the porch rail while taking several deep breaths.

The sound of the traffic masked Benjamin's arrival. At first, Elisabeth failed to recognize his presence. A familiar voice command, "Pose," drew her attention to Benjamin proudly sitting in a beautiful new carriage with a magnificent, gelded chestnut carriage horse. The exquisite and well-trained animal displayed perfect confirmation. The black carriage, with intricate red and gold painted patterns, was the finest available in Riverdale. The metal braces and leather fasteners of the tack were made of polished nickel, and the bit in the horse's mouth and controlling bit shank was plated with gold. A heavily greased black leather folding hood provided shade for driver and passenger. Benjamin sat upon a wooden bench covered with brilliant red leather.

Elisabeth, surprised, gasped, "A calash!"

Benjamin crouched and opened a small gate on the carriage side that unfolded a series of metal and wooden steps. Before he could begin his descent, he heard Elisabeth crying out his name. When he looked up, he observed a most beautiful young woman standing on the porch of the rooming house. Benjamin was very pleasantly surprised and aroused at her appearance in a pure white silk skirt and matching blouse, with the skirt loose around her legs and just long enough to cover the tops of her silk stockings. The pale green transparent chiffon overlay, slightly longer than her dress, added a modicum of modesty as well as attractiveness. The belt around her waist, made from a length of dark green ribbon, matched the green ribbon in her hair and around her neck. Her green eyes with huge pupils glowed with an almost mystical quality. Over her right arm hung a red and black coat, and in her left hand she held a pair of matching pale-green pedestal shoes. Benjamin found the raven-haired beauty simply stunning, and at that moment, he believed Elisabeth must be the most attractive woman in the world.

While Benjamin carefully descended the carriage. Elisabeth ran to him and helped him take the last few steps to the hard dirt road. Benjamin smiled, and before he spoke a single word, Elisabeth threw her arms around him and gave him the long, deep kiss of a woman deeply in love. He returned her affection, and, for a moment, the world seemed to fade away. The young lovers only saw each other.

When the all-consuming moment passed, Elisabeth stepped back and said, "Benjamin, I am so happy to see you. Is this your carriage? It is beautiful."

"Yes, I purchased it this morning. I think it best we ride in a carriage at this point in our relationship. Besides, Jeffery Porter will be returning Monday, and I will no longer be your employer. I was thinking, if you thought the time was right, I could pick you up and take you to work and bring you home after dinner. I mean—if you think that would be all right," Benjamin responded.

"I think that would be perfect," Elisabeth answered. "What a wonderful carriage horse. Why is he standing so still?"

Benjamin answered, "he has been trained to stand perfectly still when he is told, 'Pose.' Now watch, as he is told, 'Relax.'"

With the command, the carriage horse came to life. He shook his head, swished his tail, and moved side to side as he adjusted his weight. Elisabeth took Benjamin's hand, and the couple walked to the front of the highly trained carriage horse, carefully avoiding the fresh patches of horse manure along the side of the road. Elisabeth put her hand on the horse's neck and gently patted the animal. "What is your horse's name?"

"His name is Nephilim," Benjamin answered.

"What a perfectly strange name. What does it mean?" Elisabeth queried.

"Well, The Word speaks of the Nephilim as the race of

children born from parents of angelic fathers and the daughters of men," Benjamin explained. "The Nephilim were renowned philosophers and teachers, true intellectual giants who laid the foundation of modern civilization. The Word is vague about the Nephilim. I think the ancient Elders may have been the Nephilim. I mean, that is just what I think. It makes sense that children from beings beyond this world bring knowledge and moral direction to us, I suppose. I do not know, but the Elders seemed so advanced. But I am not sure of this." Benjamin prudently felt he should not verbalize his suspicions any further and changed the subject. "I think we should take this carriage somewhere now that we have it. What do you think?"

"Yes, Benjamin. Let's ride your carriage down to the ocean and explore the pier," Elisabeth responded enthusiastically. "But what of Fortune? Do you still have him?" Elisabeth continued.

"Yes. I love my old friend. The stable master has agreed to care for him in the corral in my backyard. I will be able to speak with him every day and ride him in the evening on the beach. He is very much a part of my life," Benjamin responded.

"I am happy you kept him, Benjamin," Elisabeth said, petting Nephilim's neck one last time.

The couple walked back to the carriage, and Elisabeth ascended the steps, cleaning the bottom of her stocking feet and leaning into the carriage before sitting on the red leather seat. Benjamin politely did not look up, he kept his eyes appropriately on the steps of the carriage not to take advantage of his position below Elisabeth.

Benjamin followed, placing his good leg first and raising his body until he could put his braced leg on the step and repeated the process until he entered the carriage. He then released the lock on his braced knee and sat next to Elisabeth. "I have a little surprise for you after we explore the waterfront."

Elisabeth smiled and said, "What is it—are you going to

take me to a hotel your family owns or something like that? I hope."

Benjamin was somewhat surprised by her response and said, "Well, not exactly. We are going to have dinner with my parents at my house at four o'clock this afternoon. What do you think?"

Elisabeth was horrified. "No, Benjamin! My dress is much too short for me to meet your parents. I would have never dressed like this if I knew I was going to meet your parents. Ellen Forrestal—I can't meet Ellen Forrestal in this dress!"

"Elisabeth, I have already explained to my mother that you wear short dresses and that short dresses are the current style of a young, university woman. And she is perfectly all right with the new fashion. Besides, she is extremely interested in meeting the woman I have been spending my evenings with," Benjamin reassuringly explained.

"Are you sure?" Elisabeth asked, looking down at her short dress, which exposed the top of her stocking and a few inches of her thigh, the transparent chiffon providing only a thin veil of modesty.

Benjamin put his arm around his new friend and said, "Everything will be fine. My mother is the least judgmental woman in the world, and I know she will love you when she meets you."

"Are you sure?"

"Yes, Elisabeth, I am sure." Benjamin then commanded, "Nephilim, forward," and the carriage lurched ahead.

Conrad and Ellen sat together on the sofa anxiously awaiting the arrival of their son and his new friend. "This is happening too soon. It was just a few months ago he was mourning the death of Petie. He seemed so vulnerable and innocent, and now he is bringing a young woman for dinner. How can this be happening?" asked a very caring mother.

"Well, I was sixteen when I had my first relationship with

a girl. She taught me many things. I think it is wonderful he is experiencing this normal part of life. I am happy for him," a proud father replied. "This is life."

"I know, I know," Ellen iterated.

The sound of approaching footsteps brought Conrad and Ellen to their feet. Ellen made an audible gasp as the front door opened, and in an instant, Benjamin walked around the corner of the entryway with a smile on his face. "Mother and Father, I would like you to meet Elisabeth."

Benjamin reached over and took Elisabeth's hand, bringing her into view of his parents. She stood there, holding Benjamin's hand, and said politely, "How nice to meet you."

Benjamin's parents stood frozen in stunned disbelief. Standing in the filtered afternoon light was a young woman that looked exactly like Ellen appeared nearly twenty years ago. The resemblance was uncanny. Conrad looked at the beautiful young woman with a brilliant red and black coat draped over her arm, dressed in white with attractive dark green ribbons. He thought her manner of dress provided a striking complement to her porcelain-white skin and raven hair. The eyes of the young woman were the most remarkable thing he noticed. Her emerald-green eyes seemed to glow in the foyer's soft light with unusual splendor, her pupils unnaturally large.

Benjamin's father was the first to speak: "I am Conrad, Benjamin's father, and we were not expecting such a beautiful young woman. I am glad to meet you, Elisabeth, and please feel most welcome to our home."

"Thank you, Sir. Please forgive my appearance. I would have dressed more appropriately, but Benjamin surprised me with his invitation to meet his parents when he arrived at my home this morning. I was already dressed, and he insisted I should not change," Elisabeth said, noticeably embarrassed.

"Your manner of dress is simply wonderful. Please do not be concerned. Your fashion is contemporary and most charming," Conrad said, walking forward to take Elisabeth's hand.

Conrad looked back at his wife, who remained motionless, so taken by Elisabeth's appearance. After a quiet pause, Ellen managed to say, "When I look at you, I see a mirror reflecting an image of my younger self . . . how extraordinary. I am so pleased to meet you. Benjamin has spoken of you most affectionately, and as I look upon you, his adoration seems most understandable."

Elisabeth looked at Benjamin and said, "I find your son most adorable."

In the magic of that moment, Ellen Forrestal felt complete contentment as she looked at the young couple. Her son was coming of age, and he had selected a charming and attractive woman to court. She was delighted with her son's choice and found it difficult to contain the extent of her obvious happiness.

A beaming mother stepped forward, extending Benjamin's new friend a welcoming hand of acceptance. "I am so happy to meet you."

"I am honored," Elisabeth returned, "I have read so much about you," as she reached out to take Ellen's hand.

The instant their fingers touched, a bolt of ice raced through Ellen Forrestal's veins. The world turned cold and grey. The air around her roared with the swirl of unknown forces as she was surrounded by a scorched forest of skeletonized trees and bushes—an endless crematorium of what was living now, an ashen wasteland. The tortured wind screamed like the siren of agony being sucked into a vacuum of the darkest and most unfathomable pit imaginable only a few feet in front of her. A black hole devoid of reason or purpose—the absence of all things, the antithesis of being, irresistible and forever.

As the escalating currents grabbed and pulled her body, tore and tangled her hair, Ellen stumbled upon the abomination of what could not be. At her feet, she found the fallen Raven, mutilated and lifeless. She fell to her knees and screamed into the vanishing sky, "What place is this?" She lifted and cradled the avian crown, and her tears mingled with the twisted feathers and broken beak of the vicar of heaven.

Then the Raven was torn from her arms and swallowed into the immense chasm. She could feel herself inexorably drawn into the darkness, to follow the Raven's fate. Ellen uttered a frantic gasp as she heard her only child's forlorn voice begging for his mother's grasp.

She turned to see Benjamin, standing with his back to the pit, his countenance contorted with pure horror and anguish, only an arm's reach away. He was resisting the darkness pulling him into oblivion. Benjamin leaned away from the abyss and stooped so low as to kiss the ground and cleave the stones, trapped between the forces of the wind and the will to live. Benjamin cried out, "Mother, can you save your only son?" She reached out and took his hand. In that instant, Elisabeth's cold grip grabbed Ellen's arm.

Elisabeth stood beside her with a ghastly pallor and, without speaking, snatched Benjamin by the neck with her other hand, lifting him into the howling wind and casting him into the abyss. Ellen looked upon her son for the last time, and then he was gone. Elisabeth looked coldly at Benjamin's frantic mother and released her arm. Ellen stepped back from the embodiment of death. When her hand parted Elisabeth's, Ellen returned to the parlor of her home and a young woman's smiling face that consumed her with absolute terror. She stepped back, and the room faded away as she collapsed.

"Ellen, Ellen," spoke the voice of her concerned husband while applying ammonium carbonate under her nose, slowly bringing Ellen back from the debilitating spell.

"Conrad, I must have fainted. Something has happened. I cannot explain—I feel so cold. Something has happened," Ellen repeated, trembling and frightened, looking at her husband.

Conrad took his pocket watch from his vest and measured his wife's pulse, then pulled the edge of one of her eyes to examine the underlying color. When he was satisfied that she merely fainted and was recovering, he asked, "Do you think you can walk?"

After a moment, she answered, "Yes, of course." With

Benjamin and Conrad's assistance, Ellen was able to stand. When she was stable enough to walk, she turned and looked at a distraught Elisabeth and said, "I am going upstairs for a while to lie down. Dinner will be in an hour, so please permit Benjamin to show you our home, and we will break custom and have a long conversation over dinner. Conrad, will you help me to our room?"

Conrad put his arm around his wife's waist and slowly walked her to the stairs. After taking a few steps, Ellen turned and looked back at her anxious son and assured him with an unassailable voice, "Benjamin, I am fine. I have not eaten today because I have been preoccupied with business matters, and my blood sugar was low. The excitement of meeting your charming new friend . . . well, I just fainted. I will be fine in a while. Please have the maid bring me some orange juice, and I will lie down, and I will see both of you at dinner."

"Of course, Mother," Benjamin responded, immediately pulling the long ribbon hanging from the ceiling near the entrance wall to summon the downstairs maid.

"Yes, Mr. Walker?" The maid appeared from the kitchen almost immediately.

"Martha, please bring my mother a glass of orange juice and some bread with butter. She is resting in her room with my father."

"Yes, Mr. Walker," the maid affirmed, disappearing into the kitchen and reappearing moments later, bread and juice in hand, to race across the parlor and up the stairs.

"Oh Benjamin, did I upset your mother? I am afraid I somehow upset her," a worried Elisabeth asked, reaching and grasping Benjamin's hand.

"No, not at all. My mother will always tell you exactly what she thinks. If she tells you she is suffering from low blood sugar, that's what it is. We can go up to my room until dinner, and I can show you some of my books and things," Benjamin reassured.

Conrad helped Ellen lie down on their bed and arranged the pillow to support her head. He stroked her raven black hair away from her brow and asked, "Tell me what's going on. I had breakfast with you this morning, so tell me how you are feeling. Do I need to take you to the hospital? Something has happened—please help me understand."

"Conrad, try and understand what I am going to tell you. When I touched the hand of that young woman, I had a terrible premonition, an all-consuming foreboding forewarned of what seemed the end of the world. I found myself in a dark, dead world on the edge of an endless abyss, and at my feet was the Raven's corpse. I reached down to hold the precious bird, and he was ripped from my arms and flung into the pit by unseen forces. I then heard Benjamin crying out for my help, and I saw him being drawn into the pit. As I reached to save him, a ghostly Elisabeth appeared next to me and blocked my hand, then grabbed Benjamin by the neck and cast him into the pit and to his death. When I stepped back from that ghostly Elisabeth, I returned to our parlor. The burden of the vision was too much, and I fainted. Conrad, our son was crying out for me, and I was helpless to save him. What can it mean? Am I going insane? I have faithfully taken the hydrate of lithia potion just as you prescribed for all these years. Could it be that the medication is no longer working? I am so afraid. Conrad, am I going insane?" Ellen asked her husband, nearly frantic.

"Ellen, you are taking a medication called lithium now. I switched your medication several years ago, and no, I don't think your experience is an aspect of your mood disorder. I think it is much more likely you had some form of stress reaction. Under prolonged stress, the mind will try and escape from reality. You experienced an altered state of consciousness. With all the many business activities you are engaged with and meeting your son's first courted woman who strangely could be your younger twin, well, your mind just needed to escape. Your body is telling you to slow down. What happened to you, I believe, is a stress-induced adjustment reaction caused by meeting such an unusual woman and, well, your son is growing into a man," Conrad said, attempting to reassure his wife.

Ellen looked at her loving husband and considered what he said, and after a moment she responded with somewhat pressured speech, "Conrad, please try and understand, I think you are the best physician in Kenton, and I respect your opinion. But what I experienced was not a stress reaction. My various businesses are not a source of anxiety, and while Benjamin's new friend bears an uncanny resemblance to my younger self, that does not convince me what I saw was my mind playing tricks. What I saw, what I believe I saw, was a warning of things to come. My intuition has served me well over the years, and what I received was an omen. I think you are perfectly correct. I am not going crazy. Some force is warning me of something terrible about that woman. Conrad, something is very wrong. I don't understand it, but I think something is wrong."

Conrad listened to his wife gain confidence that her experience was a premonition of a darker reality and not a failing psyche. Conrad realized her conviction eerily resembled Benjamin's inexplicable experience in the secret room in Jeffery Porter's warehouse a few months ago.

"Ellen, I had a remarkably similar conversation with Benjamin after he fainted his first day of work for Jeffery Porter. He also said he saw or felt something horrible but could not remember what before he fainted. He was most upset. . . ." Conrad continued, "He, too, thought something terrible was going to happen. He wanted me to keep the entire thing confidential. He did not want to worry you. I do not see how the two events are linked. It does seem strange, though. Very disquieting. I do not know what it means."

"I am afraid it means Elisabeth should not be in my son's life," Ellen said with a determined tone.

"Don't go there—this is all conjecture. You cannot interfere with our son's life based on this. He is enamored with Elisabeth, and what could you say to convince him to give her up? All you can do is let this relationship run its course. If you interfere with Benjamin's courting, he will think you are trying to possess him, and you will only put a wedge between yourself and your son. Ellen, what happened to you and Benjamin may not be related at all. What happened to both of you may not mean what either of you think. I want you to promise you will not interfere with Benjamin's relationship until we know more and we both agree on a course of action. Will you promise me that?" Conrad demanded.

Ellen did not respond at first. She sat up on the edge of the bed, turned away from her husband, and looked out the window. Ellen stood and walked around the room, deep in thought, and then approached the window and stared for the longest time at the Eastern Sea. She accepted her husband's opinion—she was not going insane, but she didn't accept all else he said. With deep conviction, Ellen resolved to save her son. What she experienced when she touched the hand of that strange girl was an omen. She fully realized that a mother's instincts trumped reason. Conrad would never understand. Elisabeth must be removed from Benjamin's life. Something was very wrong, and she would not forsake her son. Ellen would do what was necessary to keep her son safe. She resolved to protect him, and without her husband's knowledge if necessary. Ellen would play the part of an accepting and happy mother for all concerned but resolved she would unravel the dilemma.

Ellen began her deception with a kiss. She turned from the window, reached out to put her arms around her husband, kissed him on the lips, and said, "Of course you are right, Conrad. I may be merely a doting mother having difficulty giving her son over to another woman. Maybe I fainted because, on some level, I realize my relationship with my son is changing, and he will not be mine alone. I should think every mother must feel such things when their child first forms such an adult relationship. All of this is happening so quickly. I am close to my son. It is hard to let him go."

Conrad kissed a perfect tear from Ellen's cheek and said,

"I love you so much. I do not know what it all means, but it does seem possible that both you and Benjamin were experiencing some form of adjustment reactions to some unique set of circumstances. That conclusion may be more likely than thinking you both were reacting to a supernatural omen."

"Well, I am feeling a bit silly right now. Let's go downstairs and continue our discussion with the newest member of our family," Ellen said, acting relieved.

Ellen took Conrad's hand. They left their bedroom and returned to the formal sitting room. Her son and his new friend were absent. Ellen looked around, walked over to the dining room. She then turned and walked past Conrad and continued through the house, walked out the back door, and examined Fortune's corral. Her son and Elisabeth could not be found. She returned to the sitting room and looked out the window to determine if Benjamin's new carriage was absent. The carriage was present. She turned to Conrad, who sat down to watch his wife's search and with a smile said, "They are in Benjamin's sleep room."

Ellen walked to the bottom of the stairs, looked up at Benjamin's closed door, returned to the parlor, and sat down next to her husband. Ellen continued to look in the direction of her son's room as if she could see through the walls and ceiling of the house and simply stated, "They're having sex in our house while we are waiting for dinner."

Conrad laughed and put his arm around his wife's waist and said, "Yes, they are."

"Conrad, she is older and more experienced than our son. He is much too young for this sort of thing. How could he be attentive to that woman's needs while his mother is recovering from a condition only a few feet from his room? Conrad, that woman has cast a spell upon our son," Ellen stated unequivocally, still peering through the ceiling.

"I think they have cast a spell on each other, and it is not magic—it is hormones. Ellen, try and be reasonable. You reassured our son you were only suffering from low blood sugar, and we would see them at dinner in an hour or so.

What did you think they would do being left alone—ride Fortune around the corral?"

"I didn't expect her to ride my son all afternoon!" Ellen replied, a bit sarcastically.

"Ellen, our son is an adult with a professional vocation and independently wealthy. Explain to me why he should not be involved sexually with that beautiful young woman," Conrad asked.

"What if she gets pregnant?" a panicky Ellen asked.

"Then you will be a grandmother."

"This is not what I was thinking about when I got up this morning."

Conrad laughed and then kissed Ellen on the lips and said, "I think we should have sex and see if we can get away with it before being caught by them when they are finished."

Coldly, Ellen responded, "This is not the time. I wish you would take this a little more seriously. I don't think you understand."

✺

Elisabeth and Benjamin slowly ascended the stairs. At the landing, Benjamin paused and looked at the closed door of the master sleep room and hoped all was well. He took Elisabeth's hand, and the couple walked down the hall and into his sleep room. Elisabeth looked around at what was quintessentially a boy's room. Hanging in one of the corners was a hornet's nest Benjamin found on a summer outing when he was eight. On various shelves attached to the walls were collections of bird's nests, shells from the Eastern Sea, and rocks from the nearby mountains and riverbeds. On one wall, a series of drawings depicting the solar system's known planets. Next to the planets, Elisabeth saw several illustrations of prominent horse breeds and rare insects. Covering one entire wall was a floor to ceiling bookcase holding hundreds of leather-bound books that had entertained and educated Benjamin as he matured. A boy's library of all things beautiful, mysterious, and esoteric. A large window faced the Eastern Sea, and beneath the window was a large oak desk with a matching chair. Several leather-bound books rested near the desk's edge and a professional microscope, a gift from his father on Benjamin's fifteenth birthday. A wooden box containing hundreds of prepared slides sat near the microscope. In the corner, next to his bookcase, was a six-inch refractor telescope with a beautiful brass, clock-driven, slow-motion compensator allowing astronomical sights to hold fast in the telescope's eyepiece while being studied in the night sky. Peering through this telescope, Benjamin first saw Oceania and many other wonders of the night sky.

Elisabeth looked up at the twelve-foot-high gilded ceiling illustrated with intricate designs of animals and trees. The constellations of the winter sky, the creation of a skilled artist, decorated the center of the ceiling. A golden gas chandelier with cut glass crystal shades eclipsed many of the stars and provided the primary source of light for the room. Benjamin's bed was large and exquisite. The headboard and footboard were made from hand-carved walnut displaying imaginative ocean waves and delicate flowers. The center of the impressive headboard was a dramatic carved representation of the Raven with spread wings, a sharp bill, and deadly talons.

Elisabeth explored the room, studying every book and shell, and after a few minutes, she turned and looked at Benjamin and said, "You've filled your room with all the things you love."

Benjamin replied, "Yes, this has been my private world all my life."

"Now, you have brought me here to be part of your private world."

"As I should."

Elisabeth slowly walked over to the bedroom door, turned the lock, ensuring privacy, and said, "Will we be bothered here?"

"I have never locked my door."

She softly expressed the words, "You have never done what you are about to do."

Benjamin stared with nervous anticipation at his beautiful new friend. Elisabeth walked to him, kissed him with a long deep kiss, and then playfully forced him to his bed and pushed him down. She stepped back and kicked off her pedestal shoes and unbuttoned her sheer silk chiffon covering, carefully removed the delicate fabric, and placed the sheer cloth on the nearby desk chair. She unbuttoned her blouse and pulled it apart and out of her skirt, exposing her firm pale breasts and hard nipples, accented with red pigment. Elisabeth, without thought, dropped the crumpled blouse to the floor. She untied her silk belt and unbuttoned the row of bone-buttons on the side of her skirt, and it, too, fell to the floor. She stepped out of her skirt and stood there, allowing Benjamin to anticipate her next move. She was naked except for her stocking belt and silk stockings. Benjamin's heart and breath quickened as he watched Elisabeth's erotic display unfold before him. Elisabeth unhooked her stockings and pulled down her stocking belt and hooks, leaving her silk stockings.

Benjamin gazed at the beautiful naked woman standing before him. She had shaved her entire body. She walked to the edge of the bed. Elisabeth leaned down and kissed Benjamin with a passionate kiss. While kissing him, Elisabeth put Benjamin's hands on her breasts, and after a few seconds, she pulled her face back and directed Benjamin's mouth to one of her breasts. Benjamin covered the end of her breast with his mouth and rolled his tongue over her hardened nipple. While gently squeezing each breast, he moved his mouth to the next breast, inflaming Elisabeth's growing sexual tension as he licked and gently massaged her other nipple with his tongue. Benjamin found himself carefully, without pressure, holding her nipple between his teeth. He flicked his tongue over Elisabeth's increasingly sensitive nipple, causing the young woman to express a long, soft moan as she pressed Benjamin's face into her breast.

Elisabeth abruptly stepped back, interrupting Benjamin's foreplay. She took a deep breath and reached down and began forcefully unbuttoning his silk shirt, causing the shirt to tear and his buttons to rip and fall to the floor. She lifted his silk shirt over his head and pulled on his sleeves. Benjamin's gold cufflinks trapped his hands. She yanked each sleeve, causing the cuffs to tear and freeing his arms and hands from the entangling silk. Next, Elisabeth pulled Benjamin's boots and socks off and then focused on Benjamin's nickel brace. Benjamin helped her loosen the leather straps as Elisabeth pulled the brace from his leg. She then released Benjamin's leather belt and unbuttoned the front of his pants. Benjamin lifted himself. Elisabeth pulled his pants down over his legs.

The appearance of the prosthesis covering his deformed leg caused her to pause. Elisabeth then said, "Help me, Benjamin, to remove this."

Benjamin replied, "We can leave it. You don't have to see."

"I don't see your leg, Benjamin. I only see you."

Benjamin released the holding straps wrapped around his leg, and Elisabeth gently pulled the black wooden prosthesis from his malformed leg. Benjamin's crippled leg was only half the size of his normal leg and strangely withered from his knee down. Elisabeth did not hesitate. She ignored Benjamin's deformity and reached over and pulled his private garment down and over his legs.

Benjamin's revolver was released from his belt and disappeared in a tangle of bedding.

Elisabeth found the gun by the grip and nonchalantly dropped the weapon on the floor with a loud thud. She whispered, "Scoot over to the center of the bed."

Benjamin put both hands behind him and lifted himself backward. While moving from the edge, he lifted his compromised leg and dragged his deformity and attempted to conceal it with a blanket. Elisabeth stopped him and pushed the blanket back.

Benjamin was deeply aroused, and further excited as his naked friend crawled next to him. Elisabeth placed her hand around and gently massaged his shaft, causing Benjamin incredible pleasure. When the time was right, she leaned down and placed his erection into her mouth and moved her head up and down, arousing Benjamin close to a climax. She abruptly stopped her oral stimulation, and while facing Benjamin, lifted one of her legs over Benjamin's body, straddling him over his pelvis. Elisabeth reached under her body, placing her hands around his swollen shaft, and while lifting and straightening her body, she gently placed Benjamin inside her. Elisabeth slowly lowered herself and moaned. She began slowly raising and lowering herself, causing Benjamin's erection to rub inside the soft glove of her warm, wet body. Her movement increased in speed. Benjamin was consumed with mounting pleasure and sexual tension. Elisabeth's body dripped with sweat. On the final thrust, her body stiffened, her back and neck arched, and her eyes closed as she faced the ceiling. Elisabeth's body exploded with the most intense climax of her life. Her sexual opening contracted over and over as feminine fluid gushed and flowed from within her and soaked Benjamin's body and bed covering. At that very same instant, Benjamin's erection began to uncontrollably pulse, releasing his fluid into Elisabeth. He stiffened his body and held his breath as his climax released the tension and caused intense pleasure to flow through his entire body.

Elisabeth, covered with perspiration, relaxed her body. She lifted herself, pulling Benjamin from inside her and lying beside the man she was in love with told him, "I love you, Benjamin Walker. I love you. I have never known such intense feelings."

"I am falling in love with you, as well. How can anything so perfect be so real?" Benjamin whispered through Elisabeth's wet, tangled hair that now partially covered his face.

"It is our wonderful fate."

For a long period, the young lovers held each other with little movement and without speaking as their bodies recovered from the physical exertion of their lovemaking. Elisabeth spoke first, "I love you and desire you so much I am frightened."

Elisabeth sat up and turned, tucked her knees under her chin, brushed her wet and tangled hair from her face, wrapped her arms around her legs, and looked down at an equally disheveled Benjamin. "I have never been so attracted to any man. When I am away from you, I obsess about you. Look at me. I spent an hour shaving every hair on my body below my eyebrows. I colored my lips on my face and the nipples on my breast with wax and red pigment to heighten your desire for me . . . I have never done anything like that. I have never heard of a woman doing anything like that!"

Elisabeth looked at Benjamin's naked body covered with her feminine fluid and said, "My body has never reacted like this until I made love with you. Look how my body reacts to you! Benjamin, look at how wet your body and bedding is. I have never been this wet with a man or when I have touched myself. And Benjamin, I have never put a man's sexual organ into my mouth, but with you, I want to put my mouth on every part of your body. And when I climax—I have never felt such intensity! The way you touch me is so perfect. I cannot control myself. I must be ovulating. I made love to Ellen Forrestal's son, in Ellen Forrestal's house, when she was at home! I must be crazy. I have always been quite shy, but I am spellbound . . . possessed. Do other women react this way with you when you make love to them?"

Benjamin smiled, "I hope you never stop ovulating. Elisabeth, this was my first time. Did I not tell you that?"

Elisabeth's mouth opened as she tried to comprehend what she heard and said, "You are a phenom— "

"Thank you, so are you."

Elisabeth closed her eyes and said, "How did you know how to flick your tongue on my nipples? I went crazy when you did that!"

"I felt like doing it. I have other desires as well."

Elisabeth quickly moved to kiss Benjamin again, "If I don't get up and get cleaned up. . . . I am getting aroused again."

Elisabeth forced herself to crawl over Benjamin's body

and stand next to the bed. She cupped her hand over her opening to prevent herself from dripping onto the polished oak floor. She awkwardly removed her drooping stockings with one hand and walked across the room to Benjamin's private room. Without shutting the door, she entered and turned on the shower with her free hand and adjusted the temperature of the falling water. There was no bathtub to step over. The private room was tiled from floor to ceiling. The shower floor gently sloped to the room's center where a brass drain swallowed the streaming water falling from above. The showerhead emerged from the tiled ceiling. The private room accommodated Benjamin's unique needs. She grabbed a towel from the rack, wrapped her hair, and stepped into the water's warm stream.

Benjamin watched from his bed with complete wonder at the sight of a naked woman taking a shower in his private room. He was fascinated as he watched Elisabeth take a bar of soap and begin to rub her body to remove the perspiration. Benjamin thought it strange to hear the noise her opening made as she cleaned her private areas with a cupped hand of soapy water. He was shocked and then amused as Elisabeth put both her hands on the wall, separated her legs, and urinated in the shower. She looked up and smiled at Benjamin when she realized he was watching and seemed to giggle as she continued to clean herself. Elisabeth was totally relaxed and completely open with him as if they had been with each for years instead of two and a half days. She then walked out of the shower area and pulled the towel from her hair and began drying herself. Seeing a box of talcum on a shelf, she looked at Benjamin and asked, "Do you mind?"

Without saying a word, he shook his head no, and Elisabeth proceeded to powder her underarms and private area. When her body was sufficiently powdered, she walked farther into the sleeping room and began sorting her stockings and clothes before starting to dress.

"Your turn, Benjamin," she said with a smile.

Benjamin shifted to the side of the bed, put his good leg

on the floor, hopped over to the private room door entrance, and grabbed the doorframe. The reinforced towel bars provided secure rails. Benjamin carefully managed the slippery floor. Security rails around the shower provided enough safety to facilitate Benjamin's independence. Holding one of the rails, he maneuvered himself into the falling water. He, too, while balancing on one leg, decided to urinate, and when he completed relieving himself, he proudly turned to look at a smiling Elisabeth. Elisabeth, while dressing, continued to watch as Benjamin cleaned, powdered, and dried himself. She did not feel any pity or repulsion at his deformity, only sadness that fate gave him such a burden.

While Elisabeth replaced her stockings and belt, Benjamin went through the ritual of replacing and strapping on his prosthesis. He put on his private garments, pants, and brace. He picked up his shredded shirt and said to Elisabeth, "I better stock up."

Elisabeth laughed, "I have never done that before, either."

Benjamin stated, "It was well worth a shirt." He walked to his dresser, opened one of the drawers, and said, "No! All of my other white silk shirts are being laundered. Do you think anyone will notice I am wearing a beige shirt?"

Elisabeth made an immediate, strange, unintelligible blurting sound with her mouth before laughing at the dilemma. When she composed herself, she held up the beige shirt next to the tattered white one and, after a moment of reflection, began laughing again. Benjamin also began to laugh and continued while he unfolded and put the beige shirt on.

Elisabeth grabbed Benjamin's hairbrush and began to brush her wet hair. Starting at the bottom of her dark hair, she slowly untangled her long strands until she reached the crown of her scalp. Elisabeth now was able to take long strokes down the entire length of her sparkling hair. To her dismay, she found her mangled wet green hair ribbon still in her hair. With some effort, she retrieved the stained ribbon. "Oh, Benjamin, my hair ribbon is destroyed."

This time Benjamin laughed and pointed at the floor next

to his bed, "Your green choker is destroyed as well. Do you think anyone will notice you're not wearing your ribbons downstairs?"

"How should I answer these pressing questions?" Elisabeth began. "We meet your parents for about two minutes, and then we disappear into your room for almost an hour, and you are wondering if your parents will notice that you are wearing a different shirt and my hair is combed differently, my face free of make-up, and, in addition, sometime during our sexual melee we managed to put several tears running the length of my silk stockings, and you're asking will they notice my hair ribbon. Yes, Benjamin, they will . . . and then some."

"Well, this is all a first for me," Benjamin said. "I wonder how my mother will react to all of this."

"I can't believe I had sex in Ellen Forrestal's house! I pray she will not be angry with me?" a worried Elisabeth queried.

"My mother loves me, and I know she will love you too, so stop worrying. Let's go downstairs. Maybe mother is feeling well enough to join us. She may be waiting for us now," Benjamin said reassuringly.

After adjusting their clothing, combing their hair, and taking one last look in the full-length mirror, Benjamin unlocked his door, and the young couple walked out of the room.

Sally, the upstairs maid, was carrying a handful of clean linen down the hall. Stopping in shock, Sally froze, expressionless. Seeing Benjamin with a woman exiting his sleep room seemed impossible. Benjamin spoke first, "Sally, change my bedding and put my shower in good order."

Stoically, Sally returned, "Yes, Mr. Walker. I will place the room in good order shortly, Sir."

Without further comment, Benjamin and Elisabeth turned and walked a short distance to the stairs and began their descent. Halfway down, Benjamin noticed his parents sitting on the silk sofa in the formal parlor. The sound of the couple caused Benjamin's parents to stop their discussion and attend to Benjamin and Elisabeth's progress returning to the parlor. "How are you feeling, Mother?" Benjamin asked.

Benjamin's mother elevated her voice and looked at her approaching son, "I am doing quite well, Benjamin. Thank you for asking."

Benjamin and Elisabeth walked to the sofa, and Benjamin sat down next to his mother and continued in a most compassionate manner, "Are you sure, Mother? What do you think happened?

"Stop worrying. The orange juice and bread did the trick. The excitement of meeting your new friend and my lack of eating caused me to faint—that's all there was to it. So please, let's continue our conversation," Ellen Forrestal said, looking from Benjamin to a standing and overly concerned Elisabeth.

Benjamin stood, and while retrieving a chair for Elisabeth said, "I am so glad, Mother."

Conrad pulled up a chair for his son, and Benjamin and Elisabeth sat down in front of Benjamin's parents.

Both of Benjamin's parents noticed Benjamin that was wearing a different shirt, and Elisabeth's hair was now flowing down around her shoulder and covering her ears. In addition, and unknown to the young couple, when the shower was turned on in Benjamin's private room, the recognizable sound of the water flowing through the plumbing was very apparent to his parents. The fresh scent of talcum in the air and a patch of the powder on Elisabeth's neck also provided evidence that the couple required a shower before returning to the parlor.

After a brief awkward moment, Benjamin's father attempted to carry on their discussion that occurred before Benjamin's mother's fainting spell. His first question, not completely thought through, was somewhat unfortunate: "Did you find Benjamin's room interesting?"

Elisabeth made a slight, uncontrolled jerk and said, "Yes, I loved his books. Remarkably interesting. Your son seems to know a great deal about almost everything."

"He seems to be learning something new every day," Benjamin's mother stated as she looked at her growing boy. She then turned and looked at Elisabeth and asked, "Did you find Benjamin's insect collection interesting? It always gives me the creeps."

Before Benjamin could intercede, Elisabeth answered, "Truly fascinating. I agree, bugs give me the creeps as well."

Elisabeth was being manipulated by his mother to make falsehoods. Both parents knew he did not have an insect collection. Why would his mother ask her such a thing? Ellen's question was blatant and deliberate. His mother wanted to make Elisabeth intentionally uncomfortable or look foolish. Benjamin was perplexed and hurt.

Benjamin abruptly stood. "Our behavior this afternoon has obviously offended you, and for that I apologize. However, the mistake was mine and mine alone. Elisabeth is my closest and, yes, intimate friend. She will be treated with respect. Why would you be so offensive to someone that means so much to me? If your derision suggests she is not welcome or your question is a veiled attempt to belittle her, well then, I am also not welcomed. So, we will take our leave."

A mortified Elisabeth stared at the scene unfolding in front of her. She sat petrified, attempting to understand what had just happened. To see Benjamin angry was upsetting, and to have that anger directed at his mother was devastating. Benjamin turned and looked at Elisabeth and reached out his hand. Elisabeth stood, looking somewhat frantically at Benjamin's parents.

Ellen leaped up and said, in what appeared to be a most apologetic manner, "Please, Benjamin, don't go. I was rude, and it was uncalled for. This is all new to me. Benjamin, I am deeply sorry for my words. It was not clever or needed. Elisabeth, you are very welcome in our home, and I sincerely apologize for my remarks, neither of you has done anything wrong." But Ellen was lying. "Please, may we begin again?"

Benjamin stared at his mother sternly.

Elisabeth broke the silence, "Of course." A confused Elisabeth pulled Benjamin's hand and said, "Let's sit down, Benjamin. I would like to get to know your parents."

Benjamin's father watched before his eyes the metamorphosis of Benjamin's coming of age. Benjamin had, for the first time, openly defied his mother. His relationship with his mother had changed—he was no longer simply her child. Benjamin sat, and his father began again: "We need to agree to be open with each other, and Elisabeth, we consider you very much part of the family. Please, could you tell us about your family and what it's like to live in Kuttor?"

"Yes, Elisabeth. We would love to learn more about you," Benjamin's mother said in a most contrite manner.

So began a more subdued conversation of exploration and growing familiarity. Elisabeth spoke of her life in Kuttor, her education in Liberty, her dreams, and her aspirations. She talked of things Benjamin had taught her concerning The Word, and answered the many questions Benjamin's parents asked her about Kuttor. Elisabeth also spoke of her first year at the university, and Benjamin asked about the courses she took and what was expected of a well-ordered student. Benjamin's mother inquired about the fashions at the university, and Elisabeth explained how the female uniforms in the university library influenced how the female students were dressing. Elisabeth asked Ellen about her many businesses and what her strategy was for success. Conrad spoke of his wife's generosity and many philanthropies. Benjamin's mother, of course, spoke of her wonderful son and all of his achievements. The conversation went on for another hour, and only the insistence of the cook brought Elisabeth and Benjamin's family to the dining table to begin the formal dinner.

Benjamin and Elisabeth sat across the table from Benjamin's parents. When the maid brought out two sets of the three types of wine being served to the young couple, Benjamin again made his point that Elisabeth was his intimate partner by instructing the maid to serve Elisabeth from the same bottles of wine, the meat from the same animal, and the rest of the meal from the same dinner bowls. Nothing was said, no one looked surprised, and everyone was most thoughtful of his or her expressions.

Benjamin was no longer a boy who brought a friend home to have ice cream or to be scolded for bringing his gun to the dining table. That time was long ago, and the memory was fading. Children were no longer about the mansion. Benjamin's caveat to the maid concerning the proper method of serving the prepared meal to Elisabeth and himself clearly defined their relationship. A lengthy dinner began. The custom of silence was ignored as the conversation continued. Tempering her demeanor to facilitate her relationship with her maturing son, Ellen played her part as a respectful, intrigued parent. Benjamin had never spoken to her in the manner he displayed that evening, and Ellen was angry with herself for being so obvious. She was now aware that the slightest amount of animosity toward Elisabeth would cause her son to challenge her. Even a modicum of suspicion by Benjamin about her fear that Elisabeth represented a great threat would undoubtedly be perceived by her son as maternal jealousy and possessiveness. This would create a terrible severance between them—a source of pain, which would separate them forever.

Conrad was correct. Ellen would need to be careful about the things required of her to protect her son.

Chapter 17
The Edge of Heaven

Ellen pretended she was asleep as Conrad rose from their bed, showered, and dressed. She could hear water running through the mansion's pipes as her son also readied for the workday. She listened as the unintelligible voices of father and son emanated from the dining room. Through the open window, Ellen could hear the gentle breaking of the waves on the beach, the horses trotting, and the whine of steel wheels on cobblestones. She stared at the ceiling as the sound of horse and carriage faded into the fresh morning air. Alone, she rose and covered herself with a robe, walked down to her office, unlocked the door, looked around, and disappeared into her private world.

Sitting down in front of the telegraph key, Ellen paused. She had to be sure. Her instincts had always guided and protected her. Her innate ability to solve complex problems made her wealthy and powerful; however, this was different, this was not business, this was family. She had to be sure. Ellen moved the telegraph key into position. She ran her finger over the round ivory button on the telegraph lever as she considered the implications. Ellen began by tapping her instruction to Robert Bass. After a brief pause, he responded. He would require two weeks to complete Ellen's instructions pertaining to Elisabeth. She thanked him and set the time and date for their planning meeting. Ellen would meet with her counsel and friend at his mansion on Main Street opposite the Wolsworth mansion.

Two weeks later, in mid-morning, Elisabeth directed her carriage horse up Main Street to Robert Bass's mansion. Many Riverdale people referred to the grand mansion as the "Bachelor Mansion" because Bass had never married. Such an idea amused Ellen as if marital status should be considered significant enough to characterize a home. Upon arriving, she paused a moment and pondered the sight of her husband's death almost eighteen years ago. Her life had changed so much since that tragic day. She often thought of James during quiet times when she felt lonely or lost. She would wonder if James somehow knew how his thoughtful gift had made such an enormous difference in her and Benjamin's lives. Ellen wondered if she would be with him again in the afterlife. Ellen had her faith for such times. She could live with that.

Ellen directed her carriage horse through the massive cast-iron gate and past the twelve-foot-high iron fence, decorated with many intricate geometric patterns and topped with a phalanx of sharpened spears. The lavish fence surrounding the estate made a statement of opulence and the desire for privacy. Ellen followed the brick carriageway onto a vast and beautiful estate replete with many acres of rolling green hills decorated with the spectacle of energetic fountains, several exhibiting cascading water over marble and red granite steps into vast moats and pools of fish and flora. Giant statues of mythical gods and goddesses rising from marble pedestals provided a decorative presence among the many brick walkways that wandered the estate. Several cast-iron sculptures honored the founders of Kenton and the Elders who memorialized and shared the wisdom of the Golden Age with future generations. On a distant, green-covered hill, one statue depicted the Raven flying over Deseret, forever watching to redeem the souls of the dead. A replica of Deseret, carefully carved from red granite, displayed the seas, rivers, and geographical locations of all the landmasses and mountains of the world. The wide, brick carriageway continued to the front of the mansion. Surrounding the mansion and throughout the estate was an ocean of colorful gardens animated by the wind, which created a wave of brilliant colors. The festive visions of manicured flowers, ferns, shrubs, and sculpted topiary were shaped in the form of horses and wild animals mingling among a forest of large shade trees.

Ellen brought her carriage to the front of the mansion

where the stable master was obediently waiting. She stepped down from her carriage and thanked the stable master before he turned to walk the horse and carriage to the large stables that housed Robert Bass's extensive collection of riding and carriage horses. Ellen paused to gaze at the mansion—it was unique compared to the other elegant homes of Riverdale. Robert Bass built his home in the Londinium style, typical to Londonderry; polished red granite formed the exterior walls. The dwelling's architecture created the ambiance of a mythical castle replete with windows and doors trimmed with white marble; the spires, turrets, domes, and cupolas were made of carved granite bricks. Red granite arches leapt over many of the windows and doorways embellished with terra cotta flora and animal depictions. The peak of the high archway over the main entrance bore a detailed representation of the Raven proudly perched and forever present. The Londinium architecture design used the illusion of vertical perspective to make the structure seem taller than the actual three-story height. The red granite blocks near the top of the building were nearly one-third smaller than the blocks at the base of the building, creating the impression the dwelling reached far into the sky. Red and black bricks formed a series of two-dozen concentric half-circles surrounding the main entrance. The rooftop was covered with gold-plated, zinc-coated iron shingles. The unique shingles glistened in the sunlight, reflected the stars at night, and complemented the structure's elegant architecture with a profound sense of grandeur.

Ellen ascended the many steps and approached the massive oak door. A stained-glass panel in the center of the door depicted vines covered with green leaves energetically flowing upward as if to touch an unseen sun. Thousands of precisely trimmed pieces of glass formed the intricate artistry all united by soldered lead. Ellen grasped a large, gold doorknocker upon reaching the entrance door and announced her presence by striking the door several times. Almost immediately, Ellen saw a dark figure approaching the door through the stained glass.

Robert Bass opened the door, smiling and immaculately dressed. "Ellen, my dear friend. How may you be?"

"Pensive, Robert—most pensive, my friend," Ellen replied as she stepped through the doorway and greeted him with a strong hug and a light kiss.

"I will do my best to lift your burden, Ellen," an intensely devoted Robert assured his only client. Ellen and Robert's relationship had been mutually beneficial over many years. Robert had never married. He had known only one woman he genuinely loved, and she had been taken by fate to be married to another. He would love and be loyal to Ellen as any man betrothed, and though unspoken, Ellen was aware of the depths of Robert's feelings. In many ways, her feelings were reciprocated, and his friendship honored her. Theirs was not a physical embrace but a familial bond, rarely realized by most. What she would ask of him today could only be requested within the confines of such rapport.

Ellen stepped into the foyer. Robert took her cloak and placed the garment on the entryway hanger. Tiled with the finest black slate, walls covered with rich oak paneling, the foyer greeted the rich and powerful for many years. Next to the wall, a black leather bench provided seating so guests might comfortably remove soiled boots and shoes before entering the home. A series of ascending shelves next to the bench held sets of leather slippers to replace the soiled footwear. Ellen's slippers were on a separate shelf, contained within a polished black walnut box. As Ellen sat to exchange her shoe ware, Robert secured her red velvet slippers from the box, kneeled at her feet, and gently pulled each shoe off, and covered each foot with a slipper. Such intimate behavior between a man and a woman only occurred between lovers. "Thank you, Robert. You have always been so kind to me from the moment we met," Ellen whispered while touching Robert's face.

The grand oak staircase was the first vision a guest would see. A carved newel post with leaf-covered vines sat at the base. An ascending oak railing supported by cast-iron spindles, bound with intricate designs of flowing vines and leaves harmonized with the front entrance. On top of the newel post stood a crowning carved ornament of the Raven, ominous and proud, so placed to greet the guest that the bachelor may bid enter. The Raven stood astride, a talon on each side of the column, emblematic of the mystery of life and death, the eternal universe, never-ending and without a first cause.

Ellen and Robert turned from the foyer and stepped into the grand central room. Robert had designed his mansion with a giant room to spend most of his time during his busy day as this would limit the number of negotiations he would experience with the adverse stairs. The ceiling of the large room was two stories high. The room measured seventy feet across and a hundred and fifty feet long. The walls paneled in rich oak were in the style of a library. Wood squares, made up of vertical and horizontal oak trim, defined the design. As with the outside of the building, the illusion of immense height was incorporated into the wood-covered walls. The squares in the oak paneling near the floor were nearly three feet square, but as the patterns ascended, the squares gradually grew smaller until the square patterns near the ceiling were two-thirds the base's size. The dozen hanging stain glass gas chandeliers shared the illusion. The chains holding the chandlers had brass links nearly two inches long, and as the brass chain rose to the round nickel medallions on the gilded ceiling, the chain links grew progressively smaller. The overall illusion made the room soar many stories above the observer.

The chamber was open and divided into five areas with five distinct functions. On the far west corner, Bass managed Ellen's business empire. An enormous, triangle-shaped oak desk filled the corner of the room. From his desk, Robert was able to look out upon his estate through a corner window rising twenty feet. On the south wall next to the window was a complex telegraph-switching mechanism permitting him to communicate with many parts of the Forrestal financial empire. The giant switching mechanism sorted through hundreds of telegraph lines, making daily communication possible between the many corporate managers and employees. Only the Kenton Railroad had a more complex system of communication. On the other adjacent wall resided the vast library of legal, business, and literary books. A moveable staircase ladder resting on steel tracks towered in front of the bookcase and was necessary to retrieve many of the leather-bound volumes. Robert was much too large to climb the ladder. He would instruct one of his servants to retrieve the desired book after locating it using opera glasses.

The mansion's formal sitting area was decorated with four enormous, overstuffed leather sofas forming an open square. Four gas floor lamps on each corner of the sitting arrangement augmented the chandeliers' soft light.

Nearby rested a large dining table made of dark polished walnut and lined with fifty walnut chairs upholstered with leather cushions. On this day, the servants had prepared two settings of fine china plates and silver eating utensils. A fireside conference area contained a dozen overstuffed chairs forming a semicircle around the stone hearth. The fireplace produced gas heat from ceramic logs. A thick plate of glass enclosed the fireplace's opening, containing the blaze by capturing and radiating the heat. No filthy wood would sully the parquet floors in this grand room during Riverdale's long winter months.

The grand room's far end contained the music room, where two grand pianos and the most beautiful harpsichords were located, along with an extensive collection of musical instruments: harps, violins, violas, Kenton horns, and many others. Robert Bass would frequently invite friends and business acquaintances for an elaborate dinner, followed by an evening of music. Large oil murals depicting famous battles on land and sea taken from Deseret's rich history dominated the walls along with hanging tapestries. Robert Bass loved these paintings of the great, armed conflicts. He would often secretly entertain the thought that in another life, he may have been a triumphant, lean, and youthful general directing legions of soldiers from a grand army on a quest to vanquish the invading military of an evil aggressor.

Ellen and Robert walked from the foyer into the mansion's great room. Before progressing to the formal sitting room, Ellen stopped and turned to study one of her favorite paintings in Robert's gallery. "Robert, the detail in this painting is amazing. It seems so real. Do you know who the artist is?"

"The artist is a mystery. This is one of my favorites as well . . . the angelic wars fought in heaven. See how the unknown archangel on his great steed Proximus Centauri drives the vast army he commands directly into the rebellious army of Ha-Satin?" Robert Bass explained with animation. "The swords and shields of the Archangel army are covered with angels' blood. How could such a thing have happened?"

"I don't know. Angels in heaven fighting each other, and for what end?" Ellen had struggled with such an idea all her life. "How could an angelic war take place?"

After a moment of silence, Ellen leaned into the painting, studying the faces of anguished angels in battle so perfectly defined by the unknown artist. "This painting represents a myth or something."

"The mural depicts a war in heaven, perhaps a metaphor . . . maybe this battle took place long ago or in another reality," he stated.

"To what end, Robert, to what end? What was the artist trying to say? What subtle message is hidden in this artist's strokes?" Ellen asked while she continued studying.

Bass answered, "I don't know. You need not worry about the esoteric. You are far wiser in life than I am. You have a rare acumen for business. This artist provided us with an idea . . . a teaching moment of some sort perhaps," Robert Bass peered at Ellen. "You have been my teacher."

Ellen smiled and shook her head, "No, Robert, no. We both know that is not true."

"Do we?"

Ellen turned and looked directly at her friend. "Robert, I

come to you today to beg for your guidance and wisdom on choices I must make about my son's well-being."

"I think you will be extremely interested in the results of my investigation. Please come and sit, and I will share my findings, and you may share your concerns with me," Robert stated as he took Ellen's hand and walked her to one of the large leather sofas. She sat and watched her friend walk over to his triangle desk, secure a file, and return to sit beside her.

"I have completed my investigation of Elisabeth Zurich, and I think you will be pleased with the companion your son has chosen," Robert stated as he opened the young woman's detailed dossier. Stapled to the inside cover of the file was a large photograph of Elisabeth taken by an unseen investigator under Robert Bass's direction.

Robert began, "I must say I am struck by the amazing resemblance of Elisabeth Zurich to you at a younger age. It is an amazing coincidence—don't you think?"

Ellen sat in silence looking at the photograph and then raised her emotionless eyes to gaze at her friend.

Robert continued, "Elisabeth Zurich is twenty-three years old and in excellent health and was born into the Izdubar family clan in Dresden, Kuttor. Her birth name was Anjum Izdubar, and her father's name is Diya. Her mother died in childbirth, and she has no other siblings. Her father is a wealthy and influential merchant and exporter of exotic carpets and tapestry. In the culture of Kuttor, women are considered property and must be pledged to an infant son of a family in a similar economic caste at birth. Women are not allowed to be educated or learn a trade. The fate of females born into this repressive culture is to produce and care for children.

"Elisabeth's father refused to subject his daughter to such an outcome and secretly had his daughter educated. He also hired servants who spoke the language of Liberty and Kenton so she would be able to continue her education outside of Kuttor. Elisabeth's father bribed the family she was pledged to and the ruling religious leaders, the Locks, to permit

Elisabeth to continue her education in Liberty. Her education outside her country began at the age of fifteen when she attended the Liberty Preparatory School in Hope, and graduated with high honors. Elisabeth enrolled in the Londonderry University at the age of twenty-one and has completed her freshman year studying languages. She is a business major and an excellent student. Her instructors consider her to be highly intelligent, even gifted.

"Elisabeth has been involved with three young men while studying in Liberty. All three relationships were sexual, and the relationship lasted from a few weeks to several months," Robert Bass continued. "She was not involved when she met your son while working at the Porter Import Company. Her father arranged her employment with Jeffery Porter—they share a long business relationship. She is an excellent worker, and Jeffery Porter will most likely offer Elisabeth long-term employment after she graduates.

"Her continuing education and career after graduation are contingent on the continuation of bribes to the family she is pledged to and bribes to the Locks. If the Locks decree her guilty of apostasy, she would be killed."

"What would she have to do to be considered an apostate?" Ellen asked.

"The fact she has been educated and sexually involved with several men would be sufficient for her to be put to death," Robert answered and continued. "The Locks are aware of her activities outside Kuttor and are not likely to take action against her. This sort of thing is common among the few affluent families in Kuttor. Protecting the daughter from bondage is just a matter of paying off the right people. Elisabeth's father is extremely wealthy by Kuttor standards, and so her future seems secure."

"Still, Benjamin's wealth could guarantee her future security. I must be sure—"

"Not to worry, Ellen," Robert interrupted. "Elisabeth is independently wealthy and is quite capable of maintaining her freedom."

"What are you saying?"

"Elisabeth's father has been transferring large sums of money to several bank accounts in his daughter's name in Kenton for years," Robert explained. "Elisabeth has over three hundred thousand dollars in savings. She has complete control over the various accounts currently available to her. She is very secure financially and will maintain her expatriate status without her father's assistance indefinitely," Robert explained with a smile.

Ellen took a moment and then continued, "She is independently wealthy?"

"Yes, she will become more so if her father continues to transfer his wealth to her."

"My son knows nothing of this?" Ellen gasped.

"She is a brilliant lady, Ellen. When did you tell your husband of your wealth? I seem to recall it was after you were married."

"On the advice of counsel."

"That's right," Robert said, nodding his head.

"Is that all? What else did you find?"

"Ellen, she was brought up in an affluent family, independently wealthy, well-educated, highly intelligent, and in excellent health with no significant encumbrances. I think our Benjamin has done very well in his companion choice. She seems perfect," a happy Robert proclaimed.

Ellen did not react to Robert's pronouncement. She coldly stared at her friend and said, "I must tell you something that is not in your report. This is not what it seems."

"What do you mean?"

"You are my closest friend, and we have known each other for years, and I must ask you, do you trust my judgment?" Ellen pressed.

"Of course," Robert responded, perplexed at Ellen's insistent tone.

"Elisabeth's presence is a grave risk to my son. I know this as confidently as I know I am sitting here in front of you, and I have never been more frightened for my son," Ellen said as she leaned closer to Robert and placed her hand on his arm and began to sob.

"Ellen . . . " Robert asked, placing his hand on Ellen's, "What is it? What has happened?"

"I have had a terrible premonition. When Benjamin brought Elisabeth to our home, I reached out to shake her hand, and the moment I touched her fingers, I found myself in a dark and desolate place. At my feet was the Raven, dead. He was then swept away over a cliff by a howling, unforgiving wind, and I heard Benjamin calling out for me. I saw him on the edge of a great chasm fighting not to be swept into the abyss. As I reached out to save him, Elisabeth appeared, grabbed my hand away, and Benjamin was lost. I can still see his horrified face as he fell away to death. The next thing I knew, Conrad was reviving me as I laid upon the sitting room floor. I had collapsed into unconsciousness. Nothing like this has ever happened to me. The whole thing was so real. It is a warning, a terrible warning. Robert, you must believe me. I know this is real. I can feel it. That girl's presence is a grave danger to my son. She is a curse. Will you help me?" Ellen spoke while grasping Robert's arm with her other hand. "I must save my son . . . please help me! I will do anything to protect him!" Elisabeth continued to cry as she took her hands away from Robert and covered her face and released a slight moaning sound as she continued to sob.

"Ellen, what can be done? Your son will never give her up. They have been together nearly every night from the first day they met. You must let this run its course," Robert stated, recoiling from Elisabeth's outburst.

"We can have her sent back to Kuttor."

"That's not possible. The Locks have been bribed. They relish in a secret lifestyle unknown to the sheep they shepherd. They want their money," Robert stated in ever-increasing stern tones.

Elisabeth looked up and looked directly into Robert Bass's eyes. "I want her dead! I will pay them more. You must arrange it . . . you must."

Robert Bass stood up. Stepped back. Awful fear flowed through him. "You go too far. This is not you. I will not take life without a reason. That vision was a breakdown. Perhaps your medication needs. . . . "

Ellen, visibly angry, stood up, and for the first time in her relationship with Robert, screamed at him, "You don't understand—you can't! If you had been there, you would understand what I am telling you is the awful truth. I swear on Raven's wing, I speak the truth, and if there is no other way, she must die. Will you help me as a loving friend?"

"No!"

"We have agricultural and mineral interests in Kuttor. How is it possible we can take so much of their resources for our own enrichment?" Ellen pressed.

"We have people there we employ. . . . "

"And?"

"We bribe the Locks. No, Ellen. Do you understand what you are saying?"

Ellen stood up and repeated, with a strident voice and angry, tearful eyes, "I want my son to live, and that woman will lead to his destruction. I know this to be true. I can feel it. She is the touch of death. Help me, Robert, as my closest friend, you are my only hope."

Robert attempted to reason with his distraught friend, "Ellen, please try and understand. Benjamin is special to me, and I would do anything to protect him from potential harm. You know this is true. I would, and I have, killed to ensure his safety, and I would kill again, a hundred times if necessary, but this is not reason enough. This relationship must be allowed to continue. We can protect Benjamin. We can watch him every second of his life, if necessary. We have the resources to protect him."

"What are you saying—are you questioning my judgment? What I know to be true? I am speaking of forces beyond this world we cannot control."

"Do I question your reasoning before I have someone assassinated? A beautiful young woman that your son is deeply in love with. Yes, I must. What you are asking. . . . How can I be sure? I am not sure. Please listen to me, Ellen." Robert tried to make Ellen understand. She crossed her arms in a protective stance and prepared herself for the obvious.

Robert painfully counseled his dearest friend. "What happened to you, what you saw and felt, may be explained in several ways. Benjamin is your only child, and there is a natural concern when your son begins to make independent choices. There is also the strange coincidence of Elisabeth's appearance, so much like a younger you. I think this first meeting—"

"Enough of this! I know what I know, and this is not some sort of stress or adjustment reaction. Both you and Conrad speak without knowing what I experienced," Ellen's angry voice brought Robert's assertions to an abrupt halt.

"So, Conrad has said similar—"

"I grow weary of this conversation," Ellen proclaimed defiantly. "I am not some overly-protective mother, and I deeply resent the implications of what you suggest: that my fears are irrational. Have her taken back to Kuttor to die, or have those ignorant religious monsters kill her here. Bribe them."

"Ellen, she will not be taken back to Kuttor. That's not how the whole thing works. If the Locks reversed their course, something they never do, the Locks would not sully their sacred country with an apostate. The Locks will not take her back to Kuttor. They will come here, kill her, and take some identifying body part or clothing back as proof. Your son will be devastated. He will witness her death and burial. You know not what you ask. I am sorry, Ellen. I will do anything for you, but I will not kill this young woman. I will have no part of this," Robert stated without equivocation.

"I have a right to know who is in my employ in Kuttor, who manages our interest. I want his name and telegraph security code. I will determine his or her identity on my own if necessary. Do I have to go to such lengths?"

Without saying a word, Robert walked over to his desk

and opened a file and wrote down the information requested. He walked back to his friend and gave her the slip of paper and said, "I wash my hands of this. Now, please leave my home."

Robert turned, walked across the room, and began his labored ascension up the long flight of stairs. He did not look back. Robert did not say another word. He would honor Ellen's privilege and not speak to anyone. Bass knew his silence would make him complicit to Ellen's actions, but he was compelled to remain silent by his professional relationship with his client . . . or that is how he would try to convince himself it was morally justifiable.

Ellen watched Robert disappear up the stairs. She then looked down at the slip of paper, knowing she was holding Elisabeth's life in her hand. She walked over to the foyer, removed her slippers, laid them on the bench, and grabbed her shoes. Without putting them on, she opened the door, walked outside, and rang the stable master's bell to summon her carriage. She would never return to Robert's home.

Ellen was sitting on the silk sofa when her son entered the mansion. It had been twelve hours since she had spoken to Robert Bass, and it was late. Ellen knew what she was about to do was terrible. To save him, she would betray him. She would begin her scheme with a kiss. "Benjamin, I have been waiting for you. I have an idea I think you will like, and I want to talk to you about it."

Benjamin was surprised to see his mother up so late. He answered, "You are still up. Of course, I would love to have a word with you. I trust your day went well?"

Ellen walked up and placed her arms around her only child, kissed him on the lips, and whispered into his ear, "Very well, Benjamin. Please come and sit down beside me so we may speak."

"What is it, mother?" Benjamin asked, walking over to the silk sofa.

Ellen felt nervous and guarded. "Do you remember Petie's parent's meat market below the home I was living in when you were born?"

"Yes, I visited there often with Petie, and his father would give us greasy sausages to eat. I can still taste that awful stuff," Benjamin replied, thinking of his lost friend.

"Well, when Petie died, Mr. Passerine was not able to continue his meat market. He slipped into deep melancholia, so I purchased Mr. Passerine's shop and bought Mr. and Mrs. Passerine a small home near the sea. I set up a trust so Petie's parents would have sufficient income for the rest of their lives," Benjamin's mother softly revealed.

"I didn't know. That was truly a wonderful thing to do," Benjamin stated with a smile.

"It was a difficult time for all of us. So many things were happening. I didn't mention buying Mr. Passerine's shop. You understand?" Benjamin's mother asked.

"Of course, such a thoughtful thing."

"Mrs. Passerine was such a help when you were born, and we all loved Petie. Mrs. Passerine is such a very dear woman, her husband took the death of his child so hard. Your father has been helping Mr. Passerine with his melancholia, and he is healing. It will take time."

"I am glad father is involved."

"Yes, well, what I want to talk about is Mr. Passerine's shop and our old home. I pulled a construction crew from our home building projects on the west side of town and I had them remodel the old meat shop and our former little home above the shop. The meat shop is now a stable and carriage house. Our former home has been completely remodeled. I thought that you and Elisabeth would like a private place of your own. I know you have been using our hotels around town . . . that is, of course, completely acceptable, they are your hotels and everything, but I thought you might like a place of your own. Oh, and I had the private room modified for your special needs and, this is a little awkward, but I think Elisabeth might appreciate the discretion." Benjamin's mother explained, hoping her son's reaction would be favorable.

To her relief, Benjamin smiled and said, "That was truly kind of you. I think Elisabeth will appreciate the privacy."

"And Benjamin, you know this mansion is your true home. It will always be your home, but if your relationship with Elisabeth has sufficiently matured, you might want to consider living with her until the two of you start your studies at the university. I mean, I think she would appreciate the help of the servants."

"What a very thoughtful thing. I think Elisabeth would like to have servants. We were planning to live together at Londonderry near the university for the school year. Until then, our old home would be a wonderful place to live. We will be going to Londonderry to select a home in the next few months. I have several brokers searching for an acceptable estate. I will broach this idea to Elisabeth tomorrow. Have the servants been hired?" Benjamin asked.

"Yes, both the stable master and maid have been busy preparing the home and stable. The home has been completely stocked with food and linen, and if you or Elisabeth find fault with the servants I have selected, please feel free to terminate their services. I know Elisabeth will have her own standards and expectations. If necessary, we can always find someone more acceptable," Ellen said, looking at her son for his every reaction.

"Thank you so much, Mother," a grateful son stated as he put his arms again around his mother then gently kissed his mother on the lips.

Sitting back, Benjamin felt something that had to be said. "I want you to know, nothing will come between the two of us. You are my mother, and nothing will prevent us from having a close and loving relationship . . . nothing. Please believe me: my love for you cannot be surpassed by anyone."

"Thank you, Benjamin. No mother could ask for a finer son. I would do anything for you."

The cold, damp fog of the Eastern Sea flowed silently over the long wooden pier and the harbor's many moored ships. The tall, brilliant gas lamps at the end of the pier slowly turned into balls of fading light and then disappeared, entirely obscured by the sea's concealing hand. Far from land, hidden ships groped blindly at sea, calling out their presence with their foghorns' deep rumblings.

Ellen pulled her coat tightly together to escape the moist, penetrating cold of the night and walked quickly down the wooden pier in the direction of an iron steam freighter that had just arrived a few hours ago from Kuttor. She carried a large black attaché, and her pace was increasingly strident. It had been ten days since her conflict with Robert Bass.

Ellen's obsession with Elisabeth had not abated. The premonition of her son's death and the desperate plan to save him defined Ellen's every thought. She could still feel Elisabeth's cold touch on her hand and see the sickening, twisted smile on Elisabeth's face as Benjamin fell to his death. Ellen had not eaten for days, and when she slept, which was increasingly seldom, she would wake in night sweats, screaming in terror. Ellen's obsessive thoughts guaranteed horrific nightmares when she slept. Her living horror was driving her mad. Ellen would fight for her sanity against the irresistible force of the all-consuming curse. On the rim of the endless abyss, Ellen's persistent companion was her son's pending death. She prayed that her secret meeting tonight would bring her some relief from her all-consuming torment.

The passage of the freighter from Kuttor had been strange. The freighter carried no cargo and only one passenger, and would return to Kuttor before morning's light. Upon docking, the crew was told to leave the ship and not linger about or remain in their cabins. Most of the sailors escaped the freighter, searching for hard drink and prostitutes, and the remaining crew members found relief from their arduous duties at sea in restful sleep. The ship's company obeyed their captain's demands. The freighter appeared abandoned and ghostly quiet. There had been murmurs from the crew concerning the shadowy passenger who boarded the ship in the dead of night and was absent from all ship activities, including meals. An entire freighter used to transport one mysterious passenger across the Eastern Sea created a strange anxiety among the crew. What could be the reason for such a voyage? Quiet speculations and rumors circulated among the sailors. It was not their destiny to know the meaning of the ship's passage. If all went as planned, only Ellen Forrestal's agent from Kuttor would soon realize the reason and urgency for the freighter's clandestine journey. The mysterious passenger remained in his cabin after the docking of the freighter. He did not sleep. Ellen had called for him far from his home. He was frightened. His mission was unknown. He knew he could not fail.

The thick, swirling fog smothered the freighter in an obscuring haze. Ellen approached the dark ship, stained with streaks of flowing rust from the caustic sea, and read the ship's name proudly painted on the bow: Aberlour. The mysterious freighter moored as planned in the proper berth. It gave her a glimmer of hope. She walked up the boarding plank and found the ship deserted as planned. Teak wood planks covered the deck. She followed the promenade to the third exterior door from the boarding plank. She opened the steel door and entered a long corridor dimly lit with kerosene lamps, attached and sitting in swivel bases to compensate for the rolling sea. Numerous cabins lined both sides of the passageway. She was looking for cabin A-12. After a short while, she found the proper cabin and knocked on the wooden door. Ellen could hear approaching footsteps from within and the fumbling of the lock and the twisting of the brass knob. The door slowly opened, and Ellen saw a frail little man who seemed terrified by her presence.

The open cabin door permitted a wave of sickening stench to escape the small room, causing Ellen to gag and choke on the wretched air. After a moment, Ellen composed herself and prepared to meet her summoned employee. Ellen stood in silence, waiting for the man to identify himself. His voice broke as he pronounced his designation code, "12XY24, my Lady."

Ellen said with a slight smile, "May I enter?"

The frightened man softly responded, "Yes, of course, my Lady."

Ellen entered the small cabin. Several small kerosene lamps illuminated the cramped and vile room. A filthy bunk that hung from the wall was covered with disheveled and stained wool blankets. The room smelled of kerosene, urine, and body odor, Ellen once again choked on the thick, oppressive stench of the room and the body odor of her Kuttor agent. "Forgive my humble cabin and my unkempt state. Remain I have—in my cabin for the voyage's duration as you instructed, my Lady."

Ellen noticed a porcelain chamber pot sitting in the corner with a dish covering the top, used as a toilet by the confined man and a small metal table next to the bed covered with dirty dishes and scraps of food. "I regret this degree of secrecy was necessary. There can be no connection between us. We have never met. Do you understand?"

"Yes, my Lady."

"Do you know who I am?" Ellen asked, looking directly into the man's eyes.

"Yes, Ellen Forrestal," the strange little man appeared to tremble as he pronounced the name.

"That's right. Ellen Forrestal," she affirmed as she walked over to the small metal table, picked up the dirty dishes, placed them on the floor, and swept the crumbs of stale bread and dried pieces of unidentified tuber from the table with her attaché. She motioned for her agent to sit on the edge of the bed while arranging the table. She secured a metal chair sitting next to the wall. A small kerosene lamp on the wall above the table provided light for the conversation between the powerful and the meek.

Her agent sat down on the bed directly across from her, and for the first time she could see the man she placed all her hopes upon. His skin was a dark brown, and his hair a thick black compliment to his rugged face. His body was slight, and his shirt was stained with sweat and fallen food. His eyes were a dark brown, and through those portals, Ellen could see the deep intimidation he was enduring by her presence. "Why are you frightened?"

"Because what you are about to ask of me, my Lady. I trust such import to meet me here in these filthy confines," the little man said, not looking directly at his employer.

"Import is correct, and you will be paid for the services you provide for me."

"Yes, my Lady. Paid well am I, thank you."

"After tonight, your salary will be doubled."

"Thank you, my Lady," her agent said with a flat affect.

"What we are about to speak must not be known to anyone. Secrecy is essential. Do you understand?" Ellen leaned forward and spoke in a firm tone.

"I am not sure of the meaning of that which you require of me," he whispered.

"No one must know of this meeting or what I am going to ask of you. No one must know what you are about to do. Am I clear?" Ellen reframed her admonition.

"My word, I pledge, my Lady," the scared little man said.

"No, you pledge your life. Do you understand?" Ellen was determined to make the little man understand.

He took a moment as he looked across the table at the woman who appeared gaunt, pale, and tired, realizing his life was in her hands, and said, "Understand, I do."

"Good," Ellen said as she opened her attaché. She pulled out the dossier on Elisabeth Zurich. "As my agent in Kuttor, you have secured for me considerable agricultural, mineral, and petroleum rights from that country. Is this correct?"

"Yes, my Lady."

"How have you accomplished this?" Ellen stared through the glare of the light from the kerosene lamp.

"I bribe the Locks, my Lady."

"You bribe the Locks. That's right, and you are going to

bribe them again."

Ellen opened the file and turned it to face her agent and said, "Do you recognize this woman?"

The little man picked up the file and angled the black and white photograph directly into the light of the kerosene lamp, paused, and said, "Child of yours, she is?"

"No."

"Eyes such as yours she has, my lady?"

"Yes, green exactly like my eyes, but she is not my blood. She is not related."

"In Kuttor, this is known as a 'Kaich,' which means in our language, 'distant shadow.' Arranged from time's beginning beyond this world, such forces as has been made, a powerful curse brought to you and all you love. A powerful curse. Linked by an evil thread, the two of you. Those you love, if this girl can live, she will take from you. A curse I say, at risk your very soul," Ellen's agent explained, looking at the picture. "Touch you she has or anyone you love?"

"She has stolen my son's love, and when I touched her hand when we first met, I was given a vision of my son's death, a death she caused," Ellen said while tears filled her eyes and escaped down her pale cheeks.

"Death dance she does with your son beyond her will. A victim she is, as your son will be. A curse she carries, to your son's death. Been taken against her will, Kaich she is. Trapped this lady is. Ask of me, I will do anything. In my country, these things we know, speak to us our religion does. Powerful spell appears cast on you or a member of your family. By Raven's favored, you are led to me by him. Accident this is not, so powerful you are in this world. Raven favor you, brought to me to save your son from certain death. Why have you or your son been cursed?" Ellen's agent explained and asked with increased confidence in his voice.

"I don't know why this abomination has entered my life. Has anyone spoken to you of this woman?"

"Spoken? I don't know. Her name is?"

"In Kenton, she calls herself Elisabeth Zurich. She was

born in Kuttor twenty-three years ago and given the name Anjum Izdubar. Her father is Diya Izdubar."

"Much revered, Diya Izdubar, this man is in my country. Powerful as well, as much as you in your country. Powerful adversaries, you have been paired, from thriving forces beyond this world. Speak of her no more to me—understand I do," the little man from Kuttor said as he shut the file and said, "Kill her, I will. My fate is such. Kill her tonight, you wish of me?"

"I don't need a vulgar assassination . . . such a thing would be suspected by my husband and maybe others. This must be made to look like the Locks have deemed her an apostate by their own volition. Her death can never be traced back to me. Her spell has captured my son, and I would lose him forever without your help. Do you see why all of this must be secret?"

"Yes, my lady."

"Diya Izdubar bribed the Locks to allow her to leave Kuttor to be educated," Elllen explained.

"Yes, my lady. Unusual not for wealthy families. Many have done for favored children," the little man said while leaning forward and lifting his head.

"Well, I want you to bribe the Locks to take her back to Kuttor to be killed as an apostate. She must be killed, or my son will follow her to Kuttor to get her back. Do you understand?"

"Understand I do . . . death will not be in Kuttor. She cannot spoil the sacred soil. Locks will send the 'Lentics,' which means in the language of Kenton, 'compassionate infallibles,' will seek out the girl to kill, they will, in Riverdale, for holy law violation. Must you tell them where she can be found? In the night they will come, wearing golden robes, on horseback, always in fours. In Kuttor, they are the judge, jury, and enforcer of holy laws. Belief it is Lentics are hand of Xue and cannot make an error. By divine guidance, directed they are. For her, Lentics will come. Arrange I can, do you wish?" Ellen's agent said with a smile and a nod.

"Yes, do your best. Tell me how much money you will need to bribe the Locks?" Ellen asked, feeling encouraged.

"Much for most, not for you. It can be arranged for half million Kenton dollars in silver, I should think."

"Done. The silver certificates will arrive through the normal process. Only you will know what it is for. Do you understand?" Ellen asked.

"Yes, my lady."

"How long will it take for the Lentics to arrive in Riverdale?"

"Five, maybe six weeks."

"I want you to telegraph me on my confidential wire everything you are doing to accomplish the task I have given you. I have a map of Riverdale."

Ellen reached again into her attaché and produced the map. Ellen's home appeared on the map circled in red and designated A, and Benjamin and Elisabeth's new home was designated B, also circled on the map.

"I will inform you where she can be found. When you and the Lentics reach Riverdale, I want you to go to the telegraph office in the harbor and secure and send a runner to my home to let me know all is ready. I will send back my response with the runner to you at the telegraph office. My message will let the Lentics know where Elisabeth Zurich is located. Your message to me will inform the time the Lentics should arrive at the location or any other pertinent information. I receive many messages a day by runners in this manner. No one will suspect anything unusual. The Lentics are to remain on the ship until the time I indicate in the message. I will be at my telegraph key every night at eight o'clock; this is the time to contact me. I want you to keep me informed as to your progress. You must tell me when the ship will sail from Dresden and the expected arrival time in Riverdale. This will give me the time I need to get my son out of town and ensure my husband will be out of the way. I will try to get Elisabeth to my home where the Lentics will find her and take her away to her death by their hands. As soon as I know the date and time of the Lentics' arrival, I will be able to accomplish what I must do to ensure Elisabeth's successful demise. Do you read my language?" a somewhat rambling, stressed, and preoccupied Ellen asked.

"I read much better than I speak your language. The way you speak, different it is from my tongue. I should also tell you the Lentics would take evidence of Elisabeth's death back to Kuttor for the Locks to know the deed is completed. The body will remain. Take, they will, unique things from the girl. Her green eyes will take one or both and scalp with hair, anything else unique to her."

"She has a strange black and red coat woven by a master carpet weaver. I am sure the coat must be rare," Ellen explained to her agent.

"Coat, special it is. Such thing is quite rare. This coat is known of, very special, one of few ever made. I will speak of it to Locks so the Lentics may so be directed. Coat they will take for sure."

Elisabeth pulled a heavy cloth bag from her attaché containing nearly a pound of silver coins and placed it in front of her agent and said, "I have a pound of silver coins. Silver is the preferred form of currency in your country. Is this correct?"

"Yes, my lady."

"These coins are for you. When Elisabeth is dead and rotting in the ground, you will receive ten times this amount. Do you understand?"

"Oh, I am grateful, my lady. I may, when all is done, be able to bribe the Locks, my daughter may also escape my sad country," a thankful servant said, reaching for Ellen's hand to kiss.

Ellen pulled her hand back. She did not want anyone from Kuttor to touch her again. "You are not to touch me. I am going to leave you this file. It describes the activities of Elisabeth Zurich after she left Kuttor. I think her behavior will show she is an apostate by the laws of your country. Make your case with this information then destroy the file. If you need anything else, telegraph me. Do you understand?"

"Yes, my lady."

"And if Elisabeth should survive all I have put in motion—it would be best for all concerned that she is put to death." Ellen stood up with that threat and turned to escape the disgusting little room when he spoke again.

"Thank you, my lady. I will not fail you. Do you wish to know my name?"

Ellen turned and looked at the frail little man, and without saying another word, turned again and disappeared through the cabin into the night.

The day for Elisabeth's death had arrived. Four weeks ago, Ellen received word the Lentics had set sail for Riverdale. Earlier this evening, a runner from the Riverdale's harbor telegraph office had brought her a note from her agent indicating the freighter carrying the Lentics had arrived. The assassins, the twisted disciples of a foreign god, were waiting onboard for instructions on how to proceed. Ellen returned the runner with a simple reply: "Location A, 8:00 p.m."

Ellen had planned well. She had arranged for Benjamin to travel to Londonderry to discuss the advantages of the Benjamin Shipping Containers to potential buyers. Conrad was scheduled weeks in advance for surgery and hospital rounds. He was not expected to return home until the early morning hours. Ellen had invited Elisabeth for dinner at the Forrestal Mansion during Benjamin's absence under the guise of amenity, an opportunity to cultivate a more familiar relationship between the two women. Elisabeth was expected to arrive at 7:30. The deception had been set into motion, and if all went well, Elisabeth would be dead before dinner had grown cold.

At precisely 7:30, a very conservatively dressed Elisabeth knocked on the front door of the Forrestal Mansion, and Ellen greeted Elisabeth with a warm smile. When Elisabeth reached out to Benjamin's mother, Ellen quickly stated, "Elisabeth, I am so happy to see you. Please let me take your beautiful coat."

"Oh, thank you," Elisabeth said as she modified her behavior from a polite handshake to removing her coat. Elisabeth handed the coat to a very careful Ellen, who had no desire to touch Elisabeth.

When Ellen drew near, Elisabeth realized how gaunt and pale Benjamin's mother had become.

"How have you been?" a somewhat shocked and concerned Elisabeth asked.

"I am fine . . . a little tired. My various businesses sometimes take a toll on me. It has been one of those months. I am so glad we are getting together while Benjamin is in Londonderry."

Elisabeth replied, "I am concerned. We didn't have a particularly good start to our relationship. How long has it been, eight weeks, I think?"

"Has it been that long?" Ellen responded. "Time has gotten away from me. Love . . . we lose all our sensibilities when we fall in love. I think you are very much in love with my son."

"Very much. I have never known such feelings. Yes, I love your son very much."

"Well, I am so very happy for both of you," Ellen lied. "Let's go into the dining room. I have dismissed the help for the evening, not to be interrupted, and I had a meal prepared for us and placed in warming trays on the dining table. I hope you are hungry?"

Elisabeth turned from the foyer and looked into the dining room to see a dozen finely engraved silver covered warming trays sitting at the end of the dining table and replied, "I am famished. I am happy to be with you, and I do want to get to know you better. I cannot believe so much time has passed. I think your son put a spell on me."

"Yes, a spell. Please come in. Take a plate. I think you will find something you will enjoy," Ellen said as she directed Elisabeth to the prepared food.

"Thank you," Elisabeth stated as she walked over and picked up one of the fine china plates and began to explore the many covered silver trays.

To Ellen's surprise, Elisabeth began taking large portions of food from each warming tray she visited. Elisabeth took several large pieces of pheasant, followed by goose and prime rib. She placed the plate next to a silverware set, picked up another plate, and continued her hoarding from the bird stuffing tray, the buttered potatoes, walnut and brandy blended paste, and asparagus. She then sat down with a big smile to politely wait for her hostess to serve herself.

"Elisabeth, you are starving. I trust the maid has been providing proper nourishment?"

"The maid is wonderful, and so is the home you have provided. I cannot thank you enough for your kindness. We are incredibly happy."

"I am so happy. Would you like some wine? Dark or white?"

"Mineral water would be best."

Ellen picked up a pitcher of effervescent mineral water and filled Elisabeth's crystal goblet and said, "Please start eating while I get my plate."

With that said, Elisabeth replied, "Thank you," and began to shovel the food into her mouth.

Ellen selected several small pieces of pheasant and stuffing while she watched Elisabeth consume her food and drink the mineral water. "Are you sure you are getting enough to eat?"

Ellen waited while she chewed, swallowed, and replied, "Yes, I am sorry. I am acting like a pig. Please forgive me. The food is so wonderful, and I am famished."

"I am glad you like the food," Ellen said as she walked over to a place setting on the opposite side of the table and began pouring herself some dark wine. She then took a small watch from her pocket and placed the timepiece next to her plate. "Please forgive my preoccupation with the time. I expect a courier with some contracts I need to sign. I will be so happy when Benjamin finishes his education and is able to spend more time with our business."

"Don't let Mr. Porter hear any of that! He keeps asking Benjamin to help him with his carpet business when he finishes school."

"Mr. Porter is a lovely man."

Elisabeth shook her head in the affirmative as she placed another large forkful of pheasant into her mouth.

Elisabeth continued to eat while Ellen picked at her food and watched the minutes pass on her timepiece. Ellen was numb; she did not feel a thing except for the ominous weight of Elisabeth's presence. How she wished this evening would be over. How Ellen wished her son would be free of the terrible curse the woman in front of her had brought to her and her son's life.

Elisabeth cleared her plate and stared across the table without saying a word. Ellen was surprised by Elisabeth's abrupt change from her preoccupation with food. For a brief period, the two women looked at each other, Elisabeth with a big smile on her face.

Elisabeth blurted out, "We were planning to tell you together, but I just can't wait. . . . I am carrying your grandchild. I am so happy."

Ellen froze in total silence. There was a surreal moment of disbelief as she tried to comprehend the words that Elisabeth just spoke. "You're pregnant with Benjamin's child? How do you know? Are you sure?" Ellen felt a terrible dread.

"Yes. Benjamin and I are so happy."

"How can you be sure—I mean, are you sure?"

"Yes. I was just with your husband, who has been caring for me. The first month I had terrible morning sickness, and he prescribed some medication to help, and in the last few weeks, I have been eating everything I can get my hands on. Dr. Forrestal said this kind of thing is normal for some women. I promised Benjamin I would wait until we could tell you together, but I just can't, I am so happy."

"How far along are you?" Ellen asked, trying to comprehend.

"Eight weeks. I think the baby may have been conceived the first time we made love the day I met you."

"Up in Benjamin's room when I fainted?" Ellen asked with coldness in her voice.

"Yes, I hope you will be happy for us," Elisabeth said with growing apprehension as Ellen continued to stare without expression.

Ellen's mind began to process the implication. How could she kill her grandchild? How could she hurt her son beyond having his first love taken from him? Everything took on a strange, dreamlike quality. Ellen heard the words coming from her mouth without thought. Everything from this point on was a pure, instinctive impulse. She glanced at her watch. She had only a few moments to act. She could not kill her grandchild, not that.

"I want you to listen very carefully to what I am about to tell you."

Elisabeth was confused by Ellen's demeanor, "Are you not happy for us?"

"Now listen," Ellen snapped, "I will put on your coat and go to the corral behind the mansion and ride Fortune away from here. I want you to wait until the men that will follow me are gone, and then I want you to take your carriage to the hospital and tell Conrad to hide you there until I return. We must keep you safe."

Elisabeth was visibly frightened at the strange words coming from Benjamin's mother. "What are you talking about? What men? Why do I need to hide?"

"The Lentics will be here in a few minutes, and they are going to kill you."

"The Infallibles here? How?" Elisabeth screamed as she jumped up from the table, knocking her goblet over and spilling the contents across the table. "Is this your doing? Were you going to have me killed? You bribed the Locks, you possessive monster. You twisted—"

"Stop! There will be plenty of time for recriminations. For

now, you must survive. I am sorry. I have my reasons, and they're not what you think. When you are safe . . . "

Ellen was interrupted by the sound of approaching horses. She leaped from her chair, ran over to the foyer, grabbed Elisabeth's coat, turned one last time to her son's companion, and said, "Wait, until they are gone and go to the hospital. I will lead them as far away as possible. When they realize, they will come back for you."

With that said, Ellen was gone. Elisabeth heard the back door slam. She felt helpless. Horrified, Elisabeth sought refuge. She laid down on the floor and then crawled under the table. Her body trembled uncontrollably. She thought to herself, "This is madness. Benjamin's mother must be insane."

Ellen ran out the back door and climbed over the corral fence. Fortune jumped at the unexpected visitor and released a loud whinny, a shrill so loud she was convinced the religious assassins would hear. Ellen whispered, "Fortune, yield, yield."

The horse calmed down, tempered by the familiar voice. Ellen talked quickly to the horse and coached him to the corral gate. She climbed up on the gate and mounted the nervous horse. She released the gate and held on to Fortune's mane as she directed the horse to the street. "Run, Fortune," she commanded as she shoved her shoes into his flanks. The horse jumped and started to run.

When she was a young girl, she spent many summers riding bareback on her horse, but this was a different time. Ellen was no longer young, her strength diminished by time and stress. She had not ridden a horse for years. Ellen fought with every stride to remain centered on the animal. She held tight to Fortune's mane with her left hand, her right arm awkwardly around the horse's neck. When she reached the front of the mansion, Ellen saw the four horsemen preparing to dismount as she rode by the assassins. All four men wore golden robes, their heads wrapped with fine white silk forming the tight turban required by their faith. On their backs was the Hamonie, the curved sword of justice.

Ellen found the energy to ride from deep within her and the adrenaline-induced strength permitted her to ride hard and fast. She was riding for her unborn grandchild. Elisabeth had to survive. She rode north on Ocean Front Boulevard in front of the many mansions and homes that fenced the shoreline. The street gas lamps cast eerie twisted shadows of horse and rider as Ellen struggled to remain on the horse. The sound of the Lentics, the cries of horses, and the sound of shod hooves on cobblestone grew louder with every stride.

Ellen rode Fortune less than half a block when she began to lose her grip, and, with a few more strides from the obedient horse, she fell hard onto the cobblestone road. She landed on her left leg, snapping it like a dried twig with her fibula piercing the skin, exposing six inches of sallow bone. Ellen screamed in agony as she continued downward from the momentum of her fall, her face smashing against the hardened stone, breaking her nose and crushing one of her eye sockets. Quickly she sat up and turned in pain and panic to look upon her pursuers. The lead horseman leaned down from his horse and, with a flashing sword, Ellen's world went black.

Ellen's body continued to remain upright, sitting, for a brief instant, as blood from her severed neck sprayed into the gaslight's soft illumination. Her head rolled across the road and stopped with her face pressed against stone. The Lentic who took her life abruptly stopped his horse, dismounted, and walked over to clean his sword on Ellen's dress, as was the custom, before returning his sword to the leather scabbard on his back. The assassin then walked over to Ellen's head and kicked it with his boot, so the head was facing up. He drew his knife and plunged the blade into Ellen's undamaged eye socket, cut the muscles and nerves that held the eyeball, and plucked out her eye with his uncovered fingers. He looked at the green iris in the lamplight, then dropped the eye into a small leather pouch on his belt. The dim light obscured the identity of the corpse. The similarity of appearance between Ellen and Elisabeth would save Elisabeth and her unborn baby's life on this terrible night of deception and violence.

The assassin then grabbed a handful of her raven hair in his hand, lifted Ellen's head several feet from the ground, and freed the locks with a swift slice of the scalp. Ellen's head fell once again to the stones with a sickening thud.

The Lentic carefully folded his prize and placed his proof of death in the leather pouch. The assassin walked over to Ellen's body, grabbed one of the sleeves of the red and black coat, and, using sheer force, pulled the coat free of Ellen's limp, headless body. The religious fanatic returned to his horse. The four horsemen circled the body and, with boisterous voices, proclaimed, "The apostate is dead. May god forgive her for her treacherous ways. She is no more among the living. May she rot until she is forgiven. She is in the hands of god, the mighty and the righteous."

With that final homily, the Lentics turned their horses in the direction of the waiting freighter and began a forceful gallop. Within the hour, the rust-stained freighter with Ellen's agent and the four-horseman disappeared into the blackness of the Eastern Sea.

Elisabeth cowered beneath the dining room table, still trembling. She heard Ellen ride by the front of the mansion followed by the rumble of the many shod hooves striking the cobblestone road. She heard a faint scream and the abrupt halt of the horses. The night grew still. The muffled religious proclamation of the assassins declaring their killing of an apostate broke the silence. They were the righteous hand of Xue and could not make a mistake; they were the Infallibles. Elisabeth was free forever. The religious guardians of an imperfect god were no more in her life. To the Locks, she was dead. If seen—if she walked into a house of worship in full view of the Locks and proclaimed her presence, she would be ignored as if she were a shadow's shadow, something that could not exist, a mirage and nothing more.

Elisabeth waited. The night grew quiet again. The first sounds she heard were faint wailing and the inaudible mumbles of a gathering crowd. She ventured over to the door and looked up the street. Occupants of the many homes were walking out to investigate the troubling sounds. Elisabeth walked from the Forrestal mansion into the crowd. She pushed herself through those gathered there and looked upon the ghastly sight of the decapitated remains of Ellen Forrestal. Elisabeth heard the name repeated over and over in the confusing tangle of words. Her legs became weak as she gazed upon the sight. Elisabeth fell to the ground near Ellen's body, catching herself with her hands and soaking her dress in blood. She sat there until one of the neighbors brought a blanket to cover the body. One man among the spectators removed his coat and covered Ellen's severed head. With the terrible specter no longer visible, Elisabeth felt her strength returning. She attempted to rise. A young man in the crowd reached under her arm and picked her up. He looked at her a moment and then commented, "Are you Ellen's daughter?"

"The scorpion stings itself," Elisabeth murmured, remembering a childhood story. She then turned from facing the young man, looked upon the covered remains, and loudly declared, "I am free—she has saved my life." A new lie was born.

Elisabeth turned from all those gathered and slowly walked back to her horse and carriage in front of the Forrestal mansion. She climbed into the carriage and guided her horse in the direction of Riverdale Hospital. Elisabeth would tell Dr. Forrestal of his terrible loss. That is what she had to do.

Elisabeth slowly walked through the hospital's emergency doors and down the corridor leading to the many wards. She remained in shock. The evening's terrible events seemed like a dreary memory of a childhood nightmare: grotesque, unreal, and inescapable. Her face was pale. Her stare seemed focused far away. Her dress was soiled; she appeared to wander, looking around as if she were lost. A concerned young nurse approached her and asked, "Have you been hurt? How can I help you?"

The nurse's voice brought Elisabeth back to reality.

"I must talk to Dr. Forrestal. Something has happened."

"Yes, of course. Please follow me," the nurse said as she

led Elisabeth to one of the wards.

"Please wait here. I will tell Dr. Forrestal you are looking for him. What is your name?"

"Elisabeth."

The nurse turned and walked through the door on ward H, and Dr. Forrestal walked out into the hall within a minute. He noticed her soiled dress and bloody legs, fearing a miscarriage may have occurred. "Elisabeth, are you hurt? What has happened?"

"Please, Dr. Forrestal. We need to go somewhere private."

Dr. Forrestal took her arm and walked her down the corridor into an unoccupied examination room. Elisabeth stated, "Please sit down with me. This is going to be difficult."

Dr. Forrestal became overwhelmed with fear hearing these ominous words and sat down on a chair next to the wall. Elisabeth sat next to him and held his hand, "Your wife is dead. She died saving my life."

At first, Dr. Forrestal simply stared at Elisabeth and said, "What are you saying?"

"A group of religious fanatics from Kuttor followed me to your home, and when they arrived to kill me, your wife put on my coat and led them away. Ellen . . . they caught up with her. They killed her. She died protecting me. I just told her about the baby, then we heard the thugs outside calling me. She ran to the back corral and rode Benjamin's horse out in the street and . . . "

"What are you saying? My wife is not dead. I saw her a few hours ago. What are you talking about?"

There was a knock on the door, and Dr. Forrestal answered, "Yes."

Oboe Johnson walked into the small room, tapping his heart. He was holding his hat in his other hand, and seeing Elisabeth, he asked, "Have you told him? I am so sorry, Conrad. This is terrible. . . . I am so sorry."

Dr. Forrestal stared at Oboe and then looked at Elisabeth and began to shake. He held his hand up to his mouth, and he voiced a muffled moan as he seemed to wilt and sob. Elisabeth put her arm around him, and Oboe rushed to his other side, and Dr. Forrestal repeated, "Not Ellen . . . no, not Ellen."

For a long while, he sat there in his grief.

Then he seemed composed. He wiped the tears from his face, straightened his coat, and said, "Where is my wife?"

"We took her to Maxwell's," Oboe told him.

"I must go and see her. I must go to her."

Elisabeth said, "I will take you in my carriage."

Elisabeth stood up and took Dr. Forrestal's hand, and Oboe took his arm, and the two of them helped him through the hospital. The nurses and staff watched as he walked down the corridor realizing something terrible had happened. Dr. Forrestal seemed to be in shock and did not say a word as he left the hospital.

Elisabeth helped Dr. Forrestal to her carriage, and the two of them followed Oboe to the undertaker. After a seemingly long ride, the three of them arrived at Maxwell's Funeral Home. Oboe dismounted and immediately walked up to help his friend. He then helped Elisabeth, and they all entered the house of death.

Hearing the door open and close, Mr. Maxwell rushed from the embalming room to help his old friend. "I am so sorry, Conrad. Do you wish to see your wife before I begin to prepare her for burial?"

The undertaker's words seemed so very unreal. Conrad replied, "I must."

Mr. Maxwell took his friend's arm and led him into the white-tiled embalming room. Ellen was lying on a white porcelain mortician's table covered in a coarse muslin yellow sheet. He carefully pulled the sheet down to expose Ellen's mutilated face. He thoughtfully did not expose her severed neck. Conrad once again began to sob uncontrollably. He felt weak, and Mr. Maxwell helped him to a nearby chair.

"I am lost without her. How can I live without her? I love her so much. How can she be gone?" a grieving husband said as he looked upon his wife's remains.

Oboe remained in the coffin display room, not wishing to

look again upon the body.

Elisabeth walked into the embalming room and, without looking at the remains of the woman who wanted her dead, knelt beside the grieving husband and said, "She died saving my life, and she died saving her grandchild. She sacrificed her life so I might live. I am so sorry."

Elisabeth's words clearly moved Dr. Forrestal, and he looked away from his wife's remains and put his hand on Elisabeth's face and said, "She loved you so very much. She would have done anything for her son and you. I love you, too. I can accept her sacrifice. Thank you for your kind words."

Elisabeth lied, "I loved her, too. She was such a wonderful woman. I owe her my life."

Dr. Forrestal gazed at Elisabeth, "Yes, a special person. I love her so much. I must accept her sacrifice. I understand, and I can accept my loss knowing she died saving you and the baby. . . ."

Elisabeth began to cry as if what he had said were true.

With that, Dr. Forrestal seemed to gain his composure and stood up. "Mr. Maxwell, please use all your gifts to restore her."

"I will do my best. Ellen will be ready for viewing by tomorrow morning," Mr. Maxwell said, placing his hand on his friend's shoulder.

Dr. Forrestal turned and walked into the small rooms where the mortuary's records were kept. Dr. Forrestal signed the death certificate and wrote the death certificate number in the undertaker's record book, then signed his name in the book. "Don't be concerned with the death certificate. I will complete the paperwork tomorrow morning when I return. Will ten in the morning give you enough time to prepare my wife?"

"Yes."

"Conrad, do you wish to pick out the coffin?"

"No. Please select a nice one for her," Conrad said as he took Elisabeth's hand and walked through the display room.

Oboe opened the door, and all three walked into the night.

Elisabeth took Dr. Forrestal back to the hospital. He dismounted her carriage and asked, "Will you meet me at my home at 9:30 tomorrow morning? I need to explain to the hospital staff what has happened to ensure my patients will be taken care of for the next few days. Will you meet me tomorrow morning?"

"Yes, I will be there tomorrow, and we can go back to the funeral home. It would be best if we both met Benjamin tomorrow at the train station at 11:00. I don't want him to hear about his loss from someone other than us," Elisabeth softly stated.

"Of course. Try and get some sleep. The next few days will be difficult."

"I want you to get some rest, as well. I am so sorry for your loss, Dr. Forrestal."

"Thank you. Until tomorrow then," were Dr. Forrestal's last words before turning and walking into the hospital.

The funeral home grew eerily quiet when Conrad, Elisabeth, and Oboe left Maxwell's. In solitude, Mr. Maxwell turned to Ellen Forrestal's remains. His solemn duty was to create an illusion that she was merely in restful sleep so the survivors in her former world might look upon her one last time. Mr. Maxwell would facilitate this societal lie, the true specter of death being incomprehensible and unyielding. He began by covering his clothes with a mortician's apron and removing the course muslin sheet from Ellen's body. Only the broken and empty vessel that held Ellen's spirit in life remained before him. The greatest of care and reverence would guide his duties. Ellen's decapitated remains presented some unique challenges. Thankfully, death by decapitation was rare. Mr. Maxwell thought back to the last time he looked upon such misfortune and realized that person was her former husband, James Walker.

"How fate has linked these two souls in life and now in

death," he softly spoke to himself before he began his efforts.

After many hours of labor and artistry, Ellen appeared to lie in her coffin in peaceful sleep. Mr. Maxwell was not satisfied. Ellen's hair had to be perfect. With great care, Mr. Maxwell brushed and arranged Ellen's hair to accentuate her beauty and facilitate a natural disposition.

The body dressed and situated in the coffin, Mr. Maxwell wheeled the body through the display room and into the adjacent windowless slumber room. The slumber room had a small, low stage surrounded by luxurious, dark burgundy silk drapes. He adjusted the cart's height to match the height of the stage and slid the coffin on to the viewing platform. He adjusted the gaslights, so a soft, warm glow of light enveloped the body. Mr. Maxwell lit several small, rose-scented incense cubes, and retrieved a selection of fresh flowers from the cold room to lay around the coffin. Mr. Maxwell had completed his task.

He sat down in front of the coffin and looked at the rendition of the remains of Ellen Forrestal. Ellen looked at peace. She appeared to be sleeping, as she would appear in life. The illusion was real and convincing. Mr. Maxwell was looking at the woman he had known for years, and in the privacy of his solitude, he released his suppressed emotions. His objectivity was gone. He began to sob and mourn. He thought of the hundreds of times he contacted Ellen to provide a proper burial for a pauper family. Ellen Forrestal was kind and always generous. He would remain with his friend and benefactor for several hours before returning to his home above the funeral parlor. He would shower and dress in his most elegant suit. He would not sleep. The sun was rising from the Eastern Sea, and the survivors would be arriving soon.

Chapter 18
A Mother's Tear

Conrad Forrestal rose from a tormented sleep. He looked around the intimate room he shared with his wife, and seeing her clothes and other personal items, the terrible realization that his wife was gone struck him again. He had the countenance of a man in shock—flat in expression and robotic in motion. He showered, shaved, and dressed in formal apparel. He descended the mansion stairs and informed the staff, matter-of-factly and to their shock and sadness, of his lovely wife's demise. He stood on the curb in front of his home to receive his carriage and horse from the always prompt stable boy at the usual time of seven in the morning. Unlike all the other mornings, Conrad Forrestal directed his horse not to the hospital but the mansion of Robert Bass, Ellen's business partner, and closest friend. After a short while, he arrived at the mansion on Main street, passed through the open gate, dismounted his carriage, secured his horse, walked up to the elaborate front door, and announced his presence with a deliberate knock.

The downstairs maid opened the door. "Oh, Dr. Forrestal, please come in. I will rouse Mr. Bass from his sleep at once."

The maid directed Dr. Forrestal to the formal sitting room, but he did not progress beyond the leather bench in the foyer.

After a few minutes, Robert Bass descended the stairs and greeted his good friend. "Conrad, so good to see you. Please come into the sitting room where we might speak. May I offer you some breakfast or—"

"Please," Conrad interrupted, "sit here with me, my good friend. I have tragic news."

Mr. Bass was prepared to hear that Elisabeth was dead

and expected that Dr. Forrestal would probe him for Ellen's involvement. To his terrible dismay, he heard the words he did not expect and could not fathom.

"Robert, Ellen is dead. She died saving Elisabeth's life from some religious fanatics, and assassins from Kuttor sent to kill her. I am so sorry I have to bring this awful news."

Robert Bass did not react, trying to comprehend what he heard. "What's this—are you telling me my Ellen is dead?"

"Yes, Robert. Our Ellen is no longer with us."

Robert looked vacantly through Conrad, his eyes lacking focus. After a moment, Robert put his hand over his mouth, looked down at his feet, and remained still. "Robert, are you going to be all right?" Conrad whispered.

"No, nothing will be right again, nothing," Robert said as he stood and began wandering the foyer before regaining his composure and returning to the bench.

"I am so sorry for your loss. How may I help you? I am prepared to continue all business matters until you are—"

"Please, Robert, don't trouble yourself with such things. We will have time later to deal with all of that. . . . This is a time for grieving. A time for goodbyes. I am bringing Elisabeth with me to the undertakers at ten. Do you wish to join us?

"Yes, of course. I must prepare an obituary for the papers. Some of Ellen's businesses are publicly owned, and the shareholders must be informed. The announcement must be given in a manner that is informative and reassuring that the leadership of her many business activities will continue without faltering. Conrad, do you wish for me the honor of this task before I visit Ellen?"

"Of course, Robert. Thank you for your thoughtfulness. I was not thinking of such things. Please inform the world of their loss. I trust you with the notification. Will you say a few words at the graveside, as well? I am sorry, Robert. I know you loved Ellen as I do. I am so sorry."

"I am sorry for you. We will help each other through this terrible time, and, of course, I will eulogize my dear friend."

"Thank you. I will see you then by ten at Maxwell's," Conrad said, hugging Robert before returning to his carriage.

Robert Bass knew the duty required of him. He walked to his triangle desk and sent a confidential telegraph to his most trusted agent in Kuttor to inform Diga Izdubar that his daughter was safe and unharmed, and he would arrange for her to contact him in a few days. The Lentics had failed and taken the wrong life, and his daughter was forever free.

For the next hour, Robert, who in some ways knew Ellen more than anyone, prayed for merciful forgiveness for his dear friend. Robert asked that the burden of Ellen's horrific evil act be placed on him so her heart may be as light as a feather, so the Raven could carry her to the afterlife, so great was his love.

OBITUARY

Ellen Joy Forrestal 1849-1896

Be it known by all that dwell within the State of Kenton and beyond, that the best among us is no more. Ellen Forrestal has died. A woman that profoundly changed the world. Ellen Forrestal was the founder and chairman and chief operating officer of Forrestal Industries, the third largest multinational business conglomerate in the world. Ellen Forrestal started her business empire on the proceeds of a life insurance policy received after the death of first husband, James Walker, who died in a coaling accident when Ellen Forrestal was twenty-nine years old. With a rare acumen for business, Ellen Forrestal invested the proceeds from the policy in railroad stock, Riverdale harbor warehouses, real estate, petroleum, and mining interest. Her ability to recognize the potential for economic growth in her targeted investments, and her sophisticated management skills established the Forrestal Investment Company, a subsidiary of the privately held Forrestal Industries. In 1889, Ellen

Forrestal permitted a selected portion of her private holdings to be offered as public stocks. Forrestal Investment Industries is currently the fourth most valuable stock offered on the Kenton Stock Exchange. At the time of her death, Ellen Forrestal employed, worldwide, over 40,000 employees.

Ellen Forrestal was known for her philanthropic activities. In 1887, she established the Forrestal Medical and Mental Hygiene Research Foundations for the scientific advancement of medical and mental health treatment. The Advanced Mental Hygiene Research Hospital is the most advanced research facility in the world in the use of psychopharmacological treatment of mental illness. The Forrestal Medical Relief Foundation has provided medical treatment and surgical procedures to thousands of indigent families and paupers from Kenton and throughout the world. Forrestal Education Foundation, established in 1892, has provided scholarships for hundreds of gifted students from numerous advanced schools throughout Kenton.

Ellen Forrestal died from injuries sustained after being thrown from a horse near her mansion in Riverdale.

Ellen Forrestal was a lifetime resident of Riverdale, in Kent county. Ellen is survived by her husband, Dr. Conrad Forrestal, and her son, Benjamin Walker.

Robert Bass, Esq., President of Forrestal Industries, will continue to preside over the activities of the Forrestal Industries and subsidiaries.

Graveside services will be held, as required by The Word, within seventy-two hours of her death at the Riverdale Cemetery on May third, at noon. Robert Bass shall read from The Word and eulogize the dearly departed.

The family has asked, in lieu of flowers or memorial gifts, please send donations to one of the many Forrestal philanthropic foundations.

Robert Bass stood outside Maxwell's Undertaking, waiting for Conrad and Elisabeth to arrive. Conrad and Elisabeth appeared in Conrad's carriage just before ten, progressing slowly up the street to where Robert was standing. Upon their arrival, Robert Bass helped Conrad down from the carriage and turned his attention to the most remarkable-looking Elisabeth Zurich. He froze in disbelief. Before his eyes, he saw a young woman with an eerie resemblance to his dead friend. The black-and-white photographs failed to capture the true similarity between the two women, the brilliant green eyes, the pure white skin, the subtle similarity in the bone structure of her face, and the raven-black hair. She was the perfect image of a younger Ellen. The thought flashed through his head how such a strange, freakish thing as this must have contributed to Ellen's apparent insanity.

After Elisabeth descended, Robert introduced himself. "I am Robert Bass, Benjamin's mother's legal counsel, business associate, and friend. I am sure you are Elisabeth Zurich."

"Yes, Mr. Bass. I am Elisabeth, Benjamin's companion. I am sorry we are meeting under such circumstances," Elisabeth returned, extending her hand.

Grasping Elisabeth's hand, Robert Bass said, "I am lost for words. We were so very close. I still can't believe she is gone."

"She died saving my life. How I wonder . . . . . .how will I be able to speak of this to Benjamin? Of his mother's death? He will arrive soon on the train from Londonderry. I, too, have a loss for words. I dread that moment."

Robert Bass put his hand on her tear-stained cheek and said, "Tell him the truth, and tell him you love him."

Elisabeth put her hand on his and said, "Thank you. I will do my best."

Robert walked to the undertakers' and opened the door so Ellen's grieving husband and Elisabeth could enter. Robert followed them. Mr. Maxwell stood silently in the display room as the three of them walked in. Elisabeth and Conrad walked past Mr. Maxwell, acknowledging his presence with a subdued gesture. Robert stopped next to him and retrieved the prepared obituary from his pocket: "Will you please have Ellen's obituary telegraphed to all the major newspapers in

Kenton?"

"Of course, Mr. Bass. I will send a runner immediately," Mr. Maxwell responded.

"Thank you," Robert said as he handed the document to the mortician and continued to the slumber room.

The sad trio walked past the numerous coffins, empty and waiting, and proceeded into the dark slumber room laced with the thick scent of flowers and incense. The necessary bouquets surrounded the coffin as required by custom: white lilies, carnations, chrysanthemums, red-and-black roses, and hundreds of rare black orchids. A faint wisp of incense climbed to the hidden gas lamps, which cast a golden glow on Ellen's peaceful remains.

When Conrad Forrestal saw his restored wife once again radiating in beauty, grief and agony overwhelmed him. His body shook. He placed his hand over his mouth to soften his uncontrolled sobbing. It was simply too difficult. After a moment, he walked closer to his wife until he stood next to her. How he wanted to hold her one last time, to touch her lips and hair, but he could not. He forced himself to accept the reality that his wife was no longer there. Her current touch would feel of wax and paint, cold and empty, an imperfect facsimile of the woman he loved. The undertaker had so skillfully weaved his magical spell and turned the carnage into the perfect illusion of his love, nothing more. Ellen's dead body was no longer intended for holding and caressing. Such things were for the living. Ellen's current state was but one last recognition before she was taken from him and all the others who knew and loved her. After a moment, he stepped back and sat in a nearby chair where Elisabeth did her best to comfort him as he continued to sob.

Always pursuing an intellectual assessment of all of life's struggles, Robert resolved to be stoic, most professional at this time of terrible discontent. There would be no more uncontrolled outbursts from him. That luxury was not his. He would remain steady for the others, for Conrad. So many things were expected of him at this horrible time. As he entered the darkened room and glimpsed his beloved Ellen lying in death, Robert's mind raced with uncontrollable thoughts.

I know the truth of this tragedy. She was not in her right mind. She became engulfed in a delusion. She was preoccupied with an obsession to bring monsters from across the sea to kill Benjamin's lovely companion. She only caused her own death. Is this not divine justice? Why did she fail to heed my advice? When have I ever failed her? She was so foolish, this woman with so many gifts relying on her darkest impulses for guidance. Reckless, madness, murder, she made her choices, her cozen act killed her. Still, Elisabeth's uncanny resemblance to Ellen, with all the unspoken and obvious connotations of incest and sexual deviance, may have been too much for her to cope with. Her son's sexual cravings for the image of his mother. . . . Madness consumed her. She was driven to madness. She was perhaps merely a victim of impossible circumstances. She was pushed over the edge by her love for her son. That was her only fault. That awful vision overwhelmed her reason, her son falling into absolute depravity. I loved her so. I must reconcile and accept that the love of my life is dead. What matter the antecedents? The end is the same. My love is the same. The end is the same. . . .

Robert could no longer control his demeanor and he succumbed to the endless depth of his loss. He sobbed in a manner he had not known or realized he was capable of—his moans were pure anguish. He staggered to a nearby chair, his legs unable to support his weight. As he stumbled, Elisabeth stood and grabbed his arm so he might not fall and guided him to a chair in the darkness. She sat next to Robert and handed him her handkerchief already moistened with a thousand tears.

Elisabeth put her arm around him. "We all so loved her. We will see her soon on the other side." Robert could merely nod in acknowledgment to the beautiful young woman beside him as he bent over his knees and cried. After a while, Elisabeth walked over and whispered into Conrad's ear,

"Now we must meet Benjamin and prepare him. His train will be arriving soon, and we must be there when he arrives."

Conrad pulled himself. "Yes, of course. We must now be there for Benjamin."

Conrad stood and took Elisabeth's arm. As they walked by Robert, Conrad leaned down and put his hand on Robert's back. "I must go to tell my son. Do you wish to come with us?"

Robert continued to sob, still bent over his knees. He raised his hand to Conrad's arm and shook his head as tears covered his face.

~

Conrad and Elisabeth walked through the train station's large swinging door and continued to the station master's office. He knocked on the office door, and Samuel Peterson, the station master, opened his door and greeted them.

"Dr. Forrestal, how good to see you. May I help you with any of your concerns?"

"Yes, Samuel. My son will be arriving soon, and I was hoping we might have a private room that I may speak to him," Dr. Forrestal explained.

Samuel Peterson's happy recognition turned drawn and pale, "Oh no, Dr. Forrestal, please tell me the rumors are not true."

"Mrs. Forrestal lost her life last night, Samuel. She is gone," a sober husband responded.

"I am so sorry. Such a wonderful person, of course, you can use my office. Oh, Dr. Forrestal, my deepest condolences," Samuel said while tapping his heart.

The sound of steam and the compression of steel on steel brought a deep vibration to the station, announcing the train's arrival from Londonderry. One of the ticket clerks yelled above the noise of the train, "Eleven o'clock train from Londonderry now arriving."

Then began the sounds of shuffling feet and the stir of anticipatory voices. The animated crowd pressed through the station door, spilling onto the platform outside the building. Conrad and Elisabeth flowed along with the pressing throngs with the resolve necessary for the terrible task required of them.

Outside on the station platform, Conrad and Elisabeth searched the many exiting passengers. After a short while, Elisabeth saw the man she so deeply loved carefully stepping down from the train car. Conrad and Elisabeth quickly approached Benjamin, who was surprised by their sudden appearance. "Father, Elisabeth, what a wonderful surprise! I am so happy to see both of you. Is mother here, as well?"

They were expressionless. Then Conrad spoke, "Please, Benjamin, will you come with me? I need to speak to you in private. I have arranged a place in the station so we might speak alone." Conrad took his son's arm, leading him through the crowds to the station master's office.

Benjamin was instantly alarmed by his father's unusual behavior, "What is it, father? Has something happened?" he asked, becoming increasingly anxious.

Conrad did not answer. Father and son entered the train station, walked across the waiting room, and into the station master's office.

"Elisabeth, what has happened? Has something happened to the baby?" Benjamin continued to ask as his father shut the door to the ruckus of the waiting room.

"Please sit down, Benjamin. I have the saddest of news. Your mother is dead." Benjamin's father said, taking his son's arm while helping him sit.

Benjamin attempted to grasp the meaning of the words. He had no emotion. Looking back and forth from his father to Elisabeth, Benjamin asked, "How did she die, father?"

Benjamin's father looked to Elisabeth, who sat down beside her loving companion, and Elisabeth said, "She died saving my life."

"Go on."

"Assassins from Kuttor followed me to your home, and when your mother realized the threat to the baby and me, she took my coat and road Fortune into the street, and they followed her and killed her, thinking they were taking my life," Elisabeth explained. "I am so sorry. . . . Benjamin, I love you so very much. I am so sorry."

Without expression, Benjamin put his hand on Elisabeth's soft cheek, "She would do anything for me, even sacrifice her life. She was a wonderful mother. How strange she is gone. Nothing will be the same now . . . nothing. I am sorry, father, for your loss."

Conrad recognized his son's state of shock—the flat voice, the pallor of his skin. "Your mother is at Maxwell's. We can go there so you may see her before the funeral."

"Father, I think I would like to remember her as she was in life. Those are the memories I want of her. Try and understand," Benjamin expressed his choice.

"Benjamin, at the funeral, the casket will be open. Many from all over the world will be coming to see her. You must prepare yourself. The funeral is not the time to look upon your mother the first time in death. This will be difficult. Please come with Elisabeth and me to see your mother. I think that would best," Conrad explained to his son.

"Please come with us, Benjamin. This is the time for you to be with her. Tomorrow, hundreds of people will be passing through the funeral home, and this is the time for you to see her in her final state," Elisabeth petitioned, holding Benjamin's hand.

"Of course. I know you are right. This will be so difficult."

"Yes, it will, Benjamin. Yes, it will," Elisabeth replied while she stood to help her love to his feet.

Benjamin walked into the dark slumber room, Elisabeth holding his arm. He did not see Robert Bass sitting in the chair and crying softly. He did not see the flowers or the dark drapes framing his mother's coffin. Benjamin did not smell the burning incense. He did not see anything except the frozen face of his mother. Benjamin walked to the edge of the coffin and looked down at his dead mother. He thought she appeared strangely unreal. She was frozen in time without the slightest suggestion of life. Benjamin had seen death, and he knew he would see death again. Still, how strange to see someone so dear in such a lifeless form.

Benjamin turned to look at Elisabeth. Tears had stained her eyes. He smiled at her, "She loved you so much. I wish there had been time enough for you to know her as I have. She would have done anything for us. She gave everything for us. The world will be different now. She was a wonderful mother."

"Yes, she was," Elisabeth lied.

At that point, Benjamin realized Robert Bass was sitting near, crying, overwhelmed with grief. Benjamin sat next to her mother's dearest friend. "Robert, I know this is difficult. I know she loved you so much. Please tell me you will be all right. I know mother would want you to continue with all the wonderful things you both put into motion. She will always be with us in our memories and spirit."

Robert straightened, wiped his tears and smiled at Benjamin. "Yes, it was the shock of seeing her. We have a great deal to do. I will always love your mother. I must accept she is gone. It is so difficult."

"Yes, my friend. Nothing will be the same. Life goes on. I know she would want us to continue her work. We will get through this."

With that said, Benjamin stood and looked at his father and asked, "Do you wish to stay longer, father?"

Conrad gazed one last time at his wife in death, then turned his attention to his son. "I think I am ready. I will see her again on the other side."

Benjamin took Elisabeth's arm. Robert stood and hugged Benjamin before walking over to Conrad and embracing him. He looked one last time at the woman he loved and said, "I think I am ready to leave."

They all left the house of death, and Conrad, Benjamin, and Elisabeth said their emotional farewells to Robert. They agreed to meet the next day, and with that said, they climbed into their carriages and rode away.

Elisabeth and Benjamin entered the Forrestal mansion, followed by Conrad. Benjamin went to speak to the servants so they might share their condolences. He then walked to the sofa in the formal sitting room. As Benjamin sat, his thoughts went back to when Petie stained the silk sofa with his garbage-covered clothing, and how his mother struggled to remove the stains. How he missed Petie. How he missed that time in his life. A time of exploration and wonder, a time of childhood when he was always happy— before Petie was stolen away. Now cruel fate has brought death to him once again.

"What manner of life is this to be so unkind to take the ones we hold most precious?" Benjamin whispered to himself.

He gazed through the front window, watching the passage of the elegant carriages carrying the most proper ladies and gentlemen of Riverdale. Riverdale carried on with life as if nothing extraordinary had happened. How strange, he thought, the normalcy just outside this window. The sun will continue to rise from the Eastern Sea. The forceful storm winds will forever torment the vast, ever-moving sea. He knew the world must follow destiny's course, but he was sure that he felt the world freeze on its axis for a fleeting instant. His mother's death was such a momentous loss. Benjamin continued to sit there among all the beautiful things of his home, emotionless.

After a while, he walked into the dining room where Elisabeth and his father were quietly talking. "I will be going down to the sea for a while. I think I just want to walk along the shore. Please excuse me. . I need to be alone."

"Of course, Benjamin," his father said, looking at his only son. "Take as much time as you need. We will be here when you return."

Benjamin walked through the mansion to the servant's porch. He opened the back door to the sea and disappeared.

Conrad leaned closer to Elisabeth to prevent the servants

from hearing what he was about to say: "I think Benjamin wants to be alone to express his grief in private. He could only express his deepest feelings to his mother. Try to determine if he has been crying. The release of emotions is an essential aspect of the healing process."

"I believe you are asking me to try and help Benjamin release his feelings so he can go on with life?" Elisabeth asked, struggling with the language.

"Yes, get him to show you what he is feeling."

"I will do my best, Dr. Forrestal."

"Thank you, Elisabeth, for being in my son's life."

After a few hours, Benjamin returned home. Both Elisabeth and his father could see he remained detached. When he spoke, his eyes seemed too focused, past the person he was speaking to. His expression continued to be flat. A light meal was prepared and consumed as the three of them spoke of loss and memories. After a while, Benjamin announced he would go to bed. Elisabeth watched him climb the stairs to his boyhood sleep room.

"How strange. Benjamin seems like a child. He did not mention returning to our home. What should I do?" Elisabeth asked a concerned father.

"Go to him. Comfort him. This is going to be a difficult night for him. He needs you to be with him. He is in shock. Help him grieve. I will have the maid go to your home and bring you several days of clothing, and I will have her take your horse and carriage over to the livery stable. If you need anything else, I will send the servant out to retrieve what you need," Conrad again spoke in whispers.

"I will need the most conservative black dress."

"Of course. I will have one of the servants purchase you a selection so you may choose the most appropriate garment."

"Thank you, Dr. Forrestal."

Elisabeth rose from the table and climbed the stairs before she disappeared into Benjamin's room. A worried father went into the sitting room and sat in solitude, truly alone. After a few hours, and to his relief, he could hear his son's deep sobs.

Listening to his tortured son releasing his anguish to his loving companion brought him a modicum of comfort, knowing his son was beginning the healing process. Within a few moments of listening to his son's pain, he was once again sobbing, alone.

～

The day of Ellen Forrestal's burial had arrived. Ellen's coffin was carefully slid into an elegant black hearse made with heavy beveled glass on the roof and all four carriage sides. The hearse was designed to allow the mourners to fully view the body as the deceased was being carried to the gravesite. The day of Ellen's burial was cloudless and bright. The warm sun-bathed Ellen's body with the beautiful brilliance of the living world. The highly polished mahogany coffin was surrounded by freshly-cut white lilies symbolizing purity and the fleeting moment of life. Without roots, the graceful lilies would shrivel, turn brown, and die before the next sunrise—their beauty being as ephemeral as each short life in the span of time. Two magnificent black geldings, each adorned with black plumage of ostrich, completed the presence of a most elegant funeral vehicle. Mr. Maxwell served as the teamster, and Robert Bass sat beside him, unable to walk the distance required by the funeral procession's plan route.

That morning on the third day of Ellen's death, Mr. Maxwell, with Robert Bass at his side, drove the hearse to the green meadow cemetery on the opposite side of Crescent Hill, where in life Ellen and Conrad began their walk together and read from The Word, sealing them for all eternity. Today Conrad would walk behind his wife and beside his son. On this the saddest of days, Ellen and Conrad would not climb to the top of the hill but continue to the cemetery. It was so different from years ago when happiness ruled the world, and dreadful sorrow was unknown by all those who gathered there.

Early that morning, the mourners began to arrive to say goodbye to the woman that had touched their lives in so many ways. They had journeyed by train from Londonderry and many other cities and towns of Kenton. They had come by ship from Newhopeland, Kuttor, and Liberty. Some arrived by carriage and others by horseback, and many who knew her best, her friends and neighbors from Riverdale, walked in solemn silence to the green meadow below Crescent Hill. At first, a few hundred mourners silently stood beside the grave; as the day progressed, the gathering turned to over five hundred, and then to nearly a thousand. At noon, Mr. Maxwell commanded the team of horses to pull the hearse toward the cemetery. The Advanced School orchestra began playing, "On Raven's Wing." As the hearse proceeded, those gathered separated to form an empty column in the crowd's center to allow the procession to pass. They were all there—Ellen's many employees from her various business interests; the boilermakers and the shipwrights, the teamsters and the farmers, the carpenters and the wheelwrights, the accountants and the lawyers, the railroad workers and longshoreman, the laborers and the managers of her many companies, and many more. All stood side by side, each tapping their hearts as the survivors walked past, joined by their collective grief.

In addition to her many employees and their families, the beneficiaries of Ellen's numerous charities were also present to look tearfully upon Ellen's remains; the many students she educated, the infirmed she made whole, the doctors she supported to heal the sick, the scientists she employed to explore the unknown, the destitute she clothed, fed, and sheltered. All were united by love, admiration, and gratitude, and all were pained with the abject sorrow of such a great woman's passing.

Conrad, Benjamin, and Elisabeth held each other's hands as they walked behind the hearse. Benjamin could see his mother lying in her coffin animated only by the uneven path and the horses' gait. He wished his mother's coffin were sealed, and he prayed this last memory would soon fade. Fate would not grant his desperate pleading. She belonged to so many who wished to see her one more time. How could he deny them? Benjamin must control his feelings on this day of his mother's burial. He must suppress them for now. Benjamin was grateful for his father's advice about the importance of visiting his mother's remains before the funeral. To see her in death for the first time during this procession would have provoked an unrestrained outpouring of grief. Today he had to be strong for his father, who stood beside him, handkerchief in hand, wiping his eyes and gasping for air. Benjamin would confine his persistent grief to be expressed at a future time in solitude. This was a day for unselfish strength and devotion to his father.

Conrad's mind raced with a thousand intimate memories of his dear wife. He could see her as a young woman on his examining table when he first started practicing medicine. He recalled how she fought the darkness of melancholia, and how she mourned when he had told her of her husband's death. How beautiful she looked when she recovered from depression in the hospital. He remembered how he felt when he first fell in love with his dear wife, how complete and happy he felt when they first made love, and how their passion continued to grow until the last day of her life. So many memories of the most wonderful companion and wife a man might realize. These were the thoughts of a grieving husband on this, the saddest of all days.

Elisabeth was sorrowful about her lover's loss. She would be there for him. She had no delusions about the corpse that lay before her. Ellen may have been a genius of commerce and industry, even generous to the unfortunate, but beneath the sanguine façade, a restless monster roamed, malevolent and predacious. If not for the joy of an expecting mother compelled to share the news of new life, Elisabeth knew that she would have been the subject of the mortician's artistry. Elisabeth would play the part of a grieving companion to Ellen's son. Still, she would always know that his mother was so possessive of her son's love that she would kill to be the solitary focus of his attention. Elisabeth wished she could stand before the gathering crowd and eulogize this dead person as the grotesque fiend she truly was, a sad being without conscience or moral direction. Of course, such a thing was impossible, and Elisabeth would hide this dark reality and continue the fiction of adoration for Benjamin's mother. How she hoped the Raven would falter lifting such a heavy heart.

The hearse reached the bottom of Crescent Hill, and the teamster directed the horses to the cemetery. When the procession reached Ellen's final resting place, the horses stopped, and Robert Bass and Mr. Maxwell climbed from the carriage. As planned, Mr. Maxwell, Robert Bass, Conrad, Benjamin, and Jeffery Porter, who had walked directly behind Benjamin, pulled the coffin from the hearse and carried Ellen's remains to her prepared grave. A catafalque, draped in dark maroon velvet, suspended the coffin above the open ground. Several oak chairs designated for the immediate family sat a few feet from the grave. When the orchestra had completed the musical score, the mourners gathered around the grave. The entire world was still, save the soft sounds of whimpering. Mr. Maxwell approached a temporary wooden stage and walked up the steps. Standing above all who had gathered, he announced in his loudest voice, "Robert Bass, Ellen Forrestal's legal counsel, business partner, and a dearest friend, will say a few words of remembrance for the dearly departed and read from The Word."

Robert Bass presented the stoic image of a refined man of means. The crowd remained quiet as Robert Bass walked to the wooden stage, and climbed with some effort to the small platform from which he would say his remarks. Robert Bass stood in silence, looking across the sea of mourners standing among the rows of the dead. When the time was right, he began his eulogy.

"No sadder day can there be when life is gone, and only the still body remains, soon hidden from our view as corruption steals even that final form from the living. So, we write upon the headstone a heartfelt epitaph, enduring and concise, so in future times someone might stroll among the dead, read that brief testimony, and glimpse the grandeur of a life that is no more.

"We need not reside here among the dead. We need not read the epitaph upon the stone. No chiseled words will reveal the magnitude of the person we lay to rest on this very day. If you wish to read the epitaph of Ellen Forrestal, look no further than the faces you see among you today. They bear the countenance of reverence, respect, and even awe to have been touched by a person of such great intellect, compassion, and with the fortitude and spirit of a vast undefeated legion of angels. Ellen Forrestal was all of these things, and you bear witness to that truth. You are all the beneficiary of this woman's presence.

"How many of you have been healed by the medical institutions and the medical research she funded? How many of you craved knowledge and were educated by the scholarships she provided? How many of you were starved, naked, and homeless when she reached out to you and offered you nourishment and respect? How many of you have gained wealth by the commerce and industry she created? How many of you are gainfully employed by the opportunities she offered? You all stand witness to the answers to those questions.

"I met Ellen Forrestal several weeks after she gave birth to her first and only child, Benjamin. Her loving husband, James Walker, was taken in death the same day her child was born. Ellen Forrestal had only the most basic education. Her only work experience was a brief internship as a baker's apprentice. However, her thoughtful husband secured an accidental death insurance policy so she would have the means to survive and raise her newborn in his absence. The first thing Ellen Forrestal did with the proceeds of that policy was to donate a portion to the Riverdale Hospital. Before she invested a dime of the money she received from her husband's death, she reached out to help others. That was the heart and soul of Ellen Forrestal.

"In all the years since her first husband died, Ellen

demonstrated a rare insight for business and commerce, a true heaven-born entrepreneurial genius. When fate took our beloved Ellen from our lives, she was one the most successful and powerful individuals in the world. She built railroads and made them efficient and profitable. She owned a fleet of merchant ships carrying products manufactured and grown in her many industries and farms. She developed rich petroleum fields so we would have kerosene to bring light to the darkness, and iron mines to make steel for train rails, rims to encircle the wagon wheel, and nails by which to mend and construct our homes. The reach of her business empire is so comprehensive you cannot eat a meal, build a home, rent a room, ride in a carriage, cash a cheque, or sail upon the Eastern Sea and not be touched by Forrestal Industries. This, too, is the final epitaph of Ellen Forrestal. As the years pass and we also are condemned to the grave and forgotten through time, our survivors for the next thousand years will speak of Ellen Forrestal with the same reverence as we do today. Such is the enduring stature of Ellen Forrestal. The epitaph chiseled on her headstone will shake the world."

The crowd returned, "She will be missed," as was the custom.

Robert Bass then opened The Word and read what must be said: "O' sacred dead; we place you now in hallowed soil so your worldly substance may find peaceful sleep while your blessed spirit soars on Raven's wing."

Many in the crowd knew the passage by heart and spoke the words as Robert Bass read them: "We will wait here awhile longer among the stars and stones of this, the living realm, and mourn as we speak of you with reverence and hushed tones."

Elisabeth listened carefully to the words. The passage was new to her, and this simple lament of loss held such elegant meaning.

"Be not troubled on this your burial day when we shall weep; true, we weep that we may no longer embrace you or share our mutual burdens and joys. Please also know we weep with elation, knowing you now roam the dominion of the afterlife where pain and corruption is no more, and unlimited wisdom and knowledge is the norm."

When Benjamin heard the meaningful words, he broke. He released a mournful cry before regaining his composure.

"We accept the sanctity of fate, so we shall wait for that fateful day when we too shall soar on Raven's wing and meet again at heaven's gate."

The crowd returned, "On Raven's Wing."

When Robert Bass completed his last farewell to the woman he loved, he returned to his seat and cried again at the loss of his dear Ellen. His eyes would fill with tears many times in the years to come. He so loved Ellen.

Now those gathered, who wished to look upon the dead, formed a long queue, a cavalcade of mourners sharing the anguish of loss. Conrad, Benjamin, Elisabeth, and Robert Bass sat in solemn silence as each present walked by the open coffin, tapping their hearts, to look upon Ellen Forrestal one last time. The procession of grievers began shortly after one in the afternoon and continued for hours. Many of the mourners who noticed Elisabeth sitting next to Benjamin were both shocked and confused by the similarity of Elisabeth's appearance to that of the deceased, uncomfortable murmurs rustled through the crowd. Some speculated that she was surely Benjamin's unknown sister or cousin. Most that noticed her were merely confused.

The survivors patiently waited while the sun slipped below the horizon, and large kerosene lamps were provided to illuminate Ellen's body. When the hour of her burial grew near, Mr. Maxwell announced that the seventy-second hour had come. It was time to bury the body. The mourners knew the instructions of The Word in such matters and offered no protest.

Conrad, Benjamin, Robert Bass, and Jeffery Porter picked up the heavy muslin belt placed under the coffin. Mr. Maxwell secured the lid to the coffin and covered Ellen's remains. The belts held tight while they pulled the boards from beneath the coffin and lowered it into her grave as required by The Word. Conrad grasped a handful of soil and tossed the dirt onto the coffin. With that last gesture, the funeral came to an end. The headstone read simply: Ellen Joy Forrestal.

The Raven soared high above the world. Pressed under the majestic bird's black-feathered breast, Ellen Forrestal was held fast by the eternal being's powerful talons. The entire world was in her sight, and she felt honored by the multitude present at her funeral. She could hear the sadness of their thoughts and feel their deep pain. She listened to her closest and dearly-loved friend's kind and moving words as he spoke. She felt Elisabeth's understandable contempt. She could see and feel her son, so burdened by her death, and she felt pride knowing he was doing his best to provide strength and sustenance to his grieving father. She listened to Conrad's mournful prayers and felt the dark abyss within him caused by her absence. She felt his deep eternal love for her.

The Raven flew higher now. As Ellen approached the afterlife, clarity enlightened her mind. She was no longer blind—the veil was gone and the mystery was no more. All the questions were answered, and in that moment of overpowering lucidity, she could see the burden that would be placed on her only son. How he would suffer and falter, and how he would be sacrificed and ransomed, and how he was so very necessary. And as Ellen looked for the last time upon her son, she was permitted to shed a single tear so Benjamin would know she was still very much alive in the next realm, and all things were in proper order.

The tear rolled down Ellen's cheek and fell to the world. As the tear fell, it split into two tears, then four, and so on until the tears had become a gentle rain.

Many of the mourners did not notice the warm rain in their grief. Others thought it strange, rain falling from a cloudless sky. Benjamin held out his hand, but the rain refused to pool or moisten his palm. "How strange," Elisabeth said to Benjamin as she noticed her hair and clothing remained dry after several minutes of mild rain.

"What does it mean?" Elisabeth asked Benjamin, utterly confused by the strangeness of it.

After a moment of reflection, Benjamin put his arm around Elisabeth, and kissed her cheek, "These are mother's tears. She is telling us all is well."

Ellen now turned her eyes to the multitude. The Raven flew higher and faster. Ellen noticed the stars on the edge of her vision began to migrate toward the center, the point of her destination. All the light of the universe lay before her. She could feel the glow of heaven. Absolute love enveloped her being. Just as Ellen was about to enter the radiant glory, she heard those beautiful, soft words, "Coaling, coaling."

"James!"

Chapter 19
Brightmont

Spring grass now covered the wound in the soil at Riverdale Cemetery. Conrad was in the painful process of healing. His professional focus soon dominated his life, a welcome escape from his persistent grief. At Conrad's request, Elisabeth and Benjamin were now living in the Forrestal mansion, only to visit their home above the butcher shop on those rare occasions when the young couple desired complete privacy. Benjamin had completed the necessary licensure requirements and had earned his tenure as a member of the Certified Public Accountant Association. His mother's obsession with her son's necessity to be well-schooled in business law and accounting was clearly shown to be correct and essential. Benjamin spent many hours with Robert Bass attempting to comprehend the financial complexity of Forrestal Industries. With his mother's death, Benjamin Walker was now the chairman and chief operating officer of Forrestal Industries, a daunting and ominous responsibility for anyone.

~

One afternoon, in the company of Robert while reviewing fiscal reports for the Forrestal Shipping and Transport Company, Benjamin asked a question that had been lingering in his head for quite some time. "Robert, I have been a bit preoccupied about the strange events surrounding my mother's death. I wondered if you wouldn't mind taking a break from all of this and giving me your thoughts on a few unresolved issues I have?"

"What are your concerns, Benjamin?" Robert asked, dreading the conversation he knew was to follow.

"Well, I know my mother was very protective of me, and I am sure she would have had Elisabeth thoroughly investigated. I mean, Robert, I knew that she would do something, and I would deeply appreciate you sharing your findings with me," Benjamin asked, looking directly at Robert. Robert Bass's response, among other things, would help Benjamin have a better understanding of the man his mother was so close to. A man she explicitly trusted.

Without hesitation, Robert responded without the slightest expression of discomfort, "Of course. Your mother did a thorough investigation of Elisabeth. You were the son of one of the most affluent families in Kenton. Your mother was unable to keep her identity confidential after so much of her assets went public. She fully realized the family would be vulnerable because of her status. She often told me how important it was to have her business activities kept secret so you might have a normal life. Yes, she knew everything about Elisabeth after the third week of your relationship."

"I hope you will not feel awkward about sharing your findings with me?" Benjamin pushed.

"Not at all. As you may imagine, you have extensive resources available to investigate anyone or anything. Yes, I prepared a dossier for your mother on Anjum Izdubar—Elisabeth Zurich."

"May I see the file, please?" Benjamin continued to press.

"The dossier was given to your mother, but I recall most of it. What would you like to know?"

"I went through all my mother's files at home. I didn't find anything concerning Elisabeth. I wondered what she did with your findings. I certainly want any private information on Elisabeth to be kept confidential. I am genuinely concerned about the whole situation," Benjamin stated with some irritation in his voice.

"Of course, your mother took the only copy. I am sorry. I am sure you will find the dossier somewhere in your mother's things at home." Robert hoped Benjamin would end his inquiry with this simple explanation.

"Well, I will ask father for his assistance. Perhaps he knows of it. I would appreciate it if you would review the investigation findings with me," a determined Benjamin continued.

"Frankly, I was impressed with the young woman you had chosen to be your companion. I think you know she is the only child of one of the few affluent families in her country. Her mother died in childbirth, and her father raised her with a servant that spoke our language so she could be educated in Liberty and Kenton. Being educated put her at some risk, as you know, because a female becoming educated is considered an anathema to that culture's spiritual beliefs," Robert Bass explained.

"Yes," Benjamin replied, "she told me within the first hour of our first date there would always be a threat that she might be forced back to Kuttor or worse. She told me all about her country and how her father bribed the right people for her to escape that misogynist culture."

"That's right," Robert Bass said with an uplifting tone. "Did she tell you she was independently wealthy with over two hundred thousand dollars in several bank accounts in her name in Kenton?"

"No, she didn't. Where did she get her money—from her father?" Benjamin asked.

"Yes, he has been saving money for her all her life," Robert Bass returned.

"Oh, Robert, has her father been contacted so he will know she is all right? I completely forgot. Is there a problem letting him know?" Benjamin asked, concerned.

"I informed him within an hour after I was told of your mother's death. He was contacted by one of our confidential agents in Kuttor. Elisabeth also wrote a letter to her father as well, expressing her sadness over your mother's death," Robert Bass reassured Benjamin.

"Thank you, Robert. Elisabeth didn't tell me she had any individual financial assets."

Robert Bass smiled. "Well, your mother didn't tell your

father of her wealth until their wedding night, so you better look surprised, or she will think you were investigating her."

Benjamin knew his Elisabeth well. "She is a brilliant woman. I am sure she fully realizes mother would have to check up on her."

"Look surprised!" Robert Bass insisted.

Benjamin smiled. "All right, what else did you find?"

"I am not sure you will want to know about her previous relationships," Robert said with some hesitation. "She told me she had been with other men, and I am sure she was not involved with anyone when I met her."

Benjamin realized Elisabeth would be horrified if Ellen had known her sexual history.

"Well, then that is about it. Elisabeth did not have any other issues. The worst thing was the threat that the bribed religious leaders might change their mind."

Robert Bass could no longer look directly at Benjamin.

"It would seem they did change their minds," Benjamin stated, looking for Robert's reaction.

"There was nothing in the investigation to suggest why things might have changed in Kuttor. Try and remember Elisabeth and her father were dealing with insane people obsessed with religious dogma. Anything could have changed their minds. A new leader could have changed the rules, or a bribe was lost or embezzled."

Robert Bass began to weave a lie.

"Or perhaps," Benjamin interjected, "my mother bribed the Locks to have Elisabeth killed. I think Elisabeth is keeping things from me. It is obvious, Robert. Both of you are trying to spare me some terrible truth. This horrible suspicion haunts me, and I cannot suppress my doubts. It's like a dark cloud hanging over me—I must know, Robert. I am sorry to put you in this position. You were mother's closest friend, and I think she would have been compelled to discuss any such plan.

"Why, on that night for instance, the night my mother asked Elisabeth over for dinner? Did the religious fanatics follow her to the mansion to kill her? I think they would have waited until she was alone. Elisabeth told me she informed mother that she was carrying her grandchild just before the assassins arrived. I think she told me that to comfort me, knowing mother knew she had a grandchild before she died. Something like that would have changed my mother's plan to kill the woman I loved. Why would my mother want to kill her, Robert? My mother would have to be possessive to the point of insanity, or maybe there was something else she knew.

"Robert, I think my mother killed Jonnie York, as well. I told her I was afraid he would hurt me after father killed Jonnie's father. She told me she would never allow him to hurt me, and a few weeks later, he was dead. I think my mother would kill anyone who she believed might be a threat. Why did my mother think Elisabeth was a threat? Or was she just insane? I want you to tell me the truth, Robert. Elisabeth knows the truth. I can feel it. I think you know the truth, as well."

Robert Bass dreaded this inevitable conversation. He sat quietly, looking at Benjamin. He could not avoid Benjamin's questions and still have a working relationship with the young man without telling him what he knew. Robert began, "I think your mother was having some form of psychiatric breakdown. We both know your mother was receiving medications for her melancholia for years. I think, and I don't know, but I think when she met Elisabeth for the first time, when she saw her and realized she looked like her younger self, well, your mother couldn't mentally handle it. Benjamin, I am sorry, but I do think your mother was more mentally ill than we previously thought."

"Handle what? That I had a friend that looked like my mother twenty years ago?" Benjamin was becoming increasingly angry.

"Well, your mother may have thought she was being replaced with her younger self, and then there was also the notion of . . . well, incest . . ." Robert suggested, his voice tapering as if it were difficult to speak of the unspeakable.

Benjamin stared at Robert in disbelief of what he was hearing. "Incest . . . I thought Elisabeth reminded me of my mother for the first few seconds after I met her until she opened her mouth, and she was a totally different person from my mother. The resemblance was superficial. I never thought of her as my mother. That is crazy. Did mother say anything like that?"

"No, Benjamin. No. I am trying to understand why she may have had some kind of psychotic break."

Robert Bass was now stressed and sweating.

"I think she thought you were attracted to Elisabeth because Elisabeth looked like her. What else can explain the way she reacted when she first met Elisabeth?"

"You mean when she fainted. She said her blood sugar was low because she hadn't eaten that morning, and after some orange juice and bread, she felt fine!"

"Her explanation to me was somewhat different. . . . When she touched Elisabeth's hand, Benjamin, your mother told me she was transported to a desolate, dark world where she was surrounded by death. At her feet, she found the corpse of the Raven. She then heard your cries as you were about to be swept to your death into a bottomless abyss. She reached to save you, but your Elisabeth mystically appeared and grabbed her hand away, and you were killed. She was obsessed with this vision. She considered it a premonition. Your mother was afraid Elisabeth was going to somehow, well, destroy you. When I last saw your mother a few weeks before she was killed, she appeared gaunt and pale. She spoke to your father concerning her fears, and he also tried to explain she was having some kind of reaction to meeting Elisabeth. I told her I would have no part of what she was planning to do."

"Planning to do what? Robert!" Benjamin was now feeling disgusted at the man he had known and loved his entire life.

"She wanted to contact the Locks and use the information

from the investigation to have Elisabeth killed," Robert admitted in a quiet voice.

"Why didn't you tell someone if you thought she was going insane for whatever the reason, and she had a plan to kill my companion? Why didn't you tell father? Why didn't you do something?" Benjamin's voice elevated.

"I loved your mother, and I was blindly loyal to her. I didn't think she would actually kill Elisabeth—I told myself I was professionally bound to protect the confidentiality of our conversation. I don't know, I might have been able to save her. I think she was insane with fear for your safety," Robert struggled to explain his behavior.

Benjamin took a moment before he reacted to Robert's confession. "I have studied the confidentiality laws between client and professional. You had a duty to warn! I think it could be argued you were complicit in my mother's attempt to kill my companion. I think your actions in this matter are reprehensible."

"Yes," Robert replied.

The two men sat in silence, and then Robert continued: "I will review with you all relevant information concerning the many aspects of Forrestal Industries. I will introduce you to all the directors and the managers of the various businesses, and then I will sever all my ties to your company. I can recommend several excellent counselors—"

"No, Robert," Benjamin interrupted, "I can trust no one but you with my business. I think there are forces at work you are not able to understand. My judgment of you was intemperate and unfair. Please excuse my outburst."

Benjamin was increasingly aware of something evil now touching everyone in his life. His mother's actions were beyond her control. His mother's behavior and eventual death mirrored his experience at Jeffery Porter's warehouse. These dark forces, the antecedent to Robert Bass's compromised judgment, had influenced his decision. He would not speak of this to Robert Bass.

"No, Benjamin, I should have stopped her. I cannot think

of a circumstance when your mother and I disagreed until she foisted this terrible plan on me. I was weak. What I did was criminal."

Guilt infused Robert Bass's every word.

"No, Robert, I understand. I want you to promise me—in the years to come, if I ask you to do something you feel is wrong concerning any matter, I want you to stop me. Do what you must to convince me. If I should become ill or addled, please tell my father. Try and stop me if I do anything inconsistent with how you know me. Will you promise me, Robert?" Benjamin said, concealing his growing apprehension.

"On Raven's wing, I do so promise," he swore, confused as to what Benjamin had asked of him, but determined to honor his request.

Benjamin chose his next words carefully. "I think there is more to all this. I need some time . . . to give it some thought. I need to talk to my father, and I will share my thoughts with you at a future time. This is a difficult thing to discuss. So please accept what I am telling you. I don't hold you in any way responsible for my mother's actions and death. I need you, and I trust you."

Thinking he may have said too much, Benjamin pivoted, "We must go on from here. I know my mother could be very overpowering. I didn't realize her health was deteriorating. I was so consumed in my world. I should have been there for her. I should have known. She was my mother, and I ignored her when she needed me. I share a part in all of this."

Robert Bass did not respond at first, still confused by Benjamin's earlier statement. "I shall wait until that future time. Thank you, Benjamin. Please do not place such a burden on yourself—this is a special time in your life. Your focus was that of a young man in love. In retrospect, I should have been more proactive, and I will live with that truth until I die."

"Let us agree, Robert. We will go on from here. We have much to do. We must remain focused on those things we find ourselves about," Benjamin said, motioning to the ledgers between them. After a moment, Benjamin reached across the table and put his hand on Robert's as a show of acceptance.

"Thank you, Benjamin. Thank you."

Benjamin rubbed his fingers over the polished walnut dining table. He wondered who felled the giant tree that once reached for the sun and lived in a forest full of life. Benjamin thought, how many years did the tree live, only to be sacrificed in an afternoon, the remains of that fine perennial cut and hammered into furniture? Trees are without reason or pain, mere objects to be offered for our fixation of all things beautiful and useful, or perhaps we just cannot hear the cries of the trees we harvest, and with greater clarity, we would know the screams of their suffering.

We harvest all things we deem useful to our plan. What unknown meaning is such a life as mine? What higher plan must I fulfill, unrealized, both resplendent and frightening? Will I fall in some strange forest? Will I be cut and nailed by some unseen force? This curse that came upon me from that dark room, from an ancient carpet weaved with threads of pure evil, will cut down, I fear, everything I love. Mother was a sacrifice. Her madness brought upon her from the same evil kiss. Will I and all I love drink from the same cup of poison?

A little past ten in the morning, Benjamin's increasingly fearful thoughts were interrupted as he heard the lock releasing the front door, and the sound of his father as he entered the mansion.

"Father, I am so glad to see you. May I have a few minutes of your time? I know you are most likely exhausted from your labors at the hospital, so I will be brief. I had the servants prepare some breakfast if you should so desire," Benjamin said, rising from his seat and motioning with his hand at several covered serving trays sitting on the dining table.

"Thank you, Benjamin. I would love to have a word with you. Why warming trays? Are the servants away?"

Day K Altair

"Yes," Benjamin said, "they are accompanying Elisabeth. She is looking for baby things in town so everything will be ready when the child is born. I hope you don't mind. She has selected one of the spare sleep rooms for the baby's nursery."

"Not at all—the sound of new life is exactly what is called for in this old mansion. What is it you wish to speak of Benjamin?" Conrad asked, selecting a plate and a piece of pheasant breast and stuffing before sitting across from his son.

"I wonder if enough time has passed for me to broach some questions concerning mother's death," Benjamin asked with a hesitant tone, hoping his father would be receptive to his troubling inquiries.

Conrad hesitated. He took his knife and cut off a piece of pheasant and put the meat in his mouth. He poured red wine into an empty goblet, took a drink, looked at his son and replied, "I think this is the time for us to have this conversation. You are troubled about the unsettling circumstances of your mother's death, yes?"

"Yes, father. I must know why mother wanted to kill Elisabeth." The statement was blunt.

"I don't want to think that. Such a thing is difficult to consider. I, too, have had similar thoughts. Why do you frame your question in such a manner? You seem so sure," Benjamin's father said quietly.

"Robert told me mother came to him with some kind of vision that Elisabeth presented a danger to me. She asked him to contact the religious leaders in Kuttor to bribe them to declare Elisabeth an apostate so she would be put to death," Benjamin stated without emotion.

Conrad stared at his plate, pushing his food into little piles. His hunger evaporated. "I see. What did Robert do?"

"He told me he refused to be involved with such a thing, and he hoped she would not go through with it. I believed she used her resources in Kuttor to have the assassins sent to Riverdale. I fear she lured Elisabeth to dinner under the guise of amity to make Elisabeth accessible. I think when Elisabeth told her she was pregnant, she could not kill her grandchild. Mother could not complete her deadly scheme. So, she rode into the night so Elisabeth might live. Elisabeth has not said a word to me, but I know she is not telling the entire truth about what happened that night."

Conrad chose his words carefully. "Several months ago, I received a diagnostic manual of mental disorders, deciphered and translated from The Word. The Supplicant members have honored me with such a gift of knowledge from Oceania. This manual has greatly expanded my understanding of abnormal mental processing. I learned a great deal after reviewing the comprehensive manual. Your mother suffered from severe depression for many years. Her treatment was seemingly successful with lithium. However, some forms of mental illness can have both a symptom of depression and delusions. Your mother may have had some type of a mental break-down, and Elisabeth was the focus of her delusions. This kind of thing is exceedingly difficult to understand. Mental hygiene on this level of sophistication is so new."

"I don't understand. I do not recall a single moment when mother lacked lucidity. I know she took the potions you gave her every day. I do not remember seeing her depressed, and now I am being told she instantly became insane when she met Elisabeth? Is this what your manual is telling you?" Benjamin was skeptical.

Conrad gathered his thoughts and continued, "This is not a new idea. The information from Oceania is more refined and organized, but I know from my practice such a thing can happen. I have seen it. Your mother was under tremendous stress managing her various business interests. I think your maturity and growing independence was also a difficult transition for her. Meeting Elisabeth was the last antecedent necessary for the delusional process to emerge.

"As you know, your mother fainted when she first met Elisabeth. When I took her upstairs, she told me of a terrible vision or premonition of you falling to your death, and when she attempted to save you, Elisabeth appeared and stopped her, and you were lost. She promised me she would not act on her fears until we had a better understanding of the things she experienced. She may have never intended to keep our agreement. I am not sure. I may be wrong. . . . I am not sure of anything."

Benjamin was trying to understand what his father was telling him. "Did you see anything that made you think mother lacked sanity or appeared addled before she met Elisabeth and fainted?"

"No, nothing at all. After meeting Elisabeth, however, she appeared to weaken. She grew increasingly secretive and withdrawn. She lost her appetite and refused many meals. Toward the end, she appeared to suffer a great deal. She refused to speak of her burden. Her physical appearance seemed to decompensate."

Benjamin's father's voice softened with each word he shared with his son.

"Oh, father, forgive me. I was preoccupied with work and Elisabeth. I did not know. How could I not have known?" Benjamin reached for his father's hand.

Conrad reassured him. "Benjamin, you were preoccupied, and you were not living at home. You were starting a new life with someone you love. You were consumed with your mother's businesses. Please do not blame yourself in any way."

"Thank you, father, for those kind words," Benjamin said, welcoming the reassurance. Still, he felt he had walled his mother off from his life when she needed him. "Was there anything you could do to help her?"

Conrad continued, "I gave her some new medications to help her with the delusions. I was unable to assess the effectiveness of the medication. She never spoke to me again about the things she experienced when she met Elisabeth. She refused to talk to me about her feelings and thoughts. She withdrew. Her mind was not her own. It was a mental break."

"Father, you are an expert on mental hygiene. You have been blessed with knowledge from Oceania, so your explanation of mother's behavior would logically be drawn from your knowledge and discipline. You could not accept a different explanation, I think, and please forgive me, your mind was not open. I think there was something else going on," Benjamin challenged.

"How can you be so sure?" Conrad asked, though he knew the answer.

"Father, I still suffer from the old wound I told you of. The injury has never healed. The pain persists. It is always with me like a shadow. What I conveyed to you when you visited me at Jeffery's warehouse remains with me today," Benjamin sat back on his chair, rubbing the hand that was touched by the monster, hoping his father would accept what he was going to say.

"You are speaking of the curse—the talisman woven in the afterlife?" Benjamin's father asked, increasingly anxious.

"Yes, father. The terrible curse I brought into this home. Mother functioned so well. She was a genius in business. I have spent weeks trying to understand the complex organization she created, an extremely successful organization. Robert Bass never perceived any muddled thought in mother's mind or her actions except for her obsession with Elisabeth at the end of her life. He thought the similarity in Elisabeth and mother's appearance had sinister incestuous connotations that drove mother insane—to murder." Benjamin said with an increasingly pressured tone.

Conrad stared at Benjamin. "Is that what he told you? Did your mother ever say such a bizarre thing to him?"

"No, he came up with this on his own after meeting Elisabeth and attempting to understand mother's actions. His theory was mother was driven to madness after meeting Elisabeth because she thought I was attracted to Elisabeth by incestuous desires."

"Well, Benjamin, Robert Bass is an excellent lawyer. I would and have trusted him with my life. He knows the law. I suspect his knowledge of human behavior is somewhat lacking, however," Benjamin's father said while shaking his head.

"He was mistaken," Benjamin agreed.

"I would say he was very wrong, and his thesis had more to do with his feelings for your mother. I trust you did not take any of Robert's speculations seriously?"

"I told him the similarities between mother and Elisabeth were superficial—that their personalities were very different—and such a thought never crossed my mind."

"I don't want you to think you had anything to do with your mother's behavior or death. Your mother was an extraordinarily complex and brilliant person. She had a history of mental illness, and that was the fault that destroyed her life. She was suffering from some form of paranoid delusion, that is all!" Conrad repeated his conclusions in a most authoritative voice.

"But," Benjamin finally stated, "I think my mother was driven into insanity by that thing at Jeffery Porter's warehouse."

Conrad quietly stared for a moment at his only son and took a deep breath, "I respect your opinion. At this point, we cannot be sure. The key remains around my neck. If you are correct, and this is a well-orchestrated plot to destroy you and me and the other members of our family and the members of our organization—well, at some point, such a thing will become obvious, and I will not hesitate to destroy the talisman. I believe in you, and if you tell me you can feel that thing within you, especially after everything that has happened, I believe you," Conrad affirmed.

"Thank you, father. I believe mother was a victim of forces beyond this world. I pray I am wrong. The coincidence of Mr. Porter's tale is simply too great to be dismissed. I trust your judgment, father. You will know what the truth is when the time comes."

Benjamin now spoke in quiet tones: "It is of the strangest of coincidences that I, too, fainted and felt haunted when I looked upon that carpet from Kuttor. I was not meant to hear Jeffery Porter's tale of secret societies and evil plots. Now you know, too. Did I put you at risk? I am afraid these evil forces will drive me insane and destroy everyone I love. I was not meant to know about the purpose of that carpet. It would seem I was meant to be destroyed by it. Why was I claimed for this purpose? Will I have the strength when the time comes, or have I lost my will to that thing? I fear I am too weak. Will I be deceived by that thing and abandon what I have to do? How can I be sure? Father, am I going insane? You are my only hope." Benjamin confessed what he increasingly feared was true.

Conrad thoughtfully responded, "No, you are not insane. I cannot explain the plan for us in this world. If coincidence and mental illness can explain all of this, we must accept it. If we are caught up in something else . . . we shall act our parts."

They grew quiet. Benjamin's father continued pushing his food into piles, filled his fork, and took another bite of food followed by several swallows of wine. "All of this has made continuing on with plans for both Elisabeth and you concerning your attendance at the university unlikely this year."

"Yes, father."

Benjamin's father paused before starting the next subject with his son: "Benjamin, there is another topic I think we should discuss concerning your plans with Elisabeth."

"Yes?"

"Well, under normal circumstances, I know you would have sealed your relationship with Elisabeth. With your mother's death, I know in some ways it would be considered too soon."

"I know. With mother's death, my attentions have been drawn to mother's various businesses. I lost track of time," Benjamin welcomed his father's advice with some relief.

Benjamin's mind filled with the ramification of what he was about to say, "I understand, of course, I will ask Elisabeth to seal our relationship as soon as practical."

"Elisabeth is visibly pregnant. The delay is not fair to her. The people of Riverdale have become somewhat hostile and very judgmental of us because of who we are. There is an expectation a young man will wed the woman in such a condition," Benjamin's father advised. "Everyone in town will be talking now that Elisabeth is shopping for baby things, and, well, you understand what I am saying."

"Of course, father. Thank you for being so considerate of our situation. I will ask Elisabeth over dinner tonight. I think I will take her to the Commerce Eatery where our relationship began," Benjamin said with a serious expression on his face, "I think a small, informal wedding. I think that would be best."

"That's a wonderful idea."

Riverdale Sentinel — Societal Beacon
The Sealing of
Elisabeth Zurich to Benjamin Walker

Be it known with great delight that the sealing of the fair lady Elisabeth Zurich of Kuttor to Benjamin Walker of Riverdale has occurred with an abundance of felicity and the ambiance of most splendid joy, at the mansion of Robert Bass, also of Riverdale.

The wedding was a private affair attended only by immediate family members, friends, and business acquaintances. Of special mention, Diya Izdubar of Kuttor, father of the bride, was present to wish his only child a blissful and fruitful marriage.

The wedding march began promptly at 10:30 in the morning on October 29, with accompanying music provided by members of the Riverdale Advanced School Orchestra playing "Ascension."

The bride wore a sky-blue charmeuse silk flock, floor-length with a side slit to the waist with petite gold mesh weaved in the revealing gap, which permitted an ample view of the betrothed's leg. An exquisite cream tulle, enhanced the gown with embroidered, delicate, three-dimensional flowers with matching hair ribbon, creating a subtle theme of a summer flower garden. The dress was explicitly designed for lady Elisabeth Zurich by famed gown designer Samuel Satine of Londonderry.

The bride and groom walked the mansion's great room with hands outstretched, holding a red-covered copy of The Word for the bride and a white covered copy of The Word for the groom. Upon a small stage, the betrothed read from the copies of the sacred text in the Word so the witnesses present could attest to the reading of the proper nuptials and the exchanging of gifts to seal the couple for all eternity.

The bride received a large emerald pendant necklace from the groom, formerly worn by his mother at her wedding. The groom received a silver dagger removed from the top of the bride's stocking.

The bride and groom are from excellent lineage. Elisabeth's father is a major exporter of exquisite carpets and tapestry from Kuttor. Benjamin's father is Dr. Conrad Forrestal, a prominent physician and the chairman of the Forrestal Mental Hygiene Research Hospital of Riverdale.

Elisabeth is a student of languages at Londonderry University and is twenty four years old. Her father is Diya Izdubar. She has no siblings, and her mother, Alta Izdubar, is deceased.

Benjamin is a certified public accountant and the chairman and chief operating officer of Forrestal Industries and is eighteen years old. Benjamin is also the sole heir of the Forrestal fortune. Benjamin has no siblings and his mother, Ellen Forrestal, is deceased.

At the conclusion of the sealing, Mr. and Mrs. Walker and guests were entertained by a morceau of Kuttor traditional folk music compositions and classical art music of the Kenton mid-century tradition.

The main dish at the wedding banquet was veal of elk, royal pheasant, and prime rib prepared by Chef Socorro Watson of the Londonderry Academe of the Culinary Arts.

After the dinner, Mr. and Mrs. Walker were observed partaking of the beautiful grounds and gardens adjacent to the

Robert Bass mansion.
Mr. and Mrs. Walker will spend their marriage holiday in Newhopeland at Mr. Walker's eloquent chateau, Brightmont, in the Ural Mountains.

~

November 6, 1896

My Dear Father,

Elisabeth loves Brightmont. The enormous banquet room must be capable of seating several hundred people. The library is Elisabeth's favorite room. She spends several hours a day perusing the many books located there. She has asked me if it would be possible to make Brightmont our home. I think after the baby is born, and I have secured adequate knowledge of our financial interests and, of course, if you have no objections, such a proposition may be possible. I would have to attain a telegraph operator and the necessary telegraph lines for adequate communication with Robert and other critical personnel and contract a competent quick service. If all is in order, I think it would be possible to spend more time in this beautiful place.

I also have another thought that Brightmont might make an excellent retreat for the various managers and directors of our many businesses. I did not realize we maintain a staff of twenty people, including groundskeepers, to ensure the chateau is consistently in good order.

The surrounding forest vistas covering the adjacent mountains present such a rich scenic experience. Elisabeth and I spend hours on our sleep room balcony, enjoying the area's astonishing natural beauty. I had completely forgotten it was possible to see the enormous Colossus Volcano from Brightmont. What a truly magnificent image of that long-dormant volcano from the windows of the great room. I am so grateful that the creative architect who designed the chateau utilized such enormous windows in his or her vision; the volcano dominates the view. Utterly amazing.

I have never known so much joy as these last several weeks while on marriage holiday with my most beautiful wife. Yet beneath my happy demeanor exists a persistent melancholy for my dear mother. How strange, I feel I am walking on a wire between both happiness and absence. My beautiful companion and wife comforts me, and in so many ways I have never felt so complete. She is truly a golden light in the darkness, but the shadow of loss endures even while experiencing the intense sensations of new love and delight.

The truth is, father, I have found myself feeling guilt being away from you during this period of adjustment. I pray, father, the burden of loss will be lightened on both of us with time. How truly incomprehensible and incomplete this world is without mother; how I have missed your counsel and wise instruction. My thoughts are always with you.

Your obedient and loving son,

Benjamin

Elisabeth and Benjamin returned to the Forrestal mansion after their marriage holiday to continue their lives in Riverdale. Benjamin spent his days with Robert Bass learning the complexities of Forrestal Industries and making decisions concerning the future of the organization he was now responsible for. Elisabeth could not continue her education at the University of Londonderry due to her condition—traveling from Riverdale to Londonderry was too great a distance. Several professors from the university were hired to prepare Elisabeth to challenge several courses. With such tutoring, she would not fall behind in her education. In the afternoons, she was frequently invited to have lunch or attend other social gatherings with some of the other spouses of the rich and powerful in Kenton. Her social standing was significant, and she was treated, in some ways, like royalty by her wealthy peers. After all, she was married to the heir of the Forrestal fortune, and such a distinction made her unique in the eyes of high society. Occasionally, Elisabeth would take long walks in the afternoon through the town of Riverdale, making purchases in the many shops that lined Main Street. She kept a small purchase diary, so when she returned home, the servants would know where to retrieve her many purchases the next day.

On a beautiful fall day, several hours before Benjamin returned to the Forrestal mansion from his daily consultation with Robert Bass, Elisabeth was walking through Riverdale, enjoying the wonderful life fate had provided for her. She was wearing a simple white cotton dress and a large silk hat. She was full of joyful anticipation knowing her child was to be born in a few weeks. She was consumed with love for her husband. Everything seemed perfect.

But Fate had nothing to do with the life she was living. Her true destiny was taken from her the day Benjamin was exposed to the evil talisman in Jeffery Porter's secret room.

If Elisabeth's life had unfolded unsullied by the terrible curse, she would have known Benjamin only at a distance. She would have thought of him as an immature, deformed, little man of privilege. She would not have been attracted to him. When she walked up to his office to ask him what it was like to kill a man, she would have been merely curious about the society and culture so different from anything she had experienced. When Benjamin dismissed her for being thoughtless and crude, she would have turned away and never given Benjamin a second thought. She would have returned to the university the following semester and, in time, would have graduated with high honors. She would have fallen in love at twenty-seven years of age with a mature professor of history, and together they would work to help many of the women in Kuttor escape their terrible culture. They would have stirred dissension and rebellion in Liberty and would have been instrumental in the inevitable revolution that would destroy the corrupt regime. Their revolutionary writing and rhetoric would have secured their place in history. They would have been joyful when Liberty ceased to be a country, and the people of that repressive society were freed and absorbed into Kenton.

These things were not to be. Elisabeth's fate was stolen away from her, and she would never know the man she would have loved or the beautiful children she would have brought into the world. The true happiness of her life, robbed by such dark evil, was beyond her control. Her historical role would be given to others, and the man she would have married would live a strangely empty life, never feeling complete or understanding the endless malaise of his later years.

So, on this fall day in the twenty-fourth year of Elisabeth Walker's life, she would die.

Elisabeth attempted to cross the cobblestone thoroughfare replete with horses and drawn wagons, elegant carriages, and men riding on horseback. She found the crossing difficult. Her balance was affected by her pregnancy, and she was challenged by the rounded stone paving, numerous piles of horse manure, pools of urine, and other debris that defined passage from one side of the road to the other. She weaved and dodged the many horse-drawn wagons and carriages.

When Elisabeth was a few feet from the wooden sidewalk on the other side street, a sudden unexpected breeze picked up her wide-brim hat and tossed it a dozen feet down the road. Elisabeth turned to follow. Every time she reached to pick up the silk hat, the wind would steal it away from Elisabeth's grasp. Finally, the hat came to rest behind a mining mule in front of the Main Street Livery Stables.

The mule was a massive animal. He was rarely in sunlight, and like most mine mules, the animal was nearly blind because of his subterranean labors. Only a severe case of thrush brought the mule out of the dark, wet mine. The mule's terrible degenerative condition resulted from walking in urine and manure between the tracks pulling an iron ore cart twelve hours a day and seven days a week. The mule was in great pain.

Elisabeth reached down behind the mule to retrieve her hat, and the mule detected the movement behind him from the corner of his eye. The mule was confused, and in pain, so the unknown thing behind frightened him, and he instinctively kicked out with his powerful rear leg. The hoof of the animal stuck Elisabeth squarely in her expanded abdomen.

The powerful impact tore the placenta loose, causing a massive hemorrhage inside the uterus. The baby partially ejected through the birth canal. Elisabeth was thrown a dozen feet, landing with a sickening thud on her back. Her eyes were open and facing the sky as her pupils dilated. Her irises relaxed with the black sign of death. Her body twitched and twisted as her nervous system shut down. Then her muscles relaxed, releasing urine that mingled with the blood of the blunt force that spontaneously aborted her baby. Her heart continued an irregular beat for a few seconds as her circulatory system shut down. She died almost instantaneously after receiving the devastating kick from the powerful animal.

Elisabeth laid there among the piles of manure and pools of urine and a stranger passing through town quickly found the dead woman. He was carrying a load of baled hay, and when he saw Elisabeth, he stopped his team, opened the back of the wagon, pitched a number of the bales onto the street and picked up the dead woman and placed her in the back of his wagon and raced to the nearby hospital.

The unknown good Samaritan carried Elisabeth into the hospital and down the corridor, pleading for someone to help him. Blood mixed with urine had turned much of her white cotton dress into a crimson-stained shroud. Tears flowed down the stranger's face as he wandered through the hospital, pleading for relief from his painful burden.

Nurse Helen and Nurse Peters rushed to assist him, taking Elisabeth's corpse from him and placing her onto a nearby gurney. Elisabeth's body was rushed into emergency surgery, where the nurses began cutting away Elisabeth's clothing, and frantically attempted to find a pulse or any sign of life. Elisabeth's abdomen revealed a large contusion in the shape of a hoof. Nursing attendant Anderson, sitting at a nearby table, began taking notes of the emergency procedure. Nurse Helen attempted to place an IV into Elisabeth's arm and found the vein collapsed. Nurse Peters found the dead fetus's head and left arm protruding from the birth canal. Nurse Peters put one hand under the child's head, and her other hand under the arm and gently pulled the dark, purplish baby from Elisabeth's body. The child was cleaned and wrapped in a white towel and weighed on a nearby scale. Within a few seconds, Dr. Forrestal burst into the surgical room and looked down at his only son's dear wife. His hesitation was brief as his training immediately began to direct his actions.

Nurse Peters expressed, "Child was partially exposed from the birth canal and deceased."

Dr. Forrestal examined Elisabeth's eyes and called out to nurses, "Pallor cyanotic. Eyes are fixed and dilated."

He grabbed his stethoscope and listened to Elisabeth's chest, "No beat."

Nurse Peters, sitting next to the table, quickly strapped on a Lister blood pressure cuff around Elisabeth's arm and began pumping air into the rubber tube. The nurse listened carefully with her stethoscope for a sign of life.

"No blood pressure, doctor."

Dr. Forrestal checked Elisabeth's airway for obstruction, and finding the trachea clear, ordered the nurse to begin forcing air into Elisabeth's airway with a Lister resuscitation bag. He then began chest compressions, periodically stopping to determine if the heart had started to pump again. After five minutes without results, Dr. Forrestal asked for .05 milligrams of epinephrine dissolved in five cubic centimeters of normal saline. This was a dangerous last effort to bring Elisabeth back to life. Nurse Helen handed him the spinal needle. Dr. Forrestal carefully located the fourth intercostal space between the ribs and pushed the needle into Elisabeth's chest, attempting to pierce the ventricular chamber. The intracardiac injection failed. Her heart did not respond.

Dr. Forrestal looked at the grandfather clock standing by

the wall and stated for the medical chart, "Elisabeth Walker is dead at four thirty-two on December 6, 1896. Death was caused by blunt trauma to the abdomen from a mule's kick. She was eight months pregnant, and the fetus was found partially exposed from the mother's body and also expired after the placenta was torn loose from the uterine wall by the blunt force trauma. All standard resuscitation procedures were applied without desired results."

At that point, Dr. Forrestal asked the nursing attendant to prepare a note and send a runner to Robert Bass's mansion to inform his son that his wife had been injured and taken to the emergency room. "I don't want him to know anything else, just have the runner give the note to Benjamin. Nothing more."

"Yes, doctor," nursing attendant Anderson replied as she disappeared from the room.

Benjamin and Robert Bass were engrossed with financial projections for the coming fiscal year when the runner knocked on the door. The maid opened the door to see fourteen-year-old Toby Russet standing in the doorway, holding a note: "Important note for Mr. Walker," the young boy announced.

The maid escorted the young runner into the mansion's great room, and Toby approached Benjamin. "Mr. Walker, an important note from your father."

Benjamin quickly opened the note and read aloud the message, "Elisabeth has been taken to the Emergency Room. Come as soon as possible. Father."

Without saying another word, Benjamin stood and ran out the front door. He untied his horse, leaped into his carriage, and proceeded to the Riverdale Hospital as fast as possible. Upon arriving, he jumped from his carriage and rushed into the Emergency Room corridor, looking frantically for his father. Shortly after arriving, his father walked out of the emergency surgical room and held out his arms to his troubled son.

"Where is Elisabeth?" Benjamin repeated, "Where is Elisabeth?"

Conrad delivered the dreadful news by putting his arms around his only son. "Elisabeth and the baby are gone, son. I am so deeply sorry."

"No!" Benjamin repeated over and over as Conrad took his son to see his dead wife and child.

Benjamin and his father walked into the surgical room. Elisabeth was covered with a muslin sheet up to her neck. The baby was wrapped in a towel and placed under her arm as if she were cradling the child. The baby's head was visible, and his small face expressed the sadness of death. Elisabeth's eyes had been shut, but her mouth was slightly open, and her long, raven hair was draped around her shoulders.

Benjamin stood there in complete silence and then collapsed into unconsciousness as the trauma of the dreadful sight overwhelmed him. Conrad grabbed Benjamin to prevent him from collapsing, but he could not break the fall. Conrad did not have the strength. Benjamin began to seize as his eyes rolled back, and his body convulsed uncontrollably. Benjamin's father recognized the symptoms of a psychogenic seizure.

Chapter 20
World on Our Shoulders

The sea was warm and salty; he looked up. The surface was only a few yards away. He felt as if his lungs would burst. Breaking to the surface, Benjamin gasped for air. He swam a short distance to the sandy shore and pulled his exhausted, naked body out of the water. His labored breathing caused his ribs to ache. He rolled onto his back, opened his eyes to the night sky, and looked upon the multitude of brilliant stars. The soft, rolling waves lapped at his feet. The warm breeze swirled around him, laced with the most exquisite aroma of flowers. When his strength returned, and his breathing calmed, Benjamin looked down the beach. Slowly rolling waves glowed blue and green from bioluminescent plankton kissing the beach with surreal beauty. The sand was pure white, and some distance from the shore, Benjamin could see a vast tree line silhouette the starry sky. A massive fire in front of him caused the beach to flicker and dance with simmering light.

"How can this be?" Benjamin spoke to an unseen audience. "Is this some sort of dream?" He was confused and frightened.

At first, he was not sure. Against the backdrop of the fire, Benjamin saw a dark image walking toward him. The distorted outline of the approaching figure shimmered and danced against the flickering fire. Benjamin lifted himself and watched the enigmatic figure grow larger with every step. Finally drawing near, he heard a familiar voice, "Benjamin, you're here!"

Surprised and elated, Benjamin rose on his sound leg just as Elisabeth embraced and kissed him. Benjamin felt the warmth of Elisabeth's naked body pressed against his. After a moment passed, still holding tight, Benjamin placed his face next to Elisabeth's ear and whispered, "Oh, I love you so. I thought you were lost to me."

Elisabeth pulled back so Benjamin could see her beautiful face and dark hair glow in the firelight, "You will never lose me."

"How is this possible? I mean, what is this place? I thought you were dead. I saw you dead with our child. How can this be?" Benjamin began to tremble while attempting to unravel the mystery.

"Benjamin, I am gone from your world now . . . this is my heaven. I was permitted to share this realm with you while you sleep. I know this seems strange. My heaven would be incomplete without you," Elisabeth said, smiling, her hair flowing and dancing in the perfumed breeze.

"I am dreaming, Elisabeth . . . is this a dream?" Benjamin put his hand on Elisabeth's face for reassurance.

"No, Benjamin, this is not a dream. You are sleeping, but this is my heaven. We were meant to be together. I know how impossible this may seem. We will have many evenings together for me to explain to you. Trust me. In time all of this will be clear," Elisabeth said, taking Benjamin's arm and turning him toward the fire. "Let's go sit by the fire, and we will talk of heaven and renewal."

Benjamin began to hop on his good leg as the couple started to walk. Elisabeth abruptly stopped. "No, Benjamin. You are whole. You can walk."

Benjamin slowly brought the deformed leg he knew and placed it next to his other leg. He could stand on both legs. He had never experienced such a thing. Benjamin felt the moist sand under both feet, and his weight evenly distributed on both legs. He held his breath and took a step. "How can this be?"

"You are in my heaven now. Your body will never know pain. You will never grow old. You will never be infirm. You are whole. You can walk, run, or anything you would like to do. Just request your desire, and I will make it come true. You are in my heaven now," Elisabeth said while encouraging Benjamin to walk.

After a few halting steps, Benjamin stopped. "Our child— is our child here as well?"

Elisabeth spoke softly, "Benjamin, our child had a life to live. Our child will be born to another couple. Yes, he will have a wonderful life. This was not our child's time to pass over. He cannot be with us. He will have a wonderful life. I was allowed to glimpse what he will become, and you would be very proud."

"Will we see him in the afterlife?" a subdued Benjamin asked.

Elisabeth encouraged Benjamin to continue walking toward the fire. "Benjamin, you are still among the living, and there are some things you are not meant to know. Trust me for now, please."

Arriving at the fire, Elisabeth and Benjamin sat down on a magnificent Kuttor carpet. Benjamin pressed, "How is this real? How am I in your heaven?"

"Think of your reality when you were born. At first, you only knew the simplest sensations, and when you matured, you accepted your mother and all things that existed in your childhood. You accepted the world you were born into. As you matured, your understanding increased, yet you always accepted the reality of your life. Few ever question their existence. They just accept it. You cannot recall your life before you were born. To ask such a question is meaningless. The only thing real is the life you were born into. You must allow yourself to accept other realms of existence. This is a new life, not born into but transitioned. I am not allowed to share anything more with you in your living state," Elisabeth explained, looking into the fire.

"When will I return to my life?" Benjamin asked, looking at his beautiful wife reflecting the light of the fire.

"We will be together until dawn. At the sight of the first rays from the rising sun, you must return to the sea. You will awake and live out your day until you sleep again. You must live out your life, Benjamin. You will accomplish great things in life. I can have you only when you sleep. I will be waiting here for you when the stars come out. This is all that is permitted, and this rule cannot be violated. If I tell you any more, the night will be spoiled, and all of this will be taken away."

Tears ran down Elisabeth's cheeks, reflecting the fire's bright flicker like streaks of a falling star. They sharply contrasted her soft white skin. "No more questions for now," Elisabeth firmly decided.

Benjamin accepted the miracle and held Elisabeth tight.

Benjamin accepted what he was told from his love. "Well then, we shall make the best of the time we have until sunrise, and I will return at sunset so we can be together always."

Elisabeth and Benjamin spent the rest of the night talking, laughing, and making love. They spent a happy hour swimming in a nearby pool and eating fruits and nuts from the many trees within a short distance from their fire. Elisabeth's world glowed from the radiant beauty of a million stars. Then, at first light, Elisabeth and Benjamin walked back to the sea. The couple said their reassurances and loving goodbyes. Benjamin looked into Elisabeth's tear-filled eyes one last time, turned, and walked into the sea.

Nursing Attendant Mary sat next to Benjamin, writing her notes. Every fifteen minutes, Mary would diligently check on Benjamin's condition. She verified the IV bottle did not require changing. She examined the urine bottle beside his bed and recorded the amount of liquid present. Mary carefully observed and recorded her patient's breathing rate, blood pressure, and temperature for the doctor's review. Four times a day, Mary would pour liquid nourishment through the rubber tube placed in Benjamin's nose, which descended through the esophagus to his stomach. If Benjamin soiled himself, she would clean him. She carefully rolled Benjamin from side to side to ensure his skin would not break down under the constant pressure of his weight. Her standing orders were to notify Dr. Forrestal of any change in her patient's condition.

Mary was completing her note when she heard Benjamin stir. She heard the first whisper from Benjamin in four days, "Elisabeth."

Mary jumped and stared down at her patient. Benjamin was coming out of the coma. She ran out of the room and returned with a very frantic Dr. Forrestal. Benjamin's father took his son's hand and said, "Benjamin, Benjamin!"

With the sound of his father's voice, Benjamin opened his eyes. He stared at his father for a moment until his disorientation subsided, and the terrible image of his dead wife and child returned to his memory. Benjamin grabbed his father's arm, lifted himself, and embraced the last member of his family. Benjamin made a desperate gasp and began to wail and moan uncontrollably. Dreadful sorrow coursed through his being as he cried and called out his dear wife's name repeatedly for the next two hours.

Benjamin's father tried to comfort him. He spoke to Benjamin about loss and regret. He told him how much he loved him. Words alone could not temper such a loss. Only time might blunt the trauma. Benjamin's father realized the catharsis of such emotional release and encouraged the outpouring of grief. When Benjamin was exhausted, he released his father and laid back on his bed. He was quiet. Benjamin's father sat next to him, holding his hand until his son finally spoke, "When is the funeral?"

"I am so sorry, Benjamin. You have been unconscious for four days. I'm so sorry, the funeral was yesterday," Benjamin's father said, stroking his son's hair from his face.

"How terrible I was not there for my wife and child's funeral. I was unconscious that long. What is wrong with me? How could I have been unconscious so long?" Benjamin asked his father while sitting up.

"You had a seizure brought on by extreme stress and shock. It is called a psychogenic seizure. You were in shock, and your body and mind just shut down. You are healing. Your grief reaction will help the healing. After a while, you will feel better. You will always feel the loss, of course, but your mind will learn to cope," Dr. Forrestal tried to reassure his son without sounding too clinical.

"I want to go home, father. I will take whatever potions you conjure up. I need to go home," Benjamin insisted.

"I am sorry. It is too soon. You need to be under observation for a few days," Benjamin's father was concerned the grief might cause another seizure—or worse, Benjamin might try to hurt himself. He had treated several patients in the past that were released too soon with tragic results. Conrad was afraid he might lose his only son.

Benjamin glared at his father and, without warning, reached over and tore his IV needle out of his arm. He pulled the feeding tube out of his nose, pulled the blanket off, tossing it on the floor. Benjamin swung his legs over the bed, sat up, and sternly said, "Father, I have studied the law. You have no authority to keep me here against my will. I need to grieve at home now. Will you help me with my brace, or must I hop out of this hospital? I said I would take your medications. I will cooperate with any treatment outside the hospital. If you wish, you may have a nurse or therapist observe me at home. I will not stay in this hospital any longer."

Benjamin's father knew his son. He also knew he could not force Benjamin to stay in the hospital. "All right, I will have the apothecary send some medication for depression over to our home. I will get your brace and clothes. Let me help."

Benjamin's father retrieved Benjamin's leg brace and helped him secure the prosthesis. He helped him with the clothing. Once dressed, Conrad hugged his son, and the two of them walked out of the room and down the corridor. The doctors and nurses tapped their hearts. The carriage ride home was long and quiet. Upon entering the mansion, the staff expressed their condolences. Benjamin thanked them, and they returned to their duties.

Dr. Forrestal asked, "Benjamin, I think you may need something to eat. Something bland to help your digestive system adjust. I will have the maid bring you some beef broth and rice putting."

"Yes, thank you. I want to talk to you about something that happened to me." Benjamin was asking for guidance and help.

Father and son walked over to the dining table, and Benjamin's father summoned the downstairs maid and made the request for Benjamin's simple dinner. Benjamin sat looking at his father until the food and water were brought to the table. When the maid was gone, Benjamin leaned closer to his father across the table. "When I was unconscious in the hospital," Benjamin paused, hoping his father would accept what he was about to tell him, "I was with Elisabeth."

Benjamin's father straightened up, and his eyes widened, "Benjamin, please try to understand, you were traumatized. You experienced an extreme shock. Under such stress, your mind—"

"Stop it. What I experienced was not some delusion—this was real. Of course, you will think in terms of mental hygiene. I am asking you to hear me out, then you can diagnose me. Will you please listen?"

Conrad did not want his son to wall himself off. His son's expressions of his delusions would further help him evaluate Benjamin's mental wounds. "You can talk to me about anything. I will keep my mind open."

"I know what you are thinking. Talking will aid your assessment of me—"

"No, Benjamin, I want you to believe I am listening as a concerned father. Nothing more."

He increasingly realized he could not be his son's treating physician. His love for his son would obscure his objectivity. He knew how he might be drawn into his son's thinking, "Please tell me. My mind is always open with you."

"When I saw my dear wife and child in death, I blanked out. I found myself beneath the surface of the sea, and when I rose, I found myself on a beach. It was nighttime, and Elisabeth was standing on the shore waiting. Father, my leg was normal. Elisabeth told me I was in her heaven, and it was incomplete without me. She said I had to live out my life, but I could join her paradise when I slept. When the sun began to rise, I had to return to the sea. That is when I woke up in the hospital. It felt like only a few hours. It was not a dream. It was so real," Benjamin trusted his father unequivocally. He knew his father would not judge him.

"Benjamin, I think your mind tries to compensate with the delusion of deliverance. I want you to be open with me and tell me anything you need to." Conrad understood he needed to be direct.

Benjamin hesitated at first. "I understand. You said something similar to mother. All I am asking you is to keep your mind open; this was no dream."

"I will," he returned. "I cannot be your physician."

"I know."

Benjamin continued to speak of his journey to another realm, and all the things that he and Elisabeth did in that heavenly paradise. When he was finished with his dinner and the description of his experience, he told his father he was tired and would lie down. Conrad said he understood and would bring some medication to the room later that evening. Benjamin walked up and lifted himself onto his bed and fell asleep and dreamed. He dreamt of Elisabeth.

Elisabeth's naked body conformed perfectly to the warm white sands of the beach. She pulled Benjamin close and told him how much she loved him. The sound of the gentle waves mixed with the soft tropical breeze formed the perfect poem of contentment, complimenting the loving relationship between the young couple. The night sky crowded with a million stars created a stunning canopy: a haunting beauty of eternal mystery. Benjamin rose, cradled his head on his palm,

Un

looked down at his true love, and whispered, "I wish I could stay here forever."

Elisabeth, with moistened, sad eyes said, "In time, I promise, we will be together forever."

Elisabeth changed the subject, not wishing to spoil their remaining time. "Benjamin, what is that strange soft cloud that reaches across the sky?" she asked, tracing the outline of the misty cloud with her outstretched hand.

Benjamin following Elisabeth's direction said, "It is called the 'elephant's tusk.' See how it curves like a tusk? Well, it's not a cloud, but a collection of faraway stars. Our world and our stars are in a vast island called a galaxy, shaped like a dinner plate, and we are located on the edge of the plate. When we look into the universe from here, we see it like a soft ban of light. If we were looking down at the galaxy, it would look like a great spinning pool of water pouring down a cosmic drain."

"Your world, Benjamin . . . mine no more. Please, continue the lesson of the night sky," Elisabeth said, trying to escape the morose tide of emotion swelling up inside. "What is the galaxy draining into?"

"No one really knows. Much of the night sky is a mystery, as is everything else in life."

Elisabeth gazed across the star-filled sky, looked up, pointed at a strange blue star. "Benjamin, what is that brilliant blue star over there?"

Benjamin paused. Her question reminded him of another time. "That is a planet like ours . . . my world . . . see that dim star right next to the planet? Well, that's the world's moon. We have two small moons, but Oceania, the name of that planet, has one large moon. Oceania is really a double planet because Oceania's moon is so large. The moon is called Mortalis. Unlike Oceania, Mortalis is a lifeless world without atmosphere or water. Oceania is mostly covered with vast oceans. The way you asked me about Oceania reminded me of a close friend I once knew a long time ago. He discovered Oceania for the first time on a beautiful night like this when the planet was in full phase. He was amazed at the thought of other worlds and how so many stars existed with so many possibilities."

She pulled him closer until he was above her. "Tell me about your friend. You have never spoken to me about him."

He kissed her and ran his hand through her thick black hair whispering, "I will tell you everything. I was sixteen years old, and I had completed my tutelage at the Riverdale Advance School, but I was not allowed to continue my education at the university until I reached the age of eighteen. Children were not allowed on campus, and this child, no matter how precocious, would not be the exception no matter what my mother offered, which I am sure was considerable. My mother felt I must continue my education, and she firmly believed one day I would take over my parents' financial endeavors. So, she enrolled me in Cunningham's Correspondent School of Certified Public Accounting. She, of course, hired the appropriate tutors to ensure my success. Three days a week I endured what was undoubtedly the most tedious compendium of human knowledge compiled by civilized society, so my mother would be gratified I was not wasting my youth on trivial pursuits. On the other hand, my father, a true humanitarian, agreed to my mother's obsession with my continuing education, only if I had a more significant percentage of play days in any given week than the mental cruelty of studying bookkeeping techniques and tax law. By the way, as a derivative of my mother's fear of a wasteful childhood, I was the youngest person ever to pass the certification examination for public accountants in Kenton, but I digress.

"Ready? Here is my story of my one and only true childhood friend. I was riding Fortune through the town early one morning on a sanctioned 'play day' when I noticed a small group of kids surrounding a younger kid, harassing and teasing this poor fellow. A strange feeling of familiarity arose within me witnessing such a terrible scene. I was compelled to intervene. The commotion was at the end of an alley near

Fourth Street, so I directed my horse down the alley, and what I found was truly appalling. Five older boys were making this younger fat boy eat garbage retrieved from various garbage cans. The poor guy was badly beaten, and he was at the mercy of this gang of thugs. I rode up to the mayhem and announced my displeasure with their cruelty. I quickly found myself at odds with these five delinquents. Once they noticed my brace and deformed leg, I became the object of their deviant desire. They began calling me 'crippled boy,' 'peg leg,' 'scarface,' and dumb stuff like that. One of the older and bigger boys, he looked eighteen or nineteen, made the enormous mistake of putting his hands on me in an attempt to pull me from my horse.

"Well, my sweet mother—always looking after my best interest—had given me a nickel-plated small revolver for my sixteenth birthday with a clear understanding I would get a heavy pistol when I was a little older. Well, I pulled my shiny pistol and placed the pistol squarely in the middle of this poor sucker's forehead and said, 'I am sixteen and cannot commit a crime for another two years.' I then pulled the hammer of the gun back, which, of course, made a delightful and dramatic click as the cylinder rotated. And then I said, 'I am now going to kill you.' Well, that poor slug died a thousand deaths waiting to see what I was going to do. His buddies took off, reasoning, I am sure, I was going to kill them next. Well, the poor guy turned white and started to tremble, and, for a second, I thought I just might blow this guy's brains all over the alley and be some kind of hero like my dad when he blew away this guy who hurt my mother. Then, this tough guy lost control of his bladder and started to cry like a baby that was dropped on its head. I made some humiliating comment like, 'This is your lucky day. I'm not in the mood to shoot a baby girl today,' and pulled my gun back from the brink and said, 'The next time I catch you even looking at this guy, I will kill you as surely as the Raven can fly.' Then the guy ran off. It would have probably been better to have shot the creep and not risk having some deviant lurking around the town feeling spiteful, but I was young and hadn't killed anyone, so the guy got away.

"Well," Benjamin continued. "I got down from my horse and walked over to the poor, fat guy and asked how he was doing, and he just looked at me, his complexion turned kind of green. He vomited about a gallon of garbage the thugs made him eat. I mean, it was terrible—all kinds of coffee grounds, spoiled meat, rotten potatoes, I mean, it was disgusting. Well, I digress. So, this kid kind of looks at me, not saying a word, and faints like a wet mop dropped from the roof. I went over to this water spigot, cupped some water in my hands, went back to the guy, and threw some water on his face. Then he kind of wakes up. He was still not talking, like he was in shock or something. So, I helped him up, and with some sort of superhuman effort, I got him up in the saddle on Fortune and I told him to hang on to the saddle, and I walked him to my home.

"I am kind of carrying this guy into the house when my mother comes around the corner and gives me this look like I brought a stray cat home or something, and turns, calls the maid over and says, 'Help Benjamin with his project.' Well, she probably floated up to her secret office to type out her secret code to some secret receiver because I didn't see her again for a while. Well, I am kind of upset by my mother's vast indifference to my new friend, so I drag him over to the formal sitting room and flop him down on the silk sofa, which is totally immaculate, and this guy kind of really smells like garbage. I thought the maid was going to go through the roof. Well, I asked her to get me some baking soda and water as well as one of my father's clean shirts from the washroom and a pair of father's pants. I helped him take off his torn and smelly shirt, and the guy is still not saying a word. He just looks around the room like he just landed on Oceania or something, and the maid brings me a glass of soda water, clean clothes, and a wet wash rag. She starts scrubbing this guy's face and giving him the baking soda. We both stood back, and the kid said his first words: 'I have to go to the private room.' Well, we flopped the clean cloths and pants over his shoulder, and we wasted no time getting him down the hall, and at first sight, he bolted into the private room and disappeared for a while."

Hearing Benjamin's story Elisabeth began rolling and laughing so hard she could hardly breathe.

"What?"

Elisabeth, now coated in sand, explained, "You are talking so funny. It was like you were regressing back when you were sixteen or something. You are hilarious. Please, this is really funny, don't stop."

"Really? Well, sure. . . . So, after a few minutes, the kid comes out of the private room wearing my father's oversized clothing. He looks a lot better. I caught the maid looking into the private room with some kind of enormous trepidation, and I helped the kid back to the formal sitting room. By now, he's looking pretty good cleaned up and everything, so I asked him how he was doing, and he grinned, 'I feel a lot better now. Thank you for helping me out. I hate those mean kids. They tease me all the time because I'm fat.' I told him I knew the feeling because of my deformed leg. The kid looks down at my leg like this is the first time he noticed, and I swear this kid blurts out before he realizes what he is saying, 'Oh, I don't feel so bad now.' Well, he sounded so sincere, I just started laughing, knowing this guy is going to realize what he just said and feel really bad, and after a moment of horror on his face, he started laughing too and says, 'Wow, you're a real nice guy. You saved my life, and I insult you! I'm so sorry.' So, I tell him, it's okay. I knew what he meant. He introduces himself as Petie Passerine, and I say, 'Oh wow, you're the butcher's kid! I used to live above the butcher shop before my mother got married. I think we still own the building or something.' And Petie just laughed and said, 'I think this place is better.' And we both laughed, and I said, 'My name is Benjamin Walker. Are you feeling good enough to eat something?' And Petie said. 'Yeah, maybe some ice cream would help my stomach.' So, we went into the dining room. I rang the maid's bell, and she came running around the corner with a kind of disgusted look on her face while holding a lot of cleaning stuff in her hands, and I asked if she would get us some ice cream. She smiled and said, 'In a moment, Master Walker.' Well, Petie thought that was really neat and said, 'You are so lucky to have a nice setup like this. At my house, we eat mostly sausages. That's why I am so fat. My whole family is fat.' So, I said he could eat at my house, anytime he wanted to, and he smiled like it was Winter Solstice's Eve or something. Then, the maid brought us two huge bowls of ice cream. About that time, my mother came floating through the dining room, still looking somewhat incredulous and noticing my gun she gently reminded me, 'Benjamin, no guns at the dinner table.' So, I put my gun on the lamp table behind me. Petie thought that was the funniest thing he ever heard a mother say to a kid. He started laughing uncontrollably, and then I started laughing, and my mother just kind of stared at us and disappeared into the formal sitting room where I could hear her instructing the maid how to clean the silk sofa. It was truly a wonderful day."

Elisabeth was now sitting up with her legs pulled against her breasts. Her arms wrapped around her legs and her chin rested on her knees. She looked at Benjamin with big green eyes, fascinated with every detail of history of her lover she didn't know existed. "So that's how you found your first friend. What happens then? Did your mother ever ask his name or anything?"

"Yeah, my next play day Petie was at the front door early in the morning as we had arranged. Jane, the maid, answered the door and directed him to the dining room, which was not really the right thing to do with my new friend. She then calls out in the direction of the sleep room, 'Master Benjamin, Master Petie has arrived.' Well, I come down the stairs looking for my new friend, and he's not in the formal sitting room. I asked Jane where he was, and she said something like, 'I placed him in the dining room.' Well, I kinda lost it, and I am never loud with the servants, but I looked directly at her and said, 'You will show my friend the courtesy he deserves, is that clear?' Well, Jane looked shocked and said she was sorry to both of us. 'It will not happen again, Master Benjamin.' I then sent her away. Petie is looking like something happened but doesn't have a clue what. I told him the maid should have directed him to the formal sitting room, not the dining room, and asked if he required something while he was waiting. About that time, my mother came into the dining room asking me why I was angry with the maid, and I told her. She looked at Petie and said she was sorry, and she would discipline the maid. Petie's eyes got really big, and he didn't say anything. My mother asked him what his name was, and he said, 'Petie Passerine,' and my mother just lit up and smiled.

"'You are Martha Passerine's boy? Your mother was so helpful when Benjamin was born. How is she doing now?'

"And Petie says, 'Okay, I guess.'

"And my mother starts acting like Petie was a real person and everything, which was nice. We then went down to the stables and saddled up Fortune and our extra horse, Comet, and rode out to Old Forest Road. I showed Petie where I got stabbed by Jonnie York in the face and almost died, and told him how my father killed Jonnie's father, and Jonnie died a few weeks later. I told him I was sure my mother had him killed because she loved me. I never said anything about it. So, I looked at Petie and said, 'Whatever you do, do not try and kill me.' We both started laughing. I took Petie to my special pond in the forest that I discovered the day I was almost killed, and we just sat there on the edge of the pond. While the horses grazed, we talked about all the mysteries of the universe and stuff."

Then Benjamin looked and could see the first glimmer of the rising sun. "I must hurry, the darkness is fading."

Elisabeth said, "You're right, the sun will be rising soon. Finish telling me about your adventures with Petie before you wake up and have to go. We can figure out the universe tomorrow night."

"Okay. . . . Petie and I talked a lot about the afterlife and what to expect when we die," Benjamin said with a smile.

"And?" Elisabeth asked with anticipation.

"I think Petie and I agreed heaven would be different for different people. In life, we are subject to fate, uncontrollable forces. In death, we are subject only to our wishes, wants, and needs. The afterlife is the exact opposite of life. We can be anyone we want to be, do anything we want to do. I think the afterlife is a paradise. The afterlife is where dreams come true," Benjamin said with some certainty.

"What would the afterlife be for you, Benjamin?"

"I think you know. To be here with you for all eternity, to be healthy and whole, never be alone and be fulfilled by the one you love, and to be certain you will always be with me. This is paradise, and our love for each other makes it so," Benjamin answered as he watched her glow with happiness.

Elisabeth laid back and smiled. "I am so happy too. This is paradise when you are here with me, but when you leave me each new day, this island becomes the worst form of existence."

Benjamin could only say, "I am so sorry."

Elisabeth sat up and turned to the horizon on the Eastern Sea and stated, "No! I will not do this to you. I know this is not your fault. So please finish telling me about Petie. I refuse to allow our time together to be spoiled. Please tell me about your world before we met."

Benjamin continued, "Petie and I spent the remaining summer months exploring the world, swimming, riding horses, camping, and observing the universe with the tele- scope my father bought for me when I turned sixteen. For the first time in my life, I felt like a child. Life was more than accumulating knowledge and excelling in academics . . . it was also acting my age and enjoying life. My mother grew more comfortable with my childhood freedom as long as I continued to improve with my tutor's assistance at least three days a week and steadily progressed in my course work. I became a better student because I had so much time to be free and to enjoy my childhood. My mother began spending time with Petie's mother, discussing the future for their sons. Petie became a frequent dinner guest at our home, and with the additional activity and better food, he shed a great deal of weight, his health improved, and our frequent discussions of the world caused him to spend more time reading books on the days we could not be together. It was a perfect summer. My childhood ended that fall. Petie and I went riding on a Tuesday afternoon when Petie lost his life.

"We were riding through the forest near the Old Forest Road when Petie's horse was frightened by something in the grass. Comet bolted and threw Petie from the saddle. While Petie was falling, his left foot slipped through the stirrup and twisted, locking his foot in position, holding him upside down with his head against the ground. Comet was confused and frightened by Petie's unnatural position. He was hanging and screaming from the stirrup, his body beneath the horse, his head next to the horse's back hooves. Comet panicked and ran for the safety of his stable, dragging my helpless friend with him. I chased Comet as fast as I could, trying to save my best and only friend. I thought if I could just get close enough, I could grab the reins of the horse and save my friend's life, but that was not to be.

"When the horse reached the gravel road, I watched a few feet behind the racing horse in horror as a bloody mass of raw meat replaced Petie's face. Comet increasingly attempted to escape the dead weight hanging from his side by kicking Petie's head with his rear hoof. Each kick further crushed Petie's head, breaking his jaw and dislocating his eyes. The steel shoe repeatedly crushed his skull. When Comet reached Riverdale, my dear friend was dead. The horse ran down Third Street as Mr. Passerine, by chance, was crossing the road. Seeing a child in distress and knowing he would not have the strength to stop the horse physically, he pulled his heavy pistol and shot the horse in the head. When the horse collapsed, Petie's broken body was hoisted up on the side of the horse, battered and bloodied beyond recognition. Petie's

head seemed swollen three times its normal size. Mr. Passerine immediately came to the aid of the child he could not
recognize. Carefully releasing Petie's foot and laying the
lifeless body next to the remains of the horse. In a panic, I
rode up. . . . I was consumed by the pure horror of the ghastly
sight. Mr. Passerine looked up at me, and I saw the spirit of
life leave his body as he realized who lay dead before him. I
remembered how he looked at me and then at the impossible
countenance of his child. I saw him stare at Petie's belt
buckle, a birthday gift from father to son. Petie's father
melted into a quivering mass of anguish and hopelessness. He
didn't say a word—he simply held his child and moaned a
soft song of loss. I dismounted, released the lock on the knee
of my brace, knelt, and stared at my friend in silent despair. I
would never be a child again.

"I don't remember much about that day and the immediate days that followed. I was overwhelmed by my abject
despair next to Petie's body. The fire wagon, of course, came,
and the firemen placed the remains of Petie carefully in the
back of the wagon. Father and son were carried to my father,
who pronounced my dear friend dead. I remember my father
coming to where I was still sitting in the street in shock and
helping me into his carriage and taking Fortune to the stable,
and then we went home. I remember my mother holding me
and crying uncontrollably over the loss of the child she had
come to love. I remember standing in silence as my father
read from The Word before my friend's body escaped this
world beneath the dark, moist soil that covered his simple
wooden coffin. I remember tossing a handful of soil on the
wooden box and saying to all those gathered that Petie gave
me more happiness and hope than anyone I have ever known,
and how I hoped the Raven carried him to heaven where there
would be a place for me when fate takes me from this world. I
remember how those gathered by my friend's grave that sad
day repeated after me how much Petie would be missed. I
remember how lost I was and how my father tried to comfort
me. In reflection, I guess I remembered the important things

about losing a friend. I just could not bear to remember anything more."

Elisabeth sat quietly with tears running down her face and said, "I am so very sorry, Benjamin. I think that was the saddest story you could have told me."

"I remember asking my father how something so terrible could have happened and the meaning of fate. He told me every person in the world is born to a specific fate beyond his or her ability to control. The world is fixed, and our fate is fixed. Each of us born into riches or poverty, with gifts and deficits, intelligent or a dullard, with caring and loving parents or parents that were absent. All these things and more, millions of other things beyond our control created our existence on Deseret. Then I asked, what is the point of life if we did not have free will, if everything was fixed and determined? Were we just marionettes in some vast cosmic puppet show?

"I remember how he smiled and said no, we were not puppets but actors, all born on a stage replete with props in a theater not known to us. Actors in a vast cosmic play written by some unknown writer, but we write our own lines in the script. We choose how we will play our part, say the lines we recite, act out our character's intent along with the moral code we follow. We choose our performance regardless of the underpinnings of existence. Our fate, however, is not ours to control. We are only the masters of ourselves within the strict confines of the play. Father said he knew my fate, and I would achieve great things before I was done and to try not to understand life completely but live it. With time, I would obtain the wisdom necessary to tolerate the darkness of life and rejoice in all that was wonderful. I asked him if I could ever control my fate, choose the stage and the theater, even what actor I would play. He became profoundly serious and said if I dared to gain control of my fate and should succeed, I would not belong in this universe. He said if I could choose my own fate, this world would be flung off its axis and fall into the sun, and the stars would begin to fall. All would be hopelessly lost to me forever. The Raven would not know of my existence. I would be thrown into an abyss of my own making to suffer for eternity. He, in the firmest tone, said I should be the best I could be in every way within the fate I was born into, and to work hard to contribute to the human condition, and forgive those that have trespassed against me, and be ever mindful not to trespass on the others on this grand stage.

"The true meaning of my fate was to act my part the best I could on the stage of life, and when the play is finished, before the curtain falls, bow to the unseen audience and leave the stage content, realizing all the things I was able to achieve, and not regretting those things beyond my control."

With that, Benjamin finished his sad tale of his best and only childhood friend.

"I love you so very much," Elisabeth said. "The more you tell me about your life, the more I love you. Please never stop sharing with me who you are. Now it is time for you to go. I can see the first rays of the new day, and soon the sun will be rising from beneath the sea, and you must not be here. It is time for you to awake."

Benjamin stood up on his two strong legs and said, "I will be back as soon as possible. I love you." He leaned down and kissed his love, turned, and disappeared into the sea.

Mental Health Research Hospital

Date: January 5, 1897
Patient: Walker, Benjamin
Case: 786

Patient is an eighteen-year-old male with an appropriate age appearance. Patient suffers from a congenitally deformed leg requiring a leg brace for ambulation. Patient's weight loss is increasingly profound. Patient has lost a total of twenty-four pounds in four weeks. Patient states he has no appetite and only eats small portions of food at his father's insistence. Patient's hygiene is poor, requiring frequent encouragement to bathe. Patient remains pale and gaunt. Patient continues to be withdrawn, only communicating with encouragement. Patient is subject to hypersomnia consistent with his delusional system. Initial sessions, the patient freely expressed belief while sleeping he would visit with his deceased wife. He has become increasingly guarded concerning this delusional system. He is lethargic, fatigued, and socially withdrawn. Patient has no known underlying medical problems.

Diagnoses: Major depression with delusions (Rosenberg scale 78) brought on by death of wife four weeks ago and his mother, Ellen Forrestal, eight and a half months earlier. Patient's wife was with child. Child is also deceased. Mother and wife's deaths were sudden and under unusual circumstances. Patient consistently reports he visits his deceased wife when he sleeps. The patient's father stated that the patient's mother and wife were identical in appearance except for the age differential. Patient frequently uses a large amount of laudanum to promote sleep. Patient suffers from hypersomnia and sleeps in excess of sixteen hours in a 24-hour period.

Of considerable concern, patient has indicated deceased wife is encouraging patient to prolong his sleeping period. Patient has expressed on numerous occasions he is feeling guilty by his daily waking, causing his deceased wife to display distress manifested by wailing and sobbing. Patient is suffering from profound depression with delusional ideations. Patient is increasingly suicidal. Patient is morbidly depressed. Pharmacological intervention consists of antidepressants – Logan: 10 milligrams three times a day; Zordeen: 10 milligrams three times a day; and antipsychotic Weldram: 25 milligrams morning and evening. Patient has not responded to medications.

Patient will continuously be under observation. All food consumption will be monitored. Hygiene will be monitored.

All licit and illicit drug use will be controlled. All firearms have been removed from the home. The servants are instructed to notify patient's father or other hospital personnel of any sign of self-harm. Medication nurse will dispense medication as prescribed and chart relevant information concerning patient's behavior or statements. All medications will be secured by hospital staff away from patient's home. Patient's father has secured clandestine private detectives to observe patient when patient leaves his house. Grief therapists will visit patient four times a week for cognitive intervention to create an effective coping mechanism for depression relief. Treatment planning will occur on Mondays at three in the afternoon. Patient's father has retained legal counsel to obtain guardianship so the patient may be placed in a secure setting to prevent self-harm.

Joseph Lister: Physician

Benjamin held Elisabeth's hand. Her sobbing was uncontrollable. "How can I live like this? You are here for such a brief time, and then you are gone. I sit here for hours, anticipating your return. Benjamin, this is unbearable. I am afraid, Benjamin. What if you do not return? I am so alone here. I have lived like this for so many weeks. How can I wait a lifetime until you are always with me? Benjamin, have I made a mistake? I was warned. This bridge between life and death was not meant to be. Even in death, I wanted you with me. I was warned . . . I cannot change it back! I don't understand all of this. What have I done?" Elisabeth gasped for air as she sobbed.

"I will do my best to sleep in life so I can be with you. I, too, suffer when we are apart. How can this be your heaven?" Tears fell from Benjamin's eyes as well. "Please believe me . . . I will do my best."

Elisabeth pulled away. She laid her head on the carpet. The fire lit up her face. She did not speak again. Benjamin could see the days of stress on her face. Her countenance was increasingly emaciated and ashen. *How long can both of us take this terrible reality? Can you die twice?* Benjamin thought, looking into the face of his love. Every day is worse than the day before.

Benjamin did not say another word when he released Elisabeth's hand and stood looking at his love. He turned and walked back to the sea. On this night, he walked alone.

～

Benjamin awoke. His sleeping gown was wet with tears. He looked at his pocket watch on the nightstand. Nurse Helen would arrive soon with his morning medications. He did not have long. Benjamin slipped out of bed and stood on his good leg and hopped over to his dresser. He opened the drawer and pushed his private wear to one side. Benjamin reached far back to the very end of the drawer. His hand grasped the handle of a small-caliber pistol given to him by his mother when he was a child. He hopped over to the open window and looked at the Eastern Sea one last time, put the gun to his head, and pulled the trigger.

～

Dr. Forrestal walked out of the surgical room. Nurse Helen was in the hall, waiting for Dr. Forrestal to complete the surgery. Helen's words were direct, "Benjamin is in surgery. He shot himself in the head. I am so sorry. We did our best."

Dr. Forrestal ran to the observation room and pressed against the glass. He stood helpless as Dr. Lister attempted to stop the bleeding. He could see Dr. Lister remove a portion of Benjamin's skull to prevent further damage as the brain expanded from the trauma. The skull fragment was placed into a pan of saline for preservation. Dr. Lister completed the surgery by noon, and then he looked up at the observation room and his colleague. Dr. Lister gave the attending nurses instructions, turned, and proceeded to the observation room and to an anxious father.

Dr. Forrestal was now sitting, staring at the floor. Dr. Lister spoke, "Conrad, Benjamin is stable. I am so sorry. The brain trauma was extensive . . . he will not recover. He is in a deep coma. He will not recover. We will make him as comfortable as possible. I am so sorry I could not do more."

Dr. Lister put his arm around his friend's shoulders and tried to comfort him. Dr. Forrestal could only say, "I have lost everyone. My family is gone."

Dr. Lister spoke to his friend for a long while. Dr. Forrestal could not respond. His cherished son was gone. Everything seemed surreal—so much tragedy for one family in such a short period. After an hour, Nurse Helen entered the observation room to determine if she could be of assistance. Dr. Lister instructed her to stay with Dr. Forrestal. He knew his friend would want to be with his son for a while. "He is in shock. Please watch over him until he is ready to leave, then take him home. I will prescribe a mild sedative."

Dr. Lister spoke softly, "Conrad, Helen will stay with you and take you home when you are ready. All we can do now is wait. If there is any change in your son's condition, we will notify you. I will ensure your patients are cared for."

Dr. Forrestal stood and walked to the surgical recovery room where Benjamin had been placed. Dr. Forrestal sat next to his son for several hours before he went home. He returned the next morning and went directly to Benjamin's bedside, holding his hand and speaking to him for hours. He told Benjamin how he loved him and how proud he was as his father for all the things Benjamin had achieved in life. Benjamin's father spoke of the beautiful memories they shared. He would smile at the funny stories they experienced and cried at their shared sorrow. Mostly, Benjamin's father was saying goodbye to the son he loved so much. He tried to accept his terrible loss.

Dr. Forrestal established a daily routine. He would arrive early before seeing his patients and speak to Benjamin for a few hours before his rounds. He would sit with Benjamin during lunch and talk to him about everyday events. When Benjamin's father completed his day as a physician, he would return to Benjamin's bedside and continue his conversation with his comatose son as if he were still present. Thirty days passed, and Benjamin's father spoke to his son every day for many hours.

Dr. Lister knew it was time for Benjamin to, at the least, be moved to the long-term nursing unit of the hospital. At the end of his workday, Dr. Lister entered Benjamin's room and stood beside the grieving father and his close friend.

Conrad spoke first, "Is it hopeless, Joseph?"

Dr. Lister only said, "Yes, I am so sorry. He is in restful sleep. He will not wake again, Conrad."

Conrad looked at his friend. "Sleep—why would you say that?"

"Look at his eyelids, Conrad. You can see the small bulge of Benjamin's iris beneath the eyelids. See how his eyes are rapidly moving from side to side under the eyelid. I have been monitoring the movement, and this nystagmus repeats every ninety minutes or so. This is a typical expression of sleep—periodic rapid eye movement. You may find some comfort knowing he is in peaceful slumber. This is unusual," Joseph said, pointing his finger at Benjamin's closed eyes. "He appears to be sleeping. There was so much swelling and damage to his brain. He will not wake up. There is too much neurological damage."

Conrad looked at Benjamin's closed eyes. "This is what he wanted. I hope he has found peace. I hope somehow he is with Elisabeth."

"Please come with me to my office so we may talk," Joseph said, placing his hand on his dear friend's shoulder.

Conrad robotically obeyed. The two doctors left the room and walked to Joseph's office. Joseph motioned to a leather couch, "Please sit down, Conrad. We have some decisions to make." Joseph pulled out a bottle of whiskey and two glasses from his desk and filled each glass until they were half full.

He gave one to Conrad, grabbed a chair, and sat in front

of his friend. "Conrad, I know you have suffered so much in this last year, and I am so sorry. Benjamin's prognosis is grave. He will not recover. We must resolve Benjamin's situation or move him to the long-term nursing ward. He will be given the best care possible. With proper care, he may live a few more months, maybe a little longer. In my experience, in cases like this, your son will physically decompensate. His immune system will become compromised, and he will succumb to infection, pneumonia most likely. Conrad, you must let him go. We must think of letting go."

"Joseph, this is too soon. I am not ready for this discussion," Conrad said, taking a drink of liquor.

"Of course. The entire hospital staff will support you in any way they can. Whatever your choice. When you are ready, then."

This was a conversation both doctors had far too many times in their careers. These were dreaded moments.

Conrad whispered, "Thank you."

"My friend, you are a skilled physician. Life goes on. Your patients need you. The world needs you. You have completely changed the practice of mental hygiene. We all need you here," Joseph tried to help as he poured more whiskey into his friend's glass.

"You have always been a good friend. I was so honored when you recommended me to join the Supplicants. I have seen death and the infirm all my adult life. I will get through this. I just need some time. All of this is overwhelming," Conrad said, taking another drink from his glass.

"Conrad, we need you with us. Your role in the evolving science of mental hygiene is paramount—you will bring the knowledge from Oceania to our profession. The world needs your focus. I am so sorry, but you must accept your son is gone. He cannot hear you. You are a Supplicant. We carry the future of the modern world on our shoulders."

Conrad looked at his colleague. "If we should stumble, the world would fall." He emptied his glass and welcomed the numbing escape from his emotions. "I will continue to act the part and advance our world with knowledge from the true Elders from Oceana. I promise you I will be fine, in time. I will keep my promises to the organization."

Conrad became very still and looked directly in his friend's eyes. "Yes, it is time. . . . I commend my son to your hands. You are his physician. Use your wisdom and do what must be done."

"I will use my best judgment," Joseph said, slightly slurring his words, being increasingly numbed by the alcohol. Then he continued, hoping for some emotional relief.

"For over ten decades, we have unraveled the mystery hidden in The Word. What new beginnings will be ours?" Joseph emptied his glass, then refilled his friend's and his glass to kill the pain of the conversation. Conrad thought it strange Joseph chose this time to speak of the Supplicants, thinking the terrible conversation and the alcohol was robbing Joseph of solemnity.

Conrad took another sip from his glass and mumbled as the alcohol continued to numb the grieving father: "One hundred years—that is a long time. I didn't know that. Why did the organization take the name Supplicants? Such a strange name for something so important."

Joseph glared at the wall behind Conrad and, with some effort, focused on his friend. "So the members would have a sense of perspective. We are the messengers, not the source of the knowledge. In the beginning, some of the members became arrogant. Some members thought we were enlightened not because we were qualified to share the knowledge from Oceania, but intrinsically special. Some even thought the gifts from Oceania were theirs to profit from or gain power. This kind of conceit—vanity—would have destroyed the modern world. The entire world was meant to benefit from the knowledge hidden in The Word. Those that would not accept the simple truth were eliminated. We think that is why the encryption becomes progressively harder to solve— so society would mature as the mystery is unraveled. The organization became more circumspect in selecting members and emphasized the organization's role as being humble messengers. The Order chose the name Supplicants. The organization was not always known by that name."

Conrad felt the flow of adrenaline surge through his body. His lungs tightened—his head developed a slight tremor. He feared he knew the answer to his next question, and his words quivered through his lips, "What was the original name of the organization?"

"It was an ancient word for knowledge," Joseph hesitated, trying to fill his glass again. "Gnostics—they called themselves the Gnostics."

Conrad's vision tunneled as he processed the ramifications of Joseph's statement. His loving son had warned him long ago at Jeffery Porter's warehouse of monsters and schemes to destroy the modern world. Benjamin was correct about the warnings that fate had given him. His loving family was sacrificed because of a curse that befell his son when he looked upon the malevolence woven into that ancient carpet. His son was meant to save the modern world. Conrad no longer felt grief—the pain was gone. Conrad felt only rage and revenge. Everything fell into place. He would contain his anger so Joseph would not know of things to come and possibly try and stop him. Conrad reached up and touched his chest. He felt the key under his shirt. He would keep his promise to his son.

"Conrad, are you alright?" Joseph could see something had changed.

Conrad stared at his friend. "I remember something my son said to me a long time ago. He said, how can we believe in angels and not accept the presence of monsters?" Conrad stood and took the final sip from his glass and said, "Please excuse me, Joseph. I think I will ride down to the harbor for some fresh air."

"Of course, Conrad."

Conrad sat on the back of Demon for a while, looking at

the moving water. The corrugated sides of the carpet warehouse reached high above him, disappearing into the starry sky. Quiet. The harbor was unnaturally quiet—not the slightest breeze to wrestle the rigging or flap the loosely tied sails on nearby ships. No gulls cried out. Quiet. Conrad dismounted Demon, reached under the horse, and released the thick leather belt meant to secure the saddle. When the belt was undone, and the saddle removed, the horse was freed from the bridle and reins. "Go home, Demon. Home!" Conrad shouted.

The horse refused to move, looking back at his lifelong companion, confused and frightened. Conrad smacked the hindquarters of the horse and again commanded, "Demon, return to the stable."

Demon commenced a swift gallop. The sound of his shod hooves made a distinct hollow sound on the wooden pier, invading the silence. As the horse ran past the bright gas lamps, a shadow, a ghostly twisted semicircle of striding legs, nodding head, and forced body was cast by the obedient horse. Conrad watched his old friend disappear into the night, turned, removed the master key, and opened the door.

The gas valve for the chandeliers next to the door were turned on full. The escaping gas was ignited by the pilot flame in each chandelier. The huge showroom became brilliant with light. Treasures. Conrad looked at a room containing thousands of carpets and tapestry created by artists from a country far away. Conrad was indifferent.

He ran across the showroom and entered the immense storeroom and turned on the large, industrial gas lamps high above. The storeroom also shed the darkness to reveal hundreds of carpets. Conrad did not see them. Again, Conrad crossed the showroom to the hallway that led to the basement. The hallway gas lamp was turned on, as well as the gas lamps of the many offices that lined the hallway. Reaching the basement door, he turned on the basement industrial gas lamps using valves located in the hall just outside of the entrance. The door was locked. Using the master key, Conrad opened the door. The basement was illuminated by dozens of industrial gas ceiling lamps. The downward steps were visible. Conrad ran down the stairs, located the main gas valve, closed it and blocked the flow of gas to the entire warehouse. Starved of the gas the illumination from the gas lamps ceased; the pilot lights were extinguished. The huge warehouse fell dark. Conrad counted the ticking of his vest watch. Three hundred mechanical beats. Time enough. The main valve was opened. He waited. Conrad could hear the loud hiss throughout the building as the unburned gas escaped the many ceiling gas lamps like whispers from a large crowd. The sound was all around him.

Conrad crawled up the unseen stairs and down the darkened hall to the door leading to the showroom. He gasped for breath, the oxygen stolen from Conrad's lungs, a self-inflicted wound. The air was turning putrid from the mercaptan mixed with the gas. He vomited. He choked. His body craved air. His heart pumped like a child's drum. The showroom windows permitted the streetlights to provide a faint source of light. Conrad ran and fell, ran and fell, choked and vomited. Dry heaves. He sought the door between him and the monster. He pulled racks of tapestry and carpets away from the wall. He was weaker now. Suffocating. The door was found—the door concealing the monster, the curse. Conrad slumped to the floor in front of the door, seeking the last of the oxygen. Conrad fought to remain conscious. He could hear the muffled pounding within the room like a bird trapped in a cardboard box. He fumbled for matches from within his vest. Removed a match and placed its head against the coarse side of the small box. Conrad could hear the monster whimpering. Conrad struck the match.

The explosion was terrible and complete. Corrugated steel transformed into a million shards, wood into splinters, carpets to dust. The fire storm destroyed the wood piers. Shops and warehouses vanished in the flames. Boats and sailing ships, their wrapped sails, masts rigging neatly stowed—no more. Sleeping sailors would not awake. Sacrificed. The fire continued until the entire harbor was taken. The people of Riverdale could only watch as their livelihood was taken from them.

Newfoundland Shipping Company
February 8, 1897

The freighter: Ultimate Victory
Ships Log: 768
Time: 11:45 p.m.
Latitude: 51 degrees 16 minutes North
Longitude: 144 degrees 9 minutes South
Magnetic   .87 38 degrees true.
2 knots   Sea flat   Wind: North-West
Temperature: 72 degrees Fahrenheit
Barometric: 48 inches of mercury
Distance from port: (Riverdale) 1 mile.

Notes: 18 miles from Riverdale crew reported a bright glow on the horizon in the direction of Riverdale. I instructed the first officer to proceed with caution to our destination. One mile from port, I determined, by spyglass, the entire harbor was burning. Total destruction of piers and ware-houses were apparent. Ship was dead stopped 1 mile from the harbor to avoid glowing embers and possible deck fire. Ship's course was redirected to Newfoundland to ascertain further instructions.
Captain: Herbert Cummings, S.C.

Obituary – February 10, 1897

Conrad Gill Forrestal   1840-1897

Be it known by all that dwell within the State of Kenton and beyond, that the best among us is no more. Dr. Conrad

Forrestal was a revered physician and researcher into the human psyche and founder and director of Riverdale Hospital of Mental Hygiene. He is survived by his son, Benjamin Walker, the son of Elisabeth Forrestal (deceased) and the heir and chief executive officer of Forrestal Enterprises. Dr. Forrestal was lost in the great Riverdale harbor fire of recent days. Dr. Joseph Lister will eulogize Dr. Forrestal and read the appropriate passages from The Word. Dr. Forrestal will be buried next to his wife at the Riverdale Cemetery on February 12, at noon. Dr. Forrestal will be missed.

Benjamin struggled to reach the surface of the churning sea one last time. He had never been so deep. The terrible sound of the pistol shot faded as he struggled for the air far above him. Benjamin felt his lungs would burst as he thrust his arms in front of him and kicked violently, transitioning from life to Elisabeth's heaven. With one final thrust, Benjamin reached the surface and gasped for air. He rose and crawled out of the water, breathing heavily and looked up and down the beach, searching for his love. The starlight was blocked by long threads of rushing clouds. He thought at first the darkness of the night concealed her from him. She was not there. Ahead of him was the fire that warmed him and his beloved wife for so many nights. Elisabeth's unusual absence, he speculated, was the result of sleeping. He was sure that was why she did not greet him on the water's edge. He ran toward the fire as fast as his legs would carry him, and as Benjamin approached his love, he could see her naked body lying upon the carpet in a deep sleep. He ran to his love, shouting her name, "Elisabeth, Elisabeth, I am here." She did not respond. He knelt beside her. Only then, by the light of the fire, did he see the blood-stained carpet. She was dead, a bullet to her head.

Unclaimed Son

About the Author

DAY ALTAIR holds a bachelors degree in history from the California State University at Dominguez Hills, and a masters degree in experimental psychology from the California State University at Fullerton. He held a position of PATIENTS' RIGHTS ADVOCATE as defined by Welfare and Institutions Code of California for thirty years and represented individuals labeled mentally disabled in hundreds of administrative hearings concerning forced psychiatric treatment. The author is retired and currently living in St. George, Utah.

www.ingramcontent.com/pod-product-compliance
Lightning Source LLC
Chambersburg PA
CBHW032258020726
47495CB00001B/162